The Spir

Eden Phillpotts

Alpha Editions

This edition published in 2024

ISBN : 9789361475054

Design and Setting By
Alpha Editions
www.alphaedis.com
Email - info@alphaedis.com

Contents

BOOK I

SABINA

CHAPTER I

THE FUNERAL

The people were coming to church and one had thought it Sunday, but for two circumstances. The ring of bells at St. Mary's did not peal, and the women were dressed in black as the men.

Through the winding lanes of Bridetown a throng converged, drawn to the grey tower by a tolling bell; and while the sun shone and a riot of many flowers made hedgerows and cottage gardens gay; while the spirit of the hour was inspired by June and a sun at the zenith unclouded, the folk of the hamlet drew their faces to sadness and mothers chid the children, who could not pretend, but echoed the noontide hour in their hearts.

All were not attired for a funeral. A small crowd of women, with one or two men among them, stood together where a sycamore threw a patch of shade on a triangular space of grass near the church. There were fifty of these people—ancient women, others in their prime, and many young maidens. Some communion linked them and the few men who stood with them. All wore a black band upon their left arms. Drab or grey was their attire, but sun-bonnets nodded bright as butterflies among them, and even their dull raiment was more cheerful than the gathering company in black who now began to mass their numbers and crane their heads along the highway.

Bridetown lies near the sea in a valley under a range of grassy downs. It is the centre of a network of little lanes with cottages dotted upon them, or set back behind small gardens. The dwellings stood under thatch, or weathered tile, and their faces at this season were radiant with roses and honeysuckles, jasmine and clematis. Pinks, lilies, columbines made the garden patches gay, and, as though so many flowers were not enough, the windows, too, shone with geraniums and the scarlet tassels of great cactus, that lifted their exotic, thorny bodies behind the window panes. Not a wall but flaunted red valerian and snapdragon. Indeed Bridetown was decked with blooms.

Here and there in the midst stood better houses, with some expanse of lawn before them and flat shrubs that throve in that snug vale. Good walnut trees and mulberries threw their shadows on grass plat and house front, while the murmur of bees came from many bright borders.

South the land rose again to the sea cliffs, for the spirits of ocean and the west wind have left their mark upon Bride Vale. The white gulls float aloft;

the village elms are moulded by Zephyr with sure and steady breath. Of forestal size and unstunted, yet they turn their backs, as it were, upon the west and, yielding to that unsleeping pressure, incline landward. The trees stray not far. They congregate in an oasis about Bridetown, then wend away through valley meadows, but leave the green hills bare. The high ground rolls upward to a gentle skyline and the hillsides, denuded by water springs, or scratched by man, reveal the silver whiteness of the chalk where they are wounded.

Bride river winds in the midst, and her bright waters throw a loop round the eastern frontier of the hamlet, pass under the highway, bring life to the cottage gardens and turn more wheels than one. Bloom of apple and pear are mirrored on her face and fruit falls into her lap at autumn time. Then westward she flows through the water meadows, and so slips uneventfully away to sea, where the cliffs break and there stretches a little strand. To the last she is crowned with flowers, and the meadowsweets and violets that decked her cradle give place to sea poppies, sea hollies, and stones encrusted with lichens of red gold, where Bride flows to one great pool, sinks into the sand and glides unseen to her lover.

"They're coming!" said one of the crowd; but it was a false alarm. A flock of breeding lambs of the Dorset horned sheep pattered through the village on their way to pasture. The young, healthy creatures, with amber-coloured horns and yellow eyes, trotted contentedly along together and left an ovine reek in the air. Behind them came the shepherd—a high-coloured, middle-aged man with a sharp nose and mild, grey eyes. He could give news of the funeral, which was on the way behind him.

An iron seat stood under the sycamore on the triangular patch of grass, and a big woman sat upon it. She was of vast dimensions, broad and beamy as a Dutch sloop. Her bulk was clad in dun colour, and on her black bonnet appeared a layer of yellow dust. She spoke to others of the little crowd who surrounded her. They came from Bridetown Spinning Mill, for work was suspended because Henry Ironsyde, the mill owner, had died and now approached his grave.

"The Ironsydes bury here, but they don't live here," said Sally Groves. "They lived here once, at North Hill House; but that's when I first came to the Mill as a bit of a girl."

The big woman fanned herself with a handkerchief, then spoke a grey man with a full beard, small head, and discontented eyes. He was Levi Baggs, the hackler.

"We shall have those two blessed boys over us now, no doubt," he said. "But what know they? Things will be as they were, and time and wages the same as before."

"They'll be sure to do what their father wished, and there was a murmur of changes before he died," said Sally Groves; but Levi shook his head.

"Daniel Ironsyde is built like his father, to let well alone. Raymond Ironsyde don't count. He'll only want his money."

"Have you ever seen Mr. Raymond?" asked a girl. She was Nancy Buckler, a spinner—hard-featured, sharp-voiced, and wiry. Nancy might have been any age between twenty-five and forty. She owned to thirty.

"He don't come to Bridetown, and if you want to see him, you must go to 'The Tiger,' at Bridport," declared another girl. Her name was Sarah Northover.

"My Aunt Nelly keeps 'The Seven Stars,' in Barrack Street," she explained, "and that's just alongside 'The Tiger,' and my Aunt Nelly's very friendly with Mr. Gurd, of 'The Tiger,' and he's told her that Mr. Raymond is there half his time. He's all for sport and such like, and 'The Tiger's' a very sporting house."

"He won't be no good to the mills if he's that sort," prophesied Sally Groves.

"I saw him once, with another young fellow called Motyer," answered Sarah Northover. "He's very good-looking—fair and curly—quite different from Mr. Daniel."

"Light or dark, they're Henry Ironsyde's sons and be brought up in his pattern no doubt," declared Mr. Baggs.

People continued to appear, and among them walked an elderly man, a woman and a girl. They were Mr. Ernest Churchouse, of 'The Magnolias,' with his widowed housekeeper, Mary Dinnett, and her daughter, Sabina. The girl was nineteen, dark and handsome, and very skilled in her labour. None disputed her right to be called first spinner at the mills. She was an impulsive, ambitious maiden, and Mr. Best, foreman at the works, claimed for her that she brought genius as well as understanding to her task. Sabina joined her friend, Nancy Buckler; Mrs. Dinnett, who had been a mill hand in her youth, took a seat beside Sally Groves, and Mr. Churchouse paced alone. He was a round-faced, clean-shaven man with mild, grey eyes and iron grey hair. He looked gentle and genial. His shoulders were high, and his legs short. Walking irked him, for a sedentary life and hearty appetite had made him stout.

The fall of Henry Ironsyde served somewhat to waken Ernest Churchouse from the placid dream in which he lived, shake him from his normal quietude, and remind him of the flight of time. He and the dead man were of an age and had been boys together. Their fathers founded the Bridetown Spinning Mill, and when the elder men passed away, it was Henry Ironsyde who took over the enterprise and gradually bought out Ernest Churchouse. But while Ironsyde left Bridetown and lived henceforth at Bridport, that he might develop further interests in the spinning trade, Ernest had been well content to remain there, enjoy his regular income and live at 'The Magnolias,' his father's old-world house, beside the river. His tastes were antiquarian and literary. He wrote when in the mood, and sometimes read papers at the Mechanics' Institute of Bridport. But he was constitutionally averse from real work of any sort, lacked ambition, and found all the fame he needed in the village community with which his life had been passed. He was a childless widower. Mr. Churchouse strolled now into the churchyard to look at the grave. It opened beside that of Henry Ironsyde's parents and his wife. She had been dead for fifteen years. A little crowd peered down into the green-clad pit, for the sides, under the direction of John Best, had been lined with cypress and bay. The grass was rank, but it had been mown down for this occasion round the tombs of the Ironsydes, though elsewhere darnel rose knee deep and many venerable stones slanted out of it. Immediately south of the churchyard wall stood the Mill, and Benny Cogle, engineman at the works, who now greeted Mr. Churchouse, dwelt on the fact.

"Morning, sir," he said, "a brave day for the funeral, sure enough."

"Good morning, Benny," answered the other. His voice was weak and gentle.

"When I think how near the church and Mill do lie together, I have thoughts," continued Benny. He was a florid man of thirty, with tow-coloured hair and blue eyes.

"Naturally. You work and pray here all inside a space of fifty yards. But for my part, Benny Cogle, I am inclined to think that working is the best form of praying."

Mr. Churchouse always praised work for others and, indeed, was under the impression that he did his share.

"Same here," replied the engineman, "especially while you're young. Anyway, if I had to choose between 'em, I'd sooner work. 'Tis better for the mind and appetite. And I lay if Mr. Ironsyde, when he lies down there, could tell the truth, he'd rather be hearing the Mill going six days a week and feeling his grave throbbing to my engines, than list to the sound of the church organ on the seventh."

"Not so," reproved Mr. Churchouse. "We must not go so far as that. Henry Ironsyde was a God-fearing man and respected the Sabbath as we all should, and most of us do."

"The weaker vessels come to church, I grant," said Benny, "but the men be after more manly things than church-going of a Sunday nowadays."

"So much the worse for them," declared Mr. Churchouse. "Here," he continued, "there are naturally more women than men. Since my father and Henry Ironsyde's father established these mills, which are now justly famous in the county, the natural result has happened and women have come here in considerable numbers. Women preponderate in spinning places, because the work of spinning yarn has always been in their hands from time immemorial. And they tend our modern machinery as deftly as of old they twirled the distaff and worked the spinning-wheel; and as steadily as they used to trudge the rope walks and spin, like spiders, from the masses of flax or hemp at their waists."

"The females want religion without a doubt," said Benny. "I'm tokened to Mercy Gale, for instance; she looks after the warping wheels, and if that girl didn't say her prayers some fine morning, she'd be as useless as if she hadn't eat her breakfast. 'Tis the feminine nature that craves for support."

A very old man stood and peered into the grave. He was the father of Levi Baggs, the hackler, and people said he was never seen except on the occasion of a funeral. The ancient had been reduced to a mere wisp by the attrition of time.

He put his hand on the arm of Mr. Churchouse and regarded the grave with a nodding head.

"Ah, my dear soul," he said. "Life, how short—eternity, how long!"

"True, most true, William."

"And I ask myself, as each corpse goes in, how many more pits will open afore mine."

"'Tis hid with your Maker, William."

"Thank God I'm a good old man and ripe and ready," said Mr. Baggs. "Not," he added, "that there's any credit to me; for you can't be anything much but good at ninety-two."

"While the brain is spared we can think evil, William."

"Not a brain like mine, I do assure 'e."

A little girl ran into the churchyard—a pretty, fair child, whose bright hair contrasted with the black she wore.

"They have come and father sent me to tell you, Mr. Churchouse," she said.

"Thank you, Estelle," he answered, and they returned to the open space together. The child then joined her father, and Mr. Churchouse, saluting the dead, walked to the first mourning coach and opened the door.

It was a heavy and solid funeral of Victorian fashion proper to the time. The hearse had been drawn by four black horses with black trappings, and over the invisible coffin nodded a gloomy harvest of black ostrich plumes. There were no flowers, and some children, who crept forward with a little wreath of wild roses, were pushed back.

The men from the Mill helped to carry their master into the church; but there were not enough of them to support the massive oak that held a massive man, and John Best, Levi Baggs, Benny Cogle and Nicholas Roberts were assisted by the undertakers.

From the first coach descended an elderly woman and a youth. The lady was Miss Jenny Ironsyde, sister of the dead, and with her came her nephew Daniel, the new mill-owner. He was five-and-twenty—a sallow, strong-faced young fellow, broad in the shoulder and straight in the back. His eyes were brown and steady, his mouth and nose indicated decision; the funeral had not changed his cast of countenance, which was always solemn; for, as his father before him, he lacked a sense of humour.

Mr. Churchouse shook hands and peered into the coach.

"Where's Raymond?" he asked.

"Not come," answered Miss Ironsyde. She was a sturdy woman of five-and-fifty, with a pleasant face and kindly eyes. But they were clouded now and she showed agitation.

"Not come!" exclaimed Ernest with very genuine consternation.

Daniel Ironsyde answered. His voice was slow, but he had a natural instinct for clarity and spoke more to the point than is customary with youth.

"My brother has not come because my father has left him out of his will, Mr. Churchouse."

"Altogether?"

"Absolutely. Will you take my aunt's arm and follow next after me, please?"

Two clergymen met the coffin at the lich-gate, and behind the chief mourners came certain servants and dependents, followed by the women of the Mill. Then a dozen business men walked together. A few of his co-workers had sent their carriages; but most came themselves, to do the last honour to one greatly respected.

Mr. Churchouse paid little attention to the obsequies.

"Not at his father's funeral!" he kept thinking to himself. His simple mind was thrown into a large confusion by such an incident. The fact persisted rather than the reason for it. He longed to learn more, but could not until the funeral was ended.

When the coffin came to the grave, Mary Dinnett stole home to look after the midday dinner. It had weighed on her mind since she awoke, for Miss Ironsyde and Daniel were coming to 'The Magnolias' to partake of a meal before returning home. There were no relations from afar to be considered, and no need for funeral baked meats in the dead man's house.

When all was ended and only old William Baggs stood by the grave and watched the sextons fill it, a small company walked together up the hill north of Bridetown. Daniel went first with Mr. Churchouse, and behind them followed Miss Jenny Ironsyde with a man and a child. The man rented North Hill House. Arthur Waldron was a widower, who lived now for two things: his little daughter, Estelle, and sport. No other considerations challenged his mind. He was rich and good-hearted. He knew that his little girl had brains, and he dealt fairly with her in the matter of education.

Of the Ironsyde brothers, Raymond was his personal friend, and Mr. Waldron now permitted himself some vague expression of regret that the young man should have been absent on such an occasion.

"Yes," said Miss Ironsyde, to whom he spoke, "if there's any excuse for convention it's at a funeral. No doubt people will magnify the incident into a scandal—for their own amusement and the amusement of their friends. If Raymond had enjoyed time to reflect, I feel sure he would have come; but there was no time. His father has made no provision for him, and he is rather upset. It is not unnatural that he should be, for dear Henry, while always very impatient of Raymond's sporting tastes and so on, never threatened anything like this."

"No doubt Mr. Ironsyde would have made a difference if he had not died so suddenly."

"I think so too," she answered.

Then Waldron and his daughter went homewards; while the others, turning down a lane to the right, reached 'The Magnolias'—a small, ancient house whose face was covered with green things and whose lawn spread to the river bank.

Mrs. Dinnett had prepared a special meal of a sort associated with the mournful business of the day; for a funeral feast has its own character; the dishes should be cold and the wine should be white or brown.

Mr. Churchouse was concerned to know what Daniel meant to do for Raymond; but he found the heir by no means inclined to emotional generosity.

Daniel spoke in a steady voice, though he showed a spark of feeling presently. The fire, however, was for his dead father, not his living brother.

"I'm very sorry that Raymond could have been so small as to keep away from the funeral," he said. "It was petty. But, as Aunt Jenny says, he's built like that, and no doubt the shock of being ignored knocked him off his balance."

"He has the defects of his qualities, my dear. The same people can often rise to great heights and sink to great depths. They can do worse things—and better things—than we humdrum folk, who jog along the middle of the road. We must forgive such people for doing things we wouldn't do, and remember their power to do things we couldn't do."

The young man was frankly puzzled by this speech, which came from his aunt. He shrugged his shoulders.

"I've got to think of father first and Raymond afterwards," he said. "I owe my first duty to my father, who trusted me and honoured me, and knew very well that I should obey his wishes and carry on with my life as he would have liked to see me. He has made a very definite and clear statement, and I should be disloyal to him—dishonest to him—if I did anything contrary to the spirit of it."

"Who would wish you to?" asked Ernest Churchouse. "But a brother is a brother," he continued, "and since there is nothing definite about Raymond in the will, you should, I think, argue like this. You should say to yourself, 'my father was disappointed with my brother and did not know what to do about him; but, having a high opinion of me and my good sense and honesty, he left my brother to my care. He regarded me, in fact, as my brother's keeper, and hoped that I would help Raymond to justify his existence.' Don't you feel like that?"

"I feel that my father was very long-suffering with Raymond, and his will tells me that he had a great deal more to put up with from Raymond than anybody ever knew, except my brother himself."

"You needn't take up the cudgels for your father, Dan," interposed Miss Ironsyde. "Be sure that your dear father, from the peace which now he enjoys, would not like to see you make his quarrel with Raymond your quarrel. I'm not extenuating Raymond's selfish and unthinking conduct as a son. His own conscience will exact the payment for wrong done beyond repair. He'll come to that some day. He won't escape it. He's not built to escape it. But he's your brother, not your son; and you must ask yourself, whether as a brother, you've fairly got any quarrel with him."

Daniel considered a moment, then he spoke.

"I have not," he said—"except the general quarrel that he's a waster and not justifying his existence. We have had practically nothing to do with each other since we left school."

"Well," declared Mr. Churchouse, "now you must have something to do with each other. It is an admirable thought of your Aunt Jenny's that your father has honoured your judgment by leaving the destiny of Raymond more or less in your hands."

"I didn't say that; you said it," interrupted the lady. "Raymond's destiny is in his own hands. But I do feel, of course, that Daniel can't ignore him. The moment has come when a strong effort must be made to turn Raymond into a useful member of society."

"What allowance did dear Henry make him?" asked Mr. Churchouse.

"Father gave him two hundred a year, and father paid all his debts before his twenty-first birthday; but he didn't pay them again. Raymond has told Aunt Jenny that he's owing two hundred pounds at this moment."

"And nothing to show for it—we may be sure of that. Well, it might have been worse. Is the allowance to be continued?"

"No," said Miss Ironsyde. "That's the point. It is to cease. Henry expressly directs that it is to cease; and to me that is very significant."

"Of course, for it shows that he leaves Raymond in his brother's hands."

"I have heard Henry say that Raymond beat him," continued Miss Ironsyde. "He was a good father and a forgiving father, but temperamentally he was not built to understand Raymond. Some people develop slowly and remain children much longer than other people. Raymond is one of those. Daniel, like my dear brother before him, has developed quickly and come to man's estate and understanding."

"His father could trust his eldest son," declared Mr. Churchouse, "and, as I happen to know, Daniel, you always spoke with patience and reason about

Raymond—your father has told me so. It was natural and wise, therefore, that my late dear friend should have left Raymond to you."

"I only want to do my duty," said the young man. "By stopping away to-day Raymond hasn't made me feel any kinder to him, and if he were not so stupid in some ways, he must have known it would be so; but I am not going to let that weigh against him. How do you read the fact that my father directs Raymond's allowance to cease, Uncle Ernest?"

Mr. Churchouse bore no real connection to the Ironsydes; but his relations had always been close and cordial after he relinquished his share in the business of the mills, and the younger generation was brought up to call him 'uncle.'

"I read it like this," answered the elder. "It means that Raymond is to look to you in future, and that henceforth you may justly demand that he should not live in idleness. There is nothing more demoralising for youth than to live upon money it doesn't earn. I should say—subject to your aunt's opinion, to which I attach the greatest importance—that it is your place to give your brother an interest in life and to show him, what you know already, the value and dignity of work."

"I entirely agree," said Jenny Ironsyde. "I can go further and declare from personal knowledge that my brother had shadowed the idea in his mind."

They both regarded Daniel.

"Then leave it there," he bade them, "leave it there and I'll think it out. My father was the fairest man I ever met, and I'll try and be as fair. It's up to Raymond more than me."

"You can bring a horse to the water, though you can't make him drink," admitted Mr. Churchouse. "But if you bring your horse to the water, you've done all that reason and sense may ask you to do."

Miss Ironsyde, from larger knowledge of the circumstances, felt disposed to carry the question another step. She opened her mouth and drew in her breath to speak—making that little preliminary sound only audible when nothing follows it. But she did not speak.

"Come into the garden and see Magnolia grandiflora," said Mr. Churchouse. "There are twelve magnificent blossoms open this morning, and I should have picked every one of them for my dear friend's grave, only the direction was clear, that there were to be no flowers."

"Henry disliked any attempt to soften the edges at such a time," explained the dead man's sister. "He held that death was the skeleton at the feast of life—a wholesome and stark reminder to the thoughtless living that the grave is the end of our mortal days. He liked a funeral to be a funeral—black—black. He did not want the skeleton at the feast to be decked in roses and lilies."

"An opinion worthy of all respect," declared Mr. Churchouse.

Then he asked after the health of his guest and expressed sympathy for her sorrow and great loss.

"He'd been so much better lately that it was a shock," she said, "but he died as he wanted to die—as all Ironsydes do die—without an illness. It is a tradition that never seems to fail. That reconciled us in a way. And you—how are you? You seldom come to Bridport nowadays."

Mr. Churchouse rarely talked about himself.

"True. I have been immersed in literary work and getting on with my *magnum opus*: 'The Church Bells of Dorset.' You see one does not obtain much help here—no encouragement. Not that I expect it. We men of letters have to choose between being hermits, or humbugs."

"I always thought a hermit was a humbug," said Jenny, smiling for the first time.

"Not always. When I say 'hermit,' I mean 'recluse.' With all the will to be a social success and identify myself with the welfare of the place in which I dwell, my powers are circumscribed. Do not think I put myself above the people, or pretend any intellectual superiority, or any nonsense of that sort. No, it is merely a question of time and energy. My antiquarian work demands both, and so I am deprived by duty from mixing in the social life as much as I wish. This is not, perhaps, understood, and so I get a character for aloofness, which is not wholly deserved."

"Don't worry," said Miss Ironsyde. "Everybody cares for you. People don't think about us and our doings half as much as we are prone to fancy. I liked your last article in the *Bridport Gazette*. Only I seemed to have read most of it before."

"Probably you have. The facts, of course, were common property. My task is to collect data and retail them in a luminous and illuminating way."

"So you do—so you do."

He looked away, where Daniel stood by himself with his hands in his pockets and his eyes on the river.

"A great responsibility for one so young; but he will rise to it."

"D'you mean his brother, or the Mill?"

"Both," answered Ernest Churchouse. "Both."

Mrs. Dinnett came down the garden.

"The mourning coach is at the door," she said.

"Daniel insisted that we went home in a mourning coach," explained Miss Ironsyde. "He felt the funeral was not ended until we returned home. That shows imagination, so you can't say he hasn't got any."

"You can never say anybody hasn't got anything," declared Mr. Churchouse. "Human nature defeats all calculations. The wisest only generalise about it."

CHAPTER II

AT 'THE TIGER'

The municipal borough of Bridport stretches itself luxuriously from east to west beneath a wooded hill. Southward the land slopes to broad water-meadows where rivers meet and Brit and Asker wind to the sea. Evidences of the great local industry are not immediately apparent; but streamers and wisps of steam scattered above the red-tiled roofs tell of work, and westward, where the land falls, there stand shoulder to shoulder the busy mills.

From single yarn that a child could break, to hawsers strong enough to hold a battleship, Bridport meets every need. Her twines and cords and nets are famous the world over; her ropes, cables, cablets and canvas rigged the fleet that scattered the Spanish Armada.

The broad streets with deep, unusual side-walks are a sign of Bridport's past, for they tell of the days when men and women span yarn before their doors, and rope-walks ran their amber and silver threads of hemp and flax along the pavements. But steel and steam have taken the place of the hand-spinners, though their industry has left its sign-manual upon the township. For the great, open side-walks make for distinction and spaciousness, and there shall be found in all Dorset, no brighter, cheerfuller place than this. Bridport's very workhouse, south-facing and bowered in green, blinks half a hundred windows amiably at the noonday sun and helps to soften the life-failure of those who dwell therein. Off Barrack Street it stands, and at the time of the terror, when Napoleon threatened, soldiers hived here and gave the way its name.

Not far from the workhouse two inns face each other in Barrack Street—'The Tiger' upon one side of the way, 'The Seven Stars' upon the other; and at the moment when Henry Ironsyde's dust was reaching the bottom of his grave at Bridetown, a young man of somewhat inane countenance, clad in garments that displayed devotion to sport and indifference to taste, entered 'The Tiger's' private bar.

Behind the counter stood Richard Gurd, a middle-aged, broad-shouldered publican with a large and clean-shaven face, heavy-jaw, rather sulky eyes and mighty hands.

"The usual," said the visitor. "Ray been here?"

Mr. Gurd shook his head.

"No, Mr. Ned—nor likely to. They're burying his father this morning."

The publican poured out a glass of cherry brandy as he spoke and Mr. Neddy Motyer rolled a cigarette.

"Ray ain't going," said the customer.

"Not going to his father's funeral!"

"For a very good reason, too; he's cut off with a shilling."

"Dear, dear," said Mr. Gurd. "That's bad news, though perhaps not much of a surprise to Mr. Raymond."

"It's a devil of a lesson to the rising generation," declared the youth. "To think our own fathers can do such blackguard things, just because they don't happen to like our way of life. What would become of England if every man was made in the pattern of his father? Don't education and all that count? If my father was to do such a thing—but he won't; he's too fond of the open air and sport and that."

"Young men don't study their fathers enough in this generation, however," argued the innkeeper, "nor yet do young women study their mothers enough."

"We've got to go out in the world and play our parts," declared Neddy. "'Tis for them to study us—not us them. You must have progress. The thing for parents to do is to know they're back numbers and act according."

"They do—most of them," answered Mr. Gurd. "A back number is a back number and behaves as such. I speak impartial being a bachelor, and I forgive the young men their nonsense and pardon their opinions, because I know I was young myself once, and as big a fool as anybody, and put just the same strain on my parents, no doubt, though they lived to see me a responsible man and done with childish things. The point for parents is not to forget what it feels like to be young. That I never have, and you young gentlemen would very soon remind me if I did. But the late Mr. Henry Ironsyde found no time for all-round wisdom. He poured his brains into hemp and jute and such like. Why, he didn't even make a minute to court and wed till he was forty-five year old. And the result of that was that when his brace of boys was over twenty, he stood in sight of seventy and could only see life at that angle. And what made it worse was, that his eldest, Mister Daniel, was cut just in his own pattern. So the late gentleman never could forgive Mr. Raymond for being cut in another pattern. But if what you say is right and Mister Raymond has been left out in the cold, then I think he's been badly used."

"So he has—it's a damned shame," said Mr. Motyer, "and I hope Ray will do something about it."

"There's very little we can do against the writing of the dead," answered Mr. Gurd. Then he saluted a man who bustled into the bar.

"Morning, Job. What's the trouble?"

Job Legg was very tall and thin. He dropped at the middle, but showed vitality and energy in his small face and rodent features. His hair was black, and his thin mouth and chin clean-shaven. His eyes were small and very shrewd; his manner was humble. He had a monotonous inflection and rather chanted in a minor key than spoke.

"Mrs. Northover's compliments and might we have the big fish kettle till to-morrow? A party have been sprung on us, and five-and-twenty sit down to lunch in the pleasure gardens at two o'clock."

"And welcome, Job. Go round to the kitchen, will 'e?"

Job disappeared and Mr. Gurd explained.

"My good neighbour at 'The Seven Stars'—her with the fine pleasure gardens and swings and so on. And Job Legg's her potman. Her husband's right hand while he lived, and now hers. I have the use of their stable-yard market days, for their custom is different from mine. A woman's house and famous for her meat teas and luncheons. She does very well and deserves to."

"That old lady with the yellow wig?"

Mr. Gurd pursed his lips.

"To you she might seem old, I suppose. That's the spirit that puts a bit of a strain on the middle-aged and makes such men as me bring home to ourselves what we said and thought when we were young. 'Tis just the natural, thoughtless insolence of youth to say Nelly Northover's an old woman—her being perhaps eight-and-forty. And to call her hair a wig, because she's fortified it with home-grown what's fallen out over a period of twenty years, is again only the insolence of youth. One can only say 'forgive 'em, for they know not what they do.'"

"Well, get me another brandy anyway."

Then entered Raymond Ironsyde, and Mr. Gurd for once felt genuinely sorry to see his customer.

The young man was handsome with large, luminous, grey eyes, curly, brown hair and a beautiful mouth, clean cut, full, firm and finely modelled in the lips. His nose was straight, high in the nostril and sensitive. He resembled his brother, Daniel, but stood three inches taller, and his brow was fuller and loftier. His expression in repose appeared frank and receptive; but to-day his face wore a look half anxious, half ferocious. He was clad in tweed knickerbockers and a Norfolk jacket, of different pattern but similar material. His tie was light blue and fastened with a gold pin modelled in the shape of a hunting-horn. He bore no mark of mourning whatever.

"Whiskey and soda, Gurd. Morning, Neddy."

He spoke defiantly, as though knowing his entrance was a challenge. Then he flung himself down on a cushioned seat in the bow window of the bar-room and took a pipe and tobacco pouch from his pocket.

Mr. Gurd brought the drink round to Raymond. He spoke upon some general subject and pretended to no astonishment that the young man should be here on this day. But the customer cut him short. There was only one subject for discussion in his mind.

"I suppose you thought I should go to my father's funeral? No doubt, you'll say, with everybody else, that it's a disgrace I haven't."

"I shall mind my own business and say nothing, Mister Raymond. It's your affair, not ours."

"I'd have done the same, Ray, if I'd been treated the same," said Neddy Motyer.

"It's a protest," explained Raymond Ironsyde. "To have gone, after being publicly outraged like this in my father's will, was impossible to anybody but a cur. He ignored me as his son, and so I ignore him as my father; and who wouldn't?"

"I suppose Daniel will come up to the scratch all right?" hazarded Motyer.

"He'll make some stuffy suggestion, no doubt. He can't see me in the gutter very well."

"You must get to work, Mr. Raymond; and I can tell you, as one who knows, that work's only dreaded by them who have never done any. You'll soon find that there's nothing better for the nerves and temper than steady work."

Neddy chaffed Mr. Gurd's sentiments and Raymond said nothing. He was looking in front of him, his mind occupied with personal problems.

Neddy Motyer made another encouraging suggestion.

"There's your aunt, Miss Ironsyde," he said. "She's got plenty of cash, I've heard people say, and she gives tons away in charity. How do you stand with her?"

"Mind your own business, Ned."

"Sorry," answered the other promptly. "Only wanted to buck you up."

"I'm not in need of any bucking up, thanks. If I've got to work, I'm quite equal to it. I've got more brains than Daniel, anyway. I'm quite conscious of that."

"You've got tons more mind than him," declared Neddy.

"And if that's the case, I could do more good, if I chose, than ever Daniel will."

"Or more harm," warned Mr. Gurd. "Always remember that, Mister Raymond.
The bigger the intellects, the more power for wrong as well as right."

"He'll ask me to go into the works, I expect. And I may, or I may not."

"I should," advised Neddy. "Bridetown is a very sporting place and you'd be alongside your pal, Arthur Waldron."

"Don't go to Bridetown with an idea of sport, however—don't do that, Mister Raymond," warned Richard Gurd. "If you go, you put your back into the work and master the business of the Mill."

The young men wasted an hour in futile talk and needless drinking while Gurd attended to other customers. Then Raymond Ironsyde accepted an invitation to return home with Motyer, who lived at Eype, a mile away.

"I'm going to give my people a rest to-day," said Raymond as he departed. "I shall come in here for dinner, Dick."

"Very good, sir," answered Mr. Gurd; but he shook his head when the young men had gone.

Others in the bar hummed on the subject of young Ironsyde after his back was turned. A few stood up for him and held that he had been too severely dealt with; but the majority and those who knew most about him thought that his ill-fortune was deserved.

"For look at it," said a tradesman, who knew the facts. "If he'd been left money, he'd have only wasted the lot in sporting and been worse off after than before; but now he's up against work, and work may be the saving of him. And if he won't work, let him die the death and get off the earth and make room for a better man."

None denied the honourable obligation to work for every responsible human being.

CHAPTER III

THE HACKLER

The warehouse of Bridetown Mill adjoined the churchyard wall and its northern windows looked down upon the burying ground. The store came first and then the foreman's home, a thatched dwelling bowered in red and white roses, with the mill yard in front and a garden behind. From these the works were separated by the river. Bride came by a mill race to do her share, and a water wheel, conserving her strength, took it to the machinery. For Benny Cogle's engine was reinforced by the river. Then, speeding forward, Bride returned to her native bed, which wound through the valley south of the works.

A bridge crossed the river from the yard and communicated with the mills—a heterogeneous pile of dim, dun colours and irregular roofs huddled together with silver-bright excrescences of corrugated iron. A steady hum and drone as of some gigantic beehive ascended from the mills, and their combined steam and water power produced a tremor of earth and a steady roar in the air; while a faint dust storm often flickered about the entrance ways.

The store-house reeked with that fat, heavy odour peculiar to hemp and flax. It was a lofty building of wide doors and few windows. Here in the gloom lay bales and stacks of raw material. Italy, Russia, India, had sent their scutched hemp and tow to Bridetown. Some was in the rough; the dressed line had already been hackled and waited in bundles of long hemp composed of wisps, or 'stricks' like horses' tails. The silver and amber of the material made flashes of brightness in the dark storerooms and drew the light to their shining surfaces. Tall, brown posts supported the rafters, and in the twilight that reigned here, a man moved among the bales piled roof-high around him. He was gathering rough tow from a broken bale of Russian hemp and had stripped the Archangel matting from the mass.

Levi Baggs, the hackler, proceeded presently to weigh his material and was taking it over the bridge to the hackling shop when he met John Best, the foreman. They stopped to speak, and Levi set down the barrow that bore his load.

"I see you with him, yesterday. Did you get any ideas out of the man?"

Baggs referred to the new master and John Best understood.

"In a manner of speaking, yes," he said. "Nothing definite, of course. It's too soon to talk of changes, even if Mister Daniel means them. He'll carry on as before for the present, and think twice and again before he does anything different from his father."

"'Tis just Bridetown luck if he's the sort to keep at a dead parent's apron-strings," grumbled the other. "Nowadays, what with education and so on, the rising generation is generally ahead of the last and moves according."

"You can move two ways—backward as well as forward," answered Best. "Better he should go on as we've been going, than go back."

"He daren't go back—the times won't let him. The welfare of the workers is the first demand on capital nowadays. If it weren't, labour would very soon know the reason why."

Mr. Best regarded Levi without admiration.

"You are a grumbler born," he said, "and so fond of it that you squeal before you're hurt, just for the pleasure of squealing. One thing I can tell you, for Mister Daniel said it in so many words: he's the same in politics as his father; and that's Liberal; and since the Liberals of yesterday are the Radicals of to-morrow, we have every reason to suppose he'll move with the times."

"We all know what that means," answered Mr. Baggs. "It means getting new machinery and increasing the output of the works for the benefit of the owners, not them that run the show. I don't set no store on a man being a Radical nowadays. You can't trust nobody under a Socialist."

Mr. Best laughed.

"You wait till they've got the power, and you'll find that the whip will fall just as heavy from their hands as the masters of to-day. Better to get small money and be free, than get more and go a slave in state clothes, on state food, in a state house, with a state slave-driver to see you earn your state keep and take your state holidays when the state wills, and work as much or as little as the state pleases. What you chaps call 'liberty' you'll find is something quite different, Baggs, for it means good-bye to privacy in the home and independence outside it."

"That's a false and wicked idea of progress, John Best, and well you know it," answered Levi. "You're one of the sort content to work on a chain and bring up your children likewise; but you can't stand between the human race and freedom—no more can Daniel Ironsyde, or any other man."

"Well, meantime, till the world's put right by your friends, you get on with your hackling, my old bird, else you'll have the spreaders grumbling," answered Mr. Best. Then he went into his home and Levi trundled the wheelbarrow to a building with a tar-pitched, penthouse roof, which stuck out from the side of the mill, like a fungus on a tree stem.

Within, before a long, low window, stood the hand dresser's tools—two upturned boards set with a mass of steel pins. The larger board had tall teeth disposed openly; upon the smaller, the teeth were shorter and as dense as a hair brush. In front of them opened a grating and above ran an endless band. Behind this grille was an exhaust, which sucked away the dust and countless atoms of vegetable matter scattered by Levi's activities, and the running band from above worked it. For the authorities, he despised, considered the operations of Mr. Baggs and ordained that they should be conducted under healthy conditions.

He took his seat now before the rougher's hackle, turned up his shirt sleeves over a pair of sinewy arms and powerful wrists and set to work.

From the mass of hemp tow he drew hanks and beat the pins with them industriously, wrenched the mass through the steel teeth again and again and separated the short fibre from the long. Presently in his hand emerged a wisp of bright fibre, and now flogging the finer hackling board, he extracted still more short stalks and rubbish till the finished strick came clean and shining as a lock of woman's hair. From the hanks of long tow he seemed to bring out the tresses like magic. In his swift hand each strick flashed out from the rough hank with great rapidity, and every crafty, final touch on the teeth made it brighter. Giving a last flick or two over the small pins, Mr. Baggs set down his strick and soon a pile of these shining locks grew beside him, while the exhaust sucked away the rubbish and fragments, and the mass of short fibre which he had combed out, also accumulated for future treatment.

He worked with the swiftness and surety of a master craftsman, scourged his tow and snorted sometimes as he struggled with it. He was exerting a tremendous pressure, regulated and applied with skill, and he always exulted in the thought that he, at least, of all the workers performed hand labour far more perfectly than any machine. But still it was not the least of his many grievances that Government showed too little concern for his comfort. He was always demanding increased precautions for purifying the air he breathed. From first to last, indeed, the hemp and tow are shedding superfluities, and a layman is astonished to see how the broad strips and ribbons running through the machines and torn by innumerable systems of sharp teeth in transit, emerge at the last gasp of attenuation to trickle down the spindles and turn into the glory of yarn.

From Mr. Baggs, the long fibre and the short which he had combed out of it, proceeded to the spinning mill; and now a girl came for the stricks he had just created.

Their future under the new master was still on every tongue at Bridetown Mill, and the women turned to the few men who worked among them for information on this paramount subject.

"No, I ain't heard no more, Sarah," answered the hackler to Miss Northover's question. "You may be sure that those it concerns most will be the last to hear of any changes; and you may also be sure that the changes, when made, will not favour us."

"You can't tell that," answered Sarah, gathering the stricks. "Old Mrs. Chick, our spreader minder, says the young have always got bigger hearts than the old, and she'd sooner trust them than—"

Mr. Baggs tore a hank through the comb with such vigour that its steel teeth trembled and the dust flew.

"Tell Granny Chick not to be a bigger fool than God made her," he said. "The young have got harder hearts than the old, and education, though it may make the head bigger for all I know, makes the heart smaller. He'll be hard—hard—and I lay a week's wages that he'll get out of his responsibilities by shovelling 'em on his dead father."

"How can he?" asked Sarah.

"By letting things be as they are. By saying his father knew best."

"Young men never think that," answered she. "'Tis well known that no young man ever thought his father knew better than himself."

"Then he'll pretend to for his own convenience."

"What about all that talk of changes for the better before Mister Ironsyde died then?"

"Talk of dead men won't go far. We'll hear no more of that."

Sarah frowned and went her way. At the door, however, she turned.

"I might get to hear something about it next Sunday very like," she said. "I'm going into Bridport to my Aunt Nelly at 'The Seven Stars'; and she's a great friend of Richard Gurd at 'The Tiger'; and 'tis there Mister Raymond spends half his time, they say. So Mr. Gurd may have learned a bit about it."

"No doubt he'll hear a lot of words, and as for Raymond Ironsyde, his father knew him for a man with a bit of a heart in him and didn't trust him accordingly. But you can take it from me—"

A bell rang and its note struck Mr. Baggs dumb. He ceased both to speak and work, dropped his hank, turned down his shirt sleeves and put on his coat. Sarah at the stroke of the bell also manifested no further interest in Levi's forebodings but left him abruptly. For it was noon and the dinner-hour had come.

CHAPTER IV

CHAINS FOR RAYMOND

Raymond Ironsyde had spent his life thus far in a healthy and selfish manner. He owned no objection to hard work of a physical nature, for as a sportsman and athlete he had achieved fame and was jealous to increase it. He preserved the perspective of a boy into manhood; while his father waited, not without exasperation, for him to reach adult estate in mind as well as body. Henry Ironsyde was still waiting when he died and left Raymond to the mercy of Daniel.

Now the brothers had met to thresh out the situation; and a day came when Raymond lunched with his friend and fellow sportsman, Arthur Waldron, of North Hill House, and furnished him with particulars.

In time past, Raymond's grandfather had bought a thousand acres of land on the side of North Hill. Here he destroyed one old farmhouse and converted another into the country-seat of his family. He lived and died there; but his son, Henry, cared not for it, and the place had been let to successive tenants for many years.

Waldron was the last of these, and Raymond's ambition had always been some day to return to North Hill House and dwell in his grandfather's home.

At luncheon the party of three sat at a round table on a polished floor of oak. Estelle played hostess and gazed with frank admiration at the chattering visitor. He brought a proposition that made her feel very excited to learn what her father would think of it.

Mr. Waldron was tall and thin. He lived out of doors and appeared to be made of iron, for nothing wearied him as yet. He had high cheek-bones, and a clean-shaved, agreeable face. He took sport most seriously, was jealous for its rights and observant of its rituals even in the smallest matters. Upon the etiquette of all field sports he regarded himself, and was regarded, as an arbiter.

"Tell me how it went," he said. "I hope your brother was sporting?"

Mr. Waldron used this adjective in the widest possible sense. It embraced all reputable action and covered virtue. If conduct were 'sporting,' he demanded no more from any man; while, conversely, 'unsporting' deeds condemned the doer in all relations of life and rendered him untrustworthy from every standpoint.

"Depends what you call 'sporting,'" answered Raymond, whose estimate of the word was not so comprehensive. "You'd think it would have been rather a case for generosity, but Dan didn't seem to see that. It's unlucky for me in a way he's not larger-minded. He's content with justice—what he calls justice. But justice depends on the mind that's got to do it. There's no finality about it, and what Daniel calls justice, I call beastly peddling, if not actual bullying."

"And what did he call justice?"

"Well, his first idea was to be just to my father, who was wickedly unjust to me. That wasn't too good for a start, for if you are going to punish the living, because the dead wanted them to be punished, what price your justice anyway? But Daniel had a sort of beastly fairness too, for he recognised that my father's very sudden death must be taken into account. My Aunt Jenny supported me there; and she was sure he would have altered his will if he had had time. Daniel granted that, and I began to hope I was going to come well out of it; but I counted my chickens before they were hatched. Some people have a sort of diseased idea of the value of work and seem to think if you don't put ten hours a day into an office, you're not justifying your existence. Unfortunately for me Daniel is one of those people. If you don't work, you oughtn't to eat—he actually thinks that."

"The fallacy is that what seems to be play to a mind like Daniel's, is really seen to be work by a larger mind," explained Arthur Waldron. "Sport, for instance, which is the backbone of British character, is a thousand times more important to the nation than spinning yarn; and we, who keep up the great tradition of British sport on the highest possible plane, are doing a great deal more valuable work—unpaid, mark you—than mere merchants and people of that kind who toil after money."

"Of course; but I never yet met a merchant who would see it—certainly not Daniel. In fact I've got to work—in his way."

"D'you mean he's stopping the allowance?"

"Yes. At least he's not renewing it. He's offering me a salary if I'll work. A jolly good salary, I grant. I can be just to him, though he can't to me. But, if I'm going to draw the salary, I've got to learn the business and, in fact, go into it and become a spinner. Then, at the end of five years, if I shine and really get keen about it and help the show, he'll take me into partnership. That's his offer; and first I told him to go to the devil, and then I changed my mind and, after my aunt had sounded Daniel and found that was his ultimatum, I climbed down."

"What are you to do? Surely he won't chain an open-air man like you to a wretched desk all your time?"

"So I thought; but he didn't worry about that. I wanted to go abroad, and combine business with pleasure, and buy the raw material in Russia and India and Italy and so on. That might have been good enough; but in his rather cold-blooded way, he pointed out that to buy raw material, you wanted to know something about raw material. He asked me if I knew hemp from flax, and of course I had to say I did not. So that put the lid on that. I've got to begin where Daniel began ten years ago—at the beginning—with this difference, that I get three hundred quid a year. In fact there's such a mixture of fairness and unfairness in Daniel's idea that you don't know where to have him."

"What shall you do about it?"

"I tell you I've agreed. I must live, obviously, and I'd always meant to do something some day. But naturally my ideas were open air, and I thought when I got things going and took a scheme to my father—for horse-breeding or some useful enterprise—he would have seen I meant business and come round and planked down. But Daniel has got no use for horse-breeding, so I must be a spinner—for the time anyway."

Estelle ventured to speak.

"But only girls spin," she said. "You'd never be able to spin, Ray."

Raymond laughed.

"Everybody's got to spin, it seems," he answered.

"Except the lilies," declared Estelle gravely. "'They toil not, neither do they spin,' you know."

Mr. Waldron regarded his daughter with respect.

"Just imagine," he said, "at her age. They've made her a member of the Field Botanists' Club. Only eleven years old and invited to join a grown-up club!"

Raymond was somewhat impressed.

"Fancy a kid like you knowing anything about botany," he said.

"I don't," answered the child. "I'm only just beginning. Why, I haven't mastered the grasses yet. The flowers are easy, of course, but the grasses are ever so difficult."

They returned to Ironsyde's plans.

"And when d'you weigh in?" queried his friend.

"That's the point. That's why I invited myself to lunch. Daniel doesn't want me in the office at Bridport; he wants me here—at Bridetown—so that I can mess about in the works and see a lot of John Best, the foreman, and learn all the practical side of the business. It seems rather footling work for a man, but he did it; and he says the first thing is to get a personal understanding of the processes and all that. Of course I've always been keen on machinery."

"Good, then we shall see something of each other."

"That's what I want—more than you do, very likely. The idea was that I went to Uncle Ernest, who is willing to let me have a room at 'The Magnolias' and live with him for a year, which is the time Daniel wants me to be here; but I couldn't stick Churchouse for a year."

"Naturally."

"So what do you say? Are you game for a paying guest? You've got tons of room and I shouldn't be in the way."

"How lovely!" cried Estelle. "Do come!"

Arthur Waldron was quietly gratified.

"I'm sure I should be delighted to have a pal in the house—a kindred spirit, who understands sport. By all means come," he said.

"You're sure? I should be out most of my time at the blessed works, you know. Could I bring my horse?"

"Certainly bring your horse."

"That reminds me of one reasonable thing Dan's going to do," ran on the other. "He's going to clear me. I told Aunt Jenny it was no good beginning a new life with a millstone of debts round my neck—in fact we came down to that. I said it was a vital condition. Aunt Jenny had rather a lively time between us. She sympathises with me tremendously, however, and finally got Daniel to promise he would pay off every penny I owed—a paltry two hundred or so."

"A very sporting arrangement. Make the coffee, Estelle, then we'll take a walk on the downs."

"I'm going to Uncle Ernest to tea," explained Raymond. "I shall tell him then that I'm not coming to him, thanks to your great kindness."

"He will be disappointed," declared Estelle. "It seems rather hard of us to take you away from him, I'm afraid."

"Don't you worry, kiddy. He'll get over it. In fact he'll be jolly thankful, poor old bird. He only did it because he thought he ought to. It's the old, traditional attitude of the Churchouses to the Ironsydes."

"He's very wise about church bells, but he's rather vague about flowers," replied Estelle. "He's only interested in dead things, I think; and things that happened long, long ago."

"In a weird sort of way, a hobby is a man's substitute for sport, I believe," said Estelle's father. "Many have no feeling for sport; it's left out of them and they seem to be able to live comfortably without it. Instead they develop an instinct for something else. Generally it's deadly from the sportsman's point of view; but it seems to take the place of sport to the sportless. How old ruins, or church bells, can supersede a vital, living thing, like the sport of a nation, of course you and I can't explain; but so it is with some minds."

"It depends how they were brought up," suggested Raymond.

"No—take you; you weren't brought up to sport. But your own natural, good instinct took you to it. Same with me. The moment I saw a ball, I'm told that I shrieked till they gave it to me—at the age of one that was. And from that time forward they had no trouble with me. A ball always calmed me. Why? Because a ball, you may say, is the emblem of England's greatness. I was thinking over it not long ago. There is not a single game of the first importance that does not depend on a ball. If one had brains, one could write a book on the inner meaning of that fact. I believe that the ball has a lot to do with the greatness of the Empire."

"A jolly good idea. I'll try it on Uncle Ernest," promised Raymond.

He was cheerful and depressed in turn. His company made him happy and the thought that he would come to live at North Hill House also pleased him well; but from time to time the drastic change in his life swept his thoughts like a cloud. The picture of regular work—unloved work that would enable him to live—struck distastefully upon his mind.

They strolled over North Hill after luncheon and Estelle ran hither and thither, busy with two quests. Her sharp eyes were in the herbage for the flowers and grasses; but she also sought the feathers of the rooks and crows who assembled here in companies.

"The wing feathers are the best for father's pipes," she explained; "but the tail feathers are also very good. Sometimes I get splendid luck and find a dozen or two in a morning, and sometimes the birds don't seem to have parted with a single feather. The place to find them is round the furze clumps, because they catch there when the wind blows them."

The great hogged ridge of North Hill keeps Bridetown snug in winter time, and bursts the snow clouds on its bosom. To-day the breezes blew and shadows raced above the rolling green expanses. The downs were broken by dry-built walls and spattered with thickets of furze and white-thorn, black-thorn and elder. Blue milkwort, buttercups and daisies adorned them, with eye-bright and the lesser, quaking grass that danced over the green. Rabbits twinkled into the furzes where Waldron's three fox terriers ran before the party; and now and then a brave buck coney would stand upon the nibbled knoll above his burrow and drum danger before he darted in. It was a haunt of the cuckoo and peewit, the bunting and carrion crow.

"Here we killed on the seventeenth of January last," said Raymond's host. "A fine finish to a grand run. We rolled him over on this very spot after forty-five minutes of the best. It is always good to remember great moments in the past."

On the southern slope of North Hill there stood a ruined lime-kiln whose walls were full of fern and coated with mother o' thyme. A bank of brier and nettles lay before the mouth. They hid the foot of the kiln and made a snug and secluded spot. Bridetown clustered in its elms far below; then the land rose again to protect the hamlet from the south; and beyond stretched the blue line of the Channel.

The men sat here and smoked, while Estelle hunted for flowers and feathers.

She came back to them presently with a bee orchis. "For you," she said, and gave it to Raymond. "What the dickens is it?" he asked, and she told him. "They're rather rare, but they live happily on the down in some places. I know where." He thanked her very much.

"Never seen one before," he said. "A funny little pink and black devil, isn't it?"

"It isn't a devil," she assured him; "if anything, it's an angel. But really it's more like a small bumble-bee than anything. Perhaps you've never seen a bumble-bee either?"

"Oh, yes, I have—they don't sting." Estelle laughed.

"I thought that once. A boy in the village told me that bumble-bees have 'got no spears.' And I believed him and tried to help one out of the window once. And I very soon found that he had got a spear."

"That reminds me I must take a wasps' nest to-night," said her father. "I've not decided which way to take it yet. There are seven different ways to take a wasps' nest—all good."

They strolled homeward presently and parted at the lodge of North Hill House.

"You must come down and choose your room soon," said Estelle. "It must be one that gets the sun in it, and the moon. People always want the sun, but they never seem to want the moon."

"Don't they, Estelle! I know lots of people who want the moon," declared Raymond. "Perhaps I do."

"You can have your choice of four stalls for the horse," said Arthur Waldron. "I always ride before breakfast myself, wet or fine. Only frost stops me. I hope you will too—before you go to the works."

Raymond was soon at 'The Magnolias,' and found Mr. Churchouse expecting him in the garden. They had not met since Henry Ironsyde's death, but the elder, familiar with the situation, did not speak of Raymond's father.

He was anxious to learn the young man's decision, and proved too ingenuous to conceal his relief when the visitor explained his plans.

"I felt it my duty to offer you a temporary home," he said, "and we should have done our best to make you comfortable, but one gets into one's routine and I won't disguise from you that I am glad you go to North Hill House, Raymond."

"You couldn't disguise it if you tried, Uncle Ernest. You're thankful— naturally. You don't want youth in this dignified abode of wisdom. Besides, you've got no place for a horse—you know you haven't."

"I've no objection to youth, my dear boy, but I can't pretend that the manners and customs of youth are agreeable to me. Tobacco, for example, causes me the most acute uneasiness. Then the robustness and general exaggeration of the youthful mind and body! It rises beyond fatigue, above the middle-aged desire for calm and comfort. It kicks up its heels for sheer joy of living; it is ever in extremes; it lacks imagination, with the result that it is ruthless. All these characteristics may go with a delightful personality— as in your case, Raymond—but let youth cleave to youth. Youth understands youth. You will in fact be much happier with Waldron."

"And you will be happier without me."

"It may be selfish to say so, but I certainly shall."

"Well, you've had the virtue of making the self-denial and I think it was awfully good of you to do so."

"I am always here and always very happy and willing to befriend the grandson of my father's partner," declared Mr. Churchouse. "It is excellent news that you are going into the business."

"Remains to be seen."

The dining room at 'The Magnolias' was also the master's study. There were innocent little affectations in it and the room was arranged to create an atmosphere of philosophy and art. Books thronged in lofty book-shelves with glass doors. These were surmounted by plaster busts of Homer and Minerva, toned to mellowness by time. In the window was the writing desk of Mr. Churchouse, upon which stood a photograph of Goethe.

Tea was laid and a girl brought in the hot water when Mr. Churchouse rang for it. After she had gone Raymond praised her enthusiastically.

"By Jove, what a pretty housemaid!" he exclaimed.

"Pretty, yes; a housemaid, no," explained Mr. Churchouse. "She is the daughter of my housekeeper, Mrs. Dinnett. Mrs. Dinnett has been called to Chilcombe, to see her old mother who is, I fear, going to die, and so Sabina, with her usual kindness, has spent her half-holiday at home to look after me. Sabina lives here. She is Mrs. Dinnett's daughter and one of the spinners at the mill. In fact, Mr. Best tells me she is his most accomplished spinner and has genius for the work. In her leisure she does braiding at home, as many of the girls do."

"She's jolly handsome," declared Raymond. "She's chucked away in a place like this."

"D'you mean 'The Magnolias'?" asked the elder mildly.

"No, not 'The Magnolias' particularly, but Bridetown in general."

"And why should Bridetown be denied the privilege of numbering a beautiful girl amongst its population?"

"Oh—why—she's lost, don't you see. Working in a stuffy mill, she's lost. If she was on the stage, then thousands would see her. A beautiful thing oughtn't to be hidden away."

"God Almighty hides away a great many beautiful things," answered Mr. Churchouse. "There are many beautiful things in our literature and our flora and fauna that are never admired."

"So much the worse. When our fauna blossoms out in the shape of a lovely girl, it ought to be seen and give pleasure to thousands."

Ernest smiled.

"I don't think Sabina has any ambition to give pleasure to thousands. She is a young woman of very fine temper, with a dignified sense of her own situation and an honest pride in her own dexterity."

"Engaged to be married, of course?"

"I think not. She and her mother are my very good friends. Had any betrothal taken place, I feel sure I should have heard of it."

"Do ring for her, Mr. Churchouse, and let me look at her again. Does she know how good-looking she is?"

"Youth! Youth! Yes, not being a fool, she knows she is well-favoured— much as you do, no doubt. I mean that you cannot shave yourself every morning without being conscious that you are in the Greek mould. I could show you the engraving of a statue by Praxiteles which is absurdly like you. But this accident of nature has not made you vain."

"Me! Good Lord!"

Raymond laughed long.

"Do not be puffed up," continued Mr. Churchouse, "for, with charm, you combine to a certain extent the Greek vacuity. There are no lines upon your brow. You don't think enough."

"Don't I, by Jove! I've been thinking a great deal too much lately. I've had a headache once."

"Lack of practice, my dear boy. Sabina, being a woman of observation and intelligence, is no doubt aware of the fact that she is unusually personable. But she has brains and knows exactly what importance to attach to such an accident. If you want to learn what spinning means, she will be able to teach you."

"Every cloud has a silver lining, apparently," said Raymond, and when Sabina returned, Ernest introduced him.

The girl was clad in black with a white apron. She wore no cap.

"This is Mr. Raymond Ironsyde, Sabina, and he's coming to learn all about the Mill before long."

Raymond began to rattle away and Sabina, without self-consciousness, listened to him, laughed at his jests and answered his questions.

Mr. Churchouse gazed at them benevolently through his glasses. He came unconsciously under the influence of their joy of life.

Their conversation also pleased him, for it struck a right note—the note which he considered was seemly between employer and employed. He did not know that youth always modifies its tone in the presence of age, and that those of ripe years never hear the real truth concerning the opinions of the younger generation.

When Raymond left for home and Mr. Churchouse walked out to the gate with him, Sabina peeped out of the kitchen window which commanded the entrance, and her face was lighted with very genuine animation and interest.

Mrs. Dinnett returned at midnight tearful, for the ancient woman at Chilcombe had died in her arms—"at five after five," as she said.

Mary Dinnett was an excitable and pessimistic person. She always leapt to meet trouble half way and invariably lost her nerve upon the least opportunity to do so. The peace of 'The Magnolias' had long offered her a fitting sanctum, for here life moved with the utmost simplicity and regularity; but, though as old as he was, Mary looked ahead to the time when Mr. Churchouse might fall, and could always win an ample misery from the reflection that she must then be at the mercy of an unfriendly world.

Sabina heard the full story of her grandmother's decease with every detail of the passing, but it was the face of a young man, not the countenance of an old woman, that flitted through her thoughts as she went to sleep that night.

CHAPTER V

IN THE MILL

John Best was taking Raymond Ironsyde round the spinning mill, but the foreman had his own theory and proposed to initiate the young man by easy stages.

"You've seen the storehouses and the hacklers," he said. "Now if you just look into the works and get a general idea of the scheme of things, that's enough for one day."

In the great building two sounds deafened an unfamiliar ear: a steady roar, deep and persistent, and through it, like a staccato pulse, a louder, more painful, more penetrating din. The bass to this harsh treble arose from humming belts and running wheels; the crash that punctuated their deep-mouthed riot broke from the drawing heads of the machines.

A lofty, open roof, full of large sky-lights, covered the operating room, and in its uplifted dome supports and struts leapt this way and that, while, at the height of the walls, ran rods supporting rows of silver-bright wheels from which the power descended, through endless bands, to the machinery beneath. The floor was of stone, and upon it were disposed the various machine systems—the Card and Spreader, the Drawing Frames, Roving Frames, Gill Spinners and Spinning Frames.

The general blurred effect in Raymond's mind was one of disagreeable sound, which made speech almost impossible. The din drove at him from above and below; and it was accompanied by a thousand unfamiliar movements of flying bands and wheels and squat masses of machinery that convulsed and heaved and palpitated round him. From nearly all the machines there streamed away continuous bright ribbons of hemp or flax, that caught the light and shone. This was the 'sliver,' the wrought, textile material passing through its many changes before it came to the spinners. The amber and lint-white coils of the winding sliver made a brightness among the duns and drabs around them and their colour was caught again aloft where whisps of material hung irregularly—lumps of waste from the ends of the bobbins—and there were also colour notes of warmth in the wooden wheels on many of the machines. These struck a genial tone into the chill greys and flash of polished steel on every side.

After the mechanical activity, movement came from the irregular actions of the workers. Forty women and girls laboured here, and while some old people only sat on stools by the spouting sliver and wound it away into the tall cans that received it, other younger folk were more intensively engaged. The massive figure of Sally Groves lumbered at her ministry, where she fed the Carding Machine. She was subdued to the colour of the hemp tow with which she plied it. Elsewhere Sarah Northover flashed the tresses of long lines over her head and seemed to perform a rhythmic dance with her hands, as she tore each strick into three and laid the shining locks on her spread board. Others tended the drawers and rovers, while Sabina Dinnett, Nancy Buckler and Alice Chick, whose high task it was to spin, seemed to twinkle here, there and everywhere in a corybantic measure as they served the shouting and insatiable monsters that turned hemp and flax to yarn.

They, indeed, specially attracted Raymond, by the activity of their work and the charm of their swift, supple figures, where, never still, they danced about, with a thousand, strenuous activities of hand and foot and eye. Their work dazed him and he wanted to stop here and ask Sabina many questions. She looked much more beautiful while spinning than in her black dress and white apron—so the young man thought. Her work displayed her neat, slim shape as she twirled round, stooped, leapt up again, twisted and stood on tip-toe in a thousand fascinating attitudes. Never a dancer in the limelight had revealed so much beauty. She was rayed in a brown gown with a short skirt, and on her head she wore a grey woollen cap.

But Mr. Best forbade interest in the spinners.

"You'll not get to them for a week yet," he said. "I'll ask you to just take in the general hang of it, Mister Raymond, please. Power comes from the water-wheel and the steam engine and it's brought down to each machine. Just throw your eyes round. You ain't here to look at the girls, if you'll excuse my saying so. You're here to learn."

"You can learn more from the girls than all these noisy things put together," laughed Raymond; while Mr. Best shook his head and proceeded with his instructions.

"Those exhausts above each system suck away the dust and small rubbish," he explained. "We shouldn't be able to breathe without them."

The other looked up and saw great leaden-coloured tubes, like organ pipes, above him. Mr. Best droned on and strove to lay a foundation for future knowledge. He was skilled in every branch of the work, and a past master of all spinning mysteries. His lucid and simple exposition had very well served to introduce an attentive stranger to the complex operations going on around him, but Raymond was not attentive. He failed to concentrate and missed fundamental essentials from the desire to examine more advanced and obviously interesting operations.

He apologised to John Best before the dinner-hour.

"This is only a preliminary canter," he said. "It's all Greek to me and it will take time to get the thing clear. It looks quite different to me from what it must to you. I'll get the general scheme into my head first and then work out the details. A man's mind can't make order out of this chaos in a minute."

He stood and tried to appreciate the trend of events. He enjoyed the adventure, but at present made no effort to do more than enjoy it. He would start to work later. He began to like the din and the dusty light and the glitter and shine of polished metal and bright sliver eternally winding into the cans. Round it hovered or sat the women like dull moths. They wound the stream of hemp or flax away and snapped it when a can was full. There was no pause or slackening, nothing but the whirl of living hands and arms and bodies, dead wheels and teeth and pulleys and pins operating on the inert tow. The mediators, animate and inanimate, laboured together for its manufacture; while the masses of mingled wood and steel, leather and brass and iron, moved in controlled obedience to the giant forces liberated from steam and water that drove all. The selfsame power, gleaned from sunshine and moisture and sublimated to human flesh and blood through bread, plied in the fingers and muscles and countless, complex mental directions of the men and women who controlled. From sun-light and air, earth and water had also sprung the fields of hemp and flax in far-off lands and yielded up their loveliness to foreign scutchers. The dried death of countless beautiful herbs now represented the textile fabric on which all this immense energy was applied.

Thus far, along an obvious line of thought, Raymond's reflections took him, but there his slight mental effort ended, and even this much tired him. The time for dinner came; Mr. Best now turned certain hand-wheels and moved certain levers. They shut off the power and gradually the din lessened, the pulsing and throbbing slowed until the whole great complexity came to a stand-still. The drone of the overhead wheels ceased, the crash of the draw-heads stopped. A startling silence seemed to grow out of the noise and quell it, while a new activity manifested itself among the workers. As a bell rang they were changed in a twinkling and, amid chatter and laughter, like breaking chrysalids, they flung off their basset aprons and dun overalls, to emerge in brighter colours. Blouses of pink and blue and red flashed out, straw hats and sun-bonnets appeared, and all streamed away like magic to their neighbouring houses. It was as though its soul had passed and left a dead mill behind it.

Raymond, released for a moment from the attentions of the foreman, strolled among the machines of the minders and spinners. Then his eyes were held by an intimate and personal circumstance that linked these women to this place. He found that on the whitewashed walls beside their working corners, the girls had impressed themselves—their names, their interests, their hopes. With little picture galleries were the walls brightened, and with sentiments and ideas. The names of the workers were printed up in old stamps—green and pink—and beside them one might read, in verses, or photographs, or pictures taken from the journals, something of the history, taste and personal life of those who set them there. Serious girls had written favourite hymns beside their working places; the flippant scribbled jokes and riddles; the sentimental copied love songs that ran to many verses. Often the photograph of a maiden's lover accompanied them, and there were also portraits of mothers and sisters, babies and brothers. Some of the girls had hung up fashion-plates and decorated their workshop with ugly and mean designs for clothing that they would never wear.

Raymond found that picture postcards were a great feature of these galleries, and they contained also, of course, many private jests and allusions lost upon the visitor. Character was revealed in the collections; for the most part they showed desire for joy, and aspiration to deck the working-place with objects and words that should breed happy thoughts and draw the mind where its treasure harboured. Each heart it seemed was holding, or seeking, a romance; each heart was settled about some stalwart figure presented in the picture gallery, or still finding temporary substance for dreams in love poetry, in representations of happy lovers at stiles, in partings of soldier and sailor lads from their sweethearts. Beside some of the old workers the walls were blank. They had nothing left to set down, or hang up.

Raymond was arrested by a little rhyme round which a black border had been pasted. It was original:

"I am coiling, coiling, coiling
  Into the can,
And thinking, thinking, thinking,
  Of my dear man.

"He is toiling, toiling, toiling
  Out on the sea,
And thinking, thinking, thinking
  Only of me.

"F.H."

Mr. Best joined Ironsyde.

"These walls!" he said. "It's about time we had a coat of whitewash. Mister Daniel thinks so too."

"Why—good lord—this is the most interesting part of the whole show. This is alive! Who's F.H.?"

"The girls will keep that. They like it, though I tell them it would be better rubbed out. Poor Flossy Hackett wrote that. She was going to marry a sailor-man, but he changed his mind, and she broke her heart and drowned herself—that's all there is to it."

"The damned rascal. I hope he got what he deserved."

Mr. Best allowed his mind to peep from the shell that usually concealed it.

"If he did, he was one man in a thousand. He married a Weymouth woman and Flossy went into the river—in the deep pool beyond the works. A clever sort of girl, but a dreamer you might say."

"I'd like to have had the handling of that devil!"

"You never know. She may have had what's better than a wedding ring—in happy dreams. Reality's not the best of life. People do change their minds. He was honest and all that. Only he found somebody else he liked better."

At this moment Daniel Ironsyde came into the works, and while John Best hastened to him, Raymond pursued his amusement and studied the wall by the spinning frame where Sabina Dinnett worked. He found a photograph of her mother and a quotation from Shakespeare torn off a calendar for the date of August the third. He guessed that might be Sabina's birthday. The quotation ran:—

"To thine own self be true;
And it must follow, as the night the day,
Thou canst not then be false to any man."

There was no male in Sabina's picture gallery—indeed, no other picture but that of a girl—her fellow spinner, Nancy Buckler.

His brother approached Raymond.

"You've made a start, Ray?"

"Rather. It's jolly interesting. Best is wonderful, but he can't fathom my ignorance yet."

"It's all very simple and straightforward. Do you like your office?"

"Yes," declared the younger. "Couldn't beat it. When I want something to do, I can fling a line out of the window and fish in the river."

"You have plenty to do besides fish out of the window I should hope. Let us lunch. I'm stopping here this afternoon. Aunt Jenny wanted to know whether you'd come to Bridport to dinner on Sunday."

Daniel was entirely friendly now and he designed—if the future should justify the step—to take Raymond into partnership. But only in the event of very material changes in his brother's life would he do so. Their aunt felt sanguine that Raymond must soon recognise his responsibilities, settle to the business of justifying his existence and put away childish things; Daniel was less hopeful, but trusted that she might be right. Her imagination worked for Raymond and warned her nephew not to be too exacting at first. She pointed out that it was very improbable Daniel's brother would become a model in a moment, or settle down to the business of fixed hours and clerical work without a few lapses from the narrow and arduous path. So the elder was prepared to see his brother kick against the pricks and even warned John Best that it might be so. Brief acquaintance with Raymond had already convinced the foreman of this probability, and he found himself liking Daniel's brother from the first. The dangers, however, were not hid from him; but while he perceived the youthful instability of the newcomer and his impatience of detail, he presently discovered an interest in mechanical contrivances, a spark of originality, and a feeling for new things that might lead to results, if only the necessary application were forthcoming and the vital interest aroused.

Mr. Best had a simple formula.

"The successful spinner," he often remarked, "is the man who can turn out the best yarn from a given sample of the raw. Hand identical stuff to ten manufacturers and you'll soon see where the best yarn comes from."

He knew of better yarns than came from the Ironsyde mill, and regretted the fact. That a time might arrive when Raymond would see with him seemed exceedingly improbable; yet he felt the dim possibility by occasional flashes in the young man, and it was a quality of Mr. Best's mind to be hopeful and credit other men with his own aspirations, if any excuse existed for so doing.

CHAPTER VI

'THE SEVEN STARS'

On a Saturday in August, Sarah Northover, one of those who minded the 'spreader' at Bridetown Mill, came to see her aunt—the mistress of 'The Seven Stars,' in Barrack Street, Bridport.

She had walked three miles through the hot and dusty lanes and found the shady streets of Bridport cool by comparison, but there was work for her at 'The Seven Stars,' and Mrs. Northover proved very busy. A holiday party of five-and-twenty guests was arriving at five o'clock for tea, and Sarah, perceiving that her own tea would be a matter for the future, lent her aunt a hand.

Her tea gardens and pleasure grounds were the pride of Nelly Northover's heart. Three quarters of an acre extended here behind the inn, and she had erected swings for the children and laid a croquet lawn for those who enjoyed that pastime. Lawn tennis she would not permit, out of respect for her herbaceous border which surrounded the place of entertainment. At one corner was a large summer-house in which her famous teas were generally taken. The charge was one shilling, and being of generous disposition, Mrs. Northover provided for that figure a handsome meal.

She was a large, high-bosomed woman, powerfully built, and inclined to stoutness. Her complexion was sanguine, and her prominent eyes were very blue. Of a fair-minded and honest spirit, she suffered from an excitable temper and rather sharp tongue. But her moods were understood by her staff, and if her emotional quality did injustice, an innate sense of what was reasonable ultimately righted the wrong.

Sarah helped Job Legg and others to prepare for the coming party, while Mrs. Northover roamed the herbaceous border and cut flowers to decorate the table. While she pursued this work there bustled in Richard Gurd from 'The Tiger.' He was in his shirt-sleeves and evidently pushed for time.

"Wonders never cease," said Nelly, smiling upon him. "It's a month of Sundays since you was in my gardens. I'll lay you've come for some flowers for your dining table."

Reciprocity was practised between these best of friends, and while Mr. Gurd often sent customers to Mrs. Northover, since tea parties were not a branch of business he cared about, she returned his good service with gifts from the herbaceous border and free permission to use her spacious inn yard and stables.

"I'm always coming to have a look round at your wonderful flower-bed," said Richard, "and some Sunday morning, during church hours, I will do so; but you know how busy we all are in August. And I don't want no flowers; but I want the run of your four-stall stable. There's a 'beano' coming over from Lyme and I'm full up already."

"Never no need to ask," she answered. "I'll tell Job to set a man on to it."

He thanked her very heartily and she gave him a rose. Then he admired the grass, knowing that she prided herself upon it.

"Never seen such grass anywhere else in Bridport," he assured her. "There's lots try to grow grass like yours; but none can come near this."

"'Tis Job's work," she told him. "He's a Northerner and had the charge of a bowling-green at his uncle's public; and what he don't know about grass ain't worth knowing."

"He's a sheet-anchor, that man," confessed Richard; "a sheet-anchor and a tower of strength, as you might say."

"I don't deny it," admitted Nelly. "Sometimes, in a calm moment, I run my mind over Job Legg, and I'm almost ashamed to think how much I owe him."

"It ain't all one way, however. He's got a snug place, and no potman in Dorset draws more money, though there's some who draws more beer."

"There's no potman in Dorset with his head," she answered. "He's got a brain and it's very seldom indeed you find such an honest chap with such a lot of intellects. The clever ones are mostly the downy ones; but Job's single thought is the welfare of the house, and he pushes honesty to extremes."

"If you can say that, he must be a wonder, certainly, for none knows what honesty means better than you," said Mr. Gurd. He had put Nelly's rose into his coat.

"He's more than a potman, chiefly along of being such a good friend to my late husband. Almost the last sensible thing my poor dear said to me before he died was never to get rid of Job. And no doubt I never shall. I'm going to put up his money at Michaelmas."

"Well, don't make the man a god, and don't you spoil him. Job's a very fine chap and can carry corn as well as most of 'em—in fact far better; but a man is terrible quick to trade on the good opinion of his fellow man, and if you let him imagine you can't do without him, you may put false and fantastic ideas into his head."

"I'm not at all sure if I could do without him," she answered, "though, even if he knew it, he's far too fine a character to take advantage. A most modest creature and undervalued accordingly."

Then a boy ran in for Richard and he hastened away, while Nelly took a sheaf of flowers to the summer-house and made the table bright with them.

She praised her niece's activities.

"'Tis a shame to ring you in on your half-holiday," she said. "But you're one of the sensible sort, and you won't regret being a good girl to me in the time to come."

Then she turned to Job.

"Gurd's got a char-a-banc and a party on the way from Lyme, and he's full up and wants the four-horse stable," she told him. It was part of Job's genius never to be put about, or driven from placidity by anything.

"Then there's no time to lose," he said. "We're ready here, and now if Sarah will lend a hand at the table over there in the shade for the party of six—"

"Lord! I'd forgotten them."

"I hadn't," he answered. "They're cutting in the kitchen now and the party's due at four. So you'll have them very near off your hands before the big lot comes. I'll see to the stable and get in a bit of fresh straw and shake down some hay. Then I'll take the bar and let Miss Denman come to help with the tea."

He went his way and Sarah sat down a moment while her aunt arranged the flowers.

"There's no tea-tables like yours," she said.

"I pride myself on 'em. A lot goes to a tea beside the good food, in my opinion. Some human pigs don't notice my touches and only want to stuff; but the bettermost have an eye for everything sweet and clean about 'em. Such nicer characters don't like poultry messing round and common things in sight while they eat and drink. I know what I feel myself about a clean cloth and a bunch of fine flowers on the table, and many people are quite as particular as me. I train the girls up to take a pride in such things, and now and again a visitor will thank me for it."

"I could have brought a bunch of flowers from our little garden," said Sarah.

"It would be coals to Newcastle, my dear. We make a feature of 'em. Job Legg understands the ways of 'em, and you see the result. You can pick all day from my herbaceous border and not miss what you take."

"Nobody grows sweet peas like yours."

"Job again. He's mastered the sweet pea in a manner given to few. He'll bring out four on a stalk, and think nothing of it."

"Mister Best, our foreman, is wonderful in a garden, too," answered Sarah. "And a great fruit grower also."

"That reminds me. I've got a fine dish of greengages for this party. In the season I fling in a bit of fruit sometimes. It always comes as a pleasant surprise to tea people that they ain't called to pay extra for fruit."

She went her way and Sarah turned to a lesser entertainment under preparation in a shady corner of the garden.

A girl of the house was already busy there, and the guests had arrived. They were hot and thirsty. Some sat on the grass and fanned themselves. A young man did juggling feats with the croquet balls for the amusement of two young women.

Not until half-past six came any pause, but after that hour the tea drinkers thinned off; the big party had come and gone; the smaller groups were all attended to and tea was served in Mrs. Northover's private sitting-room behind the bar for herself, Sarah and the barmaid. Being refreshed and rested, Mrs. Northover turned to the affairs of her niece. At the same moment Mr. Legg came in.

"Sit down and have some tea," said Mrs. Northover.

"I've took a hasty cup," he answered, "but could very well do with another."

"And how's Mister Roberts, Sarah?" asked her aunt.

"Fine. He's playing in a cricket match to-day—Bridetown against Chilcombe. They've asked him to play for Bridport since Mister Raymond saw him bowl. He's very pleased about it."

"Teetotal, isn't he?" asked Mr. Job.

"Yes, Mister Legg. Nick have never once touched a drop in all his life and never means to."

"A pity there ain't more of the same way of thinking," said Mrs. Northover. "And I say that, though a publican and the wife of a publican; and so do you, don't you, Job?"

"Most steadfast," he replied. "When I took on barman as a profession, I never lifted pot or glass again to my own lips, and have stood between many a young man and the last half pint. I tell you this to your face, Missis Northover. Not an hour ago I was at 'The Tiger,' to let Richard Gurd know the stable was ready, and in the private bar there were six young men, all drinking for the pleasure of drinking. If the younger generation only lapped when 'twas thirsty, half the drinking-places would shut, and there wouldn't be no more brewers in the peerage."

He shook his head and drank his tea.

Mrs. Northover changed the subject.

"How's the works?" she asked. "Do the people like the new master?"

"Just the same—same hours, same money—everything. And Mister Daniel's brother, Mister Raymond's, come to it to learn the business. He is a cure!"

"He's over there now," said Job, waving his hand in the direction of 'The Tiger.' "Drinking port wine he is with that young sport, Motyer, and others like him. I don't like Motyer's face. He's a shifty chap, and a thorn in his family's side by all accounts. But Mister Raymond have a very open countenance and ought to have a good heart."

"What do you mean when you say he's a 'cure,' Sarah?" asked her aunt.

"He's that friendly with us girls," she answered. "He's supposed to be learning all there is to spinning, but he plays about half his time and you can't help laughing. He's so friendly as if he was one of us; but Sabina Dinnett is his pet. Wants to make her smoke cigarettes! But there's no harm to him if you understand."

"There's always harm to a chap that plays about and don't look after his own business," declared Job. "I understand his brother's been very proper about him, and now it's up to him; and he ain't at the Mill to offer the girls cigarettes."

"He's got his own room and Mister Best wishes he'd bide in it," explained Sarah, "but he says he must learn, and so he's always wandering around. But everybody likes him, except Levi Baggs. He don't like anybody. He'd like to draw us all over his hackling frames if he could."

They chattered awhile, then worked again; but Sarah stayed to supper, and it was not until half-past ten o'clock that she started for home.

Another Bridetown girl—Alice Chick, the spinner—had been spending her half holiday in Bridport. Now she met Sarah, by appointment, at the top of South Street and the two returned together.

CHAPTER VII

A WALK

The Carding Machine was a squat and noisy monster. Mr. Best confessed that it had put him in mind of a passage from Holy Writ, for it seemed to be all eyes, behind and before. The eyes were wheels, and beneath, the mass of the carder opened its mouth—a thin and hungry slit into which wound an endless band. Spread upon this leathern roller was the hemp tow—that mass of short material which Levi Baggs, the hackler, pruned away from his long strides. As for the minder, Sally Groves, she seemed built and born to tend a Carding Machine. She moved with dignity despite her great size, and although covered in tow dust from head to foot and powdered with a layer of pale amber fluff, she stood as well as another for the solemnity of toil, laboured steadfastly, was neither elated, nor cast down, and presented to younger women a spectacle of skill, resolution and good sense. The great woman ennobled her work; through the dust and din, with placid and amiable features, she peered, and ceased not hour after hour, to spread the tow truly and evenly upon the rolling board. One of less experience might have needed to weigh her material, but Sally never weighed; by long practice and good judgment, she produced sliver of even texture.

The carder panted, crashed and shook with its energies. It glimmered all over with the bright, hairy gossamer of the tow, which wound thinly through systems of fast and slow wheels. Between them the material was lashed and pricked, divided and sub-divided, torn and lacerated by thousands of pins, that separated strand from strand and shook the stuff to its integral fibres before building it up again. Despite the thunder and the suggestion of immense forces exerted upon the frail material, utmost delicacy marked the operations of the card. Any real strain must have torn to atoms the fine amber coils in which it ejected the strips of shining sliver. Enormous waste marked the operation. Beneath the machine rose mounds of dust and dirt, and fluff, light as thistledown; while as much was sucked away into the air by the exhaust above.

In a lion-coloured overall and under a hat tied beneath her chin with a yellow handkerchief, Sally Groves pursued her task. Then came to her Sabina Dinnett and, ceasing not to spread her tow the while, Sally spoke serious words.

"I asked Nancy Buckler to send you along when your machine stopped a minute. You won't be vexed with me if I say something, will you?"

"Vexed with you, Sally? Who ever was vexed with you?"

"I'm old enough to be your mother, and 'tis her work if anybody's to speak to you," explained Sally; "but she's not here, and she don't see what I can't help seeing."

"What have you seen then?"

"I've seen a very good-looking young man by the name of Raymond Ironsyde wasting a deuce of a lot of his time by your spinning frame; and wasting your time, too."

Sabina changed colour.

"Fancy you saying that!" she exclaimed. "He's got to learn the business— the practical side, Sally. And he wants to master it carefully and grasp the whole thing."

Miss Groves smiled.

"Ah. He didn't take long mastering the carder," she said. "Just two minutes was all he gave me, and I don't think he was very long at the drawing heads neither; and I ain't heard Sarah Northover say he spent much of his time at the spreader. It all depends on the minder whether Mister Raymond wants to know much about the work!"

"But the spinning is the hardest to understand, Sally."

"Granted, but he don't ask many questions of Alice Chick or Nancy Buckler, do he? I'm not blaming him, Lord knows, nor yet you, but for friendship I'm whispering to you to be sensible. He's a very kind-hearted young gentleman, and if he had a memory as big as his promises, he'd soon ruin himself. But, like a lot of other nice chaps full of generous ideas, he forgets 'em when the accident that woke 'em is out of his mind. And all I say, Sabina, is to be careful. He may be as good as gold, and I dare say he is, but he's gone on you—head over heels—he can't hide it. He don't even try to. And he's a gentleman and you're a spinner. So don't you be silly, and don't think the worse of me for speaking."

Sabina entertained the opinions concerning middle-age common to youth, but she was fond of Sally and set her heart at rest.

"You needn't be frightened," she answered. "He's a gentleman, as you say; and you know I'm not the sort to be a fool. I can't help him coming; and I can't be rude to the young man. For that matter I wouldn't. I won't forget what you've said all the same."

She hurried away and started her machine; but while her mind concentrated on spinning, some subconscious instincts worked at another matter and she found that Sally had cast a cloud upon a coming event which promised nothing but sunshine.

She had agreed to go for a walk with Raymond Ironsyde on the following Sunday, and he had named their meeting-place: a bridge that crossed the Bride in the vale two miles from the village. She meant to go, for the understanding between her and Raymond had advanced far beyond any point dreamed of by Sally Groves. Sabina's mind was in fact exceedingly full of Raymond, and his mind was full of her. Temperament had conspired to this state of things, for while the youth found himself in love for the first time in his life, and pursued the quest with that ardour and enthusiasm until now reserved for sport, Sabina, who had otherwise been much more cautious, was not only in love, but actually felt that shadowy ambitions from the past began to promise realisation. She was not vain, but she knew herself a finer thing in mind and body than most of the girls with whom she worked. She had read a great deal and learned much from Mr. Churchouse, who delighted to teach her, and from Mr. Best, with whom she was a prime favourite. She had refused several offers of marriage and preserved a steady determination not to wed until there came a man who could lift her above work and give her a home that would embrace comfort and leisure. She waited, confident that this would happen, for she knew that she could charm men. As yet none had come who awakened any emotion of love in Sabina; and she told herself that real love might alter her values and send her to a poor man's home after all. If that happened, she was willing; but she thought it improbable; because, in her experience, poor men were ignorant, and she felt very sure no ignorant man would ever make her love him.

Then came into her life one very much beyond her dreams, and from an attitude of utmost caution before a physical beauty that fascinated her, she woke into tremendous excitation of mind at the discovery that he, too, was interested. To her it seemed that he had plenty of brains. His ideas were human and beautiful. He declared the conditions of the workers to be not sufficiently considered. He was full of nebulous theories for the amelioration of such conditions. The spectacle of women working for a living caused Raymond both uneasiness and indignation. To Sabina, it seemed that he was a chivalric knight of romance—a being from a fairy story. She had heard of such men, but never met with one outside a novel. She glorified Raymond into something altogether sublime—as soon as she found that he liked her. He filled her head, and while her common-sense vainly tried to talk as Sally Groves had talked, each meeting with the young man threw her back upon the tremendous fact that he was deeply interested in her and did not care who knew it. Common-sense could not modify that; nor would she listen to common-sense, when it suggested that Raymond's record was uninspiring, and pointed to no great difference between him and other young men. She told herself that he was misunderstood; she whispered to herself that she understood him. It must be so, for he had declared it. He had said that he was an idealist. As a matter of fact he did not himself know the meaning of the word half as well as Sabina.

He filled her thoughts, and believing him to be honourable, in the everyday acceptation of the word, she knew she was safe and need not fear him. This fact added to the joy and excitement of a situation that was merely thrilling, not difficult. For she had to be receptive only, and that was easy: the vital matter rested with him. She did not do anything to encourage him, or take any step that her friends could call "forward." She just left it to him and knew not how far he meant to go, yet felt, in sanguine moments, that he would go all the way, sooner or later, and offer to marry her. Her friends declared it would be so. They were mightily interested, but not jealous, for the girls recognised Sabina's advantages.

When, therefore, he asked her to take a walk on a certain Sunday afternoon, she agreed to do so. There was no plotting or planning about it. He named a familiar place of meeting and proposed to go thence to the cliffs—a ramble that might bring them face to face with a dozen people who knew them. She felt the happier for that. Nor could Sally Groves and her warning cast her down for long. The hint that Raymond was a gentleman and Sabina a spinner touched a point in their friendship long past. The girl knew that well enough; but she also knew what Sally did not, and told herself that Raymond was a great deal more than a gentleman, just as she—Sabina— was something more than a spinner. That, however, was the precious knowledge peculiar to the young people themselves. She could not expect Sally, or anybody else, to know it yet.

As for the young man, life had cut away from him most of his former interests and amusements. He was keeping regular hours and working steadily. He regarded himself as a martyr, yet could get none to take that view. To him, then, came his love affair as a very present help in time of trouble. The emotions awakened by Sabina were real, and he fully believed that she was going to be essential to his life's happiness and completion. He knew nothing about women, for his athletic pursuits and ambitions to excel physically produced an indifference to them. But with the change in his existence, and the void thereby created, came love, and he had leisure to welcome it. He magnified Sabina, and since her intellect was as good as his own and her education better, he assured himself that she was in every respect superior to her position and worthy of any man's admiration.

He did not analyse his feelings or look ahead very far. He did not bother to ask himself what he wanted. He was only concerned to make Sabina 'a chum,' as he said, to himself. He knew this to be nonsense, even while he said it, but in the excitement of the quest, chose to ignore rational lines of thought.

They met by the little bridge over Bride, then walked southerly up a hill to a hamlet, and so on to the heights. Beneath the sponge-coloured cliffs eastward swept the grand scythe of Chesil Bank; but an east wind had brought its garment of grey-blue haze and the extremity of the Bank, with Portland Bill beyond, was hidden. The cliffs gave presently and green slopes sank to the beaches. They reached a place where, separated from the sea by great pebble-ridges, there lay a little mere. Two swans swam together upon it, and round about the grey stone banks were washed with silver pink, where the thrift prospered.

Sabina had not talked much, though she proved a good listener; but Raymond spoke fitfully, too, at first. He was new to this sort of thing and told her so.

"I don't believe I've ever been for a walk with a girl in my life before," he said.

"I can't walk fast enough for you, I'm afraid."

"Oh yes, you can; you're a very good walker."

At last he began to tell her about himself, in the usual fashion of the male, who knows by instinct that subject is most interesting to both. He dwelt on his sporting triumphs of the past, and explained his trials and tribulations in the present. He represented that he was mewed up like an eagle. He described how the tragic call to work for a living had sounded in his ear when he anticipated no such painful experience. Before this narrative Sabina affected a deeper sympathy than she felt, yet honestly perceived that to such a man, his present life of regular hours must be dreary and desolate.

"It's terrible dull for you, I'm sure," she said.

"It was," he confessed, "but I'm getting broken in, or perhaps it's because you're so jolly friendly. You're the only person I know in the whole world who has got the mind and imagination to see what a frightful jar it was for an open-air man like me to be dropped into this. People think it is the most unnatural thing on earth that I should suddenly begin to work. But it's just as unnatural really as if my brother suddenly began to play. Even my great friend, Arthur Waldron, talks rubbish about everybody having to work sooner or later—not that he ever did. But you were quick enough to see in a moment. You're tremendously clever, really."

"I wish I was; but I saw, of course, that you were rather contemptuous of it all."

"So I was at first," he confessed. "At first I felt that it was a woman's show, and that what women can do well is no work for men. But I soon saw I was wrong. It increased my respect for women in a way. To find, for instance, that you could do what you do single-handed and make light of it; that was rather an eye-opener. Whenever any pal of mine talks twaddle about what women can't do, I shall bring him to see you at work."

"I could do something better than spin if I got the chance," she said, and he applauded the sentiment highly.

"Of course you could, and I'm glad you've got the pluck to say so. I knew that from the first. You're a lot too clever for spinning, really. You'd shine anywhere. Let's sit here under this thorn bush. I must get some rabbiting over this scrub. The place swarms with them. You don't mind if I smoke?"

They rested, and he ventured to make a personal remark after Sabina had taken off her gloves to cool her hands.

"You've hurt yourself," he said, noting what seemed to be an injury. But she made light of it.

"It's only a corn from stopping the spindles. Every spinner's hands are like that. Alice Chick has chilblains in winter, then she gets a cruel, bad hand."

The slight deformity made Raymond uncomfortable. He could not bear to think of a woman suffering such a stigma in her tender flesh.

"They ought to invent something to prevent you being hurt," he said, and Sabina laughed.

"Why, there are very few manual trades don't leave their mark," she answered, "and a woman's lucky to get nothing worse than a scarred hand."

"Would it come right," he ventured to ask, "if you gave up spinning?"

"Yes, in no time. There are worse things happen to you in the mills than that—and more painful. Sometimes the wind from the reels numbs your fingers till you can't feel 'em and they go red, and then blue. And there's always grumbling about the temperature, because what suits hemp and flax don't suit humans. If some clever man could solve these difficulties, it would be more comfortable for us. Not that I'm grumbling. Our mill is about as perfect as any mill can be, and we've got the blessing of living in the country, too—that's worth a lot."

"You're fond of the country."

"Couldn't live out of it," she said. "Thanks to Mr. Churchouse, I know more about things than some girls."

"I should think you did."

"He's very wise and kind and lends me books."

"A very nice old bird. I nearly went to live with him when I came to Bridetown. Sorry I didn't, now."

She smiled and did not pretend to miss the compliment.

"As to the Mill," he went on; "don't think I'm the sort of chap that just drifts and is contented to let things be as they were in the time of his father and grandfather."

"Wouldn't you?"

"Certainly not. No doubt it's safer and easier and the line of least resistance and all that sort of thing. But when I've once mastered the business, you'll see. I didn't want to come in, but now I'm in, I'm going to the roots of it, and I shall have a pretty big say in things, too, later on."

"Fancy!" said Sabina.

"Oh yes. You mustn't suppose my brother and I see alike all round. We don't. He wants to be a copy of my father, and I've no ambition to be anything of the kind. My father wasn't at all sporting to me, Sabina, and it doesn't alter the fact because he's dead. The first thing is the workers, and whatever I am, I'm clever enough to know that if we don't do a good many things for the workers pretty soon, they'll do those things for themselves. But it will be a great deal more proper and breed a lot more goodwill between labour and capital, if capital takes the first step and improves the conditions and raises the wages all round. D'you know what I would do if I had my way? I'd go one better than the Trade Unions! I'd cut the ground from under their feet! I'd say to Capital 'instead of whining about the Trades Unions, get to work and make them needless.'"

But these gigantic ideas, uttered on the spur of the moment by one who knew less than nothing of his subject, did not interest Sabina as much as he expected. The reason, however, he did not know. It was that he had called her by her name for the first time. It slipped out without intention, though he was conscious of it as he spoke it; but he had no idea that it had greatly startled her and awoke mingled feelings of delight and doubt. She was delighted, because it meant her name must have been often in his thoughts, she was doubtful, because its argued perhaps a measure less of that respect he had always paid her. But, on the whole, she felt glad. He waited for her to speak and did not know that she had heard little, but was wondering at that moment if he would go back to the formal 'Miss Dinnett' again, or always call her 'Sabina' in future.

After a pause Raymond spoke.

"Now tell me about yourself," he said. "I'm sure you've heard enough about me."

"There's nothing to tell."

"How did you happen to be a spinner?"

"Mother was, so I went into it as a matter of course."

"I should have thought old Churchouse would have seen you're a genius, and educated you and adopted you."

"Nothing of a genius about me. I'm like most other girls."

"I never saw another girl like you," he said.

"You'd spoil anybody with your compliments."

"Never paid a compliment in my life," he declared.

Their conversation became desultory, and presently Sabina said she must be going home.

"Mother will be wondering."

On the way back they met another familiar pair and Sabina speculated as to what Raymond thought; but he showed no emotion and took off his hat to Sarah Northover and Nicholas Roberts, the lathe worker, as they passed by. Sarah smiled, and Nicholas, a thin, good-looking man, took off his hat also.

"I must go and study the lathes," said Raymond after they had passed. "That's a branch of the work I haven't looked at yet. Roberts seems a good chap, and he's a very useful bowler, I find."

"He's engaged to Sarah; they're going to be married when he can get a house."

"That's another thing that must be looked to. There are scores of cottages that want pulling down here. I shall point that out to the Lord of the Manor when I get a chance."

"You're all for changes and improvements, Mister Ironsyde."

"Call me Raymond, Sabina."

"I couldn't do that."

"Why not? I want you to. By the way, may I call you Sabina?"

"Yes, if you care to."

They parted at the entrance gate of 'The Magnolias,' and Raymond thanked her very heartily for her company.

"I've looked forward to this," he said. "And now I shall look forward to the next time. It's very sporting of you to come and I'm tremendously grateful and—good-bye, Sabina—till to-morrow."

He went on up the road to North Hill House and felt the evening had grown tasteless without her. He counted the hours to when he would see her again. She went to work at seven o'clock, but he never appeared at the Mill until ten, or later.

He began to see that this was the most serious thing within his experience. He supposed that it must be enduring and tend to alter the whole tenor of his life. Marriage was one of the stock jokes in his circle, yet, having regard for Sabina, this meant marriage or nothing. He felt ill at ease, for love had not yet taken the bit and run away with him. Other interests cried out to him—interests that he would have to give up. He tried to treat the matter as a joke with himself, but he could not. He felt melancholy, and that night at supper Waldron asked what was wrong, while Estelle told him he must be ill, because he was so dull.

"I don't believe the spinning works are good for you," she said.

"Ask for a holiday and distract your mind with other things," suggested Waldron. "If you'd come out in the mornings and ride for a couple of hours before breakfast, as I do, you'd be all right."

"I will," promised Raymond. "I want bucking up."

He pictured Sabina on horseback.

"I wish to God I was rich instead of being a pauper!" he exclaimed.

"My advice is that you stick it out for a year or more, till you've convinced your brother you'll never be any good at spinning," said Arthur Waldron. "Then, after he knows you're not frightened of work, but, of course, can't excel at work that isn't congenial, he'll put money into your hands for a higher purpose, and you will go into breeding stock, or some such thing, to help keep up the sporting instincts of the country."

With that bright picture still before him Raymond retired. But he was not hopeful and even vague suggestions on Waldron's part that his friend should become his bailiff and study agriculture did not serve to win from the sufferer more than thanks. The truth he did not mention, knowing that neither Waldron, nor anybody else, would offer palatable counsel in connection with that.

CHAPTER VIII

THE LECTURE

Daniel Ironsyde sat with his Aunt Jenny after dinner and voiced discontent. But it was not with himself and his personal progress that he felt out of tune. All went well at the Mill save in one particular, and he found no fault either with the heads of the offices at Bridport, or with John Best, who entirely controlled the manufacture at Bridetown. His brother caused the tribulation of his mind.

Miss Ironsyde sympathised, but argued for Raymond.

"He has an immense respect for you and would not willingly do anything to annoy you, I'm sure of that. You must remember that Raymond was not schooled to this. It takes a boy of his temperament a long time to find the yoke easy. You were naturally studious, and wise enough to get into harness after you left school; Raymond, with his extraordinary physical powers, found the fascination of sport over-mastering. He has had to give up what to your better understanding is trivial and unimportant, but it really meant something to him."

"He hasn't given up as much as you might think," answered Daniel. "He's always taking holidays now for cricket matches, and he rides often with Waldron. It was a mistake his going there. Waldron is a person with one idea, and a foolish idea at that. He only thinks a man is a man when he's tearing about after foxes, or killing something, or playing with a ball of some sort. He's a bad influence for Raymond. But it's not that. It's not so much what Raymond doesn't do as what he does do. He's foolish with the spinners and minders at the Mill."

"He might be," said Jenny Ironsyde, "but he's a gentleman."

"He's an idiot. I believe he'd wreck the whole business if he had the power. Best tells me he talks to the girls about what he's going to do presently, and tells them he will raise all their wages. He suggests to perfectly satisfied people that they are not getting enough money! Well, it's only human nature for them to agree with him, and you can easily see what the result of that would be. Instead of having the hands willing and contented, they'll grow unsettled and grumble, and then work will suffer and a bad spirit appear in the Mill. It is simply insane."

"I quite agree," answered his aunt. "There's no excuse whatever for nonsense of that sort, and if Raymond minded his own business, as he should, it couldn't happen. Surely his own work doesn't throw him into the company of the girls?"

"Of course it doesn't. It's simply a silly excuse to waste his time and hear his own voice. He ought to have learned all about the mechanical part weeks ago."

"Well, I can only advise patience," said Miss Ironsyde. "I don't suppose a woman would carry much weight with him, an old one I mean—myself in fact. But failing others I will do what I can. You say Mr. Waldron's no good. Then try Uncle Ernest. I think he might touch Raymond. He's gentle, but he's wise. And failing that, you must tackle him yourself, Daniel. It's your duty. I know you hate preaching and all that sort of thing, but there's nobody else."

"I suppose there isn't. It can't go on anyway, because he'll do harm. I believe asses like Raymond make more trouble than right down wicked people, Aunt Jenny."

"Don't tell him he's an ass. Be patient—you're wonderfully patient always for such a young man, so be patient with your brother. But try Uncle Ernest first. He might ask Raymond to lunch, or tea, and give him a serious talking to. He'll know what to say."

"He's too mild and easy. It will go in at one ear and come out of the other," prophesied Daniel.

But none the less he called on Mr. Churchouse when next at Bridetown.

The old man had just received a parcel by post and was elated.

"A most interesting work sent to me from 'A Well Wisher,'" he said. "It is an old perambulation of Dorsetshire, which I have long desired to possess."

"People like your writings in the *Bridport Gazette*," declared Daniel. "Can you give me a few minutes, Uncle Ernest? I won't keep you."

"My time is always at the service of Henry Ironsyde's boys," answered the other, "and nothing that I can do for you, or Raymond, is a trouble."

"Thank you. I'm grateful. It is about Raymond, as a matter of fact."

"Ah, I'm not altogether surprised. Come into the study."

Mr. Churchouse, carrying his new book, led the way and soon he heard of the younger man's anxieties. But the bookworm increased rather than allayed them.

"Do you see anything of Raymond?" began Daniel.

"A great deal of him. He often comes to supper. But I will be frank. He does not patronise my simple board for what he can get there, nor does he find my company very exciting. He wouldn't. The attraction, I'm afraid, is my housekeeper's daughter, Sabina. Sabina, I may tell you, is a very attractive girl, Daniel. It has been my pleasure during her youth to assist at her education, and she is well informed and naturally clever. She is inclined to be excitable, as many clever people are, but she is of a charming disposition and has great natural ability. I had thought she would very likely become a schoolmistress; but in this place the call of the mills is paramount and, as you know, the young women generally follow their mothers. So Sabina found the thought of the spinning attractive and is now, Mr. Best tells me, an amazingly clever spinner—his very first in fact. And it cannot be denied that Raymond sees a good deal of her. This is probably not wise, because friendship, at their tender ages, will often run into emotion, and, naturally flattered by his ingenuous attentions, Sabina might permit herself to spin dreams and so lessen her activities as a spinner of yarn. I say she might. These things mean more to a girl than a boy."

"What can I do about it? I was going to ask you to talk sense to Raymond."

"With all the will, I am not the man, I fear. Sense varies so much from the standpoint of the observer, my dear Daniel. You, for example, having an old head on young shoulders, would find yourself in agreement with my sentiments; Raymond, having a young and rather empty head on his magnificent shoulders, would not. I take the situation to be this. Raymond's life has been suddenly changed and his prodigious physical activities reduced. He bursts with life. He is more alive than any youth I have ever known. Now all this exuberance of nature must have an outlet, and what more natural than that, in the presence of such an attractive young woman, the sex instinct should begin to assert itself?"

"You don't mean he is in love, or anything like that?"

"That is just exactly what I do mean," answered Mr. Churchouse.

"I thought he probably liked to chatter to them all, and hear his own voice, and talk rubbish about what he'll do for them in the future."

"He has nebulous ideas about wages and so on; but women are quicker than men, and probably they understand perfectly well that he doesn't know what he's talking about so far as that goes. How would it be if you took him into the office at Bridport, where he would be more under your eye?"

"He must learn the business first and nobody can teach him like Best."

"Then I advise that you talk to him yourself. Don't let the fact that you are only a year and three months older than Raymond make you too tolerant. You are really ten, or twenty, years older than he is in certain directions, and you must lecture him accordingly. Be firm; be decisive. Explain to him that life is real and that he must approach it with the same degree of earnestness and self-discipline as he devotes to running and playing games and the like. I feel sure you will carry great weight. He is far from being a fool. In fact he is a very intelligent young man with excellent brains, and if he would devote them to the business, you would soon find him your right hand. The machinery does honestly interest him. But you must make it a personal thing. He must study political economy and the value of labour and its relations to capital and the market value of dry spun yarns. These vague ideas to better the lot of the working classes are wholly admirable and speak of a good heart. But you must get him to listen to reason and the laws of supply and demand and so forth."

"What shall I say about the girls?"

"It is not so much the girls as the girl. If he had manifested a general interest in them, you need have said nothing; but, with the purest good will to Raymond and a great personal affection for Sabina, I do feel that this friendship is not desirable. Don't think I am cynical and worldly and take too low a view of human nature—far from it, my dear boy. Nothing would ever make me take a low view of human nature. But one has not lived for sixty years with one's eyes shut. Unhappy things occur and Nature is especially dangerous when you find her busy with such natural creatures as your brother and Sabina. A word to the wise. I would speak, but you will do so with far greater weight."

"I hate preaching and making Raymond think I'm a prig and all that sort of thing. It only hardens him against me."

"He knows better. At any rate try persuasion. He has a remarkably good temper and a child could lead him. In fact a child sometimes does. He'd do anything for Waldron's little girl. Just say you admire and share his ambitions for the welfare of the workers. Hint at supply and demand; then explain that all must go according to fixed laws, and amelioration is a question of time and combination, and so on. Then tackle him fearlessly about Sabina and appeal to his highest instincts. I, too, in my diplomatic way will approach him with modern instances. Unfortunately it is only too easy to find modern instances of what romance may end in. And to say that modern instances are exceedingly like ancient ones, is merely to say, that human nature doesn't change."

Fired by this advice, Daniel went straight to the works, and it was about eleven o'clock in the day when he entered his brother's office above the Mill—to find it empty.

Descending to the main shop, he discovered Raymond showing a visitor round the machines. Little Estelle Waldron was paying her first visit to the spinners and, delighted at the distraction, Raymond, on whose invitation she had come, displayed all the operation of turning flax and hemp into yarn. He aired his knowledge, but it was incomplete and he referred constantly to the operators from stage to stage.

Round-eyed and attentive, Estelle poured her whole heart and soul into the business. She showed a quick perception and asked questions that interested the girls. Some, indeed, they could not answer. Estelle's mind approached their work from a new angle and saw in it mysteries and points calling for solution that had never challenged them. Neither had her problems much struck Raymond, but he saw their force when she raised them and pronounced them most important.

"Why, that's fundamental, really," he said, "and yet, be shot, if I ever thought of it! Only Best will know and I shouldn't be surprised if he doesn't."

They stood at the First Drawing Frame when Daniel appeared. They had followed the flat ribbon of sliver from the Carding Machine. At the Drawing Frame six ribbons from the Carder were all brought together into one ribbon and so gained in quality, while losing more impurities during a second severe process of combing out.

"And even now it's not ready for spinning," explained Raymond. "Now it goes on to the Second Drawing Frame, and four of these ribbons from the First Drawer are brought together into one ribbon again. So you see that no less than twenty-four ribbons from the Carder are brought together to make stuff good enough to spin."

"What do the Drawing Frames do to it?" asked Estelle; "it looks just the same."

"Blessed if I know," confessed Raymond. "What do they do to it, Mrs. Chick?"

A venerable old woman, whose simple task was to wind away the flowing sliver into cans, made answer. She was clad in a dun overall and had a dim scarlet cap of worsted drawn over her white hair. The remains of beauty homed in her brown and wrinkled face; her grey eyes were gentle, and her expression wistful and kindly.

"The Drawing Heads level the 'sliver,' and true it, and make it good," she said. "All the rubbish is dragged out on the teeth and now, though it seems thinner and weaker, it isn't really. Now it goes to the Roving Frame and that makes it still better and ready for the spinners."

Then came Daniel, and Raymond, leaving Estelle with Mrs. Chick, departed at his brother's wish. The younger anticipated trouble and began to excuse himself.

"Waldron's so jolly friendly that I thought you wouldn't mind if I showed his little girl round the works. She's tremendously clever and intelligent."

"Of course I don't mind. That's nothing, but I want to speak to you on the general question. I do wish, Raymond, you'd be more dignified."

"Dignified! Me? Good Lord!"

"Well, if you don't like that word, say 'self-respecting.' You might take longer views and look ahead."

"You may bet your boots I do that, Dan. This life isn't so delightful that I am content to live in the present hour, I assure you. I look ahead all right."

"I mean look ahead for the sake of the business, not for your own sake. I don't want to preach, or any nonsense of that kind; but there's nobody else to speak, so I must. The point is that you don't see in the least what you are doing here. In the future my idea was—and yours, too, I suppose—that you came into the business as joint partner with me in everything."

"Jolly sporting of you, Dan."

"But that being so, can't you see you ought to support me in everything?"

"I do."

"No, you don't. You're not taking the right line in the least, and what's more, I believe you know it yourself. Don't think I'm selfish and careless about our people, or indifferent to their needs and rights. I'm quite as keen about their welfare as you are; but one can't do everything in a moment. And you're not helping them and only hindering me by talking a lot of rubbish to them."

"It isn't rubbish, Dan. I had all the facts from Levi Baggs, the hackler. He understands the claims of capital and what labour is entitled to, and all the rest of it."

"Baggs is a sour, one-sided man and will only give you a biased and wrong view. If you want to know the truth, you can come into Bridport and study it. Then you'll see exactly what things are worth, and what we get paid in open market for our goods. All you do by listening to Levi is to waste your time and waste his. And then you wander about among the women talking nonsense. And remember this: they know it's nonsense. They understand the question very much better than you do, and instead of respecting you, as they ought to respect a future master, they only laugh at you behind your back. And what will the result be? Why, when you come to have a voice in the thing, they'll remind you of all your big talk. And then you've got to climb down and they'll not respect you, or take you seriously."

"All right, old chap—enough said. Only you needn't think the people wouldn't respect me. I get on jolly well with them as a matter of fact. And I do look ahead—perhaps further than you do. I certainly wouldn't promise anything I wouldn't try to perform. In fact, I'm very keen about them. And I believe if we scrapped all the machinery and got new—"

"When you've mastered the present machinery, it will be time to talk about scrapping it," answered Daniel. "People are always shouting out for new things, and when they get them—and sacrifice a year's profits very likely in doing so—often the first thing they hear from the operatives is, that the old machinery was much better. Our father always liked to see other firms make the experiments."

"That's the way to get left, if you ask me."

"I don't ask you," answered the master. "I'm telling you, Raymond; and you ought to remember that I very well know what I'm talking about and you don't. You must give me some credit. To question me is to question our father, for I learned everything from him."

"But times change. You don't want to be left high and dry in the march of progress, my dear chap."

"No—you needn't fear that. If you're young, you're a part of progress; you belong to it. But you must get a general knowledge of the present situation in our trade before you can do anything rational in the shape of progress. I've been left a very fine business with a very honoured name to keep up, and if I begin trying to run before I can walk, I should very soon fall down. You must see that."

Raymond nodded.

"Yes, that's all right. I'm a learner and I know you can teach me a lot."

"If you'd come to me instead of to the mill people."

"You don't know their side."

"Much better than you do. I've talked with our father often and often about it. He was no tyrant and nobody could ever accuse him of injustice."

Raymond flashed; but he kept his mouth shut on that theme. The only bitter quarrels between the brothers had been on the subject of their father, and the younger knew that the ground was dangerous. At this moment the last thing he desired was any difference with Daniel.

"I'll keep it all in mind, Dan. I don't want to do anything to annoy you, God knows. Is there any more? I must go and look after young Estelle."

"Only one thing; and this is purely personal, and so I hope you'll excuse me. I've just been seeing Uncle Ernest, and nobody wished us better fortune than he does."

"He's a good old boy. I've learned a lot about spinning from him."

"I know. But—look here, Raymond, I do beg of you—I implore of you not to be too friendly with Sabina Dinnett. You can't think how I should hate anything like that. It isn't fair—it isn't fair to the woman, or to me, or to the family. You must see yourself that sort of thing isn't right. She's a very good girl—our champion spinner Best says; and if you go distracting her and taking her out of her station, you are doing her a very cruel turn and upsetting her peace of mind. And the others will be jealous, of course, and so it will go on. It isn't playing the game—it really isn't. That's all. I know you're a sportsman and all that; so I do beg you'll be a sportsman in business too, and take a proper line and remember your obligations. And if I've said a harsh, or unfair word, I'm sorry for it; but you know I haven't."

Seeing that Sabina Dinnett was now in paramount and triumphant possession of Raymond's mind, he felt thankful that his brother, by running on over this subject and concluding upon the whole question, had saved him the necessity for any direct reply. Whether he would have lied or no concerning Sabina, Raymond did not stop to consider. There is little doubt that he would. But the need was escaped; and so thankful did he feel, that he responded to the admonishment in a tone more complete and with promises more comprehensive than Daniel expected.

"You're dead right. Of course I know it! I've been a silly fool all round. But I won't open my mouth so wide in future, Dan. And don't think I'm wasting my time. I'm working like the devil, really, and learning everything from the beginning. Best will tell you that's true. He's a splendid teacher and I'll see more of him in future. And I'll read all about yarn and get the hang of the markets, and so on."

"Thank you—you can't say more. And you might come into Bridport oftener, I think. Aunt Jenny was saying she never sees you now."

"I will," promised Raymond. "I'm going to dine with you both on my birthday. I believe she'll be good for fifty quid this year. Father left her a legacy of a thousand."

They parted, and Raymond returned to Estelle, who was now watching the warping, while Daniel went into his foreman's office.

Estelle was radiant. She had fallen in love with the works.

"The girls are all so kind and clever," she said.

"Rather so. I expect you know all about everything now."

"Hardly anything yet. But you must let me come again. I do want to know all about it. It is splendidly interesting."

"Of course, come and go when you like, kiddy."

"And I'm going to ask some of them to tea with me," declared Estelle. "They all love flowers, and I'm going to show them our garden and my pets. I've asked seven of them and two men."

"Ask me, too."

She brought out a piece of paper and showed him that she had written down nine names.

"And if they like it, they'll tell the others and I shall ask them too," she said. "Father is always wanting me to spend money, so now I'll spend some on a beautiful tea."

Raymond saw the name of Sabina Dinnett.

"I'll be there to help you," he promised.

"Nicholas Roberts is the lover of Miss Northover," explained Estelle, "and Benny Cogle is the lover of Miss Gale. That's why I asked them. I very nearly went back and asked Mister Baggs to come, because he seems a silent, sad man; but I was rather frightened of him."

"Don't ask him; he's an old bear," declared Raymond.

Thus, forgetting his brother as though Daniel had ceased to exist, he threw himself into Estelle's enterprise and planned an entertainment that must at least have rendered the master uneasy.

CHAPTER IX

THE PARTY

Arthur Waldron did more than love his daughter. He bore to her almost a superstitious reverence, as for one made of superior flesh and blood. He held her in some sort a reincarnation of his wife and took no credit for her cleverness himself. Yet he did not spoil her, for her nature was proof against that.

Estelle, though old for her age, could not be called a prig. She developed an abstract interest in life as her intellect unfolded to accept its wonders and mysteries, yet she remained young in mind as well as body, and was always very glad to meet others of her own age. The mill girls were indeed older than she, but Mr. Waldron's daughter found their minds as young as her own in such subjects as interested her, though there were many things hidden from her that life had taught them.

Her father never doubted Estelle's judgment or crossed her wishes. Therefore he approved of the proposed party and did his best to make it a success. Others also were glad to aid Estelle and, to her delight, Ernest Churchouse, with whom she was in favour, yielded to entreaty and joined the company on the lawn of North Hill House. Tea was served out of doors, and to it there came nine workers from the mill, and two of Mr. Best's own girls, who were friends of Estelle. Nicholas Roberts arrived with his future wife, Sarah Northover; Sabina Dinnett came with Nancy Buckler and Sally Groves from the Carding Machine, while Alice Chick brought old Mrs. Chick; Mercy Gale came too—a fair, florid girl, who warped the yarn when it was spun.

Mr. Waldron was not a ladies' man, and after helping with the tea, served under a big mulberry tree in the garden, he turned his attention to Mr. Roberts, already known favourably to him as a cricketer, and Benny Cogle, the engine man. They departed to look at a litter of puppies and the others perambulated the gardens. Estelle had a plot of her own, where grew roses, and here, presently, each with a rose at her breast, the girls sat about on an old stone seat and listened to Mr. Churchouse discourse on the lore of their trade.

Some, indeed, were bored by the subject and stole away to play beside a fountain and lily pond, where the gold fish were tame and crowded to their hands for food; but others listened and learned surprising facts that set the thoughtful girls wondering.

"You mustn't think, you spinners, that you are the last word in spinning," he said; "no, Alice and Nancy and Sabina, you're not; no more are those at other mills, who spin in choicer materials than flax and hemp—I mean the workers in cotton and silk. For the law of things in general, called evolution, seems to stand still when machinery comes to increase output and confuse our ideas of quality and quantity. Missis Chick here will tell you, when she was a spinner and the old rope walks were not things of the past, that she spun quite as good yarn from the bundle of tow at her waist as you do from the regulation spinners."

"And better," said Mrs. Chick.

"I believe you," declared Ernest, "and before your time the yarn was better still. For, though some of the best brains in men's heads have been devoted to the subject, we go backwards instead of forwards, and things have been done in spinning that I believe will never be done again. In fact, the further you go back, the better the yarn seems to have been, and I'm sure I don't know how the laws of evolution can explain that. The secret is this: machinery, for all its marvellous improvements, lags far behind the human hand, and the record yarns were spun in the East, while our forefathers still went about in wolf-skins and painted their faces blue. You may laugh, but it is so."

"Tell us about them, Mister Churchouse," begged Estelle.

"For the moment we needn't go back so far," he said. "I'll remind you what a girl thirteen years old did in Ireland a hundred years ago. Only thirteen was Catherine Woods—mark that, Sabina and Alice—but she was a genius who lived in Dunmore, County Down, and she spun a hank of linen yarn of such tenuity that it would have taken seven hundred such hanks to make a pound of yarn."

He turned to Estelle.

"Sabina and the other spinners will appreciate this," he said, "but to explain the marvel of such spider-like spinning, Estelle, I may tell you that seventeen and a half pounds of Catherine's yarn would have sufficed to stretch round the equator of the earth. No machine-spun yarn has ever come within measurable distance of this astounding feat, and I have never heard of any spinner in Europe or America equalling it; yet even this has been beaten when we were painting our noses blue."

"Where?" asked Estelle breathlessly.

"In the land of all wonders: Egypt. Herodotus tells us of a linen corselet, presented to the Lacedemonians by King Amasis, each thread of which commanded admiration, for though very fine, each was twisted of three hundred and sixty others! And if you decline to believe this—"

"Oh, Mister Churchouse, we quite believe it I'm sure, sir, if you say so," interrupted Mrs. Chick.

"Well, a later authority, Sir Gardiner Wilkinson, tells us of equal wonders. The linen which he unwound from Egyptian mummies has proved as delicate as silk, and equal, if not superior, to our best cambrics. Five hundred and forty threads went to the warp and a hundred and ten to the weft; and I'm sure a modern weaver would wonder how they could produce quills fine enough for weaving such yarn through."

"There's nothing new under the sun, seemingly," said old Mrs. Chick.

"Indeed there isn't, my dear, and so, perhaps, in the time to come, we shall spin again as well as the Egyptians five or six thousand years ago," declared Ernest.

"And even then the spiders will always beat us I expect," said Estelle.

"True—true, child; nor has man learned the secret, of the caterpillar's silken spinning. Talking of caterpillars, you may, or may not, have observed—"

It was at this point that Raymond, behind the speaker's back, beckoned Sabina, and presently, as Mr. Churchouse began to expatiate on Nature's spinning, she slipped away. The garden was large and held many winding paths and secluded nooks. Thus the lovers were able to hide themselves from other eyes and amuse themselves with their own conversation.

Sabina praised Estelle.

"She's a dear little lady and ever so clever, I'm sure."

"So she is, and yet she loses a lot. Though her father's such a great sportsman, she doesn't care a button about it. Wouldn't ride on a pony even."

"I can very well understand that. Nor would I if I had the chance."

"You're different, Sabina. You've not been brought up in a sporting family. All the same you'd ride jolly well, because you've got nerve enough for anything and a perfect figure for riding. You'd look fairly lovely on horseback."

"Whatever will you say next?"

"I often wonder myself," he answered. "This much I'll say any way: it's meat and drink to me to be walking here with you. I only wish I was clever and could really amuse you and make you want to see me, sometimes. But the things I understand, of course, bore you to tears."

"You know very well that isn't so," she said. "You've told me heaps of things well worth knowing—things I should never have heard of but for you. And—and I'm sure I'm very proud of your friendship."

"Good Lord! It's the other way about. Thanks to Mister Churchouse and your own wits, you are fearfully well read, and your cleverness fairly staggers me. Just to hear you talk is all I want—at least that isn't all. Of course, it is a great score for an everyday sort of chap like me to have interested you."

Sabina did not answer and after a silence which drew out into awkwardness, she made some remark on the flowers. But Raymond was not interested about the flowers. He had looked forward to this occasion as an opportunity of exceptional value and now strove to improve the shining hour.

"You know I'm a most unlucky beggar really, Sabina. You mightn't think it, but I am. You see me cheerful, and joking and trying to make things pleasant for us all at the works; but sometimes, if you could see me tramping alone over North Hill, or walking on the beach and looking at the seagulls, you'd be sorry for me."

"Of course, I'd be sorry for you—if there was anything to be sorry for."

"Look at it. An open-air man brought up to think my father would leave me all right, and then cut off with nothing and forced to come here and stew and toil and wear myself out struggling with a most difficult business—difficult to me, any way."

"I'm sure you're mastering it as quickly as possible."

"But the effort. And my muscles are shrinking and I'm losing weight. But, of course, that's nothing to anybody but myself. And then, another side: I want to think of you people first and raise your salaries and so on—especially yours, for you ought to have pounds where you have shillings. And my wishes to do proper things, in the line of modern progress and all that, are turned down by my brother. Here am I thinking about you and worrying and knowing it's all wrong—and there's nobody on my side—not a damned person. And it makes me fairly mad."

"I'm sure it's splendid of you to look at the Mill in such a high-minded way," declared Sabina. "And now you've told me, I shall understand what's in your mind. I'm sure I thank you for the thought at any rate."

"If you'd only be my friend," he said.

"It would be a great honour for a girl—just a spinner—to be that."

"The honour is for me. You've got such tons of mind, Sabina. You understand all the economical side, and so on."

"A thing is only worth what it will fetch, I'm afraid."

"That's the point. If you would help me, we would go into it and presently, when I'm a partner, we could bring out a scheme; and then you'd know you'd been instrumental in raising the tone of the whole works. And probably, if we set a good example, other works would raise their tone, too, and gradually the workers would find the whole scheme of things changing, to their advantage."

Sabina regarded this majestic vision with due reverence. She praised his ideals and honestly believed him a hero.

They discussed the subject while the dusk came down and he prophesied great things.

"We shall live to see it," he assured her, "and it may be largely thanks to you. And when you have a home of your own and—and—"

It was then that she became conscious of his very near presence and the dying light.

"They'll all have gone, and so must I," she said, "and I hope you'll thank Miss Waldron dearly for her nice party."

"This is only the first; she'll give dozens more now that this has been such a success. She loves the Mill. If you come this way I can let you out by the bottom gate—by the bamboo garden. You've bucked me up like anything—you always do. You're the best thing in my life, Sabina. Oh, if I was anything to you—if—but of course it's all one way."

His voice shook a little. He burned to put his arms round her, and Nature shouted so loud in his humming ears that he hardly heard her answer. For she echoed his emotion.

"What can I say to that? You're so kind—you don't know how kind. You can't guess what such friendship means to a girl like me. It's something that doesn't come into our lives very often. I'm only wondering what the world will be like when you've gone again."

"I shan't go—I'm never going. Never, Sabina. I—I couldn't live without you. Kiss me, for God's sake. I must kiss you—I must—or I shall go mad."

His arms were round her and he felt her hot cheek against his. They were young in love and dared not look into each other's eyes. But she kissed him back, and then, as he released her, she ran away, slipped through the wicket, where they stood and hastened off by the lane to Bridetown. He glowed at her touch and panted at his triumph. She had not rebuked him, but let him see that she loved him and kissed him for his kiss. He did not attempt to follow her then but turned full of glory. Here was a thing that dwarfed every interest of life and made life itself a triviality by comparison. She loved him; he had won her; nothing else that would be, or had been, in the whole world mattered beside such a triumph. His head had touched the stars.

And he felt amazingly grateful to her. His thoughts for the moment were full of chivalry. Her life must be translated to higher terms and new values. She should have the best that the world could offer, and he would win it for her. Her trust was so pathetic and beautiful. To be trusted by her made him feel a finer thing and more important to the cosmic scheme.

In itself this was a notable sensation and an addition of power, for nobody had ever trusted him until now. And here was a radiant creature, the most beautiful in the world, who trusted him with herself. His love brought a sense of splendour; her love brought a sense of strength.

He swung back to the house feeling in him such mastery as might bend the whole earth to his purposes, take Leviathan with a hook, and hang the constellations in new signs upon the void of heaven.

CHAPTER X

WORK

Sarah Northover and another young woman were tending the Spread Board. To this came the 'long line' from the hackler—those strides of amber hemp and lint-white flax that Mr. Baggs prepared in the hackler's shop. The Spread Board worked upon the long line as the Carder on the tow. Over its endless leathern platform, or spreading carriage, the long fibre was drawn into the toothed gills of the machine and converted into sliver for the Drawing Frames.

With swift and rhythmic flinging apart of her arms over her head, Sarah separated the stricks into three and laid them overlapping on the carriage. The ribbon thus created was never-ending and wound away into the torture chambers of wheels and teeth within, while from the rear of the Spreader trickled out the new-created sliver. Great scales hung beside Sarah and from time to time she weighed fresh loads of long line and recorded the amount.

Her arms flashed upwards, the divided stricks came down to be laid in rotation on the running carriage, and ceaselessly she and her fellow worker chattered despite the din around them.

"My Aunt Nelly's coming to see me this morning," said Sarah. "She's driving over to talk to Mister Waldron about his apple orchard and have a look round. Last year she bought the whole orchard for cider; and if she thinks well of it, she'll do the same this year."

"I wonder you stop here," answered the other girl, "when you might go to your aunt and work in her public-house. I'd a long sight sooner be there than here."

"You wouldn't if you was engaged to Mister Roberts," answered Sarah. "Of course seeing him every day makes all the difference. And as to work, there's nothing in it, for everybody's got to work at 'The Seven Stars,' I can tell you, and the work's never done there."

"It's the company I should like," declared the other. "I'd give a lot to see new people every day. In a public they come and go, before you've got time to be sick of the sight of 'em. But here, you see the same people and hear the same voices every day of your blessed life; and sometimes it makes me feel right down wicked."

"It's narrowing to the mind I dare say, unless you've got a man like Mister Roberts with a lot of general ideas," admitted Sarah. "But you know very well for that matter you could have a man to-morrow. Benny Cogle's mate is daft for you."

The other sniffed.

"It's very certain he ain't got no general ideas, beyond the steam engine. He can only talk about the water wheel to-day and the boilers to-morrow. When I find a chap, he'll have to know a powerful lot more about life than that chap—and shave himself oftener also."

"He'd shave every day if you took him, same as Mister Roberts does," said Sarah.

Elsewhere Mr. Best was starting a run of the Gill Spinner, a machine which took sliver straight from the Drawing Frames and spun it into a large coarse yarn. A novice watched him get the great machine to work, make all ready and then, at a touch, connect it with the power and set it crashing and roaring. Its voice was distinctive and might be heard by a practised ear above the prevailing thunder.

Then came Mrs. Nelly Northover to this unfamiliar scene, peeped in at a door or two and failed to see Sarah, who laboured at the other end of the Mill. But the hostess of 'The Seven Stars' knew Sabina Dinnett and now shook hands with her and then stood and watched in bewildered admiration before a big frame of a hundred spindles.

Sabina was spinning with a heart very full of happiness. On the previous evening she had promised to wed Raymond Ironsyde, and her thoughts to-day were winged with over-mastering joy. For life had turned into a glorious triumph; the man who had asked her to marry him was not only a gentleman, but far above the power of any wrong-doing. She knew in the very secret places of her soul, that he could never act away from his honest and noble character; that he was a knight above reproach, incapable of wronging any living thing. There was an element of risk for most girls who fell in love with those better born than themselves; but none for her. Other men might deceive and abuse, and suffer outer influences to chill their love, when the secret of it became known; but not this man. His rare nature had been revealed to her; he desired the welfare of all people; he was moved with nothing but the purest principles and loftiest feeling. He would not willingly have brought sorrow to a child. And she had won this unique spirit! He loved her with the love that only such a man was great enough to show; and she echoed it and knew that such a passion must be unchanging, everlasting, built not only to make their united lives unspeakably happy and gloriously content, but to run over also into the lives of others, less blessed, and leave the sad world happier for their happiness. There was not a cloud in the sky of her romance and she shared with him for the moment the joy of secrecy. But that would not be long. They had determined to hug their delicious knowledge for a little while and then proclaim the great tidings to the world.

So she followed the old road, along which her sisters had tramped from immemorial time, and would still tramp through the generations to come, when her journey was ended and the wonderful country of man's love explored—its oases visited, its antres endured.

Now Sabina played priestess to the Spinning Machine—a monster reared above her, stupendous and insatiable.

Along the summit of the Spinning Frame, just within reach of tall Sabina's uplifted hand, there perched a row of reels from which the finished material descended through series of rollers. The retaining roller aloft gave it to the steel delivery roller which drew the thin, sad-looking stuff with increased speed downward. And here at its moment of most shivering tenuity, when the perfected and purified material seemed reduced to an extremity of weakness, came the magic change. Unseen in the whirring complexity of the spinner, it received the momentous gift that translates fibre to yarn. In a moment it changed from stuff a baby's finger could break to thread capable of supporting fifteen pounds of pressure. For now came the twist—that word of mighty significance—and the tiny thread of new-born yarn descended to the spindle, vanished in the whirl of the flier and reappeared, an accomplished miracle, winding on the bobbin beneath.

Upon the spindle revolved the flier—a fork of steel with guide eye at one leg of the fork—and through the guide eye came the twisted yarn to wind on the bobbin below. There, as the bobbin frame rose and fell, the thread was perfectly delivered to the reel and coiled off layer by layer upon it.

Mrs. Northover stared to see the nature of a Spinner's duties and the ease with which she controlled the great, pulsing, roaring frame of a hundred spindles. Sabina's eyes were everywhere; her hands were never still; her feet seemed to dance a measure to the thunder of the Frame. Now she marked a roving reel aloft that was running out, and in a moment she had broken the sliver, swept away the empty reel and hung up a full one. Then she drew the new sliver down to the point of the break and, in a moment, the two merged and the thread ran on. Now her fingers touched the spindles, as a musician touches the keys, and at a moment's pressure the machine obeyed and the yarn flew on its way obedient. Now she cleared a snarl, or catch, where a spindle appeared to have run amuck or created hopeless confusion; now she readjusted the weights that kept a drag on the humming bobbins. Her twinkling hands touched and calmed and fed the monster. She knew its whims, corrected its errors, brought to her insensate machine the complement of brain that made it trustworthy. And when the bobbins were all full, she hastened along the Frame, turned off the driving power and silenced the huge activity in a moment. Then, like lightning, she cut her hundred threads and lifted the bobbins from their spindles until she had a pile upon her shoulder. In a marvellously short time she had doffed the bobbins and set up a hundred empty ones. Then the cut threads were readjusted, the power turned on and all was motion again.

Sabina had never calculated her labours, until Raymond took the trouble to do so; then she learned a fact that astonished her. He found that it took a hundred and fifty minutes to spin one thousand and fifty yards; and as each spindle spun two and a half miles in ten hours, her daily accomplishment was two hundred and fifty miles of yarn.

"You spin from seventy to eighty thousand miles of single yarn a year," he told her, and the fact expressed in these terms amazed her and her sister spinners.

Now Nelly Northover praised the performance.

"To think that you slips of girls can do anything so wonderful!" she said. "We talk of the spinners of Bridport as if they were nobodies; but upon my conscience, Sabina, I never will again. I've always thought I was a pretty busy woman; but I'd drop to the earth I'm sure after an hour of your job, let alone ten hours."

Sabina laughed.

"It's use, Mrs. Northover. Some take to it like a duck to water. I did for one. But some never do. If you come to the Frame frightened, you never make a spinner. They're like humans, the Spinning Frames; if they think you're afraid of them, they'll always bully you, but if you show them you're mistress, it's all right. They have their moods and whims, just as we have. They vary, and you never know how the day will go. Sometimes everything runs smoothly; sometimes nothing does. Some days you're as fresh at the end as the beginning; some days you're dog-tired and worn out after a proper fight."

"There's something hungry and cruel and wicked about 'em to my eye," declared Mrs. Northover.

"We're oftener in fault than the Frames, however. Sometimes the spinner's to blame herself—she may be out of sorts and heavy-handed and slow on her feet and can't put up her ends right, or do anything right; and often it's the fault of the other girls and the 'rove' comes to the spinner rough; and often, again, it's just luck—good or bad. If the machine always ran perfect, there'd be nothing to do. But you've got to use your wits from the time it starts to the time it stops."

"The creature would best me every time," said the visitor, regarding Sabina's machine with suspicion and something akin to dislike.

The spinner stopped a fouled spindle and rubbed her hand.

"Sometimes the yarn's always snarling and your drag weights are always burning off and the stuff is full of kinks and the sliver's badly pieced up—that's the drawing minder's fault—and a bad drawing minder means work for me. Your niece, Sarah, is a very good drawing minder, Mrs. Northover. Then you'll get ballooning, when the thread flies round above the flier, and that means too little strain on the jamb and the bobbin has got to be tempered. And often it's too hot, or else too cold, for hemp and flax must have their proper temperature. But to-day my machine is as good and kind as a nice child, that only asks to be fed and won't quarrel with anybody."

Mrs. Northover, however, saw nothing to praise, for Sabina's speech had been broken a dozen times.

"If that's what you call working kindly, I'd like to see the wretch in a nasty mood," she said. "I lay you want to slap it sometimes."

Sabina was mending a drag that had burned off. The drags were heavy weights hanging from strings that pressed upon the side of the bobbins and controlled their speed. The friction often burned these cords through and the weights had to be lifted and retied again and again.

"We want a clever invention to put this right," she said. "A lot of good time's wasted with the weights. Nobody's thought upon the right thing yet."

"I'm properly dazed," confessed Nelly Northover. "You live and learn without a doubt—nothing's so true as that."

Her niece had seen her and approached, as the machinery began to still for the dinner-hour.

"Morning, Sarah. Can you do such wonders as Miss Dinnett?" she asked.

"No, Aunt Nelly. I'm a spreader minder. But I'll be a spinner some day, if Mr. Roberts likes for me to stop, here after I'm married."

"Sarah would soon learn to spin," declared Sabina.

Then she turned to bid Raymond Ironsyde good morning. His brother was away from Bridport on a tour with one of his travellers, that he might become acquainted with many of his more important customers. Raymond, therefore, felt safe and was wasting a good deal of his time. He had brought a basket of fruit from North Hill House—a present from Estelle—and he began to dispense plums and pears as the women streamed away to dinner.

They knew him very well now and treated him with varying degrees of familiarity. Early doubts had vanished, and they took him as a good natured, rather 'soft' young man, who meant well and was friendly and harmless. The ill-educated are always suspicious, and Levi Baggs declared from the first that Raymond was nothing better than his brother's spy, placed here for a time to inquire into the ambitions and ideas of the workers and so help the firm to combat the lawful demands of those whom they employed; but this theory was long exploded save in the mind of Mr. Baggs himself. The people of Bridetown Mill held Raymond on their side, and all were secretly interested to know what would spring of his frank friendship with Sabina.

In serious moments Raymond felt uneasy at the relations he had established with the workers, and Mr. Best did not hesitate to warn him again and again that discipline was ill served by such easy terms between employer and employed; but his moments of perspicuity were rare, for now his mind and soul were poured into one thought and one only. He was riotously happy in his love affair and could not pretend to his fellow creatures anything he did not feel. Always amiable and accessible, his romance made him still more so, and he was constitutionally unable at this moment to take a serious view of anything or anybody.

One ray of hope, however, Mr. Best recognised: Raymond did show an honest and genuine interest in the machines. He had told the foreman that he believed the great problem lay there, and where machinery was concerned he could be exceedingly intelligent and rational. This trait in him had a bearing on the future and, in time to come, John Best remembered its inception and perceived how it had developed.

Now, his fruit dispensed, Raymond talked with Sabina about the Spinning Frame and instructed Mrs. Northover, who was an acquaintance of his, in its mysteries.

"These are old-fashioned frames," he declared, "and I shan't rest till I've turned them out of the works and got the latest and best. I'm all for the new things, because they help the workers and give good results. In fact, I tell my brother that he's behind the times. That's the advantage of coming to a subject fresh, with your mind unprejudiced. Daniel's all bound up in the past and, of course, everything my father did must be right; but I know better. You have to move with the times, and if you don't you'll get left."

"That's true enough, Mr. Ironsyde, whatever your business may be," answered Mrs. Northover.

"Of course—look at 'The Seven Stars.' You're always up to date, and why should my spinners—I call them mine—why should they have to spin on machines that come out of the ark, when, by spending a few thousand, they could have the latest?"

"You've got to balance cost against value," answered the innkeeper. "It don't do to dash at things. One likes for the new to be tried on its merits first, and then, if it proves all that's claimed for it, you go in and keep abreast of the times according; but the old will often be found as good as the new; and so Mr. Daniel no doubt looks before he leaps."

"That's cowardly in my opinion," replied Raymond. "You must take the chances. Of course if you're frightened to back your judgment, then that shows you're a second class man with a second class sort of mind; but if you believe in yourself, as everybody does who is any good, then you go ahead, and if you come a purler now and again, that's nothing, because you get it back in other ways. I'm not frightened to chance my luck, am I, Sabina?"

"Never was such a brave one, I'm sure," she said, conscious of their secret.

"If you haven't got nerve, you're no good," summed up the young man; "and if you have got nerve, then use it and break out of the beaten track and welcome your luck and court a few adventures for your soul's sake."

"All very well for you men," said Mrs. Northover. "You can have adventures and no great harm done; but us women, if we try for adventures, we come to a bad end."

"Nobody's more adventurous than you," answered Raymond. "Look at your gardens and your teas for a bob ahead. Wasn't that an adventure—to give a better tea than anybody in Bridport?"

"I believe women have quite as many adventures as men," declared Sarah Northover, who was waiting for her aunt, "only we're quieter about 'em."

"We've got to be," answered Mrs. Northover. "Now come on to your mother's, Sarah. There's Mr. Roberts waiting for us outside."

In the silent and empty mill Raymond dawdled for a few minutes with Sabina, talked love and won a caress. Then she put on her sunbonnet and he walked with her to the door of her home, left her at 'The Magnolias' and went his way with Estelle's fruit basket.

A great expedition had been planned by the lovers for a forthcoming public holiday. They were going to rise in the dawn, before the rest of the world was awake, and tramp out through West Haven to Golden Cap—the supreme eminence of the south coast, that towers with bright, sponge-coloured precipices above the sea, nigh Lyme.

CHAPTER XI

THE OLD STORE-HOUSE

Through a misty morning, made silver bright by the risen sun, Sabina and Raymond started for their August holiday. They left Bridetown, passed through a white fog on the water-meadows and presently climbed to the cliffs and pursued their way westward. Now the sun was over the sea and the Channel gleamed and flashed under a wakening, westerly breeze.

To West Haven they came, where the cliffs break and the rivers from Bridport flow through sluices into the little harbour.

Among the ancient, weather-worn buildings standing here with their feet in the sand drifts, was one specially picturesque. A long and lofty mass it presented, and a hundred years of storm and salt-laden winds had toned it to rich colour and fretted its roof and walls with countless stains. It was a store, three stories high, used of old time for merchandise, but now sunk to rougher uses. In its great open court, facing north, were piled thousands of tons of winnowed sand; its vaults were barred and empty; its glass windows were shattered; rust had eaten away its metal work and rot reduced its doors and sashes to powder. Rich red and auburn was its face, with worn courses of brickwork like wounds gashed upon it. A staircase of stone rose against one outer wall, and aloft, in the chambers approached thereby, was laid up a load of sweet smelling, deal planks brought by a Norway schooner. Here too, were all manner of strange little chambers, some full of old nettings, others littered with the marine stores of the fishermen, who used the ruin for their gear. The place was rat-haunted and full of strange holes and corners. Even by day, with the frank sunshine breaking through boarded windows and broken roof, it spoke of incident and adventure; by night it was eloquent of the past—of smugglers, of lawless deeds, of Napoleonic spies.

Raymond and Sabina stood and admired the old store. To her it was something new, for her activities never brought her to West Haven; but he had been familiar with it from childhood, when, with his brother, he had spent school holidays at West Haven, caught prawns from the pier, gone sailing with the fisher folk, and spent many a wet day in the old store-house.

He smiled upon it now, told her of his childish adventures and took her in to see an ancient chamber where he and Daniel had often played their games.

"Our nurse used to call it a 'cubby hole,'" he said. "And she was always; jolly thankful when she could pilot us in here from the dangers of the cliffs and the old pier, or the boats in the harbour. The place is just the same— only shrunk. The plaster from the walls is all mouldering away, or you might see the pictures we used to draw upon them with paint from the fishermen's paint pots. Down below they bring the sand and grade it for the builders. They've carted away millions of tons of sand from the foreshore in the last fifty years and will cart away millions more, no doubt, for the sea always renews it."

She wandered with him and listened half-dreaming. The air for them was electric with their love and they yearned for each other.

"I wish we could spend the whole blessed day in this little den together," he said suddenly putting his arms round her; and that brought her to some sense of reality, but none of danger. Not a tremor of peril in his company had she ever felt, for did not perfect love cast out fear, and why should a woman hesitate to trust herself with one, to her, the most precious in the world?

He suggested dawdling awhile; but she would not.

"We are to eat our breakfast at Eype Beach," she reminded him, "and that's a mile or two yet."

So they went on their way again, breasted the grassy cliffs westward of the haven, admired the fog bank touched with gold that hung over the river flats, praised Bridport wakening under its leafy woods, marked the herons on the river mud in the valley and the sparrow-hawk poised aloft above the downs. She took his arm up the hill and, like birds themselves, they went lightly together, strong, lissome, radiant in health and youth and the joy of a shared worship that made all things sweet.

They talked of the great day when the world was to know their secret. The secret itself proved so attractive to both that they agreed to keep it a little longer. Their shared knowledge proved amusing and each told the other of the warnings and advice and fears imparted by careful friends of both sexes, who knew not the splendid truth.

How small the wisdom of the wise appeared—how peddling and foolish and mean—contrasted with their superb trust. How sordid were the ways of the world, its fears and suspicions, from the vantage point to which they had climbed. Material things even suggested this thought to Raymond, and when before noon, they stood on the green crown of Golden Cap, with the earth and sea spread out around them in mighty harmonies of blue and green, he told Sabina so.

"We ought to be perched on a place like this," he said, "because we are to the rest of the world, in mind and in happiness, as we are here in body too."

"Only the sea gulls can go higher, and I always feel they're more like spirits than birds," she answered.

"I've got no use for spirits," he told her. "The splendid thing about us is that we're flesh and blood and spirit too. That's the really magnificent combination for happy creatures. A spirit at best can only be an unfinished thing. People make such a fuss about escaping from the flesh. What the deuce do you want to escape from your flesh for, if it's healthy and tough and fine?"

"When they get old, they feel like that."

"Let the old comfort the old then," he said. "I'm proud of my flesh and bones, and so are you, and so we ought to be; and if I had to give them up and die, I should hate it. And if I found myself in another world, a poor shivering idea and nothing else, without flesh and bones to cover me, or clothes to cover them, I should feel ashamed of myself. And they might call it Paradise as much as they liked, but it would be Hades to me. Of course many of the ghosts would pretend that they liked it; but I bet none would really—so jolly undignified to be nothing but an idea."

She laughed.

"That's just what I feel too; and of course it's utterly wrong of us," she said. "It shows we have got a lot to learn. We only feel like this because we're young. Perhaps young ghosts begin like that; but I expect they soon get past it."

"I should never want to get past it," he said.

He rolled over on the grass and played with her hand.

"How could you love and cuddle a ghost?"

"No doubt you could love it. I don't suppose you could cuddle it. You wouldn't want to."

"No—that's true, Sabina. If this cliff carried away this moment, and we were both smashed to pulp and arrived together in another world without any clothes and both horribly down on our luck—but it's too ghastly a picture. I should howl all through eternity—to think what I'd missed."

They talked nonsense, played with their thoughts and came nearer and nearer together. One tremendous and masterful impulse drew them on—a raging hunger and thirst on his part and something not widely different on hers. Again and again they caught themselves in each other's arms, then broke off, grew serious and strove to steady the trend of their desires.

Golden Cap was a lonely spot and few visited it that day. Once a middle-aged man and woman surprised them where they sat behind a rock near the edge of the great precipices. The man had grown warm and mopped his face and let the wind cool it.

He was ugly, clumsily built, and displayed large calves in knickerbockers and a hot, bald head.

"How hideous human beings can be," said Raymond after they had gone.

"He wasn't hideous in his wife's eyes, I expect."

"Middle-age is mercifully blind no doubt to its own horrors," he said. "You can respect and even admire old age, like other ruins, if it's picturesque, but middle-age is deadly always."

He smoked and they dawdled the hours away until Sabina declared it was tea time. Then they sought a little inn at Chidcock and spent an hour there.

The weather changed as the sun went westerly; the wind sank to a sigh and brought with it rain clouds. But they were unconscious of such accidents. Sabina longed for the cliffs again, so they turned homeward by Seaton and Thorncombe Beacon and Eype Mouth. Their talk ran upon marriage and Raymond swore that he could not wait long, while she urged the importance to him of so doing.

"'Twould shake your brother badly if you wed yet awhile, be sure of that," she said. "He would say that you weren't thinking of the work, and it might tempt him to change his mind about making you a partner."

"Oh damn him. Don't talk about him—or work either. I shall never want to work again, or think of work, or anything else on earth till—till—What does he matter anyway—or his ideas? It's a free country and a man has the right to plan his life his own way. If he wants to get the best out of me, he'd better give me five hundred a year to-morrow and tell me to marry you."

"We don't want five hundred. That's a fortune. I'm a good manager and know very well how far money can go. With your money and mine."

"Yours? You won't have any—except mine. You'll stop work then and live—not at Bridetown anyway."

"I was forgetting. It will be funny not to spin."

"You'll spin my happiness and my life and my fate and my children. You'll have plenty of spinning. I'll spin for you and you'll spin for me."

"You darling boy! I know you'll spin for me."

"Work! What's the good of working for yourself?" he asked. "Who the devil cares about himself? It's because I don't care a button for myself that I haven't bothered about the Mill. But when it comes to you—! You're worth working for! I haven't begun to work yet. I'll surprise Daniel presently and everybody else, when I fairly get into my stride. I didn't ask for it and I didn't want it; but as I've got to work, I will work—for you. And you'll live to see that my brother and his ways and plans and small outlook are all nothing to the way I shall grasp the business. And he'll see, too, when I get the lead by sheer better understanding. And that won't be my work, Sabina. It will be yours. Nothing's worth too much toil for you. And if you couldn't inspire a man to wonderful things, then no woman could."

This fit of exaltation passed and the craving for her dominated him again and took psychological shape. He grew moody and abstracted. His voice had a new note in it to her ear. He was fighting with himself and did not guess what was in her mind, or how unconsciously it echoed to his.

At dusk the rain came and they ran before a sudden storm down the green hills back to West Haven. The place already sank into night and a lamp or two twinkled through the grey. It was past eight o'clock and Raymond decided for dinner.

"We'll go to the 'Brit Arms,'" he said, "and feed and get dry. The rain won't last."

"I told mother I should be home by nine."

"Well, you told her wrong. D'you think I'm going to chuck away an hour of this day for a thousand mothers?"

When they sauntered out into the night again at ten o'clock, the Haven had nearly gone to sleep and the rain was past. In the silence they heard the river rushing through the sluices to the sea; and then they set their faces homeward.

But they had to pass the old store-house. It loomed a black, amorphous pile heaved up against the stars, and the man's footsteps dragged as he came to the gaping gates and silent court.

He stopped and she stopped.

His voice was gruff and queer and half-choked.

"Come," he said, "I'm in hell, and you've got to turn it to heaven."

She murmured something, but he put his arm round her and they vanished into the mass of silent darkness.

It was past midnight when they parted at the door of Sabina's home and he gave her the cool kiss of afterwards.

"Now we are one, body and soul, for ever," she whispered to him.

"By God, yes," he said.

CHAPTER XII

CREDIT

The mind of Raymond Ironsyde was now driven and tossed by winds of passion which, blowing against the tides of his own nature, created unrest and storm. A strain of chivalry belonged to him and at first this conquered. He felt the magnitude of Sabina's sacrifice and his obligation to a love so absolute. In this spirit he remained for a time, during which their relations were of the closest. They spoke of marriage; they even appointed the day on which the announcement of their betrothal should be made. And though he had gone thus far at her entreaty, always recognising when with her the reasonableness of her wish, after she was gone, the cross seas of his own character, created a different impression and swept the pattern of Sabina's will away.

For a time the intrigue of meeting her, the planning and the plotting amused him. He imagined the world was blind and that none knew, or guessed, the truth. But Bridetown, having eyes as many and sharp as any other hamlet, had long been familiar with the facts. The transparent veil of their imagined secrecy was already rent, though the lovers did not guess it.

Then Raymond's chivalry wore thinner. Ruling passions, obscured for a season by the tremendous experience of his first love and its success, began by slow degrees to rise again, solid and challenging, through the rosy clouds. His love, while he shouted to himself that it increased rather than diminished, none the less assumed a change of colour and contour. The bright vapours still shone and Sabina could always kindle ineffable glow to the fabric; but she away, they shrank a little and grew less radiant. The truth of himself and his ambitions showed through. At such times he dinned on the ears of his heart that Sabina was his life. At other times when the fading fire astonished him by waking a shiver, he blamed fate, told himself that but for the lack of means, he would make a perfect home for Sabina; worship and cherish her; fill her life with happiness; pander to her every whim; devote a large portion of his own time to her; do all that wit and love could devise for her pleasure—all but one thing.

He did not want to marry her. With that deed demanding to be done, the necessity for it began to be questioned sharply. He was not a marrying man and, in any case, too young to commit himself and his prospects to such a course. He assured himself that he had never contemplated immediate marriage; he had never suggested it to Sabina. She herself had not suggested it; for what advantage could be gained by such a step? While a thousand disasters might spring therefrom, not the least being a quarrel with his brother, there was nothing to be said for it. He began to suspect that he could do little less likely to assure Sabina's future. He clung to his strand of chivalry at this time, like a drowning man to a straw; but other ingredients of his nature dragged him away. Selfishness is the parent of sophistry, and Raymond found himself dismissing old rules of morality and inherited instincts of religion and justice for more practical and worldly values. He told himself it was as much for Sabina's sake as for his own that he must now respect the dictates of common-sense.

There came a day in October, when the young man sat in his office at the mills, smoking and absorbed with his own affairs. The river Bride was broken above the works, and while her way ran south of them, the mill-race came north. Its labour on the wheel accomplished, the current turned quickly back to the river bed again. From Raymond's window he could see the main stream, under a clay bank, where the martins built their nests in spring, and where rush and sedge and an over-hanging sallow marked her windings. The sunshine found the stickles, and where Bride skirted the works lay a pool in which trout moved. Water buttercups shone silver white in this back-water at spring-time and the water-voles had their haunts in the bank side.

Beyond stretched meadow-lands and over the hill that rose behind them climbed the road to the cliffs. Hounds had ascended this road two hours before and their music came faintly from afar to Raymond's ear, then ceased. Already his relations with Sabina had lessened his will to pleasure in other directions. His money had gone in gifts to her, leaving no spare cash for the old amusements; but the distractions, that for a time had seemed so tame contrasted with the girl, cried louder and reminded how necessary and healthy they were.

Life seemed reduced to the naked question of cash. He was sorry for himself. It looked hard, outrageous, wrong, that tastes so sane and simple as his own, could not be gratified. A horseman descended the hill and Raymond recognised him. It was Neddy Motyer. His horse was lame and he walked beside it. Raymond smiled to himself, for Neddy, though a zealous follower of hounds, lacked judgment and often met with disaster.

Ten minutes later Neddy himself appeared.

"Come to grief," he said. "Horse put his foot into a rabbit hole and cut his knee on a flint. I've just taken him to the vet, here to be bandaged, so I thought I'd look you up. Why weren't you out?"

"I've got more important things to think about for the minute."

Neddy helped himself to a cigarette.

"Growing quite the man of business," he said. "What will power you've got! A few of us bet five to one you wouldn't stick it a month; but here you are. Only I can tell you this, Ray: you're wilting under it. You're not half the man you were. You're getting beastly thin—looking a worm in fact."

Raymond laughed.

"I'm all right. Plenty of time to make up for lost time."

"It's metal more attractive, I believe," hazarded Motyer. "A little bird's been telling us things in Bridport. Keep clear of the petticoats, old chap—the game's never worth the candle. I speak from experience."

"Do you? I shouldn't think any girl would have much use for you."

"Oh yes, they have—plenty of them. But once bit, twice shy. I had an adventure last year."

"I don't want to hear it."

Neddy showed concern.

"You're all over the shop, Ray. These blessed works are knocking the stuffing out of you and spoiling your temper. Are you coming to the 'smoker' at 'The Tiger' next month?"

"No."

"Well, do. You want bucking. It'll be a bit out of the common. Jack Buckler's training at 'The Tiger' for his match with Solly Blades. You know—eliminating round for middle-weight championship. And he's going to spar three rounds with our boy from the tannery—Tim Chick."

"I heard about it from one of our girls here—a cousin of Tim's. But I'm off that sort of thing."

"Since when?"

"You can't understand, Ned; but life's too short for everything. Perhaps you'll have to turn to work someday. Then you'll know."

"You don't work from eight o'clock at night till eleven anyway. Take my tip and come to the show and make a night of it. Waldron's going to be there. He's hunting this morning."

"I know."

The dinner bell had rung and now there came a knock at Raymond's door. Then Sabina entered and was departing again, but her lover bade her stay.

"Don't go, Sabina. This is my friend, Mr. Motyer—Miss Dinnett."

Motyer, remembering Raymond's recent snub, was exceedingly charming to Sabina. He stopped and chatted another five minutes, then mentioned the smoking concert again and so took his departure. Raymond spoke slightingly of him when he had gone.

"He's no good, really," he said. "An utter waster and only a hanger-on of sport—can't do anything himself but talk. Now he'll tell everybody in Bridport about you coming up here in the dinner-hour. Come and cheer me up. I'm bothered to death."

He kissed her and put his arms round her, but she would not stop.

"I can't stay here," she said. "I want to walk up the hill with you. If you're bothered, so am I, my darling."

He put on his hat and they went out together.

"I've had a nasty jar," she told him. "People are beginning to say things, Raymond—things that you wouldn't like to think are being said."

"I thought we rose superior to the rest of the world, and what it said and what it thought."

"We do and we always have. We're not moral cowards either of us. But there are some things. You don't want me to be insulted. You don't want either of us to lose the respect of people."

"We can't have our cake and eat it too, I suppose," he said rather carelessly. "Personally I don't care a straw whether people respect me, or despise me, as long as I respect myself. The people that matter to me respect me all right."

"Well, the people that matter to me, don't," she answered with a flash of colour. "We'll leave you out, Raymond, since you're satisfied; but I'm not satisfied. It isn't right, or fair, that I should begin to get sour looks from the women here, where I used to have smiles; and looks from the men— hateful looks—looks that no decent woman ought to suffer. And my mother has heard a lot of lies and is very miserable. So I think it's high time we let everybody know we're engaged. And you must think so, too, after what I've told you, Ray dear."

"Certainly," he answered, "not a shadow of doubt about it. And if I saw any man insult you, I should delight to thrash him on the spot—or a dozen of them. How the devil do people find out about one? I thought we'd been more than clever enough to hoodwink a dead alive place like this."

"Will you let me tell mother, to-day? And Sally Groves, and one or two of my best friends at the Mill? Do, Raymond—it's only fair to me now."

Had she left unspoken her last sentence, he might have agreed; but it struck a wrong note on his ear. It sounded selfish; it suggested that Sabina was concerned with herself and indifferent to the complications she had brought into his life. For a moment he was minded to answer hastily; but he controlled himself.

"It's natural you should feel like that; so do I, of course. We must settle a date for letting it out. I'll think about it. I'd say this minute, and you know I'm looking forward quite as much as you are to letting the world know my luck; but unfortunately you've just raised the question at an impossible moment, Sabina."

"Why? Surely nothing can make it impossible to clear my good name, Raymond?"

"I've got a good name, too. At least, I imagine so."

"Our names are one, or should be."

"Not yet, exactly. I wanted to spare you bothers. I do spare you all the bothers I can; but, of course, I've got my own, too, like everybody else. You see it's rather vital to your future, which you're naturally so keen about, Sabina, that I keep in with my brother. You'll admit that much. Well, for the moment I'm having the deuce of a row with him. You know what an exacting beggar he is. He will have his pound of flesh, and he has no sympathy for anything on two legs but himself. I asked him for a fortnight's holiday."

"A fortnight's holiday, Raymond!"

"Yes—that's not very wonderful, is it? But, of course, you can't understand what this work is to me, because you look at it from a different angle. Anyway I want a holiday—to get right away and consider things; and he won't let me have it. And finding that, I lost my temper. And if, at the present moment, Daniel hears that we're engaged to be married, Sabina, it's about fifty to one that he'd chuck me altogether and stop my dirty little allowance also."

They had reached the gate of 'The Magnolias,' and Sabina did a startling thing. She turned from him and went down the path to the back entrance without another word. But this he could not stand. His heart smote him and he called her with such emotion that she also was sorrowful and came back to the gate.

"Good God! you frightened me," he said. "This is a quarrel, Sabina—our first and last, I hope. Never, never let anything come between us. That's unthinkable and I won't have it. You must give and take, my precious girl. And so must I. But look at it. What on earth happens to us if Daniel fires me out of the Mill?"

"He's a just man," she answered. "Dislike him as we may, he's a just man and you need not fear him, or anybody else, if you do the right thing."

"You oppose your will to mine, then, Sabina?"

"I don't know your will. I thought I did; I thought I understood you so well by now and was learning better and better how to please you. But now I tell you I am being wronged, and you say nothing can be done."

"I never said so. I'm not a blackguard, Sabina, and you ought to know that as well as the rest of the world. I'm poor, unfortunately, and the poor have got to be politic. Daniel may be just, but it's a narrow-minded, hypocritical justice, and if I tell him I'm engaged to you, he'll sack me. That's the plain English of it."

"I don't believe he would."

"Well, I know he would; and you must at least allow me to know more about him than you do. And so I ask you whether it is common-sense to tell him what's going to happen, for the sake of a few clod-hoppers, who matter to nobody, or—"

"But, but, how long is it to go on? Why do you shrink from doing now what you wanted to do at first?"

"I don't shrink from it at all. I only intend to choose the proper time and not give the show away at a moment when to do so will be to ruin me."

"'Give the show away,'" she quoted bitterly. "You can look me in the face and say a thing like that! It's only 'a show' to you; but it's my life to me."

"I'm sorry I used the expression. Words aren't anything. It's my life to me, too. And I've got to think for both of us. In a week, or ten days, I'll eat humble pie and climb down and grovel to Daniel. Then, when I'm pardoned, we'll tell everybody. It won't kill you to wait another fortnight anyway. And in the meantime we'd better see less of each other, since you're getting so worried about what your friends say about us."

Now he had said too much. Sabina would have agreed to the suggestion of a fortnight's waiting, but the proposal that they should see less of each other both hurt and angered her. The quarrel culminated.

"Caution seems to me rather a cowardly thing, Raymond, from you to me. I tell you that your wife's good name is at stake. For, since you've called me your wife so often, I suppose I may do the same. And if you're so careless for my credit, then I must be jealous for it myself."

"And my credit can go to the devil, I suppose?"

Then she flamed, struck to the root of the matter and left him.

"If the fact that you're engaged to me, by every sacred tie of honour, ruins your credit—then tell yourself what you are," she said, and her voice rose to a note he had never heard before.

This time he did not call her back, but went his own way up the hill.

CHAPTER XIII

IN THE FOREMAN'S GARDEN

Mr. Best was a good gardener and cultivated fruit and flowers to perfection. His rambling patch of ground ran beside the river and some of his apple trees bent over it. Pear trees also he grew, and a medlar and a quince. But flowers he specially loved. His house was bowered in roses to the thatched roof, and in the garden grew lilies and lupins, a hundred roses and many bright tracts of shining, scented blossoms. Now, however, they had vanished and on a Saturday afternoon John Best was tidying up, tending a bonfire and digging potatoes.

He was generous of his treasures and the girls never hesitated to ask him for a rose in June. Ancient Mrs. Chick, too, won an annual gift from the foreman. Down one side of his garden ranged great elder bushes, and Mrs. Chick made of the blooth in summer time, a decoction very precious for throat troubles.

Now Best stood for a moment and regarded a waste corner where grew nettles. Somebody approached him in this act of contemplation and he spoke.

"I often wonder if it would be worth while making an experiment with stinging nettles," he said to Ernest Churchouse, who was the visitor.

"They have a spinnable fibre, John, without a doubt."

"They have, Mister Churchouse, and they scutch well and can be wrought into textiles. But there's no temptation to make trial. I'm only thinking in a scientific spirit."

He swept up the fallen nettles for his bonfire.

"I've come for a few balls of the rough twine," said Mr. Churchouse.

"And welcome."

An unusual air of gloom sat on Mr. Best and the other was quick to observe it.

"All well, I hope?" he said.

"Not exactly. I'm rather under the weather; but I dare say it's my own fault."

"It often is," admitted Ernest; "but in my experience that doesn't make it any better. In fact, the most disagreeable sort of depression is that which we know we are responsible for ourselves. When other people annoy us, we have the tonic effect of righteous indignation; but not when we annoy ourselves and know ourselves to blame."

"I wouldn't go so far as to say it's all my own fault, however," answered Mr. Best. "It is and it isn't my fault. To be a father of children is your own fault in a manner of speaking; and yet to be a father is not any wrong, other things being as they should."

"On the contrary, it's part of the whole duty of man—other things being equal, as you say."

"We look to see ourselves reflected in our offspring, yet how often do we?" asked the foreman.

"Perhaps we might oftener, if we didn't suffer from constitutional inability to recognise ourselves, John. I've thought of this problem, let me tell you, for you are one of many who feel the same. So far as I can see, parents worry about what their children look like to them; but never about what they look like to their children."

"You speak as a childless widower," answered the other. "Believe me, Mister Churchouse, children nowadays never hesitate to tell us what we look like to them—or what they think of us either. Even my sailor boy will do it."

"It's the result of education," said Ernest. "There is no doubt that education has altered the outlook of the child on the parent. The old relation has disappeared and the fifth commandment does not make its old appeal. Children are better educated than their parents."

"And what's the result? They'd kill the home goose that lays the golden eggs to-morrow, if they could. In fact, they're doing it. Those that remain reasonable and obedient to their fathers and mothers feel themselves martyrs. That's the best sort; but it ain't much fun having a house full of martyrs whether or no; and it ain't much fun to know that your offspring are merely enduring you, as a necessary affliction. As for the other sort, who can't stick home life and old-fashioned ideas, they just break loose and escape as quick as ever they know how—and no loss either."

"A gloomy picture," admitted Mr. Churchouse; "but, like every other picture, it has two sides. I think time may be trusted to put it right. After the young have left the nest, and hopped out into the world, and been sharply pecked now and again, they begin to see home in its true perspective and find that there is nothing like the affection of a mother and father."

"They don't want anything of that," declared John. "If you stand for sense and experience and try to learn them, they think you're a fossil and out of sight of reality; and if you attempt to be young and interest yourself in their wretched little affairs and pay the boy with the boys and the girl with the girls, they think you're a fool."

"No doubt they see through any effort on the part of the middle-aged to be one with them," admitted Ernest. "And for my part I deprecate such attempts. Let us grow old like gentlemen, John, and if they cannot perceive the rightness and stateliness of age, so much the worse for them. Some of us, however, err very gravely in this matter. There are men who have not the imagination to see themselves growing old; they only feel it. And they try to hide their feelings and think they are also hiding the fact. Such men, of course, become the laughing-stocks of the rising generation and the shame of their own."

"All the young are alike, so I needn't grumble at my own family for that matter," confessed Mr. Best. "Their generation is all equally headstrong and opinionated—high and low, the same. If I've hinted to Raymond Ironsyde once, I've hinted a thousand times, that he's not going about his business in a proper spirit."

"He is at present obviously in love, John, and must not therefore be judged. But I share your uneasiness."

"It's wrong, and he knows it, and she ought to know it, too. Sabina, I mean. I should have given her credit for more sense myself. I thought she had plenty of self-respect and brains too."

"Things are coming to a crisis in that quarter," prophesied Ernest. "It is a quality of love that it doesn't stand still, John; and something is going to happen very shortly. Either it will be given out that they are betrothed, or else the thing will fade away. Sabina has very fine instincts; and on his side, he would, I am sure, do nothing unbecoming his family."

"He has—plenty," declared Mr. Best.

"Nothing about which there would not be two opinions, believe me. The fact that he has let it go so far makes me think they are engaged. The young will go their own way about things."

"If it was all right, Sabina Dinnett wouldn't be so miserable," argued John Best. "She was used to be as cheerful as a bird on a bough; and now she is not."

"Merely showing that the climax is at hand. I have seen myself lately that Sabina was unhappy and even taxed her with it; but she denied it. Her mother, however, knows that she is a good deal perturbed. We must hope for the best."

"And what is the best?" asked John.

"There is not the slightest difficulty about that; the best is what will happen," replied Mr. Churchouse. "As a good Christian you know it perfectly well."

But the other shook his head.

"That won't do," he answered, "that's only evasion, Mister Ernest. There's lots and lots of things happen, and the better the Christian you are, the better you know they ought not to happen. And whether they are engaged to be married, or whether they quarrel, trouble must come of it. If people do wrong, it's no good for Christians to say the issue must be right. That's simply weak-minded. You might as well argue nothing wrong ever does happen, since nothing can happen without the will of God."

"In a sense that's true," admitted Ernest. "So true, in fact, that we'd better change the subject, John. We thinking and religious men know there's a good deal of thin ice in Christianity, where we've got to walk with caution and not venture without a guide. One needs professional theologians to skate over these dangerous places safely. But, for my part, I have my reason well under control, as every religious person should. I can perfectly accept the fact that evil happens, and yet that nothing happens without the sanction of an all powerful and all good God."

"You'd better come and get your string then," said Mr. Best. "And long may your fine faith flourish. You're a great lesson to us people cursed with too much common-sense, I'm sure."

"Where our religion is concerned, we should be too proud to submit it to common-sense," declared Ernest. "Common-sense is all very well in everyday affairs; in fact, this world would not prosper without it; but I strongly deprecate common-sense as applied to the next world, John. The next world, from what one glimpses of it in prophecy and revelation, is outside the category of common-sense altogether."

"I stand corrected," said Mr. Best. "But it's a startler—to leave common-sense out of what matters most to thinking men."

"We shall be altered in the twinkling of an eye," explained Ernest, "and so, doubtless, will be our humble, earthly intelligence, our reliance on reason and other mundane virtues. From the heavenly standpoint, earth will seem a very sordid business altogether, I suspect, and even our good qualities appear very peddling. In fact, we may find, John, that we were in the habit of putting up statues to the wrong persons, and discover the most unexpected people at the right hand of the Throne."

"I dare say we shall," admitted Mr. Best; "for if common-sense is going by the board and the virtues all to be scrapped also, then we that think we stand had better take heed lest we fall—you and me included, Mister Churchouse. However, I'm glad to say I'm not with you there. The Book tells us very clear what's good and what's evil; and whatever else Heaven will do, it won't go back on the Book. I suppose you'll grant that much?"

"Most certainly," said the elder. "Most certainly and surely, John. That, at least, we can rely upon. Our stronghold lies in the fact that we know good from evil, and though we don't know what 'infinite' goodness is, we do know that it is still goodness. Therefore, though God is infinitely good, He is still good; the difference between His goodness and ours is one of degree, not kind. So metaphysics and quibbling leave us quite safe, which is all that really matters."

"I hope you're right," answered Best. "Life puts sharp questions to religion, and I can't pretend my religion's always clever enough to answer them."

Ernest took his twine and departed; but the subject of Raymond and Sabina was not destined to slumber, for now he met Raymond on his way to
North Hill House.

He asked him to come into tea and, to his surprise, the young man refused.

"That means Sabina isn't at home then," said Mr. Churchouse blandly.

"I don't know where she is."

At this challenge Ernest spoke and struck into the matter very directly. He blamed Raymond and feared that his course of action was not that of a gentleman.

"You would be the very first to protest and criticise unfavourably, my dear boy, if you saw anybody else treating a girl in this fashion," he concluded.

"I'm going to clear it up," answered the culprit. "Don't you worry. These things can't be done in a minute. This infernal place is always so quick to think evil, apparently, and judges decent people by its own dirty opinions. I've asked Daniel to give me a holiday, so that I may go away and think over life in general. And he won't give me a holiday. It's very clear to me, Uncle Ernest, that no self-respecting man would be able to work under Daniel for long. Things are coming to a climax. I doubt if I shall be able to keep on here."

"You evade the subject, which is your friendship with Sabina, Raymond. As to Daniel, there ought to be no difficulty whatever, and you know it very well in your heart and head. Your protest deceives nobody. But Sabina?"

Here the conversation ceased abruptly, for Raymond committed an unique offence. He told Mr. Churchouse to go to the devil, and left him, standing transfixed with amazement, at the outer gate of 'The Magnolias.'

With the insult to himself Ernest was not much concerned. His regretful astonishment centred in the spectacle of Raymond's downfall.

"To what confusion and disorder must his mind have been reduced, before he could permit himself such a lapse," reflected Mr. Churchouse.

CHAPTER XIV

THE CONCERT

The effect of Raymond's attitude on Sabina's mind proved very serious. It awoke in her first anger and then dismay. She was a woman of fine feeling and quick perception. Love and ambition had pointed the same road, and the hero, being, as it seemed, without guile, had convinced her that she might believe every word that he spoke and trust everything that he did. She had never contemplated any sacrifice before marriage, and, indeed, when it came, the consummation of their worship proved no sacrifice to her, but an added joy. Less than many a married woman had she mourned the surrender, for in her eyes it made all things complete between them and bound them inseparably with the golden links of love and honour.

When, therefore, upon this perfect union, sinister light from without had broken, she felt it no great thing to ask Raymond that their betrothal should be known. Reason and justice demanded it. She did not for an instant suppose that he would hesitate, but rather expected him to blame his own blindness in delay. But finding he desired further postponement, she was struck with consternation that rose to wrath; and when he persisted, she became alarmed and now only considered what best she might do for her own sake. Her work suffered and her friends perceived that all was not well with her. With the shortening days and bad weather, the meetings with Raymond became more difficult to pursue and she saw less of him. They had patched their quarrel and were friendly enough, but the perfect understanding had departed. They preserved a common ground and she did not mention subjects likely to annoy him. He appeared to be working steadily, seldom came into the shops and was more reserved to everybody in the Mill.

Sabina had not yet spoken to her mother, though many times tempted to do so. Her loyalty proved strong in the time of trial; but the greater the strain on herself, the greater the strain on her love for the man. She told herself that no such cruel imposition should have been placed upon her; and she could not fail closely to question the need for it. Why did Raymond demand continued silence even in the face of offences put upon her by her neighbours? How could he endure to hear that people had been rude to her, and uttered coarse jests in her hearing aimed only at her ear? Would a man who loved her, as she deserved to be loved, suffer this? Then fear grew. With her he was always kind—kind and considerate in every matter but the vital matter. Yet there were differences. The future, in which he had delighted to revel, bored him now, and when she spoke of it, he let the matter drop. He was on good terms with his brother for the moment, and appeared to be winning an increasing interest in his business to the exclusion of other affairs. He would become animated on the subject of Sabina's work, rather than the subject of Sabina. He stabbed her unconsciously with many little shafts of speech, yet knew not that he was doing so. He grew more grave and self-controlled in their relations. Her personal touch began to lose power and waken his answering fire less often. It was then that she found herself with child, and knowing that despite much to cause concern, Raymond was still himself, she rejoiced, since this fact must terminate his wavering and establish her future. Here at least was an event beyond his power to evade. He loved her and had promised to wed her. He was a man who might be weak, but had never explicitly behaved in a manner to make her tremble for such a situation as the present. Procrastination ceased to be possible. What now had happened must demand instant recognition of her rights, and that given, she assured herself the future held no terrors. Now he must marry her, or contradict his own record as a gentleman and a man of honour.

Yet she told him with a tremor and, until the last moment, could not banish from her heart the shadow of fear. He had never spoken of this possibility, or taken it into account, and she felt, seeing his silence, that it would be a shock.

The news came to him as they walked from the Mill on a Saturday when the works closed at noon. He was on his way to Bridport and she went beside him for a mile through the lanes.

For a moment he said nothing, then, seeing the road empty, he put his arms round her and kissed her.

"You clever girl!" he said.

"Don't tell me you're sorry, for God's sake, or I shall go and drown myself," she answered. Her face was anxious and she looked haggard in the cold light of a sunless, winter day. But a genuine, generous emotion had touched him, and with it woke pangs of remorse and contrition. He knew very well what she had been suffering mentally on his account, and he knew that the frightened voice in which she told him the news and the trembling mouth and the tear in her eyes ought not to have been there. Every fine feeling in the man and every honest instinct was aroused. For the moment he felt glad that no further delay was possible. His self-respect had already suffered; but now life offered him swift means to regain it. He did not, however, think of himself while his arms were round her; he thought of her and her only, while they remained together.

"'Sorry'?" he said. "Can you think I'm sorry? I'm only sorry that I didn't do something sooner and marry you before this happened, Sabina. Good Lord—it throws a lot of light. I swear it does. I'm glad—I'm honestly glad—and you must be glad and proud and happy and all the rest of it. We'll be married in a month. And you must tell your mother we're engaged to-day; and I'll tell my people. Don't you worry. Damn me, I've been worrying you a lot lately; but it was only because I couldn't see straight. Now I do and I'll soon atone."

She wept with thankful heart and begged him to turn with her and tell Mrs. Dinnett himself. But that he would not do.

"It will save time if I go on to Bridport and let Aunt Jenny hear about it. Of course the youngster is our affair and nobody need know about that. But we must be married in a jiffey and—you must give notice at the mill to-day. Go back now and tell Best."

"How wonderful you are!" she said. "And yet I feared you might be savage about it."

"More shame to me that you should have feared it," he answered; "for that means that I haven't been sporting. But you shall never be frightened of me again, Sabina. To see you frightened hurts me like hell. If ever you are again, it will be your fault, not mine."

She left him very happy and a great cloud seemed to fall off her life as she returned to the village. She blamed herself for ever doubting him. Her love rose from its smothered fires. She soared to great heights and dreamed of doing mighty things for Raymond. Straight home to her mother she went and told Mrs. Dinnett of her engagement and swiftly approaching marriage. The light had broken on her darkness at last and she welcomed the child as a blessed forerunner of good. The coming life had already made her love it.

Meantime Raymond preserved his cheerful spirit for a season. But existence never looked the same out of Sabina's presence and before he had reached Bridport, his mood changed. He recognised very acutely his duty and not a thought stirred in him to escape it; but what for a little while had appeared more than duty and promised to end mean doubts and fears for ever, began now to present itself under other aspects. The joy of a child and a wife and a home faded. For what sort of a home could he establish? He leaned to the hope that Daniel might prove generous under the circumstances and believed that his aunt might throw her weight on his side and urge his brother to make adequate provision; but these reflections galled him unspeakably, for they were sordid. They argued weakness in him. He must come as a beggar and eat humble pie; he must for ever sacrifice his independence and, with it, everything that had made life worth living. The more he thought upon it, the more he began to hate the necessity of taking this story to his relations. Better men than he had lived in poverty and risen from humble beginnings. It struck him that if he went his own way, redoubled his official energies and asked for nothing more on the strength of his marriage, his own self-respect would be preserved as well as the respect of his aunt and brother. He pictured himself as a hero, yet knew that what he contemplated was merely the conduct of an honest man.

The thought of approaching anybody with his intentions grew more distasteful, and by the time he reached Bridport, he had determined not to mention the matter, at any rate until the following day. So great a thing demanded more consideration than he could give it for the moment, because his whole future depended on the manner in which he broke it to his people. It was true that the circumstances admitted of no serious delay; Sabina must, of course, be considered before everything; but twenty-four hours would make no difference to her, while it might make all the difference to him.

He reduced the courses of action to two. Either he would announce that he was going to be married immediately as a fact accomplished; or he would invite his aunt's sympathies, use diplomacy and win her to his side with a view to approaching Daniel. Daniel appeared the danger, because it was quite certain that he would strongly disapprove of Raymond's marriage. This certainty induced another element of doubt. For suppose, far from seeking to help Raymond with his new responsibilities, Daniel took the opposite course and threatened to punish him for any such stupidity? Suppose that his brother, from a personal standpoint, objected and backed his objection with a definite assurance that Raymond must leave the mill if he took this step? The only way out of that would be to tell Daniel that he was compromised and must wed Sabina for honour. But Raymond felt that he would rather die than make any such confession. His whole soul rose with loathing at the thought of telling the truth to one so frozen and unsympathetic. Moreover there was not only himself to be considered, but Sabina. What chance would she have of ever winning Daniel to acknowledge and respect her if the facts came to his ears?

Raymond thought himself into a tangle and found a spirit of great depression settling upon him. But, at last, he decided to sleep on the situation. He did not go home, but turned his steps to 'The Tiger,' ate his luncheon and drank heartily with it.

Then he went to see a boxer, who was training with Mr. Gurd, and presently when Neddy Motyer appeared, he turned into the billiard room and there killed some hours before the time of the smoking concert.

He imbibed the intensely male atmosphere of 'The Tiger' with a good deal of satisfaction; but surging up into the forefront of his mind came every moment the truth concerning himself and his future. It made him bitter. For some reason he could not guess, he found himself playing billiards very much above his form. Neddy was full of admiration.

"By Jove, you've come on thirty in a hundred," he said. "If you only gave a fair amount of time to it, you'd soon beat anybody here but Waldron."

"My sporting days are practically over," answered Raymond. "I've got to face real life now, and as soon as you begin to do that, you find sport sinks under the horizon a bit. I thought I should miss it a lot, but I shan't."

"If anybody else said that, I should think it was the fox who had lost his brush talking," replied Neddy; "but I suppose you mean it. Only you'll find, if you chuck sport, you'll soon be no good. Even as it is, going into the works has put you back a lot. I doubt if you could do a hundred in eleven seconds now."

"There are more important things than doing a hundred in eleven seconds—or even time, either, for that matter."

"You won't chuck football, anyway? You'll be fast enough for outside right for year's yet if you watch yourself."

"Damned easy to say 'watch yourself.' Yes, I shall play footer a bit longer if they want me, I suppose."

Arthur Waldron dropped in a few minutes later.

He was glad to see Raymond.

"Good," he said. "I thought you were putting in a blameless evening with your people."

"No, I'm putting in a blameless evening here."

"He's playing enormous billiards, Waldron," declared Motyer. "I suppose you've been keeping him at it. He's come on miles."

"He didn't learn with me, anyway. It's not once in a blue moon that he plays at North Hill. But if he's come on, so much the better."

They played, but Raymond's form had deserted him. Waldron was much better than the average amateur and now he gave Raymond fifty in two hundred and beat him by as much. They dined together presently, and Job Legg, who often lent a hand at 'The Tiger' on moments of extra pressure, waited upon them.

"How's your uncle, Job?" asked Arthur Waldron, who was familiar with Mr. Legg, and not seldom visited 'The Seven Stars,' when Estelle came with him to Bridport.

"He's a goner, sir. I'm off to the funeral on Monday."

"Hope the will was all right?"

"Quite all right, sir, thank you, sir."

"Then you'll leave, no doubt, and what will Missis Northover do then?"

Legg smiled.

"It's hid in the future, sir," he answered.

A comedian, who was going to perform at the smoking concert, came in with Mr. Gurd, and the innkeeper introduced him to Neddy and Raymond. He joined them and added an element of great hilarity to the meal. He abounded in good stories, and understood horse-racing as well as Neddy Motyer himself. Neddy now called himself a 'gentleman backer,' but admitted that, so far, it had not proved a lucrative profession.

Their talk ranged over sport and athletics. They buzzed one against the other, and not even the humour of the comic man was proof against the seriousness of Arthur Waldron, who demonstrated, as always, that England's greatness had sprung from the pursuit of masculine pastimes. The breed of horses and the breed of men alike depended upon sport. The Empire, in Mr. Waldron's judgment, had arisen from this sublime foundation.

"It reaches from the highest to the lowest," he declared. "The puppy that plays most is the one that always turns into the best dog."

The smoking concert, held in Mr. Gurd's large dining-room, went the way of such things with complete success. The boxing was of the best, and the local lad, Tim Chick, performed with credit against his experienced antagonist. All the comic man's songs aimed at the folly of marriage and the horrors of domesticity. He seemed to be singing at Raymond, who roared with the rest and hated the humourist all the time. The young man grew uneasy and morose before the finish, drank too much whiskey, and felt glad to get into the cold night air when all was over.

And then there happened to him a challenge very unexpected, for Waldron, as they walked back together through the night-hidden lanes, chose the opportunity to speak of Raymond's private affairs.

"You can't accuse me of wanting to stick my nose into other people's business, can you, Ray? And you can't fairly say that you've ever found me taking too much upon myself or anything of that sort."

"No; you're unique in that respect."

"Well, then, you mustn't be savage if I'm personal. You know me jolly well and you know that you're about the closest friend I've got. And if you weren't a friend and a great deal to me, I shouldn't speak."

"Go ahead—I can guess. There's only one topic in Bridetown, apparently. No doubt you've seen me in the company of Sabina Dinnett?"

"I haven't, I can honestly say. But Estelle is very keen about the mill girls. She wants to do all sorts of fine things for them; and she's specially friendly with Missis Dinnett's daughter. And she's heard things that puzzled her young ears naturally, and she told me that some people say you're being too kind to Sabina and other people say you're treating her hardly. Of course, that puzzled Estelle, clever though she is; but, as a man of the world, I saw what it meant and that kindness may really be cruelty in the long run. You'll forgive me, won't you?"

"Of course, my dear chap. If one lives in a hole like Bridetown, one must expect one's affairs to be common property."

"And if they are, what does it matter as long as they are all straightforward? I never care a button what anybody says about me, because I know they can't say anything true that is up against me; and as to lies, they don't matter."

"And d'you think I care what they say about me?"

"Rather not. Only if a girl is involved, then the case is altered. I'm not a saint; but—"

"When anybody says they're not a saint, you know they're going to begin to preach, Arthur."

Waldron did not answer for a minute. He stopped and lighted his pipe. To Raymond, Sabina appeared unmeasurably distant at this midnight hour. His volatile mind was quick to take colour from the last experience, and in the aura of the smoking concert, woman looked a slight and inferior thing; marriage, a folly; domestic life, a jest.

Waldron spoke again.

"You won't catch me preaching. I only venture to say that in a little place like this, it's a mistake to be identified with a girl beneath you in every way. It won't hurt you, and if she was a common girl and given to playing about, it wouldn't hurt her; but the Dinnetts are different. However, you know a great deal more about her than I do, and if you tell me she's not all she seems and you're not the first and won't be the last, then, of course I'm wrong and enough said. But if she's all right and all she's thought to be, and all Estelle thinks her—for Estelle's a jolly good student of character—then, frankly, I don't think it's sporting of you to do what you're doing."

The word 'sporting' summed the situation from Waldron's point of view and he said no more.

Raymond grew milder.

"She's all Estelle thinks her. I have a great admiration for her. She's amazingly clever and refined. In fact, I never saw any girl a patch on her in my life."

"Well then, what follows? Surely she ought to be respected in every way."

"I do respect her."

"Then it's up to you to treat her as you'd treat anybody of your own class, and take care that nothing you do throws any shadow on her. And, of course, you know it. I'm not suggesting for a second you don't. I'm only suggesting that what would be quite all right with a girl in your own set, isn't exactly fair to Sabina—her position in the world being what it is."

It was on Raymond's tongue to declare his engagement; but he did not. He had banished Sabina for that night and the subject irked him. The justice of Waldron's criticism also irked him; but he acknowledged it.

"Thank you," he answered. "It's jolly good of you to say these things, Arthur, because they're not in your line, and I know you hate them. But you're dead right. I dare say I'll tell you something that will astonish you before long. But I'm not doing anything to be ashamed of. I haven't made any mistake; and if I had, I shouldn't shirk the payment."

"You can't, my dear chap. A mistake has always got to be paid for in full— often with interest added. As a sportsman you know that, and it holds all through life in my experience."

"I shan't make one. But if I do, I'm quite prepared to pay the cost."

"We all say that till the bill comes along. Better avoid the mistake, and I'm glad you're going to."

Far away from the scrub on North Hill came a sharp, weird sound.

"Hark!" said Waldron. "That's a dog fox! I hope the beggar's caught a rabbit."

CHAPTER XV

A VISIT TO MISS IRONSYDE

On the following day Raymond did not appear at breakfast, and Estelle wondered at so strange an event.

"He's going for a long walk with me this afternoon," she told her father. "It's a promise; we're going all the way to Chilcombe, for me to show him that dear little chapel and the wonderful curiosity in it."

"Not much in his line, but if he said he'll go, he'll go, no doubt," answered her father.

They went to church together presently, for Waldron observed Sunday. He held no definite religious opinions; but inclined to a vague idea that it was seemly to go, because it set a good example and increased your authority. He believed that church-going was a source of good to the proletariat, and though he did not himself accept the doctrine of eternal punishment, since it violated all sporting tenets, he was inclined to think that acceptation of the threat kept ignorant people straight and made them better members of society. He held that the parson and squire must combine in this matter and continue to claim and enforce, as far as possible, a beneficent autocracy in thorpe and hamlet; and he perceived that religion was the only remaining force which upheld their sway. That supernatural control was crumbling under the influences of education he also recognised; but did his best to stem the tide, and trusted that the old dispensation would at least last out his time.

On returning from worship they found Raymond in the garden, and when Estelle reminded him of his promise, he agreed and declared that he looked forward to the tramp. He was cheerful and apparently welcomed Estelle's programme, but there happened that which threatened to interfere with it.

Waldron had retired to his study and a new book on 'The Fox Terrier,' which he reserved for Sabbath reading, and Estelle and Raymond were just setting out for Chilcombe when there came Sabina. She had called to see her lover and entered the garden in time to stop him. She had never openly asked to see him in this manner before, and Raymond was quick to mark the significance of the change. It annoyed him, while inwardly he recognised its reasonableness. He turned and shook hands with her, and Estelle did the same.

"We're just starting for Chilcombe," she said.

Sabina looked her surprise. She had been expecting Raymond all the morning, to bring the great news to Ernest Churchouse, and was puzzled to know why he had not come. She could not wait longer, and while her mother advised delay, found herself unable to delay.

Now she perceived that Raymond had made plans independently of her.

"I was coming in this evening," he said, in answer to her eyes.

"May I speak to you a moment before you start with Miss Waldron?" she asked, and together they strolled into Estelle's rose garden where still a poor blossom or two crowned naked sprays.

"I don't understand," began the girl. "Surely—surely after yesterday?"

"I'd promised to go for this walk with her."

"What then? Wasn't there all the morning? My mother and I didn't go to church—expecting you every minute."

"You must keep your nerve, Sabina—both of us must. You mustn't be hysterical about it."

She perceived how mightily his mood had changed since their leave-taking of the day before.

"What's the matter?" she asked. "I suppose your people have not taken this well."

"They don't know yet—nobody does."

"You didn't tell them?"

"Things prevented it. We must choose the right moment to spring this. It's bound to knock them over for a minute. I'm thinking it all out. Probably you don't quite realise, Sabina, what this means from their point of view. The first thing is to get my aunt on my side; Daniel's hopeless, of course."

She stared at him.

"What in God's name has come over you? You talk as though you hadn't a drop of blood in your veins. Were you deaf yesterday? Didn't you hear me tell you I was with child by you? 'Their point of view'! What about my point of view?"

"Don't get excited, my dear girl. Do give me credit for some sense. This is a very ticklish business, and the whole of our future—yours, of course, quite as much as mine—will depend on what I do during the next few days. Do try to realise that. If I make a mistake now, we may repent it for fifty years."

"What d'you call making a mistake? What choice of action have you got if you're a gentleman? It kills me—kills me to hear you talking about making a mistake; and your hard voice means that you think you've made one. What have I done but love you with all my heart and soul? What have I ever done to make you put other people's points of view before mine?"

"I'm not—I'm not, Sabina."

"You are. You used to understand me so well and know what was in my mind before I spoke, and now—now before this—the greatest thing in the world for me—you—"

"Talk quietly, for goodness' sake. You don't want all Bridetown to hear us."

"You can say that? And you go out walking with a child and—"

"Look here, Sabina, you must pull yourself together, or else you stand a very good chance of bitching up our show altogether," he answered calmly. "This thing has got to be carried out by me, not you; and if you are not going to let me do it my own way, then so much the worse for both of us. I won't be dictated to by you, or anybody, and if you're not contented to believe in me, then I can only say you're making a big mistake and you'll very soon find it out."

"What are you going to do, then?" she asked, "and when are you going to do it? I've a right to know that, I suppose?"

"To think you can talk in that tone of voice to me—to me of all people!"

"To think you can force me to! And now you'll say you've seen things in me you never thought were there, and turn it over in your mind—and—and oh, it's cowardly—it's cruel. And you call yourself an honourable man and could tell me and swear to me only yesterday that I was more to you than anything else in the world!"

"D'you know what you're doing?" he asked. "D'you want to make me—there—I won't speak it—I won't come down to your level and forget myself and say things that I'd break my heart to think of afterwards. I must go now, or that girl will be wondering what the deuce has happened. She's told her father already that you weren't happy or something; so I suppose you must have been talking. I'll come in this evening. You'd better go home now as quick as you can."

He left her abruptly and she sat down shaking on a stone seat, to prevent herself from falling. Grief and terror shared her spirit. She watched him hurry away and, after he was gone, arose to find her legs trembling under her. She went home slowly; then thoughts came to her which restored her physical strength. Her anger gave place to fear and her fear beckoned her to confide in somebody with greater power over Raymond than her own.

She returned to her mother, described her repulse and then declared her intention of going immediately to see Miss Ironsyde. She concentrated her thoughts on the lady, of whom Raymond had often spoken with admiration and respect. She argued with herself that his aunt would only have to hear her story to take her side; she told herself and her mother that since Raymond had feared to approach his aunt, Sabina might most reasonably do so. She grew calm and convinced herself that not only might she do this, but that when Raymond heard of it, he would very possibly be glad that the necessity of confession was escaped. His Aunt Jenny was very fond of him, and would forgive him and help him to do right. Sabina found herself stronger than Raymond, and that did not astonish her, for she had suspected it before.

Her mother, now in tears, agreed with her and she started on foot for Bridport, walked quickly, and within an hour, reached the dwelling of the Ironsydes—a large house standing hidden in the trees above the town.

Miss Ironsyde was reading and looking forward to her tea when Sabina arrived. She had heard of the girl through Ernest Churchouse, but she had never met her and did not connect her in any way with Raymond. Jenny received her and was impressed with her beauty, for Sabina, albeit anxious and nervous, looked handsome after her quick walk.

"I've heard of you from your mother and Mr. Churchouse," said Miss Ironsyde, shaking hands. "You come from him, I expect. I hope he is well? Sit down by the fire."

Her kindly manner and gentle face set the younger at ease.

"He's quite well, thank you, miss. But I'm here for myself, not him. I'm in a great deal of terrible anxiety, and you'll excuse me for coming, I do hope, when I explain why I've come. It was understood between me and Mr. Raymond Ironsyde very clearly yesterday that he was going to tell you about it. He left me yesterday to do so. But I've seen him to-day and I find he never came, so I thought I might venture to come even though it was Sunday."

"The better the day, the better the deed. Something is troubling you. Why did not my nephew come, if he started to come?"

"I don't know. Indeed, he should have come."

"I'm afraid he starts to do a great many things he doesn't carry through," said Jenny, and the words, lightly spoken, fell sinister on Sabina's ear.

"There are some things a man must carry through if he starts to do them," she said quietly, and her tone threw light for Raymond's aunt. She grew serious.

"Tell me," she said. "I know my nephew very well and have his interests greatly at heart. He is somewhat undisciplined still and has had to face certain difficulties and problems, not much in themselves, but much to one with his temperament."

Then Sabina, who felt that she might be fighting for her life, set out to tell her story. She proved at her best and spoke well. She kept her temper and chose her words. The things that she had thought to speak, indeed, escaped her, but her artless and direct narrative did not fail to convince the listener.

"You're more to him than anybody in the world, but me," she said; "but I'm first, Miss Ironsyde. I must be first now. Even if to-day he had been different—but what seemed so near yesterday is far off to-day. He was harsh to-day. He terrified me, and I felt you'd think no worse of me than you must, if I ventured to come. I don't ask you to believe anything I say until you have seen him; but I'm not going to tell you anything but the sacred truth. Thanks to Mr. Churchouse I was well educated, and he took kind pains to teach me when I was young and helped me to get fond of books. So when Mr. Raymond came to the Mill, he found I was intelligent and well mannered. And he fell in love with me and asked me to marry him. And I loved him very dearly, because I had never seen or known a man with such a beautiful face and mind. And I promised to marry him. He wished it kept secret and we loved in secret and had great joy of each other for a long time. Then people began to talk and I begged him to let it be known we were engaged; but he would not. And then I told him—yesterday—that it must be known and that he must marry me as quickly as he could, for right and honour. And he seemed very glad—almost thankful I thought. He rejoiced about it and said it was splendid news. Then he left me to come straight to you and I was happy and thankful. But to-day I went to see him and he had changed and was rough to me and said he must choose his own time! This to me, who am going to be mother of his child next year! I nearly fainted when he said that. He told me to go; and I went. But I could not sit down under the shock; I had to do something and thought of you. So I came to implore you to be on my side—not only for my sake, but his. It's a very fearful thing—only I know how fearful, because I know all he's said and promised; and well I know he meant every word while he was saying it. And I do humbly beg you, miss, for love of him, to reason with him and hear what he's got to say. And if he says a word that contradicts what I've said, then I'll be content for you to believe him and I'll trouble you no more. But he won't. He'll tell you everything I've told you. He couldn't say different, for he's truthful and straight. And if it was anything less than the whole of my future life I wouldn't have come. But I feel there are things hidden in his mind I can't fathom—else after what I told him yesterday, he never, never could have been cruel to me, or changed his mind about coming to see you. And please forgive me for taking up your time. Only knowing that you cared for him so much made me come to you."

Miss Ironsyde did not answer immediately. Her intuition inclined her to believe every word at its face value; but her very readiness to do so made her cautious. The story was one of every day and bore no marks of improbability; yet among Raymond's faults she could not remember any unreasonable relations with the other sex. It had always been one bright spot in his dead father's opinion that the young man did not care about drink or women, and was not intemperate, save in his passion for athletic exercises and his abomination of work. It required no great perception to see that Sabina was not the type that entangles men. She had a beautiful face and a comely figure, but she belonged not to the illusive, distracting type. She was obvious and lacked the quality which attracts men far more than open features, regular modelling and steady eyes. It was, in fact, such a face as Raymond might have admired, and Sabina was such a girl as he might have loved—when he did fall in love. She was apparently his prototype and complement in directness and simplicity of outlook; that Miss Ironsyde perceived, and the more she reflected the less she felt inclined to doubt.

Sabina readily guessed the complex thoughts which kept the listener silent after she had finished, and sat quietly without more speech until Jenny chose to answer her. That no direct antagonism appeared was a source of comfort. Unconsciously Sabina felt happier for the presence of the other, though as yet she had heard no consoling word. Miss Ironsyde regarded her thoughtfully; then she rose and rang the bell. Sabina's heart sank for she supposed that she was to be immediately dismissed, and that meant defeat in a quarter very dangerous. But her mind was set at rest, for Jenny saw the fear in her eyes.

"I'm ringing for tea," she said. "I will ask you to stop and drink a cup with me. You've had a long walk."

Then came tears; but Sabina felt such weakness did not become her and smothered them.

"Thank you, gratefully, Miss Ironsyde," she said.

Tea was a silent matter, for Jenny had very little to say. Her speech was just and kind, however. It satisfied Sabina, whose only concern was justice now. She had spoken first.

"I think—I'm sure it's only some hitch in Mr. Raymond's mind. He's been so wonderful to me—so tender and thoughtful—and he's such a gentleman in all he does and says, that I'm sure he never could dream of going back on his sacred word. He wants to marry me. He'll never tell you different from that. But he cannot realise, perhaps, the need—and yet I won't say that neither, for, of course, he must realise."

"Say nothing more at all," answered Jenny. "You have said everything there was to say and I'm glad you have come to me and told me about it. But I'm not going to say anything myself until I've seen my nephew. You are satisfied that he will tell me the truth?"

"Yes, I am. Don't think I don't trust him. Only if there's something hidden from me, he might explain to you what it is, and what I've done to anger him."

Miss Ironsyde did not lack experience of men and could have thrown light on Sabina's problem; but she had not the heart. She began to suspect it was the girl's own compliance and his easy victory that had made Raymond weary before the reckoning. There is nothing more tasteless than paying after possession, unless the factors combine to make the payment a pleasure and possession an undying delight. Miss Ironsyde indeed guessed at the truth more accurately than she knew; but her sympathies were entirely with Sabina and it was certain that if Raymond, when the time came, could offer no respectable and sufficient excuse for a change of mind, he would find little support from her.

Of her intentions, however, she said nothing, nor indeed while Sabina drank a cup of tea had Miss Ironsyde anything to say. She was not unsympathetic, but she was guarded.

"I will see Raymond to-morrow without fail," she said when Sabina departed. "I share your belief, Miss Dinnett, that he is a truthful and straightforward man. At least I have always found him so. And I feel very sure that you are truthful and straightforward too. This will come right. I will give you one word of advice, if I may, and ask one question. Does anybody know of your engagement except my nephew and myself?"

"Only my mother. Yesterday he told me to go straight home and tell her. And I did. Whether he's told anybody, I don't know."

"Be sure he has not. He would tell nobody before me, I think. My advice, then, is to say nothing more until you hear from him, or me."

"I shouldn't, of course, Miss Ironsyde."

"Good-bye," said the other kindly. "Be of good heart and be patient for a few hours longer. It's hard to ask you to be, but you'll understand the wisdom."

When Sabina had gone, Miss Ironsyde nibbled a hot cake and reflected deeply on an interview full of pain. The story—so fresh and terrific to the teller—was older than the hills and presented no novel feature whatever to her who listened. But in theory, Jenny Ironsyde entertained very positive views concerning the trite situation. Whether she would be able to sustain them before her nephew remained to be seen. She already began to fear. She saw the dangers and traversed the arguments. Though free from class prejudice, she recognised its weight in such a situation. A break must mean Sabina's social ruin; but would union mean ruin to Raymond? And if the problem was reduced to that, what became of her theories? She decided that since her theories were based in righteousness and justice, she must prefer his downfall to the woman's. For if, indeed, he fell as the result of a mistaken marriage, he would owe the fall to himself and his attitude after the event. He need not fall. A tendency to judge him hardly, however, drew Jenny up. He had yet to be heard.

She went to her writing-desk and wrote him a letter directing him to see her on the following day without fail. "It is exceedingly important, my dear boy," she said, "and I shall expect you not later than ten o'clock to-morrow morning."

CHAPTER XVI

AT CHILCOMBE

Meantime Raymond had kept his promise and devoted some hours to Estelle's pleasure. The girl was proud of such an event, anticipated it for many days and won great delight from it when it came. She perceived, as they started, that her friend was perturbed and wondered dimly a moment as to what Sabina could have said to annoy him; but he appeared to recover quickly and was calm, cheerful and attentive to her chatter after they had gone a mile.

"To think you've never been to Chilcombe, Ray," she said. "You and father go galloping after foxes, or shooting the poor pheasants and partridges and don't care a bit for the wonderful tiny church at Chilcombe—the tiniest in England almost, I do believe. And then there's a beautiful thing in it—a splendid treasure; and many people think it was a piece of one of the ships of the Spanish Armada, that was wrecked on the Chesil Bank; and I dare say it is."

"You must tell me about it."

"I'm going to."

"Not walking too fast for you?"

"Not yet, but still you might go a little slower, or else I shall get out of breath and shan't be able to tell you about things."

He obeyed.

"There are no flowers for you to show me now," he said.

"No, but there are interesting things. For instance, away there to the right is a wonderful field. And the old story is that everything that is ever planted in it comes up red—red."

"What nonsense."

"Yes, it is, but it's creepy, nice nonsense. Because of the story. Once there were two murderers at Swire village, and one turned upon the other and told the secret of the murder and got his friend caught and hanged. And the bad murderer was paid a great deal of money for telling the Government about the other murderer; and that was blood-money, you see. Then the bad murderer bought a field, and because he bought it with blood-money, everything he planted came up red. I wish it was true; but, of course, I know it can't be, though a good many things would come up red, like sanfoin and scarlet clover and beetroots."

"A jolly good yarn," declared Raymond.

They tramped along through a network of winding lanes, and presently Estelle pointed to a lofty hillock that rose above the high lands on which they walked.

"That's Shipton Hill," she said, pointing to the domelike mound. "And I believe it's called so, because from one point it looks exactly like a ship upside down."

"I'll bet it is, and a very good name for it."

The diminutive chapel of Chilcombe stood in a farmyard beside a lofty knoll of trees. It was a stout little place of early English architecture, lifted high above the surrounding country and having a free horizon of sea and land. It consisted of a chancel, nave and south porch. Its bell cote held one bell; and within was a Norman font, a trefoil headed piscina, and sitting room for thirty-four people.

"Isn't it a darling little church?" asked Estelle, her voice sunk to a whisper; and Raymond nodded and said that it was 'ripping.'

Then they examined the medieval treasure of the reredos—a panel of cedar wood, some ten feet in length, that surmounted the altar. It was set in a deep oaken frame, and displayed two circular drawings with an oblong picture in the midst. In the left circle was the scourging of Christ; in the right, the Redeemer rose from the tomb; while between them the crucifixion had been depicted, with armies of mail-clad soldiers about the cross. The winged symbols of the evangelists appeared in other portions of the panel with various separate figures, and there were indications that the work was unfinished.

Estelle, who had often studied every line of it, gave her explanations and ideas to Raymond, while he listened with great attention. Then they went to the ancient manor house now converted into a farm; and there the girl had friends who provided them with tea. She made no attempt to hide her pride at her companion, for she was a lonely little person and the expedition with Raymond had been a great event in her life.

Exceedingly happy and contented, she walked beside him homeward in the fading light and ceased not to utter her budding thoughts and reflections. He proved a good listener and encouraged her, for she amused him and really interested him. In common with her father, Raymond was often struck by the fact that a child would consider subjects which had never entered his head; but so it was, since Estelle's mind had been wrought in a larger plan and compassed heights and depths, even in its present immaturity, to which neither Waldron's nor Raymond's had aspired. Yet the things she said were challenging, though often absurd. Facts which he knew, though Estelle as yet did not, served to block her ideals and explain her mysteries, yet he recognised the girl's simple dreams, unvexed by practical considerations, or the 'nay' that real life must make to them, were beautiful.

She spoke a good deal about the Mill, where now her chief interest centred; and Raymond spoke about it too. And presently, after brisk interchange of ideas, she pointed out a fact that had not struck him.

"It's a funny thing, Ray," she said, "but what you love best about the works is the machinery; and what I love best about them is the people. Yet I don't see how a machine can be as interesting as a girl."

"Perhaps you're wrong, Estelle. Perhaps I wish you were right. If I hadn't found a girl more interesting—" He broke off and turned from the road she had innocently opened into his own thoughts.

"Of course the people are more interesting, really. But because I'm keen about the machines, you mustn't think I'm not keener still about the people. You see the better the machines, the better time the people will have, and the less hard and difficult and tiring for them will be their work."

She considered this and suddenly beamed.

"How splendid! Of course I see. You *are* clever, Ray. And it's really the people you think of all the time."

She gave him a look of admiration.

"I expect presently they'll all see that; and gradually you'll get them more and more beautiful machines, till their work is just pleasure and nothing else. And do invent something to prevent Sabina and Nancy and Alice hurting their hands. They have to stop the spindles so often, and it wounds them, and Nancy gets chilblains in the winter, so it's simply horrid for her."

"That's right. It's one of the problems. I'm not forgetting these things."

"And if I think of anything may I tell you?"

"I hope you will, Estelle."

She talked him into a pleasant humour, and it took a practical form unknown to Estelle, for before they had reached home again, there passed through Raymond's mind a wave of contrition. The contrast between Estelle's steadfast and unconscious altruism and his own irresolution and selfishness struck into him. She made him think more kindly of Sabina, and when he considered the events of that day from Sabina's standpoint, he felt ashamed of himself. For it was not she who had done anything unreasonable. The blame was his. He had practically lied to her the day before, and to-day he had been harsh and cruel. She had a right—the best possible right—to come and see him; she had good reason to be angry on learning that he had not kept his word.

He determined to see Sabina as quickly as possible, and about seven o'clock in the evening after the return from the walk, he went down to 'The Magnolias' and rang the bell. Mrs. Dinnett came to the door, and said something that hardened the young man's heart again very rapidly.

Sabina's mother was unfriendly. Since her daughter returned, she had learned all there was to know, and for the moment felt very antagonistic. She had already announced the betrothal to certain of her friends, and the facts that day had discovered made her both anxious and angry. She was a woman of intermittent courage, but her paroxysms of pluck soon passed and between them she was craven and easily cast down. For the moment, however, she felt no fear and echoed the mood in which Sabina had returned from Bridport an hour earlier.

"Sabina can't be seen to-night," she said. "You wouldn't have anything to do with her this afternoon, Mr. Ironsyde, and treated her like a stranger; and now she won't see you."

"Why not, Missis Dinnett?"

"She's got her pride, and you've wounded it—and worse. And I may tell you we're not the people to be treated like this. It's a very ill-convenient business altogether, and if you're a gentleman and a man of honour—"

He cut her short.

"Is she going to see me, or isn't she?"

"She is not. She's very much distressed, and every reason to be, God knows; and she's not going to see you to-night."

Raymond took it quietly and his restraint instantly alarmed Mrs. Dinnett.

"It's not my fault, Mr. Ironsyde. But seeing how things are between you, she was cruel put about this afternoon, and she's got to think of herself if you can do things like that at such a moment."

"She must try and keep her nerve better. There was no reason why I should break promises. She ought to have waited for me to come to her."

Mary Dinnett flamed again.

"You can say that! And didn't she wait all the morning to see if you'd come to her—and me? And as to promises—it don't trouble you to break promises, else you'd have seen your family yesterday, as you told Sabina you were going to do."

"Is she going to the mill to-morrow?" he asked, ignoring the attack.

"No, she ain't going to the mill. It isn't a right and fitting thing that the woman you're going to marry and the mother of your future child should be working in a spinning mill; and if you don't know it, others do."

"She told you then—against my wishes?"

"And what are your wishes alongside of your acts? You're behaving very wickedly, Mr. Ironsyde, and driving my daughter frantic; and if she can't tell her mother her sorrows, who should know?"

"She has disobeyed me and done a wrong thing," he said quietly. "This may alter the whole situation, and you can tell her so."

"For God's sake don't talk like that. Would you ruin the pair of us?"

"What am I to do if I can't trust her?" he asked, and then went abruptly away before Mary could answer.

She was terribly frightened and soon drowned in tears, for when she returned to Sabina and related the conversation, her daughter became passionate and blamed her with a shower of bitter words.

"I only told you, because I thought you had sense enough to keep your mouth shut about it," she cried. "Now he'll think it's common news and hate me—hate me for telling. You've ruined me—that's what you've done, and I may as well go and make a hole in the water as not, for he'll never marry me now."

"You told Miss Ironsyde," sobbed the mother.

"That was different. She'll keep it to herself, and I had to tell her to show how serious it was for me. For anything less than that, she'd have taken his side against me. And now he'll find I've been to her, and that may—oh, my God, why didn't I keep quiet a little longer, and trust him?"

"You had every right to speak, when you found he was telling lies," said Mrs. Dinnett.

And while they quarrelled, Raymond returned to North Hill in a mood that could not keep silence. He and Arthur Waldron smoked after supper, and when Estelle had gone to bed, the younger spoke and took up the conversation of the preceding night where he had dropped it. The speech that now passed, however, proceeded on a false foundation, for Raymond only told Arthur what he pleased and garbled the facts by withholding what was paramount.

"You were talking of Sabina Dinnett last night," he said. "What would you think if I told you I was going to marry her, Waldron?"

"A big 'if.' But you're not going to tell me so. You would surely have told me yesterday if you had meant that."

"Why shouldn't I if I want to?"

"I always keep out of personal things—even with pals. I strained a point with you last night for friendship, Ray. Is the deed done, or isn't it? If it is, there is nothing left but to congratulate you and wish you both luck."

"If it isn't?"

Mr. Waldron was cautious.

"You're not going to draw me till I know as much as you know, old chap. Either you're engaged, or you're not."

"Say it's an open question—then what?"

"How can I say it's an open question after this? I'm not going to say a word about it."

"Well, I thought we were engaged; but it seems there's a bit of doubt in the air still."

"Then you'd better clear that doubt, before you mention the subject again. Until you and she agree about it, naturally it's nobody else's business."

"And yet everybody makes it their business, including you. Why did you advise me to look out what I was doing last night?"

"Because you're young, boy, and I thought you might make a mistake and do an unsporting thing. That was nothing to do with your marrying her. How was I to know such an idea was in your mind? Naturally nobody supposed any question of that sort had arisen."

"Why not?"

Waldron felt a little impatient.

"You know as well as I do. Men in your position don't as a rule contemplate marriage with women, however charming and clever, who—. But this is nonsense. I'm not going to answer your stupid questions."

"Then you'd say—?"

"No, I wouldn't. I'll say nothing about it. You're wanting to get something for nothing now, and presently I daresay you'd remind me of something I had said. We can go back to the beginning if you like, but you're not going to play lawyer with me, Ray. It's in a nutshell, I suppose. You're going to marry Miss Dinnett, or else you're not. Of course, you know which. And if you won't tell me which, then don't ask me to talk about it."

"I've not decided."

"Then drop it till you have."

"You're savage now."

"I'm never savage—you know that very well. Or, if I am, it's only with men who are unsporting."

"Let's generalise, then. I suppose you'd say a man was a fool to marry out of his own class."

"As a rule, yes. Because marriage is difficult enough at best without complicating it like that. But there are exceptions. You can't find any rule without exceptions."

"I'll tell you the truth then, Arthur. I meant to marry Sabina. I believed that she was the only being in the world worth living for. But things have happened and now I'm doubtful whether it would be the best possible."

"And what about her? Is she doubtful too?"

"I don't know. Anyway I've just been down to see her and she wouldn't see me."

"See her to-morrow then and clear it up. If there's a doubt, give yourselves the benefit of the doubt. She's tremendously clever, Estelle says, and she may be clever enough to believe it wouldn't do. And if she feels like that, you'll be a fool to press it."

They talked on and Waldron, despite his caution, was too ingenuous to hide his real opinions. He made it very clear to Raymond that any such match, in his judgment, would be attended by failure. But he spoke in ignorance of the truth.

The younger went to bed sick of himself. His instincts of right and honour fought with his desires to be free. His heart sank now at the prospect of matrimony. He assured himself that he loved Sabina as steadfastly as ever he had loved her; but that there might yet be a shared life of happiness for them without the matrimonial chains. He considered whether it would be possible to influence Sabina in that direction; he even went so far as to speculate on what would be his future feelings for her if she insisted upon the sanctity of his promises.

CHAPTER XVII

CONFUSION

Mr. Churchouse was standing in his porch, when a postman brought him a parcel. It was a book, and Ernest displayed mild interest.

"What should that be, I wonder?" he said. Then he asked a question.

"Have you seen Bert, the newspaper boy? For the second morning he disappoints me."

But Bert himself appeared at the same moment and the postman went his way.

"No newspaper on Saturday—how was that?" asked Mr. Churchouse.

"I was dreadful ill and my mother wouldn't let me go outdoors," explained the boy. "I asked Neddy Prichard to go down to the baker's and get it for you; but he wouldn't."

"Then I say no more, except to hope you're better."

"It's my froat," explained Bert, a sturdy, flaxen youngster of ten.

"One more point I should like to raise while you are here. Have you noticed that garden chair in the porch?"

"Yes, I have, and wondered why 'twas left there."

"Wonder no more, Bert. It is there that you may put the paper upon it, rather than fling the news on a dirty door-mat."

"Fancy!" said Bert. "I never!"

"Bear it in mind henceforth, and, if you will delay a moment, I will give you some black currant lozenges for your throat."

A big black cat stood by his master listening to this conversation and Bert now referred to him.

"Would thicky cat sclow me?" he asked.

"No, Bert—have no fear of Peter Grim," answered Mr. Churchouse. "His looks belie him. He has a forbidding face but a friendly heart."

"He looks cruel fierce."

"He does, but though a great sportsman, he has a most amiable nature."

Having ministered to Bert, Mr. Churchouse retired with his book and paper. Then came Mary Dinnett, red-eyed and in some agitation. But for a moment he did not observe her trouble. He had opened his parcel and revealed a volume bound in withered calf and bearing signs of age and harsh treatment.

"A work I have long coveted—it is again 'a well-wisher,' Missis Dinnett, who has sent it to me. There is much kindness in the world still."

But Mrs. Dinnett was too preoccupied with her own affairs to feel interest in Ernest's pleasant little experience. By nature pessimistic, original doubts, when she heard of Sabina's engagement, were now confirmed and she felt certain that her daughter would never become young Ironsyde's wife. Regardless of the girl's injunction to silence, and feeling that both for herself and Sabina this disaster might alter the course of their lives and bring her own hairs with sorrow to the grave, Mary now took the first opportunity to relate the facts to Mr. Churchouse. They created in him emotions of such deep concern that neither his book nor his newspaper were opened on the day of the announcement.

Mrs. Dinnett rambled through her disastrous recital, declared that for her own part, she had already accepted the horror of it and was prepared to face the worst that could happen, and went so far as to predict what Ernest himself would probably do, now that the scandal had reached his ears. She was distraught and for the moment appeared almost to revel in the accumulated horrors of the situation.

She told the story of promise and betrayal and summed up with one agonised prophecy.

"And now you'll cast her out—you'll turn upon us and throw us out—I know you will."

"'Cast her out'? Good God of Mercy! Who am I to cast anybody out, Missis Dinnett? Shall an elderly and faulty fellow creature rise in judgment at the weakness of youth? What have I done in the past to lead you to any such conclusion? I feel very certain, indeed, that you are permitting yourself a debauch of misery—wallowing in it, Mary Dinnett—as misguided wretches often wallow in drink out of an unmanly despair at their own human weakness. Fortify yourself! Approach the question on a higher plane. Remember no sparrow falls to the ground without the cognisance of its Creator! As for Sabina, I love her and have devoted many hours to her education. I also love Raymond Ironsyde—for his own sake as well as his family's. I am perfectly certain that you exaggerate the facts. Such a thing is quite incredible. Shall I quarrel with a gracious flower because a wandering bee has set a seed? He may be an inconsiderate and greedy bee—but—"

Mr. Churchouse broke off, conscious that his simile would land him in difficulties.

"No," he said, "we must not pursue this subject on a pagan or poetical basis. We are dealing with two young Christians, Missis Dinnett—a man and a woman of good nurture and high principle. I will never believe—not if he said it himself—that Raymond Ironsyde would commit any such unheard-of outrage. You say that he has promised to marry her. That is enough for me. The son of Henry Ironsyde will keep his promise. Be sure of that. For the moment leave the rest in my hands. Exercise discretion, and pray, pray keep silence about it. I do trust that nobody has heard anything. Publicity might complicate the situation seriously."

As a matter of fact Mrs. Dinnett had told everything to her bosom friend—a woman who dwelt in a cottage one hundred yards from 'The Magnolias.' She did not mention this, however.

"If you say there's hope, I'll try to believe it," she answered. "The man came here last night and Sabina wouldn't see him, and God knows what'll be the next thing."

"Leave the next thing to me."

"She's given notice at the works. He told her to."

"Of course—quite properly. Now calm down and fetch me my walking boots."

In half an hour Ernest was on his way to Bridport. As Sabina, before him, his instinct led to Miss Ironsyde and he felt that the facts might best be imparted to her. If anybody had influence with Raymond, it was she. His tone of confidence before Mrs. Dinnett had been partly assumed, however. His sympathies were chiefly with Sabina, for she was no ordinary mill hand; she had enjoyed his tuition and possessed native gifts worthy of admiration. But she was as excitable as her mother, and if this vital matter went awry, there could be no doubt that her life must be spoiled.

Mr. Churchouse managed to get a lift on his way from a friendly farmer, and he arrived at Bridport Town Hall soon after ten o'clock. While driving he put the matter from his mind for a time, and his acquaintance started other trains of thought. One of them, more agreeable to a man of his temperament than the matter in hand, still occupied his mind when he stood before Jenny Ironsyde.

"You!" she said. "I had an idea you never came into the world till afternoon."

"Seldom—seldom. I drove a good part of the way with Farmer Gate, and he made a curious remark. He said that a certain person might as well be dead for all the good he was. Now what constitutes life? I've been asking myself that."

"It's certainly difficult to decide about some people, whether they're alive or dead. Some make you doubt if they ever were alive."

"A good many certainly don't know they're born; and plenty don't know they're dead," he declared.

"To be in your grave is not necessarily to be dead, and to be in your shop, or office, needn't mean that you're alive," admitted the lady.

"Quite so. Who doesn't know dead people personally, and go to tea with them, and hear their bones rattle? And whose spirit doesn't meet in their thoughts, or works, the dead who are still living?"

"Most true, I'm sure; but you didn't come to tell me that?"

"No; yet it has set me wondering whether, perhaps, I am dead—at any rate deader than I need be."

"We are probably all deader than we need be."

"But to-day there has burst into my life a very wakening thing. It may have been sent. For mystery is everywhere, and what's looking exceedingly bad for those involved, may be good for me. And yet, one can hardly claim to win goodness out of the threatened misfortunes to those who are dear to one."

"What's the matter? Something's happened, or you wouldn't come to see me so early."

"Something has happened," he answered, "and one turns to you in times of stress, just as one used to turn to your dear brother, Henry. You have character, shrewdness and decision."

Miss Ironsyde saw light.

"You've come for Raymond," she said.

"Now how did you divine that? But, as a matter of fact, I've come for somebody else. A very serious thing has happened and if we older heads—"

"Who told you about it?"

"This morning, an hour ago, it was broken to me by Sabina's mother."

"Tell me just what she told you, Ernest."

He obeyed and described the interview exactly.

"I cannot understand that, for Sabina saw me last night and explained the situation. I impressed upon her the importance of keeping the matter as secret as possible for the present."

"Nevertheless Mary Dinnett told me. She is a very impulsive person—so is Sabina; but in Sabina's case there is brain power to control impulse; in her mother's case there is none."

"I'm much annoyed," declared Miss Ironsyde—"not of course, that you should know, but that there should be talking. Please go home and tell them both to be quiet. This chattering is most dangerous and may defeat everything. Last night I wrote to Raymond directing him to come and see me immediately. I did not tell him why; but I told him it was urgent. I made the strongest appeal possible. When you arrived, I thought it was he. He should have been here an hour ago."

"If he is coming, I will go," answered Ernest. "I don't wish to meet him at present. He has done very wrongly—wickedly, in fact. The question is whether marriage with Sabina—"

"There is no question about that in my opinion," declared the lady. "I am a student of character, and had she been a different sort of girl—. But even as it is I suspend judgment until I have seen Raymond. It is quite impossible, however, after hearing her, to see what excuse he can offer."

"She is a very superior girl indeed, and very clever and refined. I always hoped she would marry a schoolmaster, or somebody with cultured tastes. But her great and unusual beauty doubtless attracted Raymond."

"I think you'd better go home, Ernest. I'll write to you after I've seen the boy. Do command silence from both of them. I'm very angry and very distressed, but really nothing can be done till we hear him. My sympathy is entirely with Sabina. Let her go on with her life for a day or two and—"

"She's changed her life and left the Mill. I understand Raymond told her to do so."

"That is a good sign, I suppose. If she's done that, the whole affair must soon be known. But we talk in the dark."

Mr. Churchouse departed, forgot his anxieties in a second-hand book shop and presently returned home.

But he saw nothing of Raymond on the way; and Miss Ironsyde waited in vain for her nephew's arrival. He did not come, and her letter, instead of bringing him immediately as she expected, led to a very different course of action on his part.

For, taken with Sabina's refusal to see him, he guessed correctly at what had inspired it. Sabina had threatened more than once in the past to visit Miss Ironsyde and he had forbidden her to do so. Now he knew from her mother why she had gone, and while not surprised, he clutched at the incident and very quickly worked it into a tremendous grievance against the unlucky girl. His intelligence told him that he could not fairly resent her attempt to win a powerful friend at this crisis in her fortunes; but his own inclinations and growing passion for liberty fastened on it and made him see a possible vantage point. He worked himself up into a false indignation. He knew it was false, yet he persevered in it, as though it were real, and acted as though it were real.

He tore up his aunt's letter and ignored it.

Instead of going to Bridport, he went to his office and worked as usual.

At dinner time he expected Sabina, but she did not come and he heard from Mr. Best that she was not at the works.

"She came in here and gave notice on Saturday afternoon," said the foreman, shortly, and turned away from Raymond even as he spoke.

Then the young man remembered that he had bade Sabina do this. His anger increased, for now everybody must soon hear of what had happened.

In a sort of subconscious way he felt glad, despite his irritation, at the turn of events, for they might reconcile him with his conscience and help to save the situation in the long run.

CHAPTER XVIII

THE LOVERS' GROVE

A little matter now kindled a great fire, and a woman's reasonable irritation, which he had himself created, produced for Raymond Ironsyde a very complete catastrophe.

His aunt, indeed, was not prone to irritation. Few women preserved a more level mind, or exhibited that self-control which is a prime product of common-sense; but, for once, it must be confessed that Jenny broke down and did that which she had been the first to censure in another. The spark fell on sufficient fuel and the face of the earth was changed for Raymond before he slept that night.

For his failure to answer her urgent appeal, his contemptuous disregard of the strongest letter she had ever written, annoyed her exceedingly. It argued a callous indifference to her own wishes and a spirit of extraordinary unkindness. She had been a generous aunt to him all his life; he had very much for which to thank her; and yet before this pressing petition he could remain dumb. That his mind was disordered she doubted not; but nothing excused silence at such a moment.

After lunch on this day Daniel spent some little while with his aunt, and then when a post which might have brought some word from Raymond failed to do so, Jenny's gust of temper spoke. It was the familiar case of a stab at one who has annoyed us; but to point such stabs, the ear of a third person is necessary, and before she had quite realised what she was doing, Miss Ironsyde sharply blamed her nephew to his brother.

"The most inconsiderate, selfish person on earth is Raymond," she said as a servant brought her two letters, neither from the sinner. "I asked him—and prayed him—to see me to-day about a subject of the gravest importance to him and to us all; and he neither comes nor takes the least notice of my letter. He is hopeless."

"What's he done now?"

"I don't know exactly—at least—never mind. Leave it for the minute. Sorry, I was cross. You'll know what there is to know soon enough. If there's trouble in store, we must put a bold face on it and think of him."

"I rather hoped things were going smoother. He seems to be getting more steady and industrious."

"Perhaps he reserved his industry for the works and leaves none for anything else, then," she answered; "but don't worry before you need."

"You'll tell me if there's anything I ought to know, Aunt Jenny."

"He'll tell you himself, I should hope. And if he doesn't, no doubt there will be plenty of other people to do so. But don't meet trouble half way. Shall you be back to tea?"

"Probably not. I'm going to Bridetown this afternoon. I have an appointment with Best. He was to see some machinery that sounded all right; but he's very conservative and I can always trust him to be on the safe side. One doesn't mean to be left behind, of course."

"Always ask yourself what your father would have thought, Daniel. And then you'll not make any mistakes."

He nodded.

"I ask myself that often enough, you may be sure."

* * * * *

An hour later the young man had driven his trap to the Mill and listened to John Best on the subject of immediate interest. The foreman decided against any innovation for the present and Daniel was glad. Then he asked for his brother.

"Is Mister Raymond here?"

"He was this morning; but he's not down this afternoon. At least he wasn't when I went to his office just before you came."

"Everything's all right, I suppose?"

Mr. Best looked uncomfortable.

"I'm afraid not, sir; but I hate talking. You'd better hear it from him."

Daniel's heart sank.

"Tell me," he said. "You're one of us, John—my father's right hand for twenty years—and our good is your good. If you know of trouble, tell me the truth. It may be better for him in the long run. Miss Ironsyde was bothered about him, to-day."

"If it's better for him, then I'll speak," answered Best. "He's a very clever young man and learning fast now. He's buckling to and getting on with it. But—Sabina Dinnett, our first spinner, gave notice on Saturday. She's not here to-day."

"What does that mean?"

"You'd better ask them that know. I've heard a lot of rumours, and they may be true or not, and I hope they're not. But if they are, I suppose it means the old story where men get mixed up with girls."

Daniel was silent, but his face flushed.

"Don't jump to the conclusion it's true," urged the foreman. "Hear both sides before you do anything about it."

"I know it's true."

Mr. Best did not answer.

"And you know it's true," continued the younger.

"What everybody says nobody should believe," ventured Best. "What happened was this—Sabina came in on Saturday afternoon, when I was working in my garden, and gave notice. Not a month, but to go right away. Of course I asked her why, but she wouldn't tell me. She was as happy as a lark about it, and what she said was that I'd know the reason very soon and be the first to congratulate her. Of course, I thought she was going to be married. And still I hope she is. That's all you can take for truth. The rest is rumour. You can guess how a place like this will roll it over their tongues."

"I'll go and see Mister Churchouse."

"Do, sir. You can trust him to be charitable."

Daniel departed; but he did not see Ernest Churchouse. The antiquary was not at home and, instead, he heard Mrs. Dinnett, who poured the approximate truth into his ears with many tears. His brother had promised to marry Sabina, but on hearing the girl was with child, had apparently refused to keep his engagement.

Then it was Daniel Ironsyde's turn to lose his temper. He drove straight to North Hill House, found his brother in the garden with Estelle Waldron, took him aside and discharged him from the Mill.

Raymond had been considering the position and growing a little calmer. With a return of more even temper, he had written to Miss Ironsyde and promised to be with her on the following evening without fail. He had begged her to keep an open mind so far as he was concerned and he hoped that when the time came, he might be able to trust to her lifelong friendship. What he was going to say, he did not yet know; but he welcomed the brief respite and was in a good temper when his brother challenged him.

The attack was direct, blunt and even brutal. It burst like a thunder-bolt on Raymond's head, staggered him, and then, of course, enraged him.

"I won't keep you," said Daniel. "I only want to know one thing. Sabina Dinnett's going to have a baby. Are you the father of it, or aren't you?"

"What the devil business is that of yours?"

"As one of my mill hands, I consider it is my business. One thinks of them as human beings as well as machines—machines for work, or amusement—according to the point of view. So answer me."

"You cold-blooded cur! What are you but a machine?"

"Answer my question, please."

"Go to hell."

"You blackguard! You do a dirty, cowardly thing like this, despite my warnings and entreaties; you foul our name and drag it in the gutter and then aren't man enough to acknowledge it."

The younger trembled with passion.

"Shut your mouth, or I'll smash your face in!" he cried.

His sudden fury calmed his brother.

"You refuse to answer, and that can only mean one thing, Raymond. Then I've done with you. You've dragged us all through the mud—made us a shame and a scandal—proud people. You can go—the further off, the better. I dismiss you and I never want to see your face again."

"Don't worry—you never shall. God's my judge, I'd sooner sweep a crossing than come to you for anything. I know you well enough. You always meant to do this. You saved your face when my father robbed me from the grave and left me a pauper—you saved your face by putting me into the works; but you never meant me to stop there. You only waited your chance to sack me and keep the lot for yourself. And you've jumped at this and were glad to hear of this—damned glad, I'll bet!"

Daniel did not answer, but turned his back on his brother, and a minute or two later was driving away. When he had gone, the panting Raymond went to his room and flung himself on his bed. Under his cooling anger again obtruded the old satisfaction—amorphous, vile, not to be named—that he had felt before. This brought ultimate freedom a step nearer. If ostracism and punishment were to be his portion, then let him earn them. If the world—his world—was to turn against him, let the reversal be for something. Poverty would be a fair price for liberty, and those who now seemed so ready to hound him out of his present life and crush his future prospects, should live to see their error. For a time he felt savagely glad that this had happened. He regretted his letter to his aunt; he thought of packing his portmanteau on the instant and vanishing for ever; yet time and reflection abated his dreams. He began to grow a little alarmed. He even regretted his harsh words to his brother before the twilight fell.

Then his mind was occupied with Sabina; but Sabina had wounded him to the quick, for it was clear she and her mother had shamelessly published the truth. Sabina, then, had courted ruin. She deserved it. He soon argued that the disaster of the day was Sabina's work, and he dismissed her with an oath from his thoughts. Then he turned to Miss Ironsyde and found keen curiosity waken to know what she was thinking and feeling about him. Did she know that Daniel had dismissed him? Could she have listened to so grave a determination on Daniel's part and taken no step to prevent it?

He found himself deeply concerned at being flung out of his brother's business. The more he weighed all that this must mean and its effect upon his future, the more overwhelmed he began to be. He had worked very hard of late and put all his energy and wits into spinning. He was beginning to understand its infinite possibilities and to see how, Daniel's trust once won, he might have advanced their common welfare.

From this point he ceased to regret his letter to Miss Ironsyde, but was glad that he had written it. He now only felt concerned that the communication was not penned with some trace of apology for his past indifference to her wishes. He began to see that his sole hope now lay with his aunt, and the supreme point of interest centred in her attitude to the situation.

He despatched a second letter, confirming the first, and expressing some contrition at his behaviour to her. But this rudeness he declared to have been the result of peculiarly distressing circumstances; and he assured her, that when the facts came to her ears, she would find no difficulty in forgiving him.

Their meeting was fixed for the following evening, and until it had taken place, Raymond told nobody of what had happened to him. He went to work next morning, to learn indirectly whether Best had heard of his dismissal; but it seemed the foreman had not. The circumstance cheered Raymond; he began to hope that his brother had changed his mind, and the possibility put him into a sanguine mood at once. He found himself full of good resolutions; he believed that this might prove the turning point; he expected that Daniel would arrive at any moment and he was prepared frankly to express deep regret for his conduct if he did so. But Daniel did not come.

Sabina constantly crossed Raymond's mind, to be as constantly dismissed from it. He was aware that something definite must be done; but he determined not even to consider the situation until he had seen his aunt. A hopeful mood, for which no cause existed, somehow possessed him upon this day. For no reason and spun of nothing in the least tangible, there grew around him an ambient intuition that he was going to get out of this fix with the help of Jenny Ironsyde. The impression created a wave of generosity to Sabina. He felt a large magnanimity. He was prepared to do everything right and reasonable. He felt that his aunt would approve the line he purposed to take. She was practical, and he assured himself that she would not consent to pronounce the doom of marriage upon him.

In this sanguine spirit Raymond went to Bridport and dined at 'The Tiger' before going to see his aunt at the appointed time. And here there happened events to upset the level optimism that had ruled him all day. Raymond had the little back-parlour to himself and Richard Gurd waited upon him. They spoke of general subjects and then the older man became personal.

"If you'll excuse me, Mister Raymond," he said, "if you'll excuse me, as one who's known you ever since you went out of knickers, sir, I'd venture to warn you as a good friend, against a lot that's being said in Bridetown and Bridport, too. You know how rumours fly about. But a good deal more's being said behind your back than ought to be said; and you'll do well to clear it up. And by the same token, Mister Motyer's opening his mouth the widest. As for me, I got it from Job Legg over the way at 'The Seven Stars'; and he got it from a young woman at Bridetown Mills, niece of Missis Northover. So these things fly about."

Raymond was aware that Richard Gurd held no puritan opinions. He possessed tolerance and charity for all sorts and conditions, and left morals alone.

"And what did you do, Dick? I should think you'd learned by this time to let the gossip of a public-house go in at one ear and out of the other."

"Yes—for certain. I learned to do that before you were born; but when things are said up against those I value and respect, it's different. I've told three men they were liars, to-day, and I may have to tell thirty so, to-morrow."

Raymond felt his heart go slower.

"What the deuce is the matter?"

"Just this: they say you promised to marry a mill girl at Bridetown and—the usual sort of thing—and, knowing you, I told them it was a lie."

The young man uttered a scornful ejaculation.

"Tell them to mind their own business," he said. "Good heavens—what a storm in a teacup it is! They couldn't bleat louder if I'd committed a murder."

"There's more to it than to most of these stories," explained Richard. "You see it sounds a very disgraceful sort of thing, you being your brother's right hand at the works."

"I'm not that, anyway."

"Well, you're an Ironsyde, Mister Raymond, and to have a story of this sort told about an Ironsyde is meat and drink for the baser sort. So I hope you'll authorise me to contradict it."

"Good God—is there no peace, even here?" burst out Raymond. "Can even a man I thought large-minded and broad-minded and all the rest of it, go on twaddling about this as if he was an old washer-woman? Here—get me my bill—I've finished. And if you're going to begin preaching to people who come here for their food and drink, you'd better chuck a pub and start a chapel."

Mr. Gurd was stricken dumb. A thousand ghosts from the grave had not startled him so much as this rebuke. Indeed, in a measure, he felt the rebuke deserved, and it was only because he held the rumour of Raymond's achievements an evil lie, that he had cautioned the young man, and with the best motives, desired to put him on his guard. But that the story should be true—or based on truth—as now appeared from Raymond's anger, had never occurred to Richard. Had he suspected such a thing, he must have deplored it, but he certainly would not have mentioned it.

He went out now without a word and held it the wisest policy not to see his angry customer again that night. He sent Raymond's account in by a maid, and the young man paid it and went out to keep his appointment with Miss Ironsyde.

But again his mood was changed. Gurd had hit him very hard. Indeed, no such severe blow had been struck as this unconscious thrust of Richard's. For it meant that an incident that Raymond was striving to reconcile with the ways of youth—a sowing of wild oats not destined to damage future crops—had appeared to the easy-going publican as a thing to be stoutly contradicted—an act quite incompatible with Raymond's record and credit. Coming from Gurd this attitude signified a great deal; for if the keeper of a sporting inn took such a line about the situation, what sort of line were others likely to take? Above all, what sort of line would his Aunt Jenny take? His nebulous hopes dwindled. He began to fear that she would find the honour of the family depended not on his freeing himself from Sabina, but the contrary.

And he was right. Miss Ironsyde welcomed him kindly, but left no shadow of doubt as to her opinion; and the fact that the situation had been complicated by publicity, which in the last resort he argued, by no means turned her from her ultimatum.

"Sit down and smoke and listen to me, Raymond," she began, after kissing him. "I forgive you, once for all, that you could be so rude to me and fail to see me despite my very pressing letter. No doubt some whim or suspicion inspired you to be unkind. But that doesn't matter now. That's a trifle. We've got to thresh out something that isn't a trifle, however, for your honour and good name are both involved—and with yours, ours."

"I argue that a great deal too much is being made of this, Aunt Jenny."

"I hope so—I hope everything has been exaggerated through a misunderstanding. Delay in these cases is often simply fatal, Raymond, because it gives a lie a start. And if you give a lie a start, it's terribly hard to catch. Sabina Dinnett came to see me on Sunday afternoon and I trust with all my heart she told me what wasn't true."

He felt a sudden gleam of hope and she saw it.

"Don't let any cheerful feeling betray you; this is far from a cheerful subject for any of us. But again, I say, I hope that Sabina Dinnett has come to wrong conclusions. What she said was this. Trust me to be accurate, and when I have done, correct her statement if it is false. Frankly, I thought her a highly intelligent young woman, with grace of mind and fine feeling. She was fighting for her future and she did it like a gentlewoman."

Miss Ironsyde then related her conversation with Sabina and Raymond knew it to be faithful in every particular.

"Is that true, or isn't it?" she concluded.

"Yes, it's perfectly true, save in her assumption that I had changed my mind," he said. "What I may have done since, doesn't matter; but when I left her, I had not changed my mind in the least; if she had waited for me to act in my own time, and come to see you, and so on, as I meant to do, and broken it to Daniel myself, instead of hearing him break it to me and dismiss me as though I were a drunken groom, then I should have kept my word to her. But these things, and her action, and the fact that she and her fool of a mother have bleated the story all over the county—these things have decided me it would be a terrible mistake to marry Sabina now. She's not what I thought. Her true character is not trustworthy—in fact—well, you must see for yourself that they don't trust me and are holding a pistol to my head. And no man is going to stand that. We could never be married now, because she hates me. There's another reason too—a practical one."

"What?"

"Why, the best. I'm a pauper. Daniel has chucked me out of the works."

Miss Ironsyde showed very great distress.

"Do you honestly mean that you could look the world in the face if you ruin this woman?"

"Why use words like that? She's not ruined, any more than thousands of other women."

"I'm ashamed of you, Raymond. I hope to God you've never said a thing so base as that to anybody but me. And if I thought you meant it, I think it would break my heart. But you don't mean it. You loved the girl and you are an honourable man without a shadow on your good name so far. You loved Sabina, and you do love her, and if you said you didn't a thousand times, I should not believe it. You're chivalrous and generous, and that's the precious point about you. Granted that she made a mistake, is her mistake to wreck her whole life? Just think how she felt—what a shock you gave her. You part with her on Saturday the real Raymond, fully conscious that you must marry her at once—for her own honour and yours. Then on Sunday, you are harsh and cruel—for no visible reason. You frighten her; you raise up horrible fears and dangers in her young, nervous spirit. She is in a condition prone to terrors and doubts, and upon this condition you came in a surly mood and imply that you yourself are changed. What wonder she lost her head? Yet I do not think that it was to lose her head to come to me. She had often heard you speak of me. She knew that I loved you well and faithfully. She felt that if anybody could put this dreadful fear to rest, I should be the one. Don't say she wasn't right."

He listened attentively and began to feel something of his aunt's view.

"Forgive her first for coming to me. If mistaken, admit at least it was largely your own fault that she came. She has nothing but love and devotion for you. She told nothing but the truth."

He asked a question, which seemed far from the point, but none the less indicated a coming change of attitude. At any rate Jenny so regarded it.

"What d'you think of her?"

"I think she's a woman of naturally fine character. She has brains and plenty of sense and if she had not loved you unspeakably and been very emotional, I do not think this could have happened to her."

She talked on quietly, but with the unconscious force of one who feels her subject to the heart. The man began to yield—not for love of Sabina, but for love of himself. For Miss Ironsyde continued to make him see his own position must be unbearable if he persisted, while first she implied and finally declared, that only through marriage with Sabina could his own position be longer retained.

But he put forward his dismissal as an argument against marriage.

"Whatever I feel, it's too late now," he explained. "Daniel heard some distorted version of the truth in Bridetown, and, of course, believed it, and came to me white with rage and sacked me. Well, you must see that alters the case if nothing else does. Granted, for the sake of argument, that I can overlook the foolish, clumsy way she and her mother have behaved and go on as we were going, how am I to live and keep a wife on nothing?"

"That is a small matter," she answered. "You need not worry about it in the least. And you know in your heart, my dear, you need not. I have had plenty of time to think over this, and I have thought over it. And I am very ready and willing to come between you and any temporal trouble of that sort. As to Daniel, when he hears that you are going to marry and always meant to do so, it must entirely change his view of the situation. He is just and reasonable. None can deny that."

"You needn't build on Daniel, however. I'd rather break stones than go back to the Mill after what he said to me."

"Leave him, then. Leave him out of your calculation and come to me. As I tell you, I've thought about it a great deal, and first I think Sabina is well suited to be a good wife to you. With time and application she will become a woman that any man might be proud to marry. I say that without prejudice, because I honestly think it. She is adaptable, and, I believe, would very quickly develop into a woman in every way worthy of your real self. And I am prepared to give you five hundred a year, Raymond. After all, why not? All that I have is yours and your brother's, some day. And since you need it now, you shall have it now."

At another time he had been moved by this generosity; to-night, knowing what it embraced, he was not so grateful as he might have been. His instinct was to protest that he would not marry Sabina; but shame prevented him from speaking, since he could advance no decent reason for such a change of mind. He felt vaguely, dimly at the bottom of his soul that, despite events, he ought not to marry her. He believed, apart from his own intense aversion from so doing now, that marriage with him would not in the long run conduce to Sabina's happiness. But where were the words capable of lending any conviction to such a sentiment? Certainly he could think of none that would change his aunt's opinion.

Sullenly he accepted her view with outward acknowledgment and inward resentment. Then she said a thing that nearly made him rebel, since it struck at his pride, indicated that Miss Ironsyde was sure of her ground, showed that she had assumed the outcome of their meeting before the event.

First, however, he thanked her.

"Of course, it is amazingly good and kind. I don't like to accept it. But I suppose it would hurt you more if I didn't than if I do. It's a condition naturally that I marry Sabina—I quite understand that. Well, I must then. I might have been a better friend to her if I hadn't married; and might love her better and love her longer for that matter. But, of course, I can't expect you to understand that. I only want to be sporting, and a man's idea of being sporting isn't the same—"

"Now, now—you're forgetting and talking nonsense, Raymond. You really are forgetting. A man's idea of being 'sporting' does not mean telling stories to a trusting and loving girl, does it? I don't want anybody to judge you but yourself. I am perfectly content to leave it to your own conscience. And very sure I am that if you ask yourself the question, you'll answer it as it should be answered. So sure, indeed, that I have done a definite thing about it, which I will tell you in a moment. For the rest you must find a house where you please and be married as soon as you can. And when Daniel understands what a right and proper thing you're doing, I think you'll very soon find all will be satisfactory again in that quarter."

"Thank you, I'm sure. But don't speak to him yet. I won't ask for favours nor let you, Aunt Jenny. If he comes to me, well and good—I certainly won't go to him. As to Sabina, we'll clear out and get married in a day or two."

"Not before a Registrar," pleaded Miss Ironsyde.

"Before the Devil I should think," he said, preparing to leave her.

She chid him and then mentioned certain preparations made for this particular evening.

"Don't be cross any more, and let me see you value my good will and love, Ray, by doing what I'm going to ask you to do, now. So sure was I that, when the little details were cleared up, you would feel with me, and welcome your liberty from constraint, and return to Sabina with the good news, that I asked her to meet you to-night—this very night, my dear, so that you might go home with her and make her happy. She had tea with me—I made her come, and then she went to friends, and she will be in the Lovers' Grove waiting for you at ten o'clock—half an hour from now."

His impulse was to protest, but he recognised the futility for so doing. He felt baffled and cowed and weary. He hated himself because, weakened by poverty, an old woman had been too much for him. He clutched at a hope.

Perhaps by doing as his aunt desired and going through with this thing, he would find his peace of mind return and a consciousness that, after all, to keep his promise was the only thing which would renew his self-respect. It might prove the line of least resistance to take this course. He felt not sorry at the immediate prospect of meeting Sabina. In his present mood that might be a good thing to happen. Annoyance passed, and when he did take leave it was with more expressions of gratitude.

"I don't know why you are so extraordinarily good to me," he said. "I certainly don't deserve it. But the least I can do is throw up the sponge and do as you will, and trust your judgment. I don't say I agree with you, but I'm going to do it; and if it's a failure, I shan't blame you, Aunt Jenny."

"It won't be a failure. I'm as sure as I'm sure of anything that it will be a splendid success, Raymond. Come again, very soon, and tell me what you decide about a house. And remember one thing—don't fly away and take a house goodness knows where. Always reckon with the possibility—I think certainty—that Daniel will soon be friendly, when he hears you're going to be married."

He left her very exhausted, and if her spirits sank a little after his departure, Raymond's tended to rise. The night air and moonlight brisked him up; he felt a reaction towards Sabina and perceived that she must have suffered a good deal. He threw the blame on her mother. Once out of Bridetown things would settle down; and if his brother came to his senses and asked him to return, he would make it a condition that he worked henceforth at Bridport. A feeling of hatred for Bridetown mastered him.

He descended West Street until the town lay behind him, then turned to the left through a wicket, crossed some meadows and reached a popular local tryst and sanctity: the Lovers' Grove. A certain crudity in the ideas of Miss Ironsyde struck Raymond. How simple and primitive she was after all. Could such an unworldly and inexperienced woman be right? He doubted it. But he went on through the avenue of lime and sycamore trees which made the traditional grove. Beneath them ran pavement of rough stones, that lifted the pathway above possible inundation, and, to-night, the pattern of the naked boughs above was thrown down upon the stones in a black lace work by the moon. The place was very still, but half a mile distant there dreamed great woods, whence came the hooting of an owl.

Raymond stood to listen, and when the bird was silent, he heard a footfall ring on the paving-stones and saw Sabina coming to him. At heart she had been fearful that he would not appear; but this she did not whisper now. Instead she pretended confidence and said, "I knew you'd come!"

He responded with fair ardour and tried to banish his grievances against her. He assured her that all her alarm and tribulation were not his fault, but her own; and her responsive agreement and servile tact, by its self-evidence defeated its own object and fretted the man's nerves, despite his kindly feelings. For Sabina, in her unspeakable thankfulness at the turn of events, sank from herself and was obsequious. When they met he kissed her and presently, holding his hand, she kissed it. She heaped blame upon herself and praised his magnanimity; she presented the ordinary phenomena of a happy release from affliction and fear; but her intense humility was far from agreeable to Raymond, since its very accentuation served to show his own recent actions in painful colours.

He told her what his aunt was going to do; and where a subtler mind had held its peace, Sabina erred again and praised Miss Ironsyde. In truth, she was not at her best to-night and her excitement acted unfavourably on Raymond. He fought against his own emotions, and listened to her high-strung chatter and plans for the future. A torrent of blame had better suited the contrite mood in which she met him; but she took the blame on her own shoulders, and in her relief said things sycophantic and untrue.

He told her almost roughly to stop.

"For God's sake don't blackguard yourself any more," he said. "Give me a chance. It's for me to apologise to you, surely. I knew perfectly well you meant nothing, and I ought to have had more imagination and not given you any cause to be nervous. I frightened you, and if a woman's frightened, of course, she's not to be blamed for what she does, any more than a man's to be blamed for what he does when he's drunk."

This, however, she would not allow.

"If I had trusted you, and known you could not do wrong, and remembered what you said when I told you about the child—then all this would have been escaped. And God knows I did trust you at the bottom of my heart all the time."

She talked on and the man tired of it and, looking far ahead, perceived that his life must be shared for ever with a nature only now about to be revealed to him. He had seen the best of her; but he had never seen the whole truth of her. He knew she was excitable and passionate; but the excitation and passion had all been displayed for him till now. How different when she approached other affairs of life than love, and brought her emotional characteristics to bear upon them! A sensation of unutterable flatness overtook Raymond. She began talking of finding a house, and was not aware that his brother had dismissed him.

He snatched an evil pleasure from telling her so. It silenced her and made her the more oppressively submissive. But through this announcement he won temporary release. There came a longing to leave her, to go back to Bridport and see other faces, hear other voices and speak of other things. They had walked homeward through the valley of the river and, at West Haven, Raymond announced that she must go the remainder of the way alone. He salved the unexpected shock of this with a cheerful promise.

"I sleep at Bridport, to-night," he said, "and I'll leave you here, Sabina; but be quite happy. I dare say Daniel will be all right. He's a pious blade and all that sort of thing and doesn't understand real life. And as some fool broke our bit of real life rather roughly on his ear, it was too much for his weak nerves. I shan't take you very far off anyway. We'll have a look round soon. I'll go to a house agent or somebody in a day or two."

"You must choose," she said.

"No, no—that's up to you, and you mustn't have small ideas about it either. You're going to live in a jolly good house, I promise you."

This sweetened the parting. He kissed her and turned his face to Bridport, while she followed the road homeward. It took her past the old store— black as the night under a roof silvered by the moon. A strange shiver ran through her as she passed it. She could have prayed for time to turn back.

"Oh, my God, if I was a maiden again!" she said in a low voice to herself.

Then, growing calmer and musing of the past rather than the future, she asked herself whether in that case she would still be caring for Raymond; but she turned from such a thought and smothered the secret indignation still lying red-hot and hidden under the smoke of the things she had said to him that night.

On his way to Bridport, the man also reflected, but of the future, not the past.

"I must be cruel to be kind," he told himself. What he exactly meant by the assurance, he hardly knew. But, in some way, it assisted self-respect and promised a course of action likely to justify his coming life.

CHAPTER XIX

JOB LEGG'S AMBITION

A disquieting and wholly unexpected event now broke into the strenuous days of the mistress of 'The Seven Stars.' It followed another, which was now a thing of the past; but Mrs. Northover had scarcely finished being thankful that the old order was restored again, when that occurred to prove the old order could never be restored.

Job Legg had been called away to the deathbed of an aged uncle. For a fortnight he was absent, and during that time Nelly Northover found herself the victim of a revelation. She perceived, indeed, startling truths until then hidden from her, and found the absence of Job created undreamed-of complications. At every turn she missed the man and discovered, very much to her own surprise, that this most unassuming person appeared vital to the success of her famous house. On every hand she heard the same words; all progress was suspended; nothing could advance until the return of Mr. Legg. 'The Seven Stars' were arrested in their courses while he continued absent.

Thus his temporary disappearance affected the system and proved that around the sun of Job Legg, quite as much as his mistress, the galaxy revolved; but something more than this remained to be discovered by Mrs. Northover herself. She found that not only had she undervalued his significance and importance in her scheme of things; but that she entertained a personal regard for the man, unsuspected until he was absent. She missed him at every turn; and when he came back to her, after burying his uncle, Mrs. Northover could have kissed him.

This she did not do; but she was honest; she related the suspension of many great affairs for need of Job; she described to him the dislocation that his departure had occasioned and declared her hearty thankfulness that her right hand had returned to her.

"You was uppermost in my mind a thousand times a day, Job; and when it came to doing the fifty thousand things you do, I began to see what there is to you," said Nelly Northover. "And this I'll say: you haven't been getting enough money along with me."

He was pleased and smiled and thanked her.

"I've missed 'The Stars,'" he said, "and am very glad to be back."

Then when things were settled down and Mrs. Northover happy and content once more, Mr. Legg cast her into much doubt and uncertainty. Indeed his attitude so unexpected, awoke a measure of dismay. Life, that Nelly hoped was becoming static and comfortable again, suddenly grew highly dynamic. Changes stared her in the face and that was done which nothing could undo.

On the night that Raymond Ironsyde left Sabina at West Haven and returned to Bridport, Mr. Legg, the day's work done, drank a glass of sloe gin in Mrs. Northover's little parlour and uttered a startling proposition— the last to have been expected.

The landlady herself unconsciously opened the way to it, for she touched the matter of his wages and announced her purpose to increase them by five shillings a week. Then he spoke.

"Before we talk about that, hear me," he said. "You were too nice-minded to ask me if I got anything by the death of my old man; but I may tell you, that I got everything. And there was a great deal more than anybody knew. In short he's left me a shade over two hundred pounds per annum, and that with my own savings—for I've saved since I was thirteen years old—brings my income somewhere near the two hundred and fifty mark—not counting wages."

"Good powers, Job! But I am glad. Never none on earth deserved a bit better than you do."

"And yet," he said, "I only ask myself if all this lifts me high enough to say what I want to say. You know me for a modest man, Mrs. Northover."

"None more so, Job."

"And therefore I've thought a good deal about it and come to it by the way of reason as well as inclination. In fact I began to think about what I'm going to say now, many years ago after your husband died. And I just let the idea go on till the appointed time, if ever it should come; and when my uncle died and left a bit over four thousand pounds to me, I felt the hour had struck!"

Nelly's heart sank.

"You're going?" she said. "All this means that you are going into business on your own, Legg."

"Let me finish. But be sure of one thing; I'm not going if I can stay with peace and honour. If I can't, then, of course, I must go. To go would be a terrible sad thing for me, for I've grown into this place and feel as much a part of it as the beer engine, or the herbaceous border. But I had to weigh the chances, and I may say my cautious bent of mind showed very clearly what they were. And, so, first, I'll tell what a flight I've took and what a thought I've dared, and then I'll ask you, being a woman with a quick mind and tongue, to answer nothing for the moment, and say no word that you may wish to recall after."

"All very wise and proper, I'm sure."

"If it ain't, God forgive me, seeing I've been working it out in my mind for very near twenty years. And I say this, that being now a man of capital, and a healthy and respectable man, and well thought of, I believe, and nothing against me to my knowledge, I offer to marry you, Nelly Northover. The idea, of course, comes upon you like a bolt from the blue, as I can see by your face; but before you answer 'No,' I must say I've loved you in a respectful manner for many years, and though I knew my place too well to say so, I let it appear by faithful service and very sharp eyes always on your interests—day and night you may say."

"That is true," she said. "I didn't know my luck."

"I don't say that. Any honourable man would have done so much, very likely; but perhaps—however, I'm not here to praise myself but to praise you; and I may add I never in a large experience saw the woman—maid, wife or widow—to hold a candle to you for brains and energy and far-reaching fine qualities in general. And therefore I never could be worthy of you, and I don't pretend to it, and the man who did would be a very vain and windy fool; but such is my high opinion and great desire to be your husband that I risk, you may say, everything by offering myself."

"This is a very great surprise, Job."

"So great that you must do me one good turn and not answer without letting it sink in, if you please. I have a right to beg that. Of course I know on the spur of the moment the really nice-minded woman always turns down the adventurous male. 'Tis their delicate instinct so to do. But you won't do that—for fairness to me. And there's more to it yet, because we've got to think of fairness to you also. I wouldn't have you buy a pig in a poke and take a man of means without knowing where you stood. So I may say that if you presently felt the same as I do about it, I should spend a bit of my capital on 'The Seven Stars,' which, in my judgment, is now crying for capital expenditure."

"It is," admitted Mrs. Northover, "I grant you that."

"Very well, then. It would be my pride—"

He was interrupted, for the bell of the inn rang and a moment later Raymond Ironsyde appeared in the hall. He had come for supper and bed.

"Good evening, Mrs. Northover," he said. "I'm belated and starving into the bargain. Have you got a room?"

"For that matter, yes," she answered not very enthusiastically. "But surely 'The Tiger's' your house, sir?"

"I'm not bound to 'The Tiger,' and very likely shall never go there again. Gurd is getting too big for his shoes and seems to think he's called upon to preach sermons to his customers, besides doing his duty as a publican. If I want sermons I can go to church for them, not to an inn. Give me some supper and a bottle of your best claret. I'm tired and bothered."

A customer was a customer and Mrs. Northover had far too much experience to take up the cudgels for her friend over the way. She guessed pretty accurately at the subject of Richard Gurd's discourse, yet wondered that he should have spoken. For her own part, while quite as indignant as others and more sorry than many that this cloud should have darkened a famous local name, she held it no personal business of hers.

"I'll see what cold meat we've got. Would you like a chicken, sir?"

"No—beef, and plenty of it. And let me have a room."

Job Legg, concealing the mighty matters in his own bosom, soon waited upon Raymond and found him in a sulky humour. The claret was not to his liking and he ordered spirits. He began to smoke and drink, and from an unamiable mood soon thawed and became talkative. He bade Job stay and listen to him.

"I've got a hell of a lot on my mind," he said, "and it's a relief to talk to a sensible man. There aren't many knocking about so far as I can see."

He rambled on touching indirectly, as he imagined, at his own affairs, but making it clear to the listener that a very considerable tumult raged in Raymond's own mind. Then came Mrs. Northover, told the guest that it was nearer two o'clock than one, and hoped he was soon going to bed.

He promised to do so and she departed; but the faithful Job, himself not sleepy, kept Raymond company. Unavailingly he urged the desirability of sleep, but young Ironsyde sat on until he was very drunk. Then Mr. Legg helped him upstairs and assisted him to his bed.

It was after three o'clock before he retired himself and found his mind at liberty to speculate upon the issue of his own great adventure.

CHAPTER XX

A CONFERENCE

Jenny Ironsyde came to see Ernest Churchouse upon the matter of the marriage. She found him pensive and a little weary. According to his custom he indulged in ideas before approaching the subject just then uppermost in all minds in Bridetown.

"I have been suffering from rather a severe dose of the actual," he said; "at present, in the minds of those about me, there is no room for any abstraction. We are confronted with facts—painful facts—a most depressing condition for such a mind as mine. There are three orders of intelligence, Jenny. The lowest never reaches higher than the discussion of persons; the second talks about places, which is certainly better; the third soars into the region of ideas; and when one finds a person indulge in ideas, then court their friendship, for ideas are the only sound basis of intellectual interchanges. It is so strange to see an educated person, who might be discussing the deepest mysteries and noblest problems of life, preferring to relate the errors of a domestic servant, or deplore the price of sprats."

"All very well for you," declared Miss Ironsyde; "from your isolated situation, above material cares and anxieties, you can affect this superiority; but what about Mrs. Dinnett? You would very soon be grumbling if Mrs. Dinnett put the deepest mysteries and noblest problems of life before the price of sprats. It is true that man cannot live by bread alone; and it is equally true that he cannot live without it. The highest flights are impossible without cooking, and cooking would be impossible if all aspired to the highest flights."

"As a matter of fact, Mrs. Dinnett is my present source of depression," he said. "All is going as it should go, I suppose. The young people are reconciled, and I have arranged that Sabina should be married from here a fortnight hence. Thus, as it were, I shield and protect her and support her against back-biting and evil tongues."

"It is splendid of you."

"Far from it. I am only doing the obvious. I care much for the girl. But Mary Dinnett, despite the need to be sanguine and expeditious, permits herself an amount of obstinate melancholy which is most ill-judged and quite unjustified by the situation. Nothing will satisfy her. She scorns hope. She declines to take a cheerful view. She even confesses to a premonition they are not going to be married after all. She says that her grandmother had second sight and believes that the doubtful gift has been handed down to her."

"This is very bad for Sabina."

"Of course it is. I impress that upon her mother. The girl has been through a great deal. She is highly strung at all times, and these affairs have wrought havoc with her intelligence for the moment. Her one thought and feverish longing is to be married, and her mother's fatuous prophecies that she never will be are causing serious nervous trouble to Sabina. I feel sure of it. They may even be doing permanent harm."

"You should suppress Mary."

"I endeavour to do so. I put much serving upon her; but her frame of mind is such that her energy is equal to anything. You had better see her and caution her. From another woman, words of wisdom would carry more weight than mine. As to Sabina, I have warned her against her mother—a strong thing to do, but I felt it to be my duty."

They saw Mary Dinnett then, and Miss Ironsyde quickly realised that there were subtle tribulations and shades of doubt in the mother's mind beyond Mr. Churchouse's power to appreciate. Indeed, Mrs. Dinnett, encouraged so to do by the sympathetic presence of Jenny Ironsyde, strove to give reasons for her continued gloom.

"You must be more hopeful and put a brighter face on it, Mary, if only for the sake of the young people," declared the visitor. "You're not approaching the marriage from the right point of view. We must forget the past and keep our minds on the future and proceed with this affair just as though it were an ordinary marriage without any disquieting features. We have to remember that they love each other and really are well suited. The future is chequered by certain differences between my nephews, which have not yet been smoothed out; but I am sure that they will be; and meantime you need feel no fear of any inconvenience for Sabina. I am responsible."

"I know all that," said Mrs. Dinnett, "and your name is in my prayers when I rise up and when I go to bed. But while there's a lot other people can do for 'em, there's also a deal they can only do for themselves; and, in my opinion, they are not doing it. It's no good us playacting and forgetting the past and pretending everything is just as it should be, if they won't."

"But they have."

"Sabina has. I doubt if he has. I don't know how you find him, but when I see him he's not in a nice temper and not taking the situation in the spirit of a happy bridegroom—very far from it. And my second-sight, which I get from my grandmother, points to one thing: that there won't be no wedding."

"This is preposterous," declared Miss Ironsyde. "The day is fixed and every preparation far advanced."

"That's nought to a wayward mind like his. He's got in a state now when I wouldn't trust him a yard. And I hope to God you'll hold the reins tight, miss, and not slacken till they're man and wife. Once let him see his way clear to bolt, and bolt he will."

Mr. Churchouse protested, while Jenny only sighed. Sabina's mother was echoing her own secret uneasiness, but she lamented that others had marked it as well as herself.

"He is in a very moody state, but never speaks of any change of mind to me."

"Because he well knows you hold the purse," said Mrs. Dinnett. "I don't want to say anything uncharitable against the man, though I might; but I will say that there's danger and that I do well to be a miserable woman till the danger's past. You tell me to cheer up, and I promise to cheer up quick enough when there's reason to do so. Mr. Churchouse here is the best gentleman on God's earth; but he don't understand a mother's heart—how should he? and he don't know what a lot women have got to hide from men—for their own self-respect, and because men as a body are such clumsy-minded fools—speaking generally, of course."

To see even Mrs. Dinnett dealing thus in ideas excited Ernest and filled him with interest. He forgot everything but the principle she asserted and would have discussed it for an hour; but Mary, having thus hit back effectively, departed, and Miss Ironsyde brought the master of 'The Magnolias' back to their subject.

"There's a lot of truth in what she says and it shows how trouble quickens the wits," she declared; "and I can say to you, what I wouldn't to her, that Raymond is not taking this in a good spirit, or as I hoped and expected. I feel for him, too, while being absolutely firm with him. Stupid things were done and the secret of his folly made public. He has a grudge against them and, of course, that is rather a threatening fact, because a grudge against anybody is a deadly thing to get into one's mind. It poisons character and ruins your steady outlook, if it is deep seated enough."

"Would you say that he bore Sabina a grudge?"

"I'm afraid so; but I do my best to dispel it by pointing out what she thought herself faced with. And I tell him what is true, that Sabina in her moments of greatest fear and exasperation, always behaved like a lady. But in your ear only, Ernest, I confess to a new sensation—a sickly sensation of doubt. It comes over my religious certainty sometimes, like a fog. It's cold and shivery. Of course from every standpoint of religion and honour and justice, they ought to be married. But—"

He stopped her.

"Having named religion and honour and justice, there is no room for 'but.' Indeed, Jenny, there is not."

"Let me speak, all the same. Other people can have intuitions besides Mrs. Dinnett. It's an intuition—not second sight—but it is alive. Supposing this marriage doesn't really make for the happiness of either of them?"

"If they put religion and honour and justice first, it must," he repeated. "You cannot, I venture to say, have happiness without religion and honour and justice; and if Raymond were to go back on his word now, he would be the most miserable man in the country."

"I wonder."

"Don't wonder. Be sure of it. Granted he finds himself miserable—that is because he has committed a fault. Will it make him less miserable to go on and commit a greater? Sorrow is a fair price to pay for wisdom, Jenny. He is a great deal wiser now than he was six months ago, and to shirk his responsibilities and break his word will not mend matters. Besides, there is another consideration, which you forget. These young people are no longer free. Even if they both desired to remain single, honour, justice and religion actually demand marriage. There was a doubt in my own mind once, too, whether their happiness would be assured by union. Now there is no doubt. A child is coming into the world. Need I say more?"

"I stand corrected," she answered. "There is really nothing more to be said. For the child's sake, if for no other reason, marry they must. We know too well the fate of the child born out of wedlock in this country."

"It is a shameful and cruel fate; and while the Church of England cowardly suffers the State to impose it, and selfish men care not, we, with some enthusiasm for the unborn and some indignation to see their disabilities, must do what lies in our power for them."

He rambled off into generalities inspired by this grave theme.

"'Suffer the little children to come unto Me,' said Christ; and we make it almost impossible for fifty thousand little children to come unto Him every year; and those who stand for Him, the ministers of His Church, lift not a finger. The little children of nobody they are. They grow up conscious of their handicap; they come into the world to trust and hope and find themselves pariahs. Is that conducive to a religious trust in God, or a rational trust in man for these outlawed thousands?"

She brought him back again to Raymond and Sabina.

"Apart from the necessity and justice," she said, "and taking it for granted that the thing must happen, what is your opinion of the future? You know Sabina well and ought to be in a position to say if you think she will have the wit and sense to make it a happy marriage."

"I should wish to think so. They are a gracious pair—at least they were. I liked both boy and girl exceedingly and I happened to be the one who introduced them to each other. It was after Henry's death. Sabina came in with our tea and one could almost see an understanding spring up and come to life under one's eyes. They've been wicked, Jenny; but such is my hopelessly open mind in the matter of goodness and wickedness, that I often find it harder to forgive some people for doing their duty than others for being wicked. In fact, some do their duty in a way that is perfectly unforgivable, while others fail in such an affecting and attractive manner that they make you all the fonder of them."

"I feel so, too, sometimes," she admitted, "but I never dared to confess it. Once married, I think Raymond would steady down and realise his responsibilities. We must both do what we can to bring the brothers together again. It will take a long time to make Daniel forgive this business."

"It is just the Daniel type who would take it most seriously, even if we are able soon to say 'all's well that ends well.' For that reason, one regrets he heard particulars. However, we must trust and believe the future will set all right and reinstate Raymond at the works. For my own part I feel very sure that will happen."

"Well, I always like to see hope triumphing over experience," she said, "and one need never look further than you for that."

"Thank yourself," he answered. "Your steadfast optimism always awakes an echo in me. If we make up our minds that this is going to be all right, that will at least help on the good cause. We can't do much to make it all right, but we can do something. They are in Bridport house-hunting this morning, I hear."

"They are; and that reminds me they come to lunch and, I hope, to report progress. Of course anything Raymond likes, Sabina approves; but he isn't easily satisfied. However, they may have found something. Daniel, rather fortunately, is from home just now, in the North."

"If we could get him to the wedding, it would be a great thing."

"I'm afraid we mustn't hope for that; but we can both urge him to come. He may."

"I will compose a very special letter to him," said Mr. Churchouse. "How's your rheumatism?"

"Better, if anything."

CHAPTER XXI

THE WARPING MILL

In the warping shed Mercy Gale plied her work. It was a separate building adjoining the stores at Bridetown Mill and, like them, impregnated with the distinctive, fat smell of flax and hemp. Under dusty rafters and on a floor of stone the huge warping reels stood. They were light, open frameworks that rose from floor to ceiling and turned upon steel rods. Hither came the full bobbins from the spinning machines to be wound off. Two dozen of the bobbins hung together on a flat frame or 'creel' and through eyes and slots the yarn ran through a 'hake,' which deftly crossed the strands so that they ran smoothly and freely. The bake box rose and fell and lapped the yarn in perfect spirals round the warping reels as they revolved. The length of a reel of twine varies in different places and countries; but at Bridetown, a Dorset reel was always measured, and it represented twenty-one thousand, six hundred yards.

Mercy Gale was chaining the warp off the reels in great massive coils which would presently depart to be polished and finished at Bridport. All its multiple forms sprang from the simple yarn. It would turn into shop and parcel twines; fishing twines for deep sea lines and nets; and by processes of reduplication, swell to cords and shroud laid ropes, hawsers and mighty cables.

A little figure filled the door of the shed and Estelle Waldron appeared. She shook hands and greeted the worker with friendship, for Estelle was now free of the Mill and greatly prided herself on personally knowing everybody within them.

"Good morning, Mercy," she said. "I've come to see Nancy Buckler."

"Good morning, miss. I know. She's going to run in at dinner time to sing you her song."

"It's a wonderful song, I believe," declared Estelle, "and very, very old. Her grandfather taught it to her before he died, and I want to write it down. Do you like poetry, Mercy?"

"Can't say as I do," confessed the warper. She was a fair, tall girl. "I like novels," she added. "I love stories, but I haven't got much use for rhymes."

"Stories about what?" asked Estelle. "I have a sort of an idea to start a library, if I can persuade my father to let me. I believe I could get some books from friends to make a beginning."

"Stories about adventure," declared Mercy. "Most of the girls like love stories; but I don't care so much about them. I like stories where big things happen in history."

"So do I; and then you know you're reading about what really did happen and about great people who really lived. I think I can lend you some stories like that."

Mercy thanked her and Estelle fell silent considering which book from her limited collection would best meet the other's demand. Herself she did not read many novels, but loved her books about plants and her poets. Poetry was precious food to her, and Mr. Churchouse, who also appreciated it, had led her to his special favourites. For the present, therefore, Estelle was content with Longfellow and Cowper and Wordsworth. The more dazzling light of Keats and Shelley and Swinburne had yet to dawn for her.

Nancy Buckler arrived presently to sing her song. Her looks did not belie Nancy. She was sharp of countenance, with thin cheeks and a prominent nose. Her voice, too, had a pinch of asperity about it. By nature she was critical of her fellow creatures. No man had desired her, and the fact soured her a little and led to a general contempt of the sex.

She smiled for Estelle, however, because the ingenuous child had won her friendship.

"Good morning, miss," she said. "If you've got a pencil and paper, you can take down the words."

"But sing them first," begged the listener. "I want to hear you sing them to the old tune, because I expect the tune is as old as the words, Nancy."

"It's a funny old tune for certain. I can't sing it like grandfather did, for all his age. He croaked it like a machine running, and that seemed the proper way. But I've not got much of a voice."

"'Tis loud enough, anyway," said Mercy, "and that's a virtue."

"Yes, you can hear what I'm saying," admitted Miss Buckler, then she sang her song.

"When a twister, a twisting, will twist him a twist,
With the twisting his twist, he the twine doth entwist;
But if one of the twines of the twist doth untwist,
The twine that untwisteth, untwisteth the twist,
Untwisting the twine that entwineth between,

He twists with his twister the two in a twine.
Then, twice having twisted the twines of his twine,
He twisteth the twine he had twined in twine.
The twain, that in twining before in the twine,
As twines were entwisted, he now doth untwine,
'Twixt the twain intertwisting a twine more between."

Nancy gave her remarkable performance in a clear, thin treble. It was a monotonous melody, but suited the words very well. She sang slowly and her face and voice exhibited neither light nor shade. Yet her method suited the words in their exceedingly unemotional appeal.

"It's the most curious song I ever heard," cried Estelle, "and you sing it perfectly, because I heard every word."

Then she brought out pencil and paper, sat in the deep alcove of the window and transcribed Nancy's verse.

"You must sing that to my father next time you come up," she said. "It's like no other song in the world, I'm sure."

Sally Groves came in. She had brought Estelle the seed of a flower from her garden.

"I put it by for you, Miss Waldron," said the big woman, "because you said you liked it in the fall."

They talked together while Mercy Gale doffed her overall and woollen bonnet.

"Tell me," said Estelle, "of a very good sort of wedding present for Mr. Ironsyde, when he marries Sabina next week."

"A new temper, I should think," suggested Nancy.

"He can't help being rather in a temper," explained Estelle, "because they can't find a house."

"Sabina can find plenty," answered the spinner. "It's him that's so hard to please."

Sally Groves strove to curb Nancy's tongue.

"You mind your own business," she said. "Mr. Ironsyde wants everything just so, and why not?"

"Because it ain't a time to be messing about, I should think," retorted Nancy. "And it's for the woman to be considered, not him."

Then Estelle, in all innocence, asked a shattering question.

.

"Is it true Sabina is going to have a baby? One or two girls in the mill told me she was, but I asked my father, and he seemed to be annoyed and said, of course not. But I hope it's true—it would be lovely for Sabina to have a baby to play with."

"So it would then," declared Sally Groves, "but I shouldn't tell nothing about it for the present, miss."

"Least said, soonest mended," said Mercy Gale.

"It's like this," explained Sally Groves with clumsy goodness: "they'll want to keep it for a surprise, miss, and I dare say they'd be terrible disappointed if they thought anybody knew anything about it yet."

Nancy Buckler laughed.

"I reckon they would," she said.

"So don't you name it, miss," continued Sally. "Don't you name the word yet awhile."

Estelle nodded.

"I won't then," she promised. "I know how sad it is, if you've got a great secret, to find other people know it before you want them to."

"Beastly sad," said Nancy, as she went her way, and the child looked after her puzzled.

"I believe Nancy's jealous of Sabina," she said.

Then it was Sally Groves who laughed and her merriment shook the billows of her mighty person.

Estelle found herself somewhat depressed as she went home. Not so much the words as the general spirit of these comments chilled her. After luncheon she visited her father's study and talked to him while he smoked.

"What perfectly beautiful thing can I get for Ray and Sabina for a wedding present?"

He cleaned his pipe with one of the crow's feathers Estelle was used to collect for him. They stood in vases on the mantel-shelf.

"It's a puzzler," confessed Arthur Waldron.

"D'you think Ray has grown bad-tempered, father?"

"Do you?"

"No, I'm sure I don't. He is a little different, but that's because he's going to be married. No doubt people do get a little different, then. But Nancy

Buckler at the Mill said she thought the best wedding present for him would be a new temper."

"That's the sort of insolent things people say, I suppose, behind his back. It's all very unfortunate in my opinion, Estelle."

"It's frightfully unfortunate Ray leaving us, because, after he's married, he must have a house of his own; but it isn't unfortunate his marrying Sabina, I'm sure."

"I'm not sure at all," confessed her father. His opinion always carried the greatest weight, and she was so much concerned at this announcement that Arthur felt sorry he had spoken.

"You see, Estelle—how can I explain? I think Ray in rather too young to marry."

"He's well over twenty."

"Yes, but he's young for his age, and the things that he is keen about are not the things that a girl is keen about. I doubt if he will make Sabina happy."

"He will if he likes, and I'm sure he will like. He can always make me happy, so, of course, he can make Sabina. He's really tremendously clever and knows all sorts of things. Oh, don't think it's going to be sad, father. I'm sure they're both much too wise to do anything that's going to be sad. Because if Ray—"

She stopped, for Raymond himself came in. He had left early that morning to seek a house with Sabina.

"What luck?" said Waldron.

"We've found something that'll do, I think. Two miles out towards Chidcock. A garden and a decent paddock and a stable. But he'll have to spend some money on the stable. There's a doubt if he will—the landlord, I mean. Sabina likes the house, so I hope it will be all right."

Waldron nodded.

"If it's Thornton, the horse-dealer, he'll do what you want. He's got houses up there."

"It isn't. I haven't seen the man yet."

"Well," said his friend, "I don't know what the deuce Estelle and I are going to do without you. We shall miss you abominably."

"What shall I do without you? That's more to the point. You've got each other for pals—I—"

He broke off and Arthur filled the pregnant pause.

"Look here—Estelle wants to give you a wedding present, old man; and so do I. And as we haven't the remotest idea what would be the likeliest thing, don't stand on ceremony, but tell us."

"I don't want anything—except to know I shall always be welcome when I drop in."

"We needn't tell you that."

"But you must want thousands of things," declared Estelle, "everybody does when they're married. And if you don't, I'm sure Sabina does—knives and forks and silver tea kettles and pictures for the walls."

"Married people don't want pictures, Estelle; they never look at anything but one another."

She laughed.

"But the poor walls want pictures if you don't. I believe the walls wouldn't feel comfortable without pictures. Besides you and Sabina can't sit and look at each other all day."

"What about a nice little handy 'jingle' for her to trundle about in?" asked Waldron.

"As I can't pull it, old chap, it wouldn't be much good. I'm keeping the hunter; but I shan't be able to keep anything else—if that."

"How would it be if you sold the hunter and got a nice everyday sort of horse that you could ride, or that Sabina could drive?" asked Estelle.

"No," said Waldron firmly. "He doesn't sell his hunter or his guns. These things stand for a link with the outer world and represent sport, which is quite as important as marriage in the general scheme."

"I thought to chuck all that and take up golf," said Raymond. "There's a lot in golf they tell me."

But Waldron shook his head.

"Golf's all right," he admitted, "and a great game. I'm going to take it up myself, and I'm glad it's coming in, because it will add to the usefulness of a lot of us men who have to fall out of cricket. There's a great future for golf, I believe. But no golf for you yet. You won't run any more and you'll drop out of football, as only 'pros.' play much after marriage. But you must shoot as much as possible, and hunt a bit, and play cricket still."

This comforting programme soothed Raymond.

"That's all right, but I've got to find work. I was just beginning to feel keen on work; but now—flit, Estelle, my duck. I want to have a yarn with father."

The girl departed.

"Do let it be a 'jingle,' Ray," she begged, and then was gone.

"It's my damned brother," went on Raymond.

"He'll come round and ask you to go back, as soon as you're fixed up and everything's all right."

"Everything won't be all right. Everything's confoundedly wrong. Think what it is for a proud man to be at the mercy of an aunt, and to look to her for his keep. If anything could make me sick of the whole show, it's that."

"I shouldn't feel it so. She's keen on you, and keen on Sabina; and she knows you can't live upon air. You may be sure also she knows that it won't last. Daniel will come round."

"And if he does? It's all the same—taking his money."

"You won't be taking it; you'll be earning it."

"I hate him, like hell, and I hate the thought of working under him all my life."

"You won't be under him. You've often said the time was coming when you'd wipe Daniel's eye and show you were the moving spirit of the Mill. Well now, when you go back, you must work double tides to do it."

"He may not take me back, and for many things I'd sooner he didn't. We should never be the same to one another after that row. For two pins, even now, I'd make a bolt, Arthur, and disappear altogether and go abroad and carve out my own way."

"Don't talk rot. You can't do that."

But Waldron, in spite of his advice and sanguine prophecies, hid a grave doubt at heart whether, so far as Raymond's own future was concerned, such a course might not be the wisest. He felt confident, however, that the younger man would keep his engagements. Raymond had plenty of pluck and did not lack for a heart, so far as Waldron knew. Had Sabina been no more than engaged, he must strongly have urged Raymond to drop her and endure the harsh criticism that would have followed: for an engagement broken appeared a lesser evil than an unhappy mating; but since the position was complicated, he could not feel so and stoutly upheld the marriage on principle, while extremely doubtful of its practical outcome.

They talked for two hours to no purpose and then Estelle called them to tea.

CHAPTER XXII

THE TELEGRAM

Raymond and Sabina spent a long afternoon at the house they had taken; and while he was interested with the stables and garden, she occupied herself indoors. She was very tired before they had finished, and presently, returning to Bridport, they called at 'The Seven Stars' and ordered tea.

The famous garden was dismantled now and Job Legg spent some daily hours in digging there. To-morrow Job was to hear what Mrs. Northover had to say concerning his proposal, and, meantime, the pending decision neither unsettled him nor interfered with his usual placidity and enterprise.

Nelly Northover herself waited upon the engaged couple. She was somewhat abstracted with her own thoughts, but so far banished them that she could show and feel interest in the visitors. Raymond described the house, and Sabina, glad to see Raymond in a cheerful mood, expatiated on the charms of her future home.

They delayed somewhat longer than Mrs. Northover expected and she left them presently, for she had an appointment bearing on the supreme subject of her offer of marriage. Mrs. Northover was, in fact, going to take another opinion. Such indecision seemed foreign to her character, which seldom found her in two minds; but it happened that upon one judgment she had often relied since her husband's death and, before the great problem at present challenging Nelly, she believed another view might largely assist her. That she could not decide herself, she felt to be very significant. The fact made her cautious and anxious.

She put on her bonnet now, left a maid to settle with the customers and presently stepped across the road to 'The Tiger,' for it was Richard Gurd in whom Mrs. Northover put her trust. She designed to place Job's offer before her friend and invite a candid and unprejudiced criticism. For so doing more reasons than one may have existed; we seldom seek the judgment of a friend without mixed motives; but, at any rate, Nelly believed very thoroughly in her neighbour, and if, in reality, it was as much a wish that he should know what had happened, as a desire to learn his opinion upon it, she none the less felt that opinion would be precious and probably decide her.

Richard was waiting in his office—a small apartment off the bar, to which none had access save himself.

"Come in here and we shan't be disturbed," he said. "Of course, when you tell me you want my advice on a matter of the greatest importance, all else has to stand by. My old friend's wife has a right to come to me, I should hope, and I'm glad you've done so. Sit here by the fire."

It did not take Mrs. Northover long to relate the situation, nor was Mr. Gurd much puzzled to declare his view. In brief words she told him of Job Legg's greatly increased prosperity and his proposal to wed. Having made her statement, she advanced a few words for Job.

"In fairness and beyond all this, I must tell you, Richard, that he's a very uncommon sort of man. That you know, of course, as well as I do. But what you don't know is that when he was away, I badly missed him and found out, for the first time, what an all-round, valuable creature he has become at 'The Seven Stars.' When he was along with his dying relation, I missed the man a thousand times in every twelve hours and I felt properly astonished to find how he was the prop and stay of my business. That may seem too much to say, seeing I'm a fairly clever woman and know how to run 'The Seven Stars' in a pretty prosperous way; but there is no doubt Legg is very much more than what he seems. He's a very human man and I'll go so far as to say this: I like him. There's great self-respect to him and you feel, under his level temper and unfailing readiness to work at anything and everything, that he's a power for good—in fact a man with high principles—so high as my own, if not higher."

"Stop there, or you'll over-do it," said Richard. "Higher than yours his principles won't take him and I refuse to hear you say so. You ask me in plain words if you shall marry Job Legg, or if you shan't. And before I speak, I may tell you that, as a man of the world, I shan't quarrel with you if you don't take my advice. As a rule I have found that good advice is more often given than taken and, whether or no, the giving of advice nearly always means one thing. And that is that the giver loses a friend. If the advice is bad, it is generally taken, and him that takes it finds out in due course it was bad, and so the giver makes an enemy. And if 'tis good, the same thing happens, for then 'tis not taken and, looking back, the sufferer sees his mistake, and human nature works, and instead of kicking himself, he feels like kicking the wise man that gave him the good advice. But between me and you that won't happen, for there's the ghost of William Northover to come between. You and me are high spirited, and I dare say there are some people who would say we are short tempered; but we know better."

"That's all true as gospel; and now you tell me if I ought to marry Job. Or, if 'tis too great a question to decide in a minute, as I find it myself, then leave it till to-morrow and I'll pop in again."

"No need to leave it. My mind is used to make itself up swift. First, as to Legg. Legg's a very good man, indeed, and I'd be the first to praise him. He's all you say—or nearly all—and I've often been very much impressed by him. And if he was anybody's servant but yours, I dare say I'd have tempted him to 'The Tiger' before now. But there are some that shine in the lead, like you and me, and some that only show their full worth when they've got to obey. Job can obey to perfection; but I'm not so sure if he's fitted to command."

"Remember," she said, "that if I say 'no' to the man, I lose him. He can't be my right hand no more then, because he'd leave. And my heart sinks at the thought of another potman at my age."

"When you say 'potman' you come to the root of the matter, and your age has nothing to do with it," answered Richard. "The natural instinct at such times is to advise against, and when man or woman asks a fellow creature as to the wisdom of marrying, they'll always pull a long face and find fifty good reasons why not. But I'm taking this in a larger spirit. There's no reason why you shouldn't marry again, and you'd make another as happy as you did your first, no doubt. But Job Legg is a potman; he's been a potman for a generation; he thinks like a potman, and his outlook in life is naturally the potman outlook. Mind, I'm not saying anything against him as a man when I tell you so; I'm only looking at him now as a husband for you. He's got religion and a good temper, and dollops of sense, and I'll even go so far as to say, seeing that he is now a man of money, that he was within his right to offer, if he did it in a modest manner. But I won't say more than that. He's simple and faithful and a servant worthy of all respect, but that man haven't the parts to rise to mastership. A good stick, but if he was your crutch, he'd fail you. For my part, I'm very sure that people of much greater importance than him would offer for you if they knew you were for a husband."

"I wouldn't say I was for a husband, Richard. The idea never came into my mind till Job Legg put it there."

"Just your modesty. There's no more reason why you shouldn't wed than why I shouldn't. You're a comely and highly marriageable person still, and nobody knows it better than what I do."

"You advise against, then?"

"In that quarter, yes. I'm thinking of you, and only you, and I don't believe Job is quite man enough for the part. Leave it, however, for twenty-four hours."

"He was to have his answer, to-morrow."

"He's used to waiting. Tell him you're coming to it and won't keep him much longer. It's too big a thing to be quite sure about, and you were right when you said so. I'll come across and see you in the morning."

"I'm obliged to you, Richard. And if you'll turn it over, I'll thank you. I wouldn't have come to any other than you, bachelor though you are."

"I'll weigh it," he promised, "but I warn you I'm very unlikely to see it different. What you've told me have put other side issues into my head. You'll hunt a rabbit and flush a game bird, sometimes. In fact, great things often come out of little ones."

"I know you'll be fair and not let anything influence your judgment," she said.

He promised, but with secret uneasiness, for already it seemed that his judgment was being influenced. For that reason he had postponed a final decision until the following day. Mrs. Northover departed with grateful thanks and left behind her, though she guessed it not, problems far more tremendous than any she had brought.

Meantime Raymond and Sabina, on their way to Miss Ironsyde, were met by Mr. Neddy Motyer. Neddy had not seen his friend for some time and now saluted and stopped. It was nearly dark and they stood under a lamp-post.

"Cheero!" said Mr. Motyer. "Haven't cast an eye on you for a month of Sundays, Ironsyde."

Raymond introduced Sabina and Neddy was gallant and reminded her they had met before at the Mill. Then, desiring a little masculine society, Sabina's betrothed proposed that she should go on and report that he was coming.

"Aunt Jenny will expect us to stop for dinner, so there's no hurry. I'll be up in half an hour."

She left them and Neddy suggested drinking.

"You might as well be dead and buried for all the boys see of you nowadays," he said, as they entered 'The Bull' Hotel.

"I'm busy."

"I know, but I hope you'll have a big night off before the deed is done and you take leave of freedom—what?"

"I'm not taking leave of freedom. You godless bachelors don't know you're born."

"Bluff—bluff!" declared Neddy. "You can't deceive me, old sport."

"You wait till you find the right one."

"I shall," promised Neddy. "And very well content to wait. Nothing is easier than not to be married."

"Nothing is harder, my dear chap, if you're in love with the right girl."

Neddy felt the ground delicate. He knew that Raymond had knocked down a man for insulting him a week before, so he changed the subject.

"I thought you'd be at the fight," he said. "It was a pretty spar—interesting all through. Jack Buckler won. Blades practically let him. Not because he wanted to, but because Solly Blades has got a streak of softness in his make-up. That's fatal in a fighter. If you've got a gentle heart, it don't matter how clever you are: you can't take full advantage of your skill and use the opening when you've won it. Blades didn't punish Buckler's stupidity, or weakness just when he could have done it. So he lost, because he gave Jack time to get strong again; and when Blades in his turn went weak, Buckler got it over and outed him."

"Your heart often robs you of what your head won," said another man in the bar. "Life's like prize-fighting in that respect. If you don't hit other people when you can, the time will probably come when they'll hit you."

It was an ugly philosophy and Raymond, looking within, applied to it himself. Then he put his own thoughts away.

"And how are the gee-gees?" he asked.

"As a 'gentleman backer,' I can't say I'm going very strong," confessed Neddy. "On the whole, I think it's a mug's game. Anyway, I shall chuck it when flat racing comes again. My father's getting restive. I shall have to do something pretty soon."

Raymond stayed for an hour and was again urged to give a bachelor-supper before he married; but he declined.

"Shan't chuck away a tenner on a lot of wasters," he said. "Got something better to do with it."

Several men promised to come to church and see the event, now near at hand, but he told them that they might be disappointed.

"I'm not too sure about that," he said. "I may put my foot down on that racket and be married at a registrar's. Anyway church is no certainty. I've got no use for making a show of my private affairs."

On the way to Miss Ironsyde's he grew moody and gloom settled upon him. A glimpse of the old free and easy life threw into darker colours the new existence ahead. He remembered the sentiments of the strange man in the bar—how weakness is always punished and the heart often robs the head of victory. His heart was robbing his head of freedom; and that meant victory also; for what sort of success can life offer to those who begin it by flinging liberty to the winds? Yes, he had been "bluffing," as Neddy declared; and to bluff was foreign to his nature. Nobody was deceived, for everybody knew the truth, and though none dared laugh at him in public, secretly all his acquaintance were doubtless doing so.

Sabina saw that he was perturbed when presently he joined Miss Ironsyde. He had drunk more than enough and proved irritable.

He was, however, silent at first, while his aunt discussed the wedding. She took it for granted that it would be in church and reminded Raymond of necessary steps.

"And certain people should be asked," she said. "Have you any friends you particularly wish to be there? Mr. Churchouse is planning a wedding breakfast—"

"No—none of my friends will be there if I can help it. They're not that sort."

"Have you written to Daniel?"

"'Written to Daniel'! Good God, no! What should I write to Daniel, but to tell him he's the biggest cur and hound on earth?"

"You've passed all that. You're not going back again, Raymond. You know what you said last time when we talked about it."

"If he's ever to be more than a name to me, he must apologise for being a low down brute, first. I've got plenty on my mind without thinking about him. He's going to rue the day he treated me as he has done. I'll bring him and Bridetown Mill to the gutter, yet."

"Don't, don't, please. I thought you felt last time we were talking about him—"

"Drop him—don't mention his name to me—I won't hear it. If you want me to go on with my life with self-respect, then keep his name out of my life. I've cursed him to hell once and for all, so talk of something else!"

Jenny Ironsyde saw that her nephew was in a dark temper, and while at heart she felt indignant and ashamed, more for Sabina's sake than his own, she humoured him, spoke of the future and strove to win him back into a cheerful mind.

Then as they were going to dinner, at half-past seven o'clock, the maid who announced the meal, brought with her a telegram. It was directed to 'Ironsyde' only, and, putting on her glasses, Jenny read it.

Daniel had been very seriously injured in a railway accident at York.

Remorse strikes the young with cruel bitterness. Raymond turned pale and staggered. While he had been cursing his brother, the man lay smitten, perhaps at the door of death. His aunt it was who steadied him and turned to the time-table. Then she went to her store of ready money. In an hour Raymond was on his way. It might be possible for him to catch a midnight train for the North from London and reach York before morning.

When he had gone, Jenny turned to Sabina, who had spoken no word during this scene.

"Much may come of this," she said. "God works in mysterious ways. I have no fear that Raymond will fail in his duty to dear Daniel at such a time. Come back early to-morrow, Sabina. I shall get a telegram, as soon as Raymond can despatch it, and shall hold myself in readiness to go at once and stop with Daniel. Tell Mister Churchouse what has happened."

The lady spent the night in packing. Her sufferings and anxieties were allayed by occupation; but the long hours seemed unending.

She was ready to start at dawn, but not until ten o'clock came the news from York. Mr. Churchouse was already with her when the telegram arrived. He had driven from Bridetown with Sabina. Daniel Ironsyde was dead and had passed many hours before Raymond reached him.

Sabina went home on hearing this news, and Ernest Churchouse remained with Miss Ironsyde.

She was prostrated and, for a time, he could not comfort her. But the practical nature of her mind asserted itself between gusts of grief. She despatched a telegram to Raymond at York, and begged him to bring back his brother's body as soon as it might be done. Concerning the future she also spoke to Ernest.

"He has made no will," she said, "That I know, because when last we were speaking of Raymond, he told me he felt it impossible at present to do so."

"Then the whole estate belongs to Raymond, now?" he asked.

"Yes, everything is his."

CHAPTER XXIII

A LETTER FOR SABINA

A human machine, under stress of personal tribulation and lowered vitality, had erred in a signal box five miles from York, with the result that several of his fellow creatures were killed and many injured. Daniel Ironsyde had only lived long enough to direct the telegram to his home.

Three days later Raymond returned with the body, and once more Bridetown crowded to its windows and open spaces, to see the funeral of another master of the Mill.

To an onlooker the scene might have appeared a repetition in almost every particular of Henry Ironsyde's obsequies.

The spinners crowded on the grassy triangle under the sycamore tree and debated their future. They wondered whether Raymond would come to the funeral; and a new note entered into all voices when they spoke his name, for he was master now. Mr. Churchouse attended the burial, and Arthur Waldron walked down from North Hill House with his daughter. In the churchyard, where Daniel's grave waited for him beside his father, old Mr. Baggs stood and looked down, as he had done when Henry Ironsyde came to his grave.

"Life, how short—eternity, how long," he said to John Best.

Ernest Churchouse opened the door of the mourning coach as he had done on the previous occasion, and Miss Ironsyde alighted, followed by Raymond. He had come. But he had changed even to the visible eye. The least observing were able to mark differences of voice and manner.

Raymond's nature had responded to the stroke of circumstance with lightning swiftness. The pressure of his position, thus suddenly relieved, caused a rebound, a liberation of the grinding tension. It remained to be seen what course he might now pursue; yet those who knew him best anticipated no particular reaction. But when he returned it was quickly apparent that tremendous changes had already taken place in the young man's outlook on life and that, whatever his future line of conduct might be, he realised very keenly his altered position. He was now free of all temporal cares; but against that fact he found himself faced with great new responsibilities.

Remorse hit him hard, but he was through the worst of that, and life had become so tremendous, that he could not for very long keep his thoughts on death.

At his brother's funeral he allowed his eye to rest on no familiar face and cast no recognising glance at man or woman. He was haggard and pale, but more than that: a new expression had come into his countenance. Already consciousness of possession marked him. He had grasped the fact of the change far quicker than Daniel had grasped it after their father's death.

He was returning immediately with his aunt to Bridport; but Mr. Churchouse broke through the barrier and spoke to him as he entered the carriage.

"Won't you see Sabina before you go, Raymond? You must realise that, even under these terrible conditions, we cannot delay. I understand she wrote to you when you came back; but that you have not answered her letter. As things are it seems to me you might like to be quietly and privately married away from Bridetown?"

Raymond hardly seemed to hear.

"I can't talk about that now. A great deal falls upon me at present. I am enormously busy and have to take up the threads of all poor Daniel was doing in the North. There is nobody but myself, in my opinion, who can go through with it. I return to London to-night."

"But Sabina?"

Raymond answered calmly.

"Sabina Dinnett will hear from me during the next twenty-four hours," he said.

Ernest gazed aghast.

"But, my dear boy, you cannot realise the situation if you talk like that. Surely you—"

"I realise the situation perfectly well. Good-bye, Uncle Ernest."

The coach drove away. Miss Ironsyde said nothing. She had broken down beside the grave and was still weeping.

Then came Mr. Best, where Mr. Churchouse stood at the lich-gate. He was anxious for information.

"Did he say anything about his plans?" he asked.

"Only that he is proceeding with his late brother's business in the North. I perceive a most definite change in the young man, John."

"For the better, we'll hope. What's hid in people! You never would have thought Mister Raymond would have carried himself like that. It wasn't grief at his loss, but a sort of an understanding of the change. He even looked at us differently—even me."

"He's overwrought and not himself, probably. I don't think he quite grasps the immediate situation. He seems to be looking far ahead already, whereas the most pressing matter should be a thing of to-morrow."

"Is the wedding day fixed?"

"It is not. He writes to Sabina."

"Writes! Isn't he going to see her to-day!"

"He returns to London to-night."

Arthur Waldron also asked for news, for Raymond had apparently been unconscious of his existence at the funeral. He, too, noted the change in Ironsyde's demeanour.

"What was it?" he asked, as Mr. Churchouse walked beside him homeward. "Something is altered. It's more his manner than his appearance. Of course, he looks played out after his shock, but it's not that. Estelle thinks it's his black clothes."

"Stress of mind and anxiety, no doubt. I spoke to him; but he was rather distant. Not unfriendly—he called me 'Uncle Ernest' as usual—but distant. His mind is entirely preoccupied with business."

"What about Sabina?"

"I asked him. He's writing to her. She wasn't at the funeral. She and her mother kept away at my advice. But I certainly thought he would come and see them afterwards. However, the idea hadn't apparently occurred to him. His mind is full of other things. There was a suggestion of strength—of power—something new."

"He must be very strong now," said Estelle. "He will have to be strong, because the Mill is all his and everything depends upon him. Doesn't Sabina feel she must be strong, too, Mr. Churchouse?"

"Sabina is naturally excited. But she is also puzzled, because it seems strange that anything should come between her and Raymond at a time like this—even the terrible death of dear Daniel. She has been counting on hearing from him, and to-day she felt quite sure he would see her."

"Is the wedding put off then?"

"I trust not. She is to hear from him to-morrow."

* * * * *

Raymond kept his word and before the end of the following day Sabina received a letter. She had alternated, since Daniel's sudden death, between fits of depression and elation. She was cast down, because no communication of any kind had reached her since Raymond hurried off on the day of the accident; and she was elated, because the future must certainly be much more splendid for Raymond now.

She explained his silence easily enough, for much work devolved upon him; but when he did not come to see her on the day of the funeral, she was seriously perturbed and grew excited, unstrung and full of forebodings. Her mother heard from those who had seen him that Raymond appeared to be abstracted and 'kept himself to himself' entirely; which led to anxiety on her part also. The letter defined the position.

"MY DEAREST SABINA,—A thing like the death of my brother, with all that it means to me, cannot happen without having very far-reaching results. You may have noticed for some time before this occurred that I felt uneasy about the future—not only for your sake, but my own—and I had long felt that we were doing a very doubtful thing to marry. However, as circumstances were such then, that I should have been in the gutter if I did not marry, I was going to do so. There seemed to be no choice, though I felt all the time that I was not doing the fair thing to you, or myself.

"Now the case is altered and I can do the fair thing to you and myself, because circumstances make it possible. I have got tons of money now, and it is not too much to say that I want you to share it. But not on the old understanding. I hate and loathe matrimony and everything to do with it, and now that it is possible to avoid the institution, I intend to do so.

"What you have got to do is to put a lot of stupid, conventional ideas out of your mind, and not worry about other people, and the drivel they talk, or the idiotic things they say. We weren't conventional last year, so why the dickens should we be this? I'm awfully keen about you, Sabina, and awfully keen about the child too; but let us be sane and be lovers and not a wretched married couple.

"If you will come and be my housekeeper, I shall welcome you with rejoicings, and we can go house-hunting again and find something worthier of us and take bigger views.

"Don't let this bowl you over and make you savage. It is simply a question of what will keep us the best friends, and wear best. I am perfectly certain that in the long run we shall be happier so, than chained together by a lot of cursed laws, that will put our future relations on a footing that denies freedom of action to us both. Let's be pioneers and set a good example to people and help to knock on the head the imbecile marriage laws.

"I am, of course, going to put you all right from a worldly point of view and settle a good income upon you, which you will enjoy independently of me; and I also recognise the responsibility of our child. He or she will be my heir, and nothing will be spared for the youngster.

"I do hope, my dearest girl, you will see what a sensible idea this is. It means liberty, and you can't have real love without liberty. If we married, I am certain that in a year or two we should hate each other like the devil, and I believe you know that as well as I do. Marriage is out-grown—it's a barbaric survival and has a most damnable effect on character. If we are to be close chums and preserve our self-respect, we must steer clear of it.

"I am very sure I am right. I've thought a lot about it and heard some very shrewd men in London speak about it. We are up against a sort of battle nowadays. The idea of marriage is the welfare of the community, and the idea of freedom is the welfare of the individual; and I, for one, don't see in the least why the individual should go down for the community. What has the community done for us, that we should become slaves for it?

"Wealth—at any rate, ample means—does several things for a man. It opens his eyes to the meaning of power. Power is a fine thing if it's coupled with sense. Already I see what a poor creature I was—owing to the accident of poverty. Now you'll find what a huge difference power makes. It changes everything and turns a child into a man. At any rate, I've been a child till now. You've got to be childlike if you're poor.

"So I hope you'll take this in the spirit I write, Sabina, and trust me, for I'm straight as a line, and my first thought is to make you a happy woman. That I certainly can do, if you'll let me.

"I shall be coming home presently; but, for the moment, I must stop here. There is a gigantic deal of work waiting for me; but working for myself and somebody else are two very different things. I don't grudge the work now, since the result of the work means more power.

"I hope this is all clear. If it isn't, we must thresh it out when we meet. All I want you to grasp for the moment is that I love you as well as ever—better than anything in the world—and, because I want us to be the dearest friends always, I'm not going to marry you.

"Your mother and Uncle Ernest will of course take the conventional line, and my Aunt Jennie will do the same; but I hope you won't bother about them. Your welfare lies with me. Don't let them talk you into making a martyr of yourself, or any nonsense of that sort.

"Always, my dearest Sabina,
"Your faithful pal,
"RAY."

Half an hour later Mrs. Dinnett took the letter in to Mr. Churchouse.

"Death," she said. "Death is in the air. Sabina has gone to bed and I'm going for the doctor. He's broke off the engagement and wants her to be his housekeeper. And this is a Christian country, or supposed to be. Says it's going to be quite all right and offers her money and a lifetime of sin!"

"Be calm, Mary, be calm. You must have misread the letter. Go and get the doctor by all means if Sabina has succumbed. And leave the letter with me. I will read it carefully. That is if it is not private."

"No, it ain't private. He slaps at us all. We're all conventional people, which means, I suppose, that we fear God and keep the laws. But if my gentleman thinks—"

"Go and get the doctor, Mary. Two heads are better than one in a case of this sort. I feel sure you and Sabina are making a mistake."

"The world shall ring," said Mrs. Dinnett, "and we'll see if he can show his face among honest men again. We that have abided by the law all our days—now we'll see what the law can do for us against this godless wretch."

She went off to the village and Ernest cried after her to say nothing at present. He knew, however, as he spoke that it was vain.

Then he put away his own work and read the letter very carefully twice through.

Profound sorrow came upon him and his innate optimism was over-clouded. This seemed no longer the Raymond Ironsyde he had known from childhood. It was not even the Raymond of a month ago. He perceived how potential qualities of mind had awakened in the new conditions. He was philosophically interested. So deeply indeed did the psychological features of the change occupy his reflections, that for a time he overlooked their immediate and crushing significance in the affairs of another person.

Traces of the old Raymond remained in the promises of unbounded generosity and assurances of devotion; but Mr. Churchouse set no store upon them. The word that rang truest was Raymond's acute consciousness of power and appreciation thereof. It had, as he said, opened his eyes. Under any other conditions than those embracing Sabina and right and wrong, as Ernest accepted the meaning of right and wrong, he had won great hope from the letter. It was clear that Raymond had become a man at a bound and might be expected to develop into a useful man; but that his first step from adolescence was to involve the destruction of a woman and child, soon submerged all lesser considerations in the thinker's mind. Righteousness was implicated, and to start his new career with a cold-blooded crime made Mr. Churchouse tremble for the entire future of the criminal.

Yet he saw very little hope of changing Ironsyde's decision. Raymond had evidently considered the matter, and though his argument was abominable in Ernest's view, and nothing more than a cowardly evasion of his promises, he suspected that the writer found it satisfy his conscience, since its further education in the consciousness of power. He did not suppose that any whose opinion he respected would alter Raymond. It might even be that he was honest in his theories, and believed himself when he said that marriage would end by destroying his love for Sabina. But Mr. Churchouse did not pursue that line of argument. Had not Mary Dinnett just reminded him that this was a Christian country?

It was, of course, an immoral and selfish letter. Ernest knew exactly how it would strike Miss Ironsyde; but he also knew that many people without principle would view it as reasonable.

He had to determine what he was going to do, and soon came back to the attitude he had always taken. An unborn, immortal soul must be considered, and it was idle for Raymond to talk about making the coming child his heir. Such undertakings were vain. The young man was volatile and his life lay before him. That he could make this offer argued an indifference to Sabina's honour which no promises of temporal comfort condoned. For that matter he must surely have known while he wrote that it would be rejected.

The outlook appeared exceedingly hopeless. Mr. Churchouse rose from his desk and looked out of the window. It was a grey and silent morning. Only a big magnolia leaf tapped at the casement and dripped rain from its point. And overhead, in her chamber, Sabina was lying stricken and speechless. With infinite commiseration Mr. Churchouse considered what this must mean to her. It was as though Mrs. Dinnett's hysterical words had come true. Indeed, the tender-hearted man felt that death was in his house—death of fair hopes, death of a young and trusting spirit.

"The rising generation puts a strain on Christianity that I'm sure it was never called to bear in my youth," reflected Mr. Churchouse.

CHAPTER XXIV

MRS. NORTHOVER DECIDES

When Richard Gurd began to consider the case of Nelly Northover, his mind was very curiously affected. To develop the stages by which he arrived at his startling conclusions might be attractive, but the destination is more important than the journey. After twenty-four hours devoted to this subject alone, Richard had not only decided that Nelly Northover must not marry Job Legg; he had pushed the problem of his friend far beyond that point and found it already complicated by a greater than Job.

Indeed, the sudden reminder that Nelly was a comely and personable woman had affected Richard Gurd, and the thought that she should contemplate marriage caused him some preliminary uneasiness. He could no more see her married again than he could see himself taking a wife; yet from this attitude, progress was swift, and the longer he thought upon Mrs. Northover, the more steadily did his mind drive him into an opinion that she might reasonably wed again if she desired to do so. And then he proceeded to the personal concession that there was no radical necessity to remain single himself. Because he had reached his present ripe age without a wife, it did not follow he must remain for ever unmarried. He had no objection to marriage, and continued a bachelor merely because he had never found any woman desirable in his eyes. Moreover he disliked children.

He had reached this stage of the argument before he slept, and when he woke again, he found his mind considerably advanced along the road to Nelly. He now came to the deliberate conclusion that he wanted her. The discovery amazed him, but he could not escape it; and in the light of such a surprise he became a little dazzled. Sudden soul movements of such force and complexity made Richard Gurd selfish. It is a fact, that before he went at the appointed time to see the mistress of 'The Seven Stars,' he had forgotten all about Job Legg and was entirely concerned with his own tremendous project. Full grown and complete at all vital points it sprang from his energetic brain. He had reached the high personal ambition of wanting to marry Mrs. Northover himself, and their friendship of many years had been so complete, that he felt sanguine from the moment that his great determination dawned.

But she spoke and quickly reminded him of what she was expecting.

"And how d'you think about it? Shall it be, or shan't it, Richard?"

They were in the private parlour.

"Leave that," he said. "I can assure you that little affair is already a thing of the past. In fact, my mind has moved such a long way since you came to see me yesterday, that I'd forgot what you came about. But, after all, that was the starting point. Now a very curious thing has fallen out, and looking back, I can only say that the wonder is it didn't fall out long years ago."

"It did, so far as he was concerned," explained Mrs. Northover. "Mr. Legg has been hoping for this for years."

"The Lord often chooses a fool to light the road of the wise, my dear. Not that Job's a fool, and a more self-respecting man you won't find. In fact I shall always feel kindly to your potman, for, in a manner of speaking, you may say he's helped to show me my own duty."

"I dare say he has; he's a lesson to us all."

"He is, but, all the same, it's confounding class with class to think of him as a husband for you. Not that I've got any class prejudice myself. You can't keep a hotel year in, year out, and allow yourself the luxury of class prejudice; but be that as it may, Legg, though he adorns his class, wouldn't adorn ours in my opinion. And yet I'll say this: I believe it was put to him by Providence to offer for you, so that you might be lifted to higher things."

"Speak English, my dear man. I don't exactly know what you're talking about. But I suppose you mean I'd better not?"

Mrs. Northover was a little disappointed and Richard perceived it.

"Be calm, and don't let me sweep you off your feet as I've been swept off mine," he answered. "Since I discovered marriage was a possibility in your mind, I am obliged to confess that it's grown up to be a possibility in mine. And why not?"

"No reason at all. 'Twas the wonder of Bridport, you might say for years, why you remained single."

"Well, this I'll tell you, Nelly; I'm not going to have you marrying any Dick, Tom or Harry that's daring enough to lift his eyes to you and cheeky enough to offer. And when the thought came in my mind, I very soon found that this event rose up ideas that might have slumbered till eternity, but for Job Legg. And that's why I say Providence is in it. I've felt a great admiration for your judgment, and good sense, and fine appearance, ever since the blow fell and your husband was taken. And we know each other pretty close and have got no secrets from each other. And now you may say I've suddenly seen the light; and if you've got half the opinion of me that I have of you, no doubt you'll thank your God to hear what I'm saying and answer according."

"Good powers! You want to marry me yourself?" gasped Mrs. Northover.

"By all your 'Seven Stars' I do," he said. "In fact, I want for 'The Tiger' to swallow the 'Seven Stars,' in a poetical way of speaking. I'm a downright man and never take ten minutes where five's enough, so there it is. It came over me last night as a thing that must be—like the conversion of Paul. And I'll go further; I won't have you beat about the bush, Nelly. You're the sort of woman that can make up your mind in a big thing as quick as you can in a small thing. I consider there's been a good deal of a delicate and tender nature going on between us, though we were too busy to notice it; but now the bud have burst into flower, and I see amazing clear we were made for each other. In fact, I ain't going to take 'no' for an answer, my dear. I've never asked a female to marry me until this hour; and I have not waited into greyness and ripeness to hear a negative. I'm sure of myself, naturally, and I well know that you'd only be a thought less fortunate than I shall be."

"Stop!" she said, "and let me think. I'm terrible flattered at this, and I'll go so far as to say there's rhyme and reason in it, Richard. But you run on so. I feel my will power fairly oozing out of me."

"Not at all," he answered. "Your will power's what I rely upon. You're a forceful person yourself and you naturally approve of forcefulness in others. There's no reason why you shouldn't love me as well as I love you; and, for that matter, you do."

"Well, I must have time. I must drop Legg civilly and break it to him gradual."

"I'll meet you there. You needn't tell him you're going to be married all in a minute. He'll find that out for himself very quick. So will everybody. If a thing's worth doing, try to do it—that's my motto. But, for the moment, you can say that your affections are given in another quarter."

"Of course, it's a great thing for me, Richard. I'm very proud of it."

"And so am I. And Job Legg was the dumb instrument, so I am the last to quarrel with him. Just tell him, that failing another, you might have thought on him; but that the die is cast; and when he hears his fate, he'll naturally want to know who 'tis. And then the great secret must come out. I should reckon after Easter would be a very good time for us to wed."

"I can't believe my senses," she said.

"You will in a week," he assured her; "and, meanwhile, I shall do my best to help you. In a week the joyful tidings go out to the people."

He kissed her, shook her hand and squeezed it. Then he departed leaving Mrs. Northover in the extremity of bewilderment. But pleasure and great pride formed no small part of her mingled emotions.

One paramount necessity darkened all, however. Nelly felt a very sharp pang when she thought upon Mr. Legg, and her sufferings increased as the day advanced until they quite mastered the situation and clouded the brightness of conquest. Other difficulties and doubts also obtruded as she began to estimate the immensity of the thing that Mr. Gurd's ardour had prompted her to do; but Job was the primal problem and she knew that she could not sleep until she had made her peace with him.

She determined to leave him in no doubt concerning his successful rival. The confession would indeed make it easier for them both. At least she hoped it might do so.

He came for keys after closing time and she bade him sit down in the chair which Richard Gurd had that morning filled. One notes trifles at the supremest moments of life, and the trifles often stick, while the great events which accompany them fade into the past. Mrs. Northover observed that while Richard Gurd had filled the chair—and overflowed, Mr. Legg by no means did so. He occupied but the centre of the spacious seat. There seemed a significance in that.

"Sit down, Job, and listen. I've got to say something that will hurt you, my dear man. I've made my choice, after a good bit of deep thought I assure you, and I've—I've chosen the other, Job."

He stared and his thin jaws worked. His nostrils also twitched.

"I didn't know there was another."

"More didn't I," answered she. "I'm nothing if not honest, and I tell you frankly that I didn't know it either till he offered. He was a lifelong friend, and I asked him about what I ought to be doing, and then it came out he had already thought of me as a wife and was biding his time. He had nought but praise for you, as all men have; but there it is—Richard Gurd is very wishful to marry me; and you must understand this clearly, Job. If it had been any lesser man than him, or any other man in the world, for that matter, I wouldn't have taken him. I'm very fond of you, and a finer character I've never known; but when Richard offered—well, you're among the clever ones and I'm sure you'd be the last to put yourself up against a man of his standing and fame. And my first husband's lifelong friend, you must remember. And though, after all these years, it may seem strange to a great many people, it won't seem strange to you, I hope."

"It's a very ill-convenient time to hear this," said Mr. Legg mildly.

Then he stopped and regarded her with his little, shrewd eyes. He seemed less occupied with the tremendous present than the future. Presently he went on again, while Mrs. Northover stared at him with an expression of genuine sadness.

"All I can say is that I wish Gurd had offered sooner, and not led me into this tremendous misfortune. Of course, him and me aren't in the same street and I won't pretend it, for none would be deceived if I did. But I say again it's very unfortunate he hung fire till he heard that I had made my offer. For if he'd spoke first, I should have held my peace and gone on my appointed way and stopped at 'The Seven Stars.' But now, if this happens, all is over and the course of my life is changed. In fact, it is not too much to say I shall leave Bridport, though how any person can live comfortably away from Bridport, I don't know."

Mrs. Northover felt relief that he should thus fasten on such a minor issue, and never liked him better than at that moment. "Thank God, he's took it, lying down!" she thought, then spoke.

"Don't you leave, my dear man. Bridport won't be Bridport without you, and you've always been a true and valued friend to me, and such a helpful and sensible creature that I shall only know in the next world all I owe you. And between us, I don't see no reason at all why you shouldn't go on as my potman and—more than that—why shouldn't you marry a nice woman yourself and bring her here, if you've got a mind to it!"

He expressed no indignation. Again, it seemed that the future was his sole concern and that he designed to waste no warmth on his disappointment.

"There never was but one woman for me and never will be; and as to stopping here, I might, or I might not, for I've always had my feelings under very nice control and shouldn't break the rule of a lifetime. But you won't be at 'The Seven Stars' yourself much longer, and I certainly don't serve under any other but you. In fact this house and garden would only be a deserted wilderness to my view, if you wasn't reigning over 'em."

He spoke in his usual emotionless voice, but he woke very active phenomena in Mrs. Northover. Her face grew troubled and she looked into his eyes with a frown.

"Me gone! What do you mean, Legg? Me leave 'The Seven Stars' after thirty-four years?"

"No doubt your first would turn in his grave if you did," he admitted; "but what about it? When you're mistress of 'The Tiger'—well, then you're mistress of 'The Tiger,' and you can't be in two places at once—clever as you are."

He had given her something to think about. The possibility of guile in Mr. Legg had never struck the least, or greatest, of his admirers. He was held a simple soul of transparent probity, yet, for a moment, it almost seemed as though his last remark carried an inner meaning. Nelly dismissed the suspicion as unworthy of Job; but none the less, though he had doubtless spoken without any sinister purpose, his opinions gave her pause. Indeed, they shook her. She had been too much excited to look ahead. Now she was called to do so.

Mr. Legg removed the bunch of keys from its nail and prepared to go on his way.

She felt weak.

"To play second fiddle for the rest of your life after playing first for a quarter of a century is a far-reaching thought," she said.

"Without a doubt it would be," he admitted. "Of course, with some men you wouldn't be called to do it. With Richard Gurd, you would."

"To leave 'The Seven Stars'! Somehow I'd always regarded our place as a higher class establishment than 'The Tiger'—along of the tea-gardens and pleasure ground and the class of company."

"And quite right to do so. But that's only your opinion, and mine. It won't be his. Good night."

He left her deep in thought, then five minutes afterwards thrust his long nose round the door again.

"The English of it is you can't have anything for nothing—not in this weary world," he said.

Then he disappeared.

A week later Sarah Northover came to see her aunt and congratulate her on the great news.

"Now people know it," said Sarah, "they all wonder how ever 'twas you and Mister Gurd didn't marry long ago."

"We've been wondering the same, for that matter, and Richard takes the blame—naturally, since I couldn't say the word before he asked the question. But for your ear and only yours, Sarah, I can whisper that this thing didn't go by rule. And in sober honesty I do believe if he hadn't heard another man wanted me, Mister Gurd would never have found out he did. But such are the strange things that happen in human nature, no doubt."

"Another!" said Sarah. "They're making up for lost time, seemingly."

"Another, and a good man," declared her aunt; "but his name is sacred, and you mustn't ask to know it."

Sarah related events at Bridetown.

"You've heard, of course, about the goings on? Mister Ironsyde don't marry Sabina, and her mother wants to have the law against him; but though Sabina's in a sad state and got to be watched, she won't have the law. We only hear scraps about it, because Nancy Buckler, her great friend, is under oath of secrecy. But if he shows his face at Bridetown, it's very likely he'll be man-handled. Then, against that, there's rumours in the air he'll make great changes at the Mill, and may put up all our money. In that case, I don't think he'd be treated very rough, because, as my Mister Roberts says, 'Self-preservation is the first law of nature,' and always have been; and if he's going to better us it will mean a lot."

"Don't you be too hopeful, however," warned Mrs. Northover. "There's a deal of difference between holding the reins yourself and saying sharp things against them who are. He's hard, and last time he was in this house but one, he got as drunk as a lord and Legg helped him to bed. And he quarrelled very sharp with Mister Gurd for giving him good advice; and Richard says the young man is iron painted to look like wood. And he's rarely mistook."

"But he always did tell us we never got enough money for our work," argued Sarah. "And if anything comes of it and Nicholas and me earn five bob more a week between us, it means marriage. So I'm in a twitter."

"What does John Best say?"

"Nought. We can't get a word out of him. All we know is we're cruel busy and orders flow in like a river. But that was poor Mister Daniel's work, no doubt."

"Marriage is in the air, seemingly," reflected Nelly. "It mightn't be altogether a bad thing if you and me went to the altar together, Sarah. 'Twas always understood you'd be married from 'The Seven Stars,' and the sight of a young bride and bridegroom would soften the ceremony a bit and distract the eye from me and Richard."

"Good Lord!" answered the girl. "There won't be no eyes for small folks like us on the day you take Mister Gurd. 'Twould be one expense without a doubt; but I'm certain positive he wouldn't like for us little people to be mixed up with it. 'Twould lessen the blaze from his point of view, and a man such as him wouldn't approve of that."

"Perhaps you're right," admitted her aunt, with a massive sigh. "He's a masterful piece, and the affair will be carried out as he wills."

"I can't see you away from 'The Seven Stars,' somehow, Aunt Nelly."

"That's what everybody says. More can't I see myself away for that matter. But Richard said 'The Tiger' would swallow 'The Seven Stars,' and I know what he meant now."

CHAPTER XXV

THE WOMAN'S DARKNESS

The blood of Sabina Dinnett was poisoned through an ordeal of her life when it should have run at its purest and sweetest. That the man who had promised to marry her, had exhausted the vocabulary of love for her, should thus cast her off, struck her into a frantic calenture which, for a season, threatened her existence. The surprise of his decision was not absolute and utter, otherwise such a shock might indeed have killed her; but there lacked not many previous signs to show that Raymond Ironsyde had strayed from his old enthusiasm and found the approach of marriage finally quench love. The wronged girl could look back and see a thousand such warnings, while she remembered also a dark dread in her heart as to what might possibly overtake her on the death of Daniel. True the shadow had lasted but a moment; she banished it, as unworthy, and preferred to dwell on the increased happiness and prosperity that must accrue to Raymond; but the passing fear had touched her first, and she could look back now and mark how deeply doubt tinctured all her waking hours since the necessity arose for Raymond to wed.

For a few days she raged and was only comforted with difficulty. Mr. Churchouse and Jenny Ironsyde both visited Sabina and bade her control herself and keep calm, lest worst things should happen to her. Ernest was still sanguine that the young man would regret his suggestions; but Jenny quenched this hope.

"It is all of a piece," she said, "and, looking back, I see it. His instinct and will are against any such binding thing as marriage. He wants to make her happy; but if to do so is to make himself miserable, then she must go unhappy. Some bad girls might accept his offer; but Sabina, of course, cannot. She is not made of the stuff to sink to this, and it was only because he always insisted on the vital need for her to complete his life, that she forgot her wisdom in the past and believed they were really the complement of each other. As if a woman ever was, or ever will be, the real complement of a man, or a man, the complement of a woman! They are only complementary as meat and drink to the hungry."

After some days Sabina read Raymond's letter again and it now awoke a new passion. At first she had hated herself and talked of doing herself an injury; but this was hysteria bred of suffering, since she had not the temperament to commit self-destruction. Now her rage burned against the child that she was doomed to bring into the world, and she brooded secretly on how its end might be accomplished. She knew the peril to herself of any such attempt; but while she could not have committed suicide, she faced the thought of the necessary risks. If the child lived, the hateful link must exist forever, if it perished, she would be free. So she argued.

Full of this idea, she rose from her bed, went about and found some little consolation in the sympathy of her friends. They cursed the man until they heard what he had written to her. Then a change came over their criticism, for they were not tuned to Sabina's pitch, and it seemed to them, from their more modest standards of education, combined with the diminished self-respect where ignorance obtains, that Raymond's offer was fair—even handsome. Some, indeed, still mourned with her and shared her fierce indignation; some simulated anger to please her; but most confessed to themselves that she had not much to grumble at.

A wise woman warned her against any attempt to tamper with the child. It was too late and the danger far too serious. So she passed through the second phase of her sufferings and went from hatred of herself and loathing of her load, to acute detestation of the man who had destroyed her.

His offer seemed to her more villainous than his desertion. His ignorance of her true self, the insolence and contempt that prompted such a proposal, the view of her—these thoughts lashed her into fury. She longed for some one to help her against him and treat him as he deserved to be treated. She felt equal to making any sacrifice, if only he might be debased and scorned and pointed at as he deserved to be. She felt that her emotions must be shared by every honourable woman and decent man. Her spirit hungered for a great revenge.

At first she dreamed of a personal action. She longed to tear him with her nails, outrage him in people's eyes and make him suffer in his flesh; but that passed: she knew she could not do it. A man was needed to extort punishment from Raymond. But no man existed who would undertake the task. She must then find such a man. She even sought him. But she did not find him. The search led to bitter discoveries. If women could forgive her betrayer; if women could say, as presently they said, that she did not know her luck, men were still more indifferent.

The attitude of the world to her sufferings horrified Sabina. She had none to love her—none, at least, to show his love by assaulting and injuring her enemy. Only a certain number even took up the cudgels for her in speech. Of these Levi Baggs, the hackler, was the strongest. But his misanthropy embraced her also. He had said harsh things of his new master; but neither had he spared the victim.

Upon these three great periods, of rage, futile passion, and hate, there followed a lethargy from which Ernest Churchouse tried in vain to rouse Sabina. He apprehended worse results from this coma of mind and body than from the flux of her natural indignation. He spent much time with her and bade her hope that Raymond might still reconsider his future.

None had yet seen him since his brother's funeral, and his aunt received no answer to a very strenuous plea. He wrote to her, indeed, about affairs, and even asked her for advice upon certain matters; but they affected the past and Daniel rather than the future and himself. She could not fail to notice the supreme change that power had brought with it; his very handwriting seemed to have acquired a firmer line; while his diction certainly showed more strength of purpose. Could power modify character? It seemed impossible. She supposed, rather, that character, latent till this sudden change of fortune, had been revealed by power. Her first fears for the future of the business abated; but with increasing respect for Raymond, the former affection perished. She was firm in her moral standards, and to find his first use of power an evasion of solemn and sacred promises, made Miss Ironsyde Raymond's enemy. That he ignored her appeals to his manhood and honesty did not modify her changed attitude. She found herself much wounded by his callous conduct, and while his past weakness had been forgiven, his new strength proved unforgivable.

Her appeal was, however, indirectly acknowledged, for Sabina received another letter from Raymond in which he mentioned Miss Ironsyde's communication.

"My aunt," he wrote, "does not realise the situation, or appreciate the fact that love may remain a much more enduring and lively emotion outside marriage than inside it. There are, of course, people who find chains bearable enough, and even grow to like them, as convicts were said to do; but you are not such a craven, no more am I. We must think of the future, not the past, and I feel very sure that if we married, the result would be death to our friendship. We had a splendid time, and we might still have a splendid time, if you could be unconventional and realise how many other women are also. But probably you have decided against my suggestions, or I should have heard from you. So I suppose you hate me, and I'm awfully sorry to think it. You won't come to me, then. But that doesn't lessen my obligations, and I'm going to take every possible care of you and your child, Sabina, whether you come or not. He is my child, too, and I shan't forget it. If you would like to see me you shall when I return to Bridport, pretty soon now; but if you would rather not do so, then let me know who represents you, and I will hear what you and your mother would wish."

She wrote several answers to this and destroyed them. They were bitter and contemptuous, and as each was finished she realised its futility. She could but sting; she could not seriously hurt. Even her sting would not trouble him much, for a man who had done what he had done, was proof against the scorn and hate of a woman. Only greater power than his own could make him feel. Her powerlessness maddened her—her powerlessness contrasted with his remorseless strength. But he used his strength like a coward.

Some of her friends urged her to take legal action against Raymond Ironsyde and demand mighty damages.

"You can hurt him there, if you can't anywhere else," said Nancy Buckler. "You say you're too weak to hurt him, but you're not. Knock his money out of him; you ought to get thousands."

Her mother, for a time, was of the same opinion. It seemed a right and reasonable thing that Sabina should not be called upon to face her ruined life without some compensation, but she found herself averse from this. The thought of touching his money, or availing herself of it in any way, was horrible to her. She knew, moreover, that such an arrangement would go far to soothe Raymond's conscience; and the more he paid, probably the happier he would feel. For other causes also she declined to take any legal steps against him, and in this decision Ernest Churchouse supported her.

He had been her prime consolation indeed, and though, at first, his line of argument only left Sabina impatient, by degrees—by very slow degrees— she inclined to him and suffered herself to hope he might not be mistaken. He urged patience and silence. He held that Raymond Ironsyde would presently return to that better and worthier self, which could not be denied him. His own abounding charity, where humanity was concerned, honestly induced Ernest to hope and almost believe that the son of Henry Ironsyde had made these proposals under excitation of mind; that he was thrown off his balance by the pressure of events; and that, presently, when he had time to remember the facts concerning Sabina, he would be heartily ashamed of himself and make the only adequate amends.

It was not unnatural that the girl should find in this theory her highest consolation. She clung to it desperately, though few but Mr. Churchouse himself accounted it of any consequence. Him, however, she had been accustomed to consider the fountain of wisdom, and though, with womanhood, she had lived to see his opinions mistaken and his trust often abused, yet disappointments did not change a sanguine belief in his fellow creatures.

So, thankful to repose her mind on another, Sabina for a while came to standing-ground in her storm-stricken journey. Each day was an eternity, but she strove to be patient. And, meantime, she wrote and posted a letter to her old lover. It was not angry, or even petulant. Indeed, she made her appeal with dignity and good choice of words. Before all she insisted on the welfare of the child, and reminded him of the cruelty inflicted from birth on any baby unlawfully born in England.

Mr. Churchouse had instructed her in this matter, and she asked Raymond if he could find it in his heart to allow the child of their common love and worship to come into the world unrecognised by the world, deprived of recognition and human rights.

He answered the letter vaguely and Mr. Churchouse read a gleam of hope into his words, but neither Sabina nor her mother were able to do so. For he spoke only of recognising his responsibilities and paternal duty. He bade her fear nothing for the child, or herself, and assured her that her future would be his care and first obligation as long as he lived.

In these assertions Mr. Churchouse saw a wakening dawn, but Mary Dinnett declared otherwise. The man was widening the gap; his original idea, that Sabina should live with him, had dearly been abandoned.

Then the contradictions of human nature appeared, and Mary, who had been the first to declare her deep indignation at Raymond's cynical proposal, began to weaken and even wonder if Sabina had done wisely not to discuss that matter.

"Not that ever you should have done it," she hastened to add; "but if you'd been a bit crafty and not ruled it out altogether, you might have built on it and got friendly again and gradually worked him back to his duty."

Then Mr. Churchouse protested, in the name of righteousness, while she argued that God helps those that help themselves, and that wickedness should be opposed with craft. Sabina listened to them helplessly and her last hope died out.

CHAPTER XXVI

OF HUMAN NATURE

Nicholas Roberts drove his lathes in a lofty chamber separated by wooden walls from the great central activities of the spinning mill. Despite the flying sparks from his emery wheels, he always kept a portrait of Sarah Northover before him; and certain pictures of notable sportsmen also hung with Sarah above the benches whereon Nicholas pursued his task. His work was to put a fresh face on the wooden reels and rollers that formed a part of the machines; for running hemp or flax will groove the toughest wood in time, and so ruin the control of the rollers and spoil the thread.

The wood curled away like paper before the teeth of the lathes, and the chisels of these, in their turn, had often to be set upon spinning stones. It was noisy work, and Nicholas now stopped his grindstone that he might hear his own voice and that of Mr. Best, who came suddenly into the shop.

The foreman spoke of some new wood for roller turning.

"It should be here this week," he said. "I told them we were running short. You may expect a good batch of plane and beech by Thursday."

They discussed the work of Roberts and presently turned to the paramount question in every mind at the Mill. All naturally desired to know when Raymond Ironsyde would make his appearance and what would happen when he did so; but while some, having regard for his conduct, felt he would not dare to appear again himself, others believed that one so insensible to honesty and decency would be indifferent to all opinions entertained of him. Such suspected that the criticisms of Bridetown would be too unimportant to trouble the new master.

And it seemed that they were right, for now came Ernest Churchouse seeking Mr. Best. He looked into the turning-shop, saw John and entered.

"He's coming next week, but perhaps you know it," he began. "And if you haven't heard, be sure you will at any moment."

"Then our fate is in store," declared Nicholas. "Some hope nothing, but, seeing that with all his faults he's a sportsman, I do hope a bit. There's plenty beside me who remember his words very well, and they pointed to an all-around rise for men and women alike."

"There was a rumour of violence against him. You don't apprehend anything of that sort, I hope?" asked Ernest of Best.

"A few—more women than men—had a plot, I believe, but I haven't heard any more about it. Baggs is the ringleader; but if there was any talk of raising the money, he'd find himself deserted. He's very bitter just now, however, and as he's got the pleasant experience of being right for once, you may be sure he's making the most of it."

"I'll see him," said Mr. Churchouse. "I always find him the most difficult character possible; but he must know that to answer violence with violence is vain. Patience may yet find the solution. I have by no means given up hope that right will be done."

"Come and tell Levi, then. Him and me are out for the moment, because I won't join him in calling down evil on Mister Ironsyde's head. But what's the sense of losing your temper in other people's quarrels? Better keep it for your own, I say."

They found Levi Baggs grumbling to himself over a mass of badly scutched flax; but when he heard that Raymond Ironsyde was coming, he grew philosophic.

"If we could only learn from what we work in," he said, "we'd have the lawless young dog at our mercy. But, of course, we shall not. Why don't the yarn teach us a lesson? Why don't it show us that, though the thread is nought, and you can break it, same as Raymond Ironsyde can break me or you, yet when you get to the twist, and the doubling and the trebling, then it's strong enough to defy anything. And if we combined as we ought, we shouldn't be waiting here to listen to what he's got to say; we should be waiting here to tell him what we've got to say. If we had the wit and understanding to twist our threads into one rope against the wickedness of the world, then we should have it all our own way."

"Yes—all your own way to do your own wickedness," declared Best. "We know very well what your idea of fairness is. You look upon capital as a natural enemy, and if Raymond Ironsyde was an angel with wings, you'd still feel to him that he was a foe and not a friend."

"The tradition is in the blood," declared Levi. "Capital is our natural enemy, as you say. Our fathers knew it, and we know it, and our children will know it."

"Your fathers had a great deal more sense than you have, Baggs," declared Mr. Churchouse. "And if you only remember the past a little, you wouldn't grumble quite so loudly at the present. But labour has a short memory and no gratitude, unfortunately. You're always shouting out what must be done for you; you never spare a thought on what has been done. You never look back at the working-class drudgery of bygone days—to the 'forties' of last century, when your fathers went to work at the curfew bell and earned eighteen-pence a week as apprentices, and two shillings a week and a penny for themselves after they had learned their business. A good spinner in those days might earn five shillings a week, Levi—and that out of doors in fair weather. In foul, he, or she, wouldn't do so well. If you had told your fathers seventy years ago that all the spinning walks would be done away with and the population better off notwithstanding, they would never have believed it."

"That's the way to look at the subject, Levi," declared John Best. "Think what the men of the past would have said to our luck—and our education."

"Machinery brought the spinning indoors," continued Ernest. "I can remember forty spinning walks in St. Michael's Lane alone. And with small wages and long hours, remember the price of things, Levi; remember the fearful price of bare necessities. Clothes were so dear that many a labourer went to church in his smock frock all his life. Many never donned broadcloth from their cradle to their grave. And tea five shillings a pound, Levi Baggs! They used to buy it by the ounce and brew it over and over again. Think of the little children, too, and how they were made to work. Think of them and feel your heart ache."

"My heart aches for myself," answered the hackler, "because I very well remember what my own childhood was. And I'm not saying the times don't better. I'm saying we must keep at 'em, or they'll soon slip back again into the old, bad ways. Capital's always pulling against labour and would get back its evil mastery to-morrow if it could. So we need to keep awake, to see we don't lose what we've won, but add to it. Now here's a man that's a servant by instinct, and it's in his blood to knuckle under."

He pointed to Best.

"I'm for no man more than another," answered John. "I stand not for man or woman in particular. I'm for the Mill first and last and always. I think of what is best for the Mill and put it above the welfare of the individual, whatever he represents—capital or labour."

"That's where you're wrong. The people are the Mill and only the people," declared Baggs. "The rest is iron and steel and flax and hemp and steam— dead things all. We are the Mill, not the stuff in it, or the man that happens to be the new master."

"Mr. Raymond has expressed admirable sentiments in my hearing," declared Ernest Churchouse. "For so young a man, he has a considerable grasp of the situation and progressive ideas. You might be in worse hands."

"Might we? How worse? What can be worse than a man that lies to women and seduces an innocent girl under promise of marriage? What can be worse than a coward and traitor, who does a thing like that, and when he finds he's strong enough to escape the consequences, escapes them?"

"Heaven knows I'm not condoning his conduct, Levi. He has behaved as badly as a young man could, and not a word of extenuation will you hear from me. I'm not speaking of him as a part of the social order; I'm speaking of him as master of the Mill. As master here he may be a successful man and you'll do well to bear in mind that he must be judged by results. Morally, he's a failure, and you are right to condemn him; but don't let that make you an enemy to him as owner of the works. Be just, and don't be prejudiced against him in one capacity because he's failed in another."

"A bad man is a bad man," answered Baggs stoutly, "and a blackguard's a blackguard. And if you are equal to doing one dirty trick, your fellow man has a right to distrust you all through. You've got to look at a question through your own spectacles, and I won't hear no nonsense about the welfare of the Mill, because the welfare of the Mill means to me—Levi Baggs—my welfare—and, no doubt, it means to that godless rip, his welfare. You mark me—a man that can ruin one girl won't be very tender about fifty girls and women. And if you think Raymond Ironsyde will take any steps to better the workers at the expense of the master, you're wrong, and don't know nothing about human nature."

John Best looked at Mr. Churchouse doubtfully.

"There's sense in that, I'm fearing," he said.

"When you say 'human nature,' Levi, you sum the whole situation," answered Ernest mildly. "Because human nature is like the sea—you never know when you put a net into it what you'll drag up to the light of day. Human nature is never exhausted, and it abounds in contradictions. You cannot make hard and fast laws for it, and you cannot, if you are philosophically inclined, presume to argue about it as though it were a consistent and unchanging factor. History is full of examples of men defeating their own characters, of falling away from their own ideals, yet struggling back to them. Careers have dawned in beauty and promise and set in blood and failure; and, again, you find people who make a bad start, yet manage to retrieve the situation. In a word, you cannot argue from the past to the future, where human nature is concerned. It is a series of surprises, some gratifying and some very much the reverse. There's always room for hope with the worst and fear with the best of us."

"It's easy for you to talk," growled Mr. Baggs. "But talk don't take the place of facts. I say a blackguard's always a blackguard and defy any man to disprove it."

"If you want facts, you can have them," replied Ernest. "My researches into history have made me sanguine in this respect. Many have been vicious in youth and proved stout enemies to vice at a later time. Themistocles did much evil. His father disowned him—and he drove his mother to take her own life for grief at his sins. Yet, presently, the ugly bud put forth a noble flower. Nicholas West was utterly wicked in his youth and committed such crimes that he was driven from college after burning his master's dwelling-house. Yet light dawned for this young man and he ended his days as Bishop of Ely. Titus Vespasianus emulated Nero in his early rascalities; but having donned the imperial purple, he cast away his evil companions and was accounted good as well as great. Henry V. of England was another such man, who reformed himself to admiration. Augustine began badly, and declared as a jest that he would rather have his lust satisfied than extinguished. Yet this man ended as a Saint of Christ. I could give you many other examples, Levi."

"Then we'll hope for the best," said John.

But Mr. Baggs only sneered.

"We hear of the converted sinners," he said; "but we don't hear of the victims that suffered their wickedness before they turned into saints. Let Raymond Ironsyde be twenty saints rolled into one, that won't make Sabina Dinnett an honest woman, or her child a lawful child."

"Never jump to conclusions," advised Ernest. "Even that may come right. Nothing is impossible."

"That's a great thought—that nothing's impossible," declared Mr. Best.

They argued, each according to his character and bent of mind, and, while the meliorists cheered each other, Mr. Baggs laughed at them and held their aspirations vain.

CHAPTER XXVII

THE MASTER OF THE MILL

Raymond Ironsyde came to Bridetown. He rode in from Bridport, and met John Best by appointment early on a March morning.

With the words of Ernest Churchouse still in his ears, the foreman felt profound interest to learn what might be learned considering the changes in his master's character.

He found a new Raymond, yet as the older writing of a parchment palimpsest will sometimes make itself apparent behind the new, glimpses of his earlier self did not lack. The things many remembered and hoped that Ironsyde would remember were not forgotten by him. But instead of the old, vague generalities and misty assurance of goodwill, he now declared definite plans based on knowledge. He came armed with figures and facts, and his method of expression had changed from ideas to intentions. His very manner chimed with his new power. He was decisive, and quite devoid of sentimentality. He feared none, but his attitude to all had changed.

They spoke in Mr. Best's office and he marked how the works came first in Raymond's regard.

"I've been putting in a lot of time on the machine question," he said. "As you know, that always interested me most before I thought I should have much say in the matter. Well, there's no manner of doubt we're badly behind the times. You can't deny it, John. You know better than anybody what we want, and it must be your work to go on with what you began to do for my brother. I don't want to rush at changes and then find I've wasted capital without fair results; but it's clear to me that a good many of our earlier operations are not done as well and swiftly as they might be."

"That's true. The Carder is out of date and the Spreader certainly is."

"The thing is to get the best substitutes in the market. You'll have to go round again in a larger spirit. I'm not frightened of risks. Is there anybody here who can take your place for a month or six weeks?"

Mr. Best shook his head.

"There certainly is not," he said.

"Then we must look round Bridport for a man. I'm prepared to put money into the changes, provided I have you behind me. I can trust you absolutely to know; but I advocate a more sporting policy than my poor brother did. After that we come to the people. I've got my business at my fingers' ends now and I found I was better at figures than I thought. There must be some changes. There are two problems: time and money. Either one or other; or probably both must be bettered—that's what I am faced with."

"It wants careful thinking out, sir."

"Well, you are a great deal more to me than my foreman, and you know it. I look to you and only you to help me run the show at Bridetown, henceforth. And, before everything, I want my people to be keen and feel my good is their good and their good is mine. Anyway, I have based changes on a fair calculation of future profits, plus necessary losses and need to make up wear and tear."

"And remember, raw products tend to rise in price all the time."

"As to that, I'm none too sure we've been buying in the best market. When I know more about it, I may travel a bit myself. Meantime, I'm changing two of our travellers."

Mr. Best nodded.

"That's to the good," he said. "I know which. Poor Mr. Daniel would keep them, because his father had told him they were all they ought to be. But least said, soonest mended."

"As to the staff, it's summed up in a word. I mean for them a little less time and a little more money. Some would like longer hours and much higher wages; some would be content with a little more money; some only talked about shorter time. I heard them all air their opinions in the past. But I've concluded for somewhat shorter hours and somewhat better money. You must rub it into them that new machinery will indirectly help them, too, and make the work lighter and the results better."

"That's undoubtedly true, but it's no good saying so. You'll never make them feel that new machinery helps them. But they'll be very glad of a little more money."

"We must enlarge their minds and make them understand that the better the machinery, the better their prospects. As I go up—and I mean to—so they shall go up. But our hope of success lies in the mechanical means we employ. They must grasp that intelligently, and be patient, and not expect me to put them before the Mill. If the works succeed, then they succeed and I succeed. If the works hang fire and get behindhand, then they will suffer. We're all the servants of the machinery. I want them to grasp that."

"It's difficult for them; but no doubt they'll get to see it," answered John.

"They must. That's the way to success in my opinion. It's a very interesting subject—the most interesting to me—always was. The machinery, I mean. I may go to America, presently. Of course, they can give us a start and a beating at machinery there."

"We must remember the driving power," said Best.

"The driving power can be raised, like everything else. If we haven't got enough power, we must increase it. I've thought of that, too, as a matter of fact."

"You can't increase what the river will do; but, of course, you can get a stronger steam engine."

"Not so sure about the river. There's a new thing—American, of course— called a turbine. But no hurry for that. We've got all the power we want for the minute. That's one virtue of some of the new machinery: it doesn't demand so much power in some cases."

But Best was very sceptical on this point. They discussed other matters and Raymond detailed his ideas as to the alteration of hours and wages. For the most part his foreman had no objections to offer, and when he did question the figures, he was overruled. But he felt constrained to praise.

"It's wonderful how you've gone into it," he said. "I never should have thought you'd have had such a head for detail, Mister Raymond."

"No more should I, John. I surprised myself. But when you are working for another person—that's one thing; when you are working for yourself— that's another thing. Not much virtue in what I've done, as it is for myself in the long run. When you tell them, explain that I'm not a philanthropist— only a man of business in future. But before all things fair and straight. I mean to be fair to them and to the machinery, too. And to the machinery I look to make all our fortunes. I should have done a little more to start with—for the people I mean; but the death duties are the devil. In fact, I start crippled by them. Tell them that and make them understand what they mean on an enterprise of this sort."

They went through the works together presently and it was clear that the new owner fixed a gulf between the past and the future. His old easy manner had vanished—and, while friendly enough, he made it quite clear that a vast alteration had come into his mind and manners. It seemed incredible that six months before Raymond was chaffing the girls and bringing them fruit. He called them by their names as of yore; but they knew in a moment he had moved with his fortunes and their own manner instinctively altered.

He was kind and pleasant, but far more interested in their work than them; and they drew conclusions from the fact. They judged his attitude with gloom and were the more agreeably surprised when they learned what advantages had been planned for them. Levi Baggs and Benny Cogle, the engineman, grumbled that more was not done; but the women, who judged Raymond from his treatment of Sabina and hoped nothing from his old promises, were gratified and astonished at what they heard. An improved sentiment towards the new master was manifest. The instinct to judge people at your own tribunal awoke, and while Sally Groves and old Mrs. Chick held out for morals, the other women did not. Already they had realised that the idle youth they could answer was gone. And with him had gone the young man who amused himself with a spinner. Of course, he could not be expected to marry Sabina. Such things did not happen out of story books; and if you tried to be too clever for your situation, this was the sort of thing that befell you.

So argued Nancy Buckler and Mercy Gale; nor did Sarah Northover much differ from them. None had been fiercer for Sabina than Nancy, yet her opinion, before the spectacle of Raymond himself and after she heard his intentions, was modified. To see him so alert, so aloof from the girls, translated to a higher interest, had altered Nancy. Despite her asperity and apparent independence of thought, her mind was servile, as the ignorant mind is bound to be. She paid the unconscious deference of weakness to power.

Raymond lunched at North Hill House—now his property. He had not seen Waldron since the great change in his fortunes and Arthur, with the rest, was quick to perceive the difference. They met in friendship and Estelle kissed Raymond as she was accustomed to do; but the alteration in him, while missed by her, was soon apparent to her father. It took the shape of a more direct and definite method of thinking. Raymond no longer uttered his opinions inconsiderately, as though confessing they were worthless even while he spoke them. He weighed his words, jested far less often, and did not turn serious subjects into laughter.

Waldron suggested certain things to his new landlord that he desired should be done; but he was amused in secret that some work Raymond had blamed Daniel for not doing, he now refused to do himself.

"I've no objection, old chap—none at all. The other points you raise I shall carry out at my own expense; but the French window in the drawing-room, while an excellent addition to the room, is not a necessity. So you must do that yourself." Thus he spoke and Arthur agreed.

Estelle only found him unchanged. Before her he was always jovial and happy. He liked to hear her talk and listen to her budding theories of life and pretty dreams of what the world ought to be, if people would only take a little more trouble for other people. But Estelle was painfully direct. She thought for herself and had not yet learned to hide her ideas, modify their shapes, or muffle their outlines when presenting them to another person. Mr. Churchouse and her father were responsible for this. They encouraged her directness and, while knowing that she outraged opinion sometimes, could not bring themselves to warn her, or stain the frankness of her views, with the caution that good manners require thought should not go nude.

Now the peril of Estelle's principles appeared when lunch was finished and the servants had withdrawn.

"I didn't speak before Lucy and Agnes," she said, "because they might talk about it afterwards."

"Bless me! How cunning she's getting!" laughed Raymond. But he did not laugh long. Estelle handed him his coffee and lit a match for his cigar; while Arthur, guessing what was coming, resigned himself helplessly to the storm.

"Sabina is fearfully unhappy, Ray. She loves you so much, and I hope you will change your mind and marry her after all, because if you do, she'll love her baby, too, and look forward to it very much. But if you don't, she'll hate her baby. And it would be a dreadful thing for the poor little baby to come into the world hated."

To Waldron's intense relief Raymond showed no annoyance whatever. He was gentle and smiled at Estelle.

"So it would, Chicky—it would be a dreadful thing for a baby to come into the world hated. But don't you worry. Nobody's going to hate it."

"I'll tell Sabina that. Sabina's sure to have a nice baby, because she's so nice herself."

"Sure to. And I shall be a very good friend to the baby without marrying Sabina."

"If she knows that, it ought to comfort her," declared Estelle. "And I shall be a great friend to it, too."

Her father bade the child be off on an errand presently and expressed his regrets to the guest when she was gone.

"Awfully sorry, old chap, but she's so unearthly and simple; and though I've often told myself to preach to her, I never can quite do it."

"Never do. She'll learn to hide her thoughts soon enough. Nothing she can say would annoy me. For that matter she's only saying what a great many other people are thinking and haven't the pluck to say. The truth is this, Arthur; when I was a poor man I was a weak man, and I should have married Sabina and we should both have had a hell of a life, no doubt. Now the death of Daniel has made me a strong man, and I'm not doing wrong as the result; I'm doing right. I can afford to do right and not mind the consequences. And the truth about life is that half the people who do wrong, only do it because they can't afford to do right."

"That's a comforting doctrine—for the poor."

"It's like this. Sabina is a very dear girl, and I loved her tremendously, and if she'd gone on being the same afterwards, I should have married her. But she changed, and I saw that we could never be really happy together as man and wife. There are things in her that would have ruined my temper, and there are things in me she would have got to hate more and more. As a matter of brutal fact, Arthur, she got to dislike me long before things came to a climax. She had to hide it, because, from her standpoint and her silly mother's, marriage is the only sort of salvation. Whereas for us it would have been damnation. It's very simple; she's got to think as I think and then she'll be all right."

"You can't make people think your way, if they prefer to think their own."

"It's merely the line of least resistance and what will pay her best. I want you to grasp the fact that she had ceased to like me before there was any reason why she should cease to like me. I'll swear she had. My first thought and intention, when I heard what had happened, was to marry her right away. And what changed my feeling about it, and showed me devilish clear it would be a mistake, was Sabina herself. We needn't go over that. But I'm not going to marry her now under any circumstances whatever, while recognising very clearly my duty to her and the child. And though you may say it's humbug, I'm thinking quite as much for her as myself when I say this."

"I don't presume to judge. You're not a humbug—no good sportsman is in my experience. If you do everything right for the child, I suppose the world has no reason to criticise."

"As long as I'm right with myself, I don't care one button what the world says, Arthur. There's nothing quicker opens your eyes, or helps you to take larger views, than independence."

"I see that."

"All the same, it's a steadying thing if you're honest and have got brains in your head. People thought I was a shallow, easy, good-natured and good-for-nothing fool six months ago. Well, they thought wrong. But don't think I'm pleased with myself, or any nonsense of that sort. Only a fool is pleased with himself. I've wasted my life till now, because I had no ambition. Now I'm beginning it and trying to get things into their proper perspective. When I had no responsibilities, I was irresponsible. Now they've come, I'm stringing myself up to meet them."

"Life's given you your chance."

"Exactly; and I hope to show I can take it. But I'm not going to start by making an ass of myself to please a few old women."

"Where shall you live?"

"Nowhere in particular for the minute. I shall roam and see all that's being done in my business and take John Best with me for a while. Then it depends. Perhaps, if things go as I expect about machinery, I shall ask you for a corner again in the autumn."

Mr. Waldron nodded; but he was not finding himself in complete agreement with Raymond.

"Always welcome," he said.

"Perhaps you'd rather not? Well—see how things go. Estelle may bar me. I'm at Bridport to-night and return to London to-morrow. But I shall be back again in a week."

"Shall you play any cricket this summer?"

"I should like to if I have time; but it's very improbable. I'm not going to chuck sport though. Next year I may have more leisure."

"You're at 'The Seven Stars,' I hear—haven't forgiven Dick Gurd he tells me."

"Did we quarrel? I forget. Seems funny to think I had enough time on my hands to wrangle with an innkeeper. But I like Missis Northover's. It's quiet."

"Shall I come in and dine this evening?"

"Wait till I'm back again. I've got to talk to my Aunt Jenny to-night. She's one of the old brigade, but I'm hoping to make her see sense."

"When sense clashes with religion, old man, nobody sees sense. I'm afraid your opinions won't entirely commend themselves to Miss Ironsyde."

"Probably not. I quite realise that I shall have to exercise the virtue of patience at Bridport and Bridetown for a year or two. But while I've got you for a friend, Arthur, I'm not going to bother."

Waldron marked the imperious changes and felt somewhat bewildered. Raymond left him not a little to think about, and when the younger had ridden off, Arthur strolled afield with his thoughts and strove to bring order into them. He felt in a vague sort of way that he had been talking to a stranger, and his hope, if he experienced a hope, was that the new master of the Mill might not take himself too seriously. "People who do that are invariably one-sided," thought Waldron.

Upon Ironsyde's attitude and intentions with regard to Sabina, he also reflected uneasily. What Raymond had declared sounded all right, yet Arthur could not break with old rooted opinions and the general view of conduct embodied in his favourite word. Was it "sporting"? And more important still, was it true? Had Ironsyde arrived at his determination from honest conviction, or thanks to the force of changed circumstances? Mr. Waldron gave his friend the benefit of the doubt.

"One must remember that he is a good sportsman," he reflected, "and he can't have enough brains to make him a bad sportsman."

For the thinker had found within his experience, that those who despised sport, too often despised also the simple ethics that he associated with sportsmanship. In fact, Arthur, after one or two painful experiences, had explicitly declared that big brains often went hand in hand with a doubtful sense of honour. He had also, of course, known numerous examples of another sort of dangerous people who assumed the name and distinction of "sportsman" as a garment to hide their true activities and unworthy selves.

CHAPTER XXVIII

CLASH OF OPINIONS

Mr. Job Legg, with a persistence inspired by private purpose, continued to impress upon Nelly Northover the radical truth that in this world you cannot have anything for nothing. He varied the precept sometimes, and reminded her that we must not hope to have our cake and eat it too; and closer relations with Richard Gurd served to impress upon Mrs. Northover the value of these verities. Nor did she resent them from Mr. Legg. He had preserved an attitude of manly resignation under his supreme disappointment. He was patient, uncomplaining and self-controlled. He did not immediately give notice of departure, but, for the present, continued to do his duty with customary thoroughness. He showed himself a most tactful man. New virtues were manifested in the light of the misfortune that had overtaken him. Affliction and reverse seemed to make him shine the brighter. Nelly could hardly understand it. Had she not regarded his character as one of obvious simplicity and incapable of guile, she might have felt suspicious of any male who behaved with such exemplary distinction under the circumstances.

It was, of course, clear that the mistress of 'The Seven Stars' could not become Mr. Gurd's partner and continue to reign over her own constellation as of old. Yet Nelly did not readily accept a fact so obvious, even under Mr. Legg's reiterated admonitions. She felt wayward—almost wilful about it: and there came an evening when Richard dropped in for his usual half hour of courting to find her in such a frame of mind. Humour on his part had saved the situation; but he lacked humour, and while Nelly, even as she spoke, knew she was talking nonsense and only waited his reminder of the inevitable in a friendly spirit, yet, when the reminder came, it was couched in words so forcible and so direct, that for a parlous moment her own sense of humour broke down.

The initial error was Mr. Gurd's. The elasticity of youth, both mental and physical, had departed from him, and he took her remarks, uttered more in mischief than in earnest, with too much gravity, not perceiving that Nelly herself was in a woman's mood and merely uttering absurdities that he might contradict her. She was ready enough to climb down from her impossible attitude; but Richard abruptly threw her down; which unchivalrous action wounded Mrs. Northover to the quick and begat in her an obstinate and rebellious determination to climb up again.

"I'm looking on ahead," she began, while they sat in her parlour together. "This is a great upheaval, Richard, and I'm just beginning to feel how great. I'm wondering all manner of things. Will you be so happy and comfortable along with me, at 'The Seven Stars,' as you are at 'The Tiger'? You must put that to yourself, you know."

It was so absurd an assumption, that she expected his laughter; and if he had laughed and answered with inspiration, no harm could have come of it. But Richard felt annoyed rather than amused. The suggestion seemed to show that Mrs. Northover was a fool—the last thing he bargained for. He exhibited contempt. Indeed, he snorted in a manner almost insulting.

"Woman comes to man, I believe, not man to woman," he said.

"That is so," she admitted with a touch of colour in her cheeks at his attitude, "but you must think all round it—which you haven't done yet, seemingly."

Then Richard laughed—too late; for a laugh may lose all its value if the right moment be missed.

"Where's the fun?" she asked. "I thought, of course, that you'd be business-like as well as lover-like and would see 'The Seven Stars' had got more to it than 'The Tiger.'"

Even now the situation might have been saved. The very immensity of her claim rendered it ridiculous; but Richard was too astonished to guess an utterance so hyperbolic had been made to offer him an easy victory.

"You thought that, Nelly? 'The Seven Stars' more to it than 'The Tiger'?"

"Surely!"

"Because you get a few tea-parties and old women at nine-pence a head on your little bit of grass?"

A counter so terrific destroyed the last glimmering hope of a peaceful situation, and Mrs. Northover perceived this first.

"It's war then?" she said. "So perhaps you'll tell me what you mean by my little bit of grass. Not the finest pleasure gardens in Bridport, I suppose?"

"Be damned if this ain't the funniest thing I've ever heard," he answered.

"You never was one to see a joke, we all know; and if that's the funniest thing you ever heard, you ain't heard many. And you'll forgive me, please, if I tell you there's nothing funny in my speaking about my pleasure gardens, though it does sound a bit funny to hear 'em called 'a bit of grass' by a man that's got nothing but a few apple trees, past bearing, and a strip of potatoes and weeds, and a fowl-run. But, as you've got no use for a garden, perhaps you'll remember the inn yard, and how many hosses you can put up, and how many I can."

"It's the number of hosses that comes—not the number you put up," he answered; "and if you want to tell me you've often obliged with a spare space in your yard, perhaps I may remind you that you generally got quite as good as you gave. But be that as it will, the point lies in one simple question, and I ask you if you really thought, as a woman nearer sixty than fifty and with credit for sense, that I was going to chuck 'The Tiger' and coming over to your shop. Did you really think that?"

Not for an instant had she thought it; but the time was inappropriate for saying so. She might have confessed the truth in the past; she might confess the truth in the future; she was not going to do so at present. He should have a stab for his stab.

"You've often told me I was the sensiblest woman in Dorset, Richard, and being that, I naturally thought you'd drop your bar-loafers' place and come over to me—and glad to come."

"Good God!" he said, and stared at her with open nostrils, from which indignant air exploded in gusts.

She began to make peace from that moment, feeling that the limit had been reached. Indeed she was rather anxious. The thrust appeared to be mortal. Mr. Gurd rolled in his chair, and after his oath, could find no further words.

She declared sorrow.

"There—forgive me—I didn't mean to say that. 'Tis a crying shame to see two old people dressing one another down this way. I'm sorry if I hurt your feelings, but don't forget you've properly trampled on mine. My pleasure grounds are my lifeblood you might say; and you knew it."

"You needn't apologise now. 'The Tiger' a bar-loafers' place! The centre of all high-class sport in the district a bar-loafers' place! Well, well! No wonder you thought I'd be glad to come and live at 'The Seven Stars'!"

"I didn't really," she confessed. "I knew very well you wouldn't; but I had to say it. The words just flashed out. And if I'd remembered a joke was nothing to you, I might have thought twice."

"I laughed, however."

"Yes, you laughed, I grant—what you can do in that direction, which ain't much."

Mr. Gurd rose to his full height.

"Well, that lets me out," he said. "We'd better turn this over in a forgiving spirit; and since you say you're sorry, I won't be behind you, though my words was whips to your scorpions and you can't deny it."

"We'll meet again in a week," said Mrs. Northover.

"Make it a fortnight," he suggested.

"No—say a month," she answered—"or six weeks."

Then it was Richard's turn to feel the future in danger. But he had no intention to eat humble pie that evening.

"A month then. But one point I wish to make bitter clear, Nelly. If you marry me, you come to 'The Tiger.'"

"So it seems."

"Yes—bar-loafers, or no bar-loafers."

"I'll bear it in mind, Richard."

The leave-taking lacked affection and they parted with full hearts. Each was smarting under consciousness of the other's failure in nice feeling; each was amazed as at a revelation. Richard kept his mouth shut concerning this interview, for he was proud and did not like to confess even to himself that he stood on the verge of disaster; but Mrs. Northover held a familiar within her gates, and she did not hesitate to lay the course of the adventure before Job Legg.

"The world is full of surprises," said Nelly, "and you never know, when you begin talking, where the gift of speech will land you. And if you're dealing with a man who can't take a bit of fun and can't keep his eyes on his tongue and his temper at the same time, trouble will often happen."

She told the story with honesty and did not exaggerate; but Mr. Legg supported her and held that such a self-respecting woman could have done and said no less. He declared that Richard Gurd had brought the misfortune on himself, and feared that the innkeeper's display revealed a poor understanding of female nature.

"It isn't as if you was a difficult and notorious sort of woman," explained Job; "for then the man might have reason on his side; but to misunderstand you and overlook your playful touch—that shows he's got a low order of brain; because you always speak clearly. Your word is as good as your bond and none can question your judgment."

He proceeded to examine the argument earnestly and had just proved that Mrs. Northover was well within her right to set 'The Seven Stars' above 'The Tiger,' when Raymond Ironsyde entered.

He returned from dining with his aunt, and an interview now concluded was of very painful and far-reaching significance. For they had not agreed, and Miss Ironsyde proved no more able to convince her nephew than was he, to make her see his purpose combined truest wisdom and humanity.

They talked after dinner and she invited him to justify his conduct if he could, before hearing her opinions and intentions. He replied at once and she found his arguments and reasons all arrayed and ready to his tongue. He spoke clearly and stated his case in very lucid language; but he irritated her by showing that his mind was entirely closed to argument and that he was not prepared to be influenced in any sort of way. Her power had vanished now and she saw how only her power, not her persuasion, had won Raymond before his brother's death. He spoke with utmost plainness and did not spare himself in the least.

"I've been wrong," he said, "but I'm going to try and be right in the future. I did a foolish thing and fell in love with a good and clever girl. Once in love, of course, everything was bent and deflected to be seen through that medium and I believed that nothing else mattered or ever would. Then came the sequel, and being powerless to resist, I was going to marry. For some cowardly reason I funked poverty, and the thought of escaping it made me agree to marry Sabina, knowing all the time it must prove a failure. That was my second big mistake, and the third was asking her to come and live with me without marrying her. I suggested that, because I wanted her and felt very keen about the child. I ought not to have thought of such a thing. It wasn't fair to her—I quite see that."

"Can anything be fair to her short of marriage?"

"Not from her point of view, Aunt Jenny."

"And what other point of view, in keeping with honour and religion, exists?"

"As to religion, I'm without it and so much the freer. I don't want to pretend anything I don't feel. I shall always be very sorry, indeed, for what I did; but I'm not going to wreck my life by marrying Sabina."

"What about her life?"

"If she will trust her life to me, I shall do all in my power to make it a happy and easy life. I want the child to be a success. I know it will grow up a reproach to me and all that sort of thing in the opinion of many people; but that won't trouble me half as much as my own regrets. I've not done anything that puts me beyond the, pale of humanity—nor has Sabina; and if she can keep her nerve and go on with her life, it ought to be all right for her, presently."

"A very cynical attitude and I wish I could change it, Raymond. You've lost your self-respect and you know you've done a wrong thing. Can't you see that you'll always suffer it if you take no steps to right it? You are a man of feeling, and power can't lessen your feeling. Every time you see that child, you will know that you have brought a living soul into the world cruelly handicapped by your deliberate will."

"That's not a fair argument," he answered. "If our rotten laws handicap the baby, it will be my object to nullify the handicap to the best of my ability. The laws won't come between me and my child, any more than they came between me and my passion. I'm not the sort to hide behind the mean English law of the natural child. But I'm not going to let that law bully me into marriage with Sabina. I've got to think of myself as well as other people. I won't say, what's true—that if Sabina married me she wouldn't be happy in the long run; but I will say that I know I shouldn't be, and I'm not prepared to pay any penalty whatever for what I did, beyond the penalty of my own regrets."

"If you rule religion out and think you can escape and keep your honour, I don't know what to say," she answered. "For my part I believe Sabina would make you a very good and loving wife. And don't fancy, if you refuse her what faithfully you promised her, she will be content with less."

"That's her look out. You won't be wise, Aunt Jenny, to influence her against a fair and generous offer. I want her to live a good life, and I don't want our past love-making to ruin that life, or our child to ruin that life. If she's going to pose as a martyr, I can't help it. That's the side of her that wrecked the show, as a matter of fact, and made it very clear to me that we shouldn't be a happy married couple."

"Self-preservation is a law of nature. She only did what any girl would have done in trying to find friends to save her from threatened disaster."

"Well, I dare say it was natural to her to take that line, and it was equally natural to me to resent it. At any rate we know where we stand now. Tell me if there's anything else."

"I only warn you that she will accept no benefits of any kind from you, Raymond. And who shall blame her?"

"That's entirely her affair, of course. I can't do more than admit my responsibilities and declare my interest in her future."

"She will throw your interest back in your face and teach her child to despise you, as she does."

"How d'you know that, Aunt Jenny?"

"Because she's a proud woman. And because she would lose the friendship of all proud women and clean thinking men if she condoned what you intend to do. It's horrible to see you turned from a simple, stupid, but honourable boy, into a hard, selfish, irreligious man—and all the result of being rich. I should never have thought it could have made such a dreadful difference so quickly. But I have not changed, Raymond. And I tell you this: if you don't marry Sabina; if you don't see that only so can you hold up your head as an honest man and a respectable member of society, worthy of your class and your family, then, I, for one, can have no more to do with you. I mean it."

"I'm sorry you say that. You've been my guardian angel in a way and I've a million things to thank you for from my childhood. It would be a great grief to me, Aunt Jenny, if you allowed a difference of opinion to make you take such a line. I hope you'll think differently."

"I shall not," she said. "I have not told you this on the spur of the moment, or before I had thought it out very fully and very painfully. But if you do this outrageous thing, I will never be your aunt any more, Raymond, and never wish to see you again as long as I live. You know me; I'm not hysterical, or silly, or even sentimental; but I'm jealous for your father's name—and your brother's. You know where duty and honour and solemn obligation point. There is no reason whatever why you should shirk your duty, or sully your honour; but if you do, I decline to have any further dealings with you."

He rose to go.

"That's definite and clear. Good-bye, Aunt Jenny."

"Good-bye," she said. "And may God guide you to recall that 'good-bye,' nephew."

Then he went back to 'The Seven Stars,' and wondered as he walked, how the new outlook had shrunk up this old woman too, and made one, who bulked so largely in his life of old, now appear as of no account whatever. He was heartily sorry she should have taken so unreasonable a course; but he grieved more for her sake than his own. She was growing old. She would lack his company in the time to come, and her heart was too warm to endure this alienation without much pain.

He suspected that if Sabina's future course of action satisfied Miss Ironsyde, she would be friendly to her and the child and, in time, possibly win some pleasure from them.

CHAPTER XXIX

THE BUNCH OF GRAPES

Raymond proceeded with his business at Bridetown oblivious of persons and personalities. He puzzled those who were prepared to be his enemies, for it seemed he was becoming as impersonal as the spinning machines, and one cannot quarrel with a machine.

It appeared that he was to be numbered with those who begin badly and retrieve the situation afterwards. So, at least, hoped Ernest Churchouse, yet, since the old man was called to witness and endure a part of the sorrows of Sabina and her mother, it demanded large faith on his part to anticipate brighter times. He clung to it that Raymond would yet marry Sabina, and he regretted that when the young man actually offered to see Sabina, she refused to see him. For this happened. He came to stop at North Hill House for two months, while certain experts were inspecting the works, and during this time he wished to visit 'The Magnolias' and talk with Sabina, but she declined.

The very active hate that he had awakened sank gradually to smouldering fires of bitter resentment and contempt. She spoke openly of destroying their babe when it should be born.

Then the event happened and Sabina became the mother of a man child.

Raymond was still with Arthur Waldron when Estelle brought the news, and the men discussed it.

"I hope she'll be reasonable now," said Ironsyde. "It bothered me when she refused to see me, because you can't oppose reason to stupidity of that sort. If she's going to take my aunt's line, of course, I'm done, and shall be powerless to help her. I spoke to Uncle Ernest about it two days ago. He says that it will have to be marriage, or nothing, and seemed to think that would move me to marriage! Some people can't understand plain English. But why should she cut off her nose to spite her face and refuse my friendship and help because I won't marry her?"

"She's that sort, I suppose. Of course, plenty of women would do the same."

"I'm not convinced it's Sabina really who is doing this. That's why I wanted to see her. Very likely Aunt Jenny is inspiring such a silly attitude, or her mother. They may think if she's firm I may yield. They don't seem to realise that love's as dead as a doornail now. But my duty is clear enough and they can't prevent me from doing it, I imagine."

"You want to be sporting to the child, of course."

"And to the mother of the child. Damn it all, I'm made of flesh and blood. I'm not a fiend. But with women, if you have a grain of common-sense and reasoning power, you become a fiend the moment there's a row. I want Sabina and my child to have a good show in the world, Arthur."

"Well, you must let her know it."

"I'll see her, presently. I'll take no denial about that. It may be a pious plot really, for religious people don't care how they intrigue, if they can bring off what they want to happen. It was very strange she refused to see me. Perhaps they never told her that I offered to come."

"Yes, they did, because Estelle heard Churchouse tell her. Estelle was with her at the time, and she said she was so sorry when Sabina refused. It may have been because she was ill, of course."

"I must see her before I go away, anyway. If they've been poisoning her mind against me, I must put it right."

"You're a rum 'un! Can't you see what this means to her? You talk as if she'd no grievance, and as though it was all a matter of course and an everyday thing."

"So it is, for that matter. However, there's no reason for you to bother about it. I quite recognise what it is to be a father, and the obligations. But because I happen to be a father, is no reason why I should be asked to do impossibilities. Because you've made a fool of yourself once is no reason why you should again. By good chance I've had unexpected luck in life and things have fallen out amazingly well—and I'm very willing indeed that other people should share my good luck and good fortune. I mean that they shall. But I'm not going to negative my good fortune by doing an imbecile thing."

"As long as you're sporting I've got no quarrel with you," declared Waldron. "I'm not very clever myself, but I can see that if they won't let you do what you want to do, it's not your fault. If they refuse to let you play the game— but, of course, you must grant the game looks different from their point of view. No doubt they think you're not playing the game. A woman's naturally not such a sporting animal as a man, and what we think is straight, she often doesn't appreciate, and what she thinks is straight we often know is crooked. Women, in fact, are more like the other nations which, with all their excellent qualities, don't know what 'sporting' means."

"I mean to do right," answered Raymond, "and probably I'm strong enough to make them see it and wear them down, presently. I'm really only concerned about Sabina and her child. The rest, and what they think and what they don't think, matter nothing. She may listen to reason when she's well again."

Two days later Raymond received a box from London and showed Estelle an amazing bunch of Muscat grapes, destined for Sabina.

"She always liked grapes," he said, "and these are as good as any in the world at this moment."

On his way to the Mill he left the grapes at 'The Magnolias,' and spoke a moment with Mr. Churchouse.

"She is making an excellent recovery," said Ernest, "and I am hoping that, presently, the maternal instinct will assert itself. I do everything to encourage it. But, of course, when conditions are abnormal, results must be abnormal. She's a very fine and brave woman and worthy of supreme admiration. And worthy of far better and more manly treatment than she has received from you. But you know that very well, Raymond. Owing to the complexities created by civilisation clashing with nature, we get much needless pain in the world. But a reasonable being should have recognised the situation, as you did not, and realise that we have no right to obey nature if we know at the same time we are flouting civilisation. You think you're doing right by considering Sabina's future. You are a gross materialist, Raymond, and the end of that is always dust and ashes and defeated hopes. I won't bring religion into it, because that wouldn't carry weight with you; but I bring justice into it and your debt to the social order, that has made you what you are and to which you owe everything. You have done a grave and wicked wrong to the new-born atom of life in this house, and though it is now too late wholly to right that wrong, much might yet be done. I blame you, but I hope for you—I still hope for you."

He took the grapes, and Raymond, somewhat staggered by this challenge, found himself not ready to answer it.

"We'll have a talk some evening, Uncle Ernest," he answered. "I don't expect your generation to see this thing from my point of view. It's reasonable you shouldn't, because you can't change; and it's also reasonable that I shouldn't see it from your point of view. If I'm material, I'm built so; and that won't prevent me from doing my duty."

"I would talk the hands round the clock if I thought I could help you to see your duty with other eyes than your own," replied the old man. "I am quite ready to speak when you are to listen. And I shall begin by reminding you that you are a father. You expect Sabina to be a mother in the full meaning of that beautiful word; but a child must have a father also."

"I am willing to be a father."

"Yes, on your own values, which ignore the welfare of the community, justice to the next generation, and the respect you should entertain for yourself."

"Well, we'll thresh it out another time. You know I respect you very much, Uncle Ernest; and I'm sure you'll weigh my point of view and not let Aunt Jenny influence you."

"I have a series of duties before me," answered Mr. Churchouse; "and not least among them is to reconcile you and your aunt. That you should have broken with your sole remaining relative is heart-breaking."

"I'd be friends to-morrow; but you know her."

He went away to the works and Ernest took the grapes to Mrs. Dinnett.

"You'd better not let her have them, however, unless the doctor permits it," said Mr. Churchouse, whereupon, Mary, not trusting herself to speak, took the grapes and departed. The affront embodied in the fruit affected a mind much overwrought of late. She took the present to Sabina's room.

"There," she said. "He's sunk to sending that. I'd like to fling them in his face."

"Take them away. I can't touch them."

"Touch them! And poisoned as likely as not. A man that's committed his crimes would stick at nothing."

"He uses poison enough," said the young mother; "but only the poison he can use safely. It matters nothing to him if I live or die. No doubt he'd will me dead, and this child too, if he could; but seeing he can't, he cares nothing. He'll heap insult on injury, no doubt. He's made of clay coarse enough to do it. But when I'm well, I'll see him and make it clear, once for all."

"You say that now. But I hope you'll never see him, or breathe the same air with him."

"Once—when I'm strong. I don't want him to go on living his life without knowing what I'm thinking of him. I don't want him to think he can pose as a decent man again. I want him to know that the road-menders and road-sweepers are high above him."

"Don't you get in a passion. He knows all that well enough. He isn't deceiving himself any more than anybody else. All honest people know what he is—foul wretch. Yes, he's poisoned three lives, if no more, and they are yours and mine and that sleeping child's."

"He's ruined his aunt's life, too. She's thrown him over."

"That won't trouble him. War against women is what you'd expect. But please God, he'll be up against a man some day—then we shall see a different result. May the Almighty let me live long enough to see him in the gutter, where he belongs. I ask no more."

They poured their bitterness upon Raymond Ironsyde; then a thought came into Mary Dinnett's mind and she left Sabina. Judging the time, she put on her bonnet presently and walked out to the road whence Raymond would return from his work at the luncheon hour.

She stood beside the road at a stile that led into the fields, and as Raymond, deep in thought, passed her without looking up, he saw something cast at his feet and for a moment stood still. With a soft thud his bunch of grapes fell ruined in the dust before him and, starting back, he looked at the stile and saw Sabina's mother gazing at him red-faced and furious. Neither spoke. The woman's countenance told her hatred and loathing; the man shrugged his shoulders and, after one swift glance at her, proceeded on his way without quickening or slackening his stride.

He heard her spit behind him and found time to regret that a woman of Mary's calibre should be at Sabina's side. Such concentrated hate astonished him a little. There was no reason in it; nothing could be gained by it. This senseless act of a fool merely made him impatient. But he smiled before he reached North Hill House to think that but for the interposition of chance and fortune, this brainless old woman might have become his mother-in-law.

CHAPTER XXX

A TRIUMPH OF REASON

Mrs. Northover took care that her interrupted conversation with Job Legg should be completed; and he, too, was anxious, that she should know his position. But he realised the danger very fully and was circumspect in his criticism of Richard Gurd's attitude toward 'The Seven Stars.'

"For my part," said Job on the evening that preceded a very important event, "I still repeat that you have a right to consider we're higher class than 'The Tiger'; and to speak of the renowned garden as a 'bit of grass' was going much too far. It shows a wrong disposition, and it wasn't a gentlemanly thing, and if it weren't such a wicked falsehood, you might laugh at it for jealousy."

"Who ever would have thought the man jealous?" she asked.

"These failings will out," declared Mr. Legg. "And seeing you mean to take him, it is as well you know it."

She nodded rather gloomily.

"Your choice of words is above praise, I'm sure, Job," she said. "For such a simple and straightforward man, you've a wonderful knowledge of the human heart."

"Through tribulation I've come to it," he answered. "However, I'm here to help you, not talk about my own bitter disappointments. And very willing I am to help you when it can be done."

"D'you think you could speak to Richard for me, and put out the truth concerning 'The Seven Stars'?" she asked. But Mr. Legg, simple though he might be, was not as simple as that.

"No," he replied. "There's few things I wouldn't do for you, on the earth or in the waters under the earth, and I say that, even though you've turned me down after lifting the light of hope. But for me to see Gurd on this subject is impossible. It's far too delicate. Another man might, but not me, because he knows that I stand in the unfortunate position of the cast out. So if there's one man that can't go to Gurd and demand reparation on your account, I'm that man. In a calmer moment, you'll be the first to see it."

"I suppose that is so. He'd think, if you talked sense to him, you had an axe to grind and treat you according. You've suffered enough."

"I have without a doubt, and shall continue to do so," he answered her.

"I think just as much of you as ever I did notwithstanding," said Mrs. Northover. "And I'll go so far as to say that your simple goodness and calm sense under all circumstances might wear better in the long run than Richard's overbearing way and cruel conceit. Be honest, Job. Do you yourself think 'The Tiger' is a finer house and more famous than my place?"

Mr. Legg perceived very accurately where Nelly suffered most.

"This house," he declared, "have got the natural advantages and Gurd have got the pull in the matter of capital. My candid opinion, what I've come to after many years of careful thought on the subject, is that if we—I say 'we' from force of habit, though I'm in the outer darkness now—if we had a few hundred pounds spending on us and an advertisement to holiday people in the papers sometimes, then in six months we shouldn't hear any more about 'The Tiger.' Cash, spent by the hand of a master on 'The Seven Stars,' would lift us into a different house and we should soon be known to cater for a class that wouldn't recognise 'The Tiger.' What we want is a bit of gold and white paint before next summer and all those delicate marks about the place that women understand and value. I've often thought that a new sign for example, with seven golden stars on a sky blue background, and perhaps even a flagstaff in the pleasure grounds, with our own flag flying upon it, would, as it were, widen the gulf between him and you. But, of course, that was before these things happened, and when I was thinking, day and night you may say, how to catch the custom."

Mrs. Northover sighed.

"In another man, it would be craft to say such clever things," she answered; "but, in you, I know it's just simple goodness of heart and Christian fellowship. 'Tis amazing how we think alike."

"Not now," he corrected her. "Too late now. I wish to God we had thought alike; for then, instead of looking at my money as I'd look at a pile of road scrapings, I should see it with very different eyes. My windfall would have been poured out here in such a fashion that the people would have wondered. This place is my life, in a manner of speaking. My earthly life, I mean; which you may say is ended now. I was, in my own opinion, as much a part of 'The Seven Stars,' as the beer engine. And when uncle died this was my first thought. Or I should say my second, because in the natural course of events, you were the first."

She sighed again and Mr. Legg left this delicate ground.

"If the man can only be brought to see he's wrong about his fanciful opinion of 'The Tiger,' all may go right for you," he continued. "I don't care for his feelings over-much, but your peace of mind I do consider. At present he dares to think you're a silly woman whose goose is a swan. That's very disorderly coming from the man who's going to marry you. Therefore you must get some clear-sighted person to open his eyes, and make it bitter clear to him that 'The Tiger' never was and never will be a place to draw nice minds and the female element like us."

"There's nobody could put it to him better than you," she said.

"At another time, perhaps—not now. I'm not clever, Nelly; but I'm too clever to edge in between a man like Gurd and his future wife. If we stood different, then nobody would open his mouth quicker than me."

"We may stand different yet," she answered. "There was a good deal of passion when we met, and not the sort of passion you expect between lovers, either."

"If that is so," he answered, "then we can only leave it for the future. But this I'll certainly say: if you tell me presently that you're free to the nation once more and have changed your mind about Richard, then I'd very soon let him know there's a gulf fixed between 'The Tiger' and 'The Seven Stars'; and if you said the word, he'd see that gulf getting broader and broader under his living eyes."

"I'd have overlooked most anything but what he actually said," she declared. "But to strike at the garden—However, I'll see him, and if I find he's feeling like what I am, it's quite in human reason that we may undo the past before it's too late."

"And always remember it's his own will you shall live at 'The Tiger,'" warned Job. "Excuse my bluntness in reminding you of his words; which, no doubt, you committed to memory long before you told me about 'em; but the point lies there. You can't be in two places at once, and so sure as you sign yourself 'Gurd,' you'll sell, or sublet 'The Seven Stars.' In fact, even a simple brain like mine can see you'll sell, for Richard will never be content to let you serve two masters; and where the treasure is, there will the heart be also. And to one of your delicate feelings, to know strange hands are in this house, and strange things being done, and liberties taken with the edifice and the garden, very likely. But I don't want to paint any such dreadful picture as that, and, of course, if you honestly love Richard, though you're the first woman that ever could—then enough said."

"The question is whether he loves me. However, I'll turn it over; and no doubt he will," she answered. "I see him to-morrow."

"And don't leave anything uncertain, if I may advise," concluded Mr. Legg. "I speak as a child in these matters; but, if he's looking at this thing same as you are, and if you both feel you'd be finer ornaments of society apart, than married, all I say is don't let any false manhood on his part, or modesty on yours, keep you to it. Better be good neighbours than bad partners. And if I've said too much, God forgive me."

Fired by these opinions Nelly went to her meeting with Richard and the first words uttered by Mr. Gurd sent a ray of warmth to her heart, for it seemed he also had reviewed the situation in a manner worthy of his high intelligence.

But he approached the subject uneasily and Mrs. Northover was too much a woman to rescue him at once. She had been through a good deal and felt it fair that the master of 'The Tiger' should also suffer.

"It's borne in upon me," he said, after some generalities and vague hopes that Nelly was well, "that, perhaps, there's no smoke without fire, as the saying is."

"Meaning what?" asked she.

"Meaning, that though we flared up a bit and forgot what we owe to ourselves, there must have been a reason for so much feeling."

"There certainly was."

"We needn't go back over the details; but you may be sure there must have lurked more behind our row than just a difference of opinion. People don't get properly hot with each other unless there's a reason, Nelly, and I'm beginning to fear that the reason lies deeper than we thought."

He waited for her to speak; but she did not.

"You mustn't think me shifty, or anything of that kind; but I do feel, where there was such a lot of smoke and us separated all these weeks, and none the worse for separation apparently, that, if we was to take the step—in a word, it's come over me stronger and stronger that we might do well to weigh what we're going to do in the balance before we do it."

Her delight knew no bounds. But still she did not reply, and Mr. Gurd began to grow red.

"If, by your silence, you mean that I'm cutting a poor figure before you, and you think I want to be off our bargain, you're wrong," he said. "Your mind ought to move quicker and I don't mind telling you so. I'm not off my bargain, because I'm a man of honour, and my word, given to man, woman or child, is kept. And if you don't know that, you're the only party in Bridport that don't. But I say again, there's two sides to it, and look before you leap, though not a maxim women are very addicted to following, is a good rule for all that. So I'll ask you how the land lies, if you please. You've turned this over same as me; and I'll be obliged if you'll tell me how you're viewing it."

"In other words you've changed your mind?"

"My mind can wait. I may have done so, or I may not; but to change my mind ain't to change my word, so you need have no anxiety on that account."

"Far from being anxious," answered Mrs. Northover, "I never felt so light-hearted since I was a girl, Richard. For why? My name for honest dealing is as high as yours, I believe, and if you'd come back to me and asked for bygones to be bygones, I should have struggled with it, same as you meant to do. But, seeing you're shaken, I'm pleased to tell, that I'm shaken also. In fact, 'shaken' isn't a strong enough word. I'm thankful to Heaven you don't want to go on with it, because, more don't I."

"If anything could make me still wish to take you, it's to hear such wisdom," declared Mr. Gurd, after a noisy expiration of thanksgiving. "I might have known you wasn't behind me in brain power, and I might have felt you'd be bound to see this quite as quick as me, if not quicker. And I'm sure nothing could make me think higher of you than to hear these comforting words."

Mrs. Northover used an aphorism from Mr. Legg.

"Our only fault was not to see each other's cleverness," she said, "or to think for a moment, after what passed between us, we could marry without loss of self-respect. It's a lot better, Richard, to be good neighbours than bad partners. And good neighbours we always have been and shall be; and whether we'd be good partners or not is no matter; we won't run the risk."

"God bless you!" he answered. "Then we part true friends, and if anything could make me feel more friendly than I always have felt, it is your high-mindedness, Nelly. For high-mindedness there never was your equal. And if many and many a young couple, that flies together and then feels the call to fly apart again, could only approach the tender subject with your fair sight and high reasoning powers, it would be a happier world."

"There's only one thing left," concluded Mrs. Northover, "and that's to let the public know we've changed our minds. With small people, that wouldn't matter; but with us, we can't forget we've been on the centre of the stage lately; and it would never do to let the people suppose that we had quarrelled, or sunk to anything vulgar."

"Leave it to me," he answered. "It only calls for a light hand. I shall pass it off with one of my jokes, and then people will treat it in a laughing spirit and not brood over it. Folk are quick to take a man's own view on everything concerning himself if he's got the art to convince."

"We'll say that more marriages are made on the tongues of outsiders than ever come to be celebrated in church," suggested Mrs. Northover, "and then people will begin to doubt if it wasn't all nonsense from the first."

"And they won't be far wrong if they do. It was nonsense; and if we say so in the public ear, none will dare to doubt it."

CHAPTER XXXI

THE OFFER DECLINED

Estelle talked to Raymond and endeavoured to interest him in Sabina's child.

"Everybody who understands babies says that he's a lovely and perfect one," declared Estelle. "I hope you're going to look at him before you go away, because he's yours. And I believe he will be like you, some day. Do the colours of babies' eyes change, like kittens' eyes, Ray?"

"Haven't the slightest idea," he answered. "You may be quite sure I shall take care of it, Estelle, and see that it has everything it wants."

"Somehow they're not pleased with you all the same," she answered. "I don't understand about it, but they evidently feel that you ought to have married Sabina. I suppose you're not properly his father if you don't marry her?"

"That's nonsense, Estelle. I'm quite properly his father, and I'm going to be a jolly good father too. But I don't want to be married. I don't believe in it."

"If Sabina knew you were going to love him and be good to him, she would be happier, I hope."

"I'm going to see her presently," he said.

"And see the baby?"

"Plenty of time for that."

"There's time, of course, Ray. But he's changing. He's five weeks old to-morrow, and I can see great changes. He can just begin to laugh now. Things amuse him we don't know. I expect babies are like dogs and can see what we can't."

"I'll look at him if Sabina likes."

"Of course she'll like. It's rather horrid of you, in a way, being able to go on with your work for so many weeks without looking at him. It's really rather a slight on Sabina, Ray. If I'd had a baby, and his father wouldn't look at him for week after week, I should be vexed. And so is Sabina."

"Next time you see her, ask her to name a day and I'll go whenever she likes."

Estelle was delighted.

"That's lovely of you and it will cheer her up very much, for certain," she answered. Then she ran away, for to arrange such a meeting seemed the most desirable thing in the world to her at that moment. To Sabina she went as fast as her legs could take her, and appreciating that he had sent this guileless messenger to ensure a meeting without preliminaries and without prejudice, Sabina hid her feelings and specified a time on the following day.

"If he'll come to see me to-morrow in the dinner-hour, that will be best. I'll be alone after twelve o'clock."

"You'll show him the baby, won't you, Sabina?"

"He won't want to see it."

"Why not?"

"Does he want to?"

"Honestly he doesn't seem to understand how wonderful the baby is," explained the child. "Ray's going to be a splendid father to him, Sabina. He's quite interested; only men are different from us. Perhaps they never feel much interest till babies can talk to them. My father says he wasn't much interested in me till I could talk, so it may be a general thing. But when Ray sees him, he'll be tremendously proud of him."

Sabina said no more, and when Raymond arrived to see her at the time she appointed, he found her waiting near the entrance of 'The Magnolias.'

She wore a black dress and was looking very well and very handsome. But the expression in her eyes had changed. He put out his hand, but she did not take it.

"Mister Churchouse has kindly said we can talk in the study, Mister Ironsyde."

He followed her, and when they had come to the room, hoped that she was quite well again. Then he sat in a chair by the table and she took a seat opposite him. She did not reply to his wish for her good health, but waited for him to speak. She was not sulky, but apparently indifferent. Her fret and fume were smothered of late. Now that the supreme injury was inflicted and she had borne a child out of wedlock, Sabina's frenzies were over. The battle was lost. Life held no further promises, and the denial of the great promise that it had offered and taken back again, numbed her. She was weary of the subject of herself and the child. She could even ask Mr. Churchouse for books to occupy her mind during convalescence. Yet the slumbering storm in her soul awoke in full fury before the man had spoken a dozen words.

She looked at Raymond with tired eyes, and he felt that, like himself, she was older, wiser, different. He measured the extent of her experiences and felt sorry for her.

"Sabina," he said. "I must apologise for one mistake. When I asked you to come back to me and live with me, I did a caddish thing. It wasn't worthy of me, or you. I'm awfully sorry. I forgot myself there."

She flushed.

"Can that worry you?" she asked. "I should have thought, after what you'd already done, such an added trifle wouldn't have made you think twice. To ruin a woman body and soul—to lie to her and steal all she's got to give under pretence of marriage—that wasn't caddish, I suppose—that wasn't anything to make you less pleased with yourself. That was what we may expect from men of honour and right bringing up?"

"Don't take this line, or we shan't get on. If, after certain things happened, I had still felt we—"

"Stop," she said, "and hear me. You're making my blood burn and my fingers itch to do something. My hands are strong and quick—they're trained to be quick. I thought I could come to this meeting calm and patient enough. I didn't know I'd got any hate left in me—for you, or the world. But I have—you've mighty soon woke it again; and I'm not going to hear you maul the past into your pattern and explain everything away and tell me how you came gradually to see we shouldn't be happy together and all the usual dirty, little lies. Tell yourself falsehoods if you like—you needn't waste time telling them to me. I'll tell you the truth; and that is that you're a low, mean coward and bully—a creature to sicken the air for any honest man or woman. And you know it behind your big talk. What did you do? You seduced me under promise of marriage, and when your brother heard what you'd done and flung you out of the Mill, you ran to your aunt. And she said, 'Choose between ruin and no money, and Sabina and money from me.' And so you agreed to marry me—to keep yourself in cash. And then, when all was changed and you found yourself a rich man, you lied again and deserted me, and wronged your child—ruined us both. That's what you did, and what you are."

"If you really believe that's the one and only version, I'm afraid we shan't come to an understanding," he said quietly. "You mustn't think so badly of me as that, Sabina."

"Your aunt does. That's how she sees it, being an honest woman."

"I must try to show you you're wrong—in time. For the moment I'm only concerned to do everything in my power to make your future secure and calm your mind."

"Are you? Then marry me. That's the only way you can make my future secure, and you well know it."

"I can't marry you. I shall never marry. I am very firmly convinced that to marry a woman is to do her a great injury nine times out of ten."

"Worse than seducing her and leaving her alone in the world with a bastard child, I suppose?"

"You're not alone in the world, and your child is my child, and I recognise the fullest obligations to you both."

"Liar! If you'd recognised your obligations, you wouldn't have let it come into the world nameless and fatherless."

She rose.

"You want everything your own way, and you think you can bend everything to your own way. But you'll not bend me no more. You've broke me, and you've broke your child. We're rubbish—rubbish on the world's rubbish heap—flung there by you. I, that was so proud of myself! We'll go to the grave shamed and outcast—failures for people to laugh at or preach over. Your child's doomed now. The State and the Church both turn their backs on such as him. You can't make him your lawful son now."

"I can do for him all any father can do for a son."

"You shall do nought for him! He's part of me—not you. If you hold back from me, you hold back from him. God's my judge he shan't receive a crust from your hands. You've given him enough. He's got you to thank for a ruined life. He shan't have anything more from you while I can stand between. Don't you trouble for him. You go on from strength to strength and the people will praise your hard work and your goodness to the workers—such a pattern master as you'll be."

"May time make you feel differently, Sabina," he answered. "I've deserved this—all of it. I'm quite ready to grant I've done wrong. But I'm not going to do more if I can help it. I want to be your friend in the highest and worthiest sense possible. I want to atone to you for the past, and I want to stand up for your child through thick and thin, and bear the reproach that he must be to me as long as I live. I've weighed all that. But power can challenge the indifference of the State and the cowardice of the Church. The dirty laws will be blotted out by public opinion some day. The child can grow up to be my son and heir, as he will be my first care and thought. Everything that is mine can be his and yours—"

"That's all one now," she said. "He touches nothing of yours while I touch nothing of yours. There's only one way to bring me and the child into your life, Raymond Ironsyde, and that's by marrying me. Without that we'll not acknowledge you. I'd rather go on the streets than do it. I'd rather tie a brick round your child's neck and drown him like an unwanted dog than let him have comfort from you. And God judge me if I'll depart from that if I live to be a hundred."

"You're being badly advised, Sabina. I never thought to hear you talk like this. Perhaps it's the fact that I'm here myself annoys you. Will you let my lawyer see you?"

"Marry me—marry me—you that loved me. All less than that is insult."

"We must leave it, then. Would you like me to see my child?"

"See him! Why? You'll never see him if I can help it. You'd blast his little, trusting eyes. But I won't drown him—you needn't fear that. I'll fight for him, and find friends for him. There's a few clean people left who won't make him suffer for your sins. He'll live to spit on your grave yet."

Then she left the room, and he got up and went from the house.

BOOK II

ESTELLE

CHAPTER I

THE FLYING YEARS

But little can even the most complete biography furnish of a man's days. It is argued that essentials are all that matter, and that since one year is often like another, and life merely a matter of occasional mountain peaks in flat country, the outstanding events alone need be chronicled with any excuse. But who knows the essential, since biographists must perforce omit the spade work of life on character, the gradual attrition or upbuilding of principles under experience, and the strain and stress, that, sooner or later, bear fruit in action? Even autobiography, as all other history, needs must be incomplete, since no man himself exactly appreciated the vital experiences that made him what he is, or turns him from what he was; while even if the secret belongs to the protagonist, and intellect and understanding have enabled him to grasp the reality of his progress, or retrogression, he will be jealous to guard such truths and, for pride, or modesty, conceal the real fountains of inspiration that were responsible for progress, or the temptations to error that found his weakest spots, blocked his advance, and rendered futile his highest hopes. The man who knows his inner defeats will not declare them honestly, even if egotism induces an autobiography; while the biographist, being ignorant of his hero's real, psychological existence, secret life, and those thousand hidden influences that have touched him and caused him to react, cannot, with all the will in the world to be true, relate more than superficial truths concerning him.

Ten years may only be recorded as lengthening the lives of Raymond Ironsyde, Sabina Dinnett and their son, together with those interested in them. Time, the supreme solvent, flows over existence, submerging here, lifting there, altering the relative attitudes of husband and wife, parent and child, friend and enemy. For no human relation is static. The ebb and flow forget not the closest or remotest connection between members of the human family; not a friendship or interest stands still, and not a love or a hate. Time operates upon every human emotion as it operates upon physical life; and ten years left no single situation at Bridetown or Bridport unchallenged. Death cut few knots; since accident willed that one alone fell among those with whom we are concerned. For the rest, years brought their palliatives and corrosives, soothed here, fretted there; here buried old griefs and healed old sores; here calloused troubles, so that they only throbbed intermittently; here built up new enthusiasms, awakened new loves, barbed new enmities.

Things that looked impossible on the day that Ironsyde heard Sabina scorn him, happened. Threats evaporated, danger signals disappeared; but, in other cases, while the jagged edges and peaks of bitterness and contempt were worn away by a decade of years, the solid rocks from which they sprang persisted and the massive reasons for emotion were not moved, albeit their sharpest expressions vanished. Some loves faded into likings, and their raptures to a placid contentment, built as much on the convenience of habit as the memories of a passionate past; other affections, less fortunate, perished and left nothing but remains unlovely. Hates also, with their sharpest bristles rubbed down, were modified to bluntness, and left a mere lumpish aversion of mind. Some dislikes altogether perished and gave place to indifference; some persisted as the shadow of their former selves; some were kept alive by absurd pride in those who pretended, for their credit's sake, a steadfastness they were not really built to feel.

Sabina, for example, was constitutionally unequal to any supreme and all-controlling passion unless it had been love; yet still she preserved that inimical attitude to Raymond Ironsyde she had promised to entertain; though in reality the fire was gone and the ashes cold. She knew it, but was willing to rekindle the flame if material offered, as now it threatened to do.

Ernest Churchouse had published his book upon 'The Bells of Dorset' and, feeling that it represented his life work, declared himself content. He had grown still less active, but found abundant interests in literature and friendship. He undertook the instruction of Sabina's son and, from time to time, reported upon the child. His first friend was now Estelle Waldron, who, at this stage of her development, found the old and childlike man chime with her hopes and aspirations.

Estelle was passing through the phase not uncommon to one of her nature. For a time her early womanhood found food in poetry, and her mind, apparently fashioned to advance the world's welfare and add to human happiness, reposed as it seemed on an interlude of reading and the pursuit of beauty. She developed fast to a point—the point whereat she had established a library and common room for the Mill hands; the point at which the girls called her 'Our Lady,' and very honestly loved her for herself as well as for the good she brought them. Now, however, her activities were turned inward and she sought to atone for an education incomplete. She had never gone to school, and her governesses, while able and sufficient, could not do for her what only school life can do. This experience, though held needless and doubtful in many opinions, Estelle felt to miss and her conscience prompted her to go to London and mix with other people, while her inclination tempted her to stop with her father. She went to London for two years and worked upon a woman's newspaper. Then she fell ill and came home and spent her time with Arthur Waldron, with Raymond Ironsyde, and with Ernest Churchouse. A girl friend or two from London also came to visit her.

She recovered perfect health, and having contracted a great new worship for poetry in her convalescence, retained it afterwards. Ernest was her ally, for he loved poetry—an understanding denied to her other friends. So Estelle passed through a period of dreaming, while her intellect grew larger and her human sympathy no less. She had developed into a handsome woman with regular features, a large and almost stately presence and a direct, undraped manner not shadowed as yet by any ray of sex instinct. Nature, with her many endowments, chose to withhold the feminine challenge. She was as stark and pure as the moon. Young men, drawn by her smile, fled from her self. Her father's friends regarded her much as he did: with a sort of uneasy admiration. The people were fond of her, and older women declared that she would never marry.

Of such was Miss Jenny Ironsyde. "Estelle's children will be good works," she told Raymond. For she and her nephew were friends again. The steady tides of time had washed away her prophecy of eternal enmity, and increasing infirmity made her seek companionship where she could find it. Moreover, she remembered a word that she had spoken to Raymond in the past, when she told him how a grudge entertained by one human being against another poisons character and ruins the steadfast outlook upon life. She escaped that danger.

It is a quality of small minds rather than of great to remain unchanged. They fossilise more quickly, are more concentrated, have a power to freeze into a mould and preserve it against the teeth of time, or the wit and wisdom of the world. The result is ugly or beautiful, according to the emotion thus for ever embalmed. The loves of such people are intuitive— shared with instinct and above, or below, reason; their hate is similarly impenetrable—preserved in a vacuum. For only a vacuum can hold the sweet for ever untainted, or the bitter for ever unalloyed. Mary Dinnett belonged to this order. She was now dead, and concerning the legacy of her unchanging attitude more will presently appear.

As for Nelly Northover, she had long been the wife of Mr. Job Legg. That pertinacious man achieved his end at last, and what his few enemies declared was guile, and his many friends held to be tact, won Nelly to him a year after her adventure with Mr. Gurd. None congratulated them more heartily than the master of 'The Tiger.' Indeed, when 'The Seven Stars' blazed out anew on an azure firmament—the least of many changes that refreshed and invigorated that famous house—'The Tiger' also shone forth in savage splendour and his black and orange stripes blazed again from a mass of tropical vegetation.

And beneath the inn signs prosperity continued to obtain. Mr. Gurd grew less energetic than of yore, while Mrs. Legg put on much flesh and daily perceived her wisdom in linking Job for ever to the enterprise for which she lived. He became thinner, if anything, and Time toiled after him in vain. Immense success rewarded his innovations, and the tea-gardens of 'The Seven Stars' had long become a feature of Bridport's social life. People hinted that Mr. Legg was not the meek and mild spirit of ancient opinion and that Nelly knew it; but this suggestion may be held no more than the penalty of fame—an activity of the baser sort, who ever drop vinegar of detraction into the oil of content.

John Best still reigned at the Mill, though he had himself already chosen the young man destined to wear his mantle in process of time. To leave the works meant to leave his garden; and that he was unprepared to do until failing energies made it necessary. A decade saw changes among the workers, but not many. Sally Groves had retired to braid for the firm at home, and old Mrs. Chick was also gone; but the other hands remained and the staff had slightly increased. Nancy Buckler was chief spinner now; Sarah Roberts still minded the spreader, and Nicholas continued at the lathes. Benny Cogle had a new Otto gas engine to look after, and Mercy Gale, now married to him, still worked in the warping chamber. Levi Baggs would not retire, and since he hackled with his old master, the untameable man, now more than sixty years old, still kept his place, still flouted the accepted order, still read sinister motives into every human activity. New machinery had increased the prosperity of the enterprise, but to no considerable extent. Competition continued keen as ever, and each year saw the workers winning slightly increased power through the advance of labour interests.

Raymond Ironsyde was satisfied and remained largely unchanged. He had hardened in opinion and increased in knowledge. He lacked imagination and, as of old, trusted to the machine; but he was rational and proved a capable, second class man of sound judgment and trustworthy in all his undertakings. Sport continued to be a living interest of his life, and since he had no ties that involved an establishment, he gladly accepted Arthur Waldron's offer of a permanent home.

It came to him after he had travelled largely and been for three years master of the works. Arthur was delighted when Raymond accepted his suggestion and made his abode at North Hill. They hunted and shot together; and Waldron, who now judged that the time for golf had come in his case, devoted the moiety of his life to that pastime.

Ironsyde worked hard and was held in respect. The circumstance of his child had long been accepted and understood. He exhausted his energy and patience in endeavours to maintain and advance the boy; and those justified in so doing lost no opportunity to urge on Sabina Dinnett the justice of his demand; but here nothing could change her. She refused to recognise Raymond, or receive from him any assistance in the education and nurture of his son. She had called him Abel, and as Abel Dinnett the lad was known. He resembled her in that he was dark and of an excitable and uneven temperament. He might be easily elated and as easily cast down. Raymond, who kept a secret eye upon the child, trusted that in a few years his turn would come, though at present denied. At first he resented the resolution that shut him out of his son's life; but the matter had long since sunk to unimportance and he believed that when Abel came to years of understanding, he would recognise his own interests and blame those responsible for ignoring them in his childhood. Upon this opinion hinged the future of not a few persons. It developed into a conviction permanently established at the back of his mind; but since Sabina and others came between, he was content to let them do so and relied upon his son's intelligence in time to come. For years he did not again seek the child's acquaintance after a rebuff, and made no attempt to interfere with the operations of Abel's grandmother and mother—to keep them wholly apart. Thus, after all, the gratification of their purpose was devoid of savour and Ironsyde's indifferent acquiescence robbed their will of its triumph. He had told Mary Dinnett, through Ernest Churchouse, that she and her daughter must proceed as they thought fit and that, in any case, the last word would be with him. Here, however, he misvalued the strength of the forces arrayed against him, and only the future proved whether the seed sowed in Abel Dinnett's youthful heart was fertile or barren—whether, by the blood in his own veins, he would offer soil of character to develop enmity to the man who got him, or reveal a nature slow to anger and impatient of wrath.

For Ernest Churchouse these problems offered occupation and he stood as an intermediary between the interests that clashed in the child. He made himself responsible for a measure of the boy's education and, sometimes, reported to Estelle such development of character as he perceived. In secret, inspired by the rival claims of heredity and environment, Ernest strove to cast a scientific horoscope of little Abel's probable future. But to-day contradicted yesterday, and to-morrow proved both untrustworthy. The child was always changing, developing new ideas, indicating new possibilities. It appeared too soon yet to say what he would be, or predict his character and force of purpose.

Thus he grew, and when he was eight years old, his first friend and ally—his grandmother—died. Mr. Churchouse, who had long deplored her influence for Abel's sake, was hopeful that this departure might prove a blessing.

Now Sabina had taken her mother's place and she looked after Ernest well enough. He always hoped that she would marry, and she had been asked to do so more than once, but felt tempted to no such step.

Thus, then, things stood, and any change of focus and altered outlook in these people, that may serve to suggest discontinuity with their past, must be explained by the passage of ten years. Such a period had renewed all physically—a fact full of subtle connotations. It had sharpened the youthful and matured the adult mind; it had dimmed the senses sinking upon nature's night time and strengthened the dawning will and opening intellect. For as a ship furls her spread of sail on entering harbour, so age reduces the scope of the mind and its energies to catch every fresh ripple of the breeze that blows out of progress and change. The centre of the stage, too, gradually reveals new performers; the gaze of manhood is turned on new figures; the limelight of human interest throws up the coming forces of activity and intellect; while those who yesterday shone supreme, slowly pass into the penumbra that heralds eclipse. And who bulk big enough to arrest the eternal march, delay their own progress from light to darkness, or stay the eager young feet tramping outward of the dayspring to take their places in the day? Life moves so fast that many a man lives to see the dust thick on his own name in the scroll of merit and taste a regret that only reason can allay.

Fate had denied Sabina Dinnett her brief apotheosis. From dark to dark she had gone; yet time had purged her mind of any large bitterness. She looked on and watched Raymond's sojourn in the light from a standpoint negative and indifferent. The future for her held interest, for she could not cease to be interested in him, though she knew that he had long since ceased to be interested in her. From the cool cloisters of her obscurity she watched and was only strong in opinion at one point. She dreamed of her son making his way and succeeding in the world; she welcomed Mr. Churchouse's assurance as to the lad's mental progress and promise; but she was determined as ever that not, if she could help it, should Abel enter terms of friendship with his father.

Thus the relations subsisted, while, strange to record, in practice they had long been accepted as part of the order of things at Bridetown. They ceased even to form matter for gossip. For Raymond Ironsyde was greater here than the lord of the manor, or any other force. The Mill continued to be the heart of the village. Through the Mill the lifeblood circulated; by the Mill the prosperity of the people was regulated; and since the master saw that on his own prosperity reposed the prosperity of those whom he employed, there was none to decry him, or echo a disordered past in the ear of the well-ordered present.

CHAPTER II

THE SEA GARDEN

Bride river still flowed her old way to her work and came, by goldilocks and grasses, by reedmace and angelica, to the mill-race and water-wheel. But now, where the old wheel thundered, there yawned a gap, for the river's power was about to be conserved to better purpose than of old, and as the new machines now demanded greater forces to drive them, so human skill found a way to increase the applied strength of a streamlet. Against the outer wall of the Mill now hung a turbine and Raymond, Estelle and others had assembled to see it in operation for the first time. Bride was bottled here, and instead of flashing and foaming over the water wheel as of yore, now vanished into the turbine and presently appeared again below it.

Raymond explained the machine with gusto, and Estelle mourned the wheel, yet as one who knew its departure was inevitable.

It was summer time, and after John Best had displayed the significance of the turbine and the increased powers generated thereby, Raymond strolled down the valley beside the river at Estelle's invitation.

She had something to show him at the mouth of the stream—a sea garden, now in all its beauty and precious to her. For though her mind had winged far beyond the joys of childhood and was occupied with greater matters than field botany, still she loved the wild flowers and welcomed them again in their seasons.

Their speech drifted to the people, and he told how some welcomed the new appliance and some doubted. Then Raymond spoke of Sabina Dinnett in sympathetic ears.

For now Estelle understood the past; but she had never wavered in her friendship with Sabina, any more than had diminished her sister-like attachment to Raymond. Now, as often, he regretted the attitude his child preserved towards him and expressed sorrow that he could not break down Abel's distrust.

"More than distrust, in fact, for the kid dislikes me," he said. "You know he does, Chicky. But I never can understand why, because he's always with his mother and Uncle Ernest, and Sabina doesn't bear me any malice now, to my knowledge. Surely the child must come round sooner or later?"

"When he's old enough to understand, I expect he will," she said. "But you'll have to be patient, Ray."

"Oh, yes—that's my strong suit nowadays."

"He's a clever little chap, so Sabina says; but he's difficult and wayward. He won't be friends with me."

Raymond changed the subject and praised the valley as it opened to the sea.

"What a jolly place! I believe there are scores of delightful spots at Bridetown within a walk, and I'm always too busy to see them."

"That's certain. I could show you scores."

"I ought to know the place I live in, better. I don't even know the soil I walk on—awful ignorance."

"The soil is oolite and clay, and the subsoil, which you see in the cliffs, is yellow sandstone—the loveliest, goldenest soil in the world," declared Estelle.

"The colour of a bath sponge," he said, and she pretended despair.

"Oh dear! And I really thought I had seen the dawning of poetry in you, Ray."

"Merely reflected from yourself, Chicky. Still I'm improving. The turbine has a poetic side, don't you think?"

"I suppose it has. Science is poetic—at any rate, the history of science is full of poetry—if you know what poetry means."

"I wish I had more time for such things," he said. "Perhaps I shall have some day. To be in trade is rather deadening though. There seems so little to show for all my activities—only hundreds of thousands of miles of string. In weak moments I sometimes ask myself if, after all, it is good enough."

"They must be very weak moments, indeed," said Estelle. "Perhaps you'll tell me how the world could get on without string?"

"I don't know. But you, with all your love of beautiful things, ought to understand me instead of jumping on me. What is beauty? No two people feel the same about it, surely? You'd say a poem was beautiful; I'd say a square cut for four, just out of reach of cover point, was beautiful. Your father would say, a book on shooting high pheasants was beautiful, if he agreed with it; John Best would say a good sample of shop twine was beautiful."

"We should all be right, beauty is in all those things. I can see that. I can even see that shooting birds with great skill, as father does, is beautiful—not the slaughter of the bird, which can't be beautiful, but the way it's done. But those are small things. With the workers you want to begin at the beginning and show them—what Mister Best knows—that the beauty of the thing they make depends on it being well and truly made."

"They're restless."

"Yes; they're reaching out for more happiness, like everybody else."

"I wouldn't back the next generation of capitalists to hold the fort against labour."

"Perhaps the next generation won't want to," she said. "Perhaps by that time we shall be educated up to the idea that rich people are quite as anti-social as poor people. Then we shall do away with both poverty and riches. To us, educated on the old values, it would come as a shock, but the generation that is born into such a world would accept it as a matter of course and not grumble."

He laughed.

"Don't believe it, Chicky. Every generation has its own hawks and eagles as well as its sheep. The strong will always want the fulness of the earth and always try to inspire the weak to help them get it. With great leadership you must have equivalent rewards."

"Why? Cannot you imagine men big enough to work for humanity without reward? Have there not been plenty of such men—before Christ, as well as since?"

"Power is reward," he answered. "No man is so great that he is indifferent to power, for his greatness depends upon it; and if power was dissipated to-morrow and diluted until none could call himself a leader, we should have a reaction at once and the sheep would grow frightened and bleat for a shepherd. And the shepherd would very soon appear."

They stood where the cliffs broke and Bride ended her journey at the sea. She came gently without any splendid nuptials to the lover of rivers. Her brief course run, her last silver loop wound through the meadows, she ended in a placid pool amid the sand ridges above high-water mark. The yellow cliffs climbed up again on either side, and near the chalice in the grey beach whence, invisible, the river sank away to win the sea by stealth, spread Estelle's sea garden—an expanse of stone and sand enriched by many flowers that seemed to crown the river pool with a garland, or weave a wreath for Bride's grave in the sand. Here were pale gold of poppies, red gold of lotus and rich lichens that made the sea-worn pebbles shine. Sea thistle spread glaucous foliage and lifted its blue blossoms; stone-crops and thrifts, tiny trefoils and couch grasses were woven into the sand, and pink storks-bill and silvery convolvulus brought cool colour to this harmony spread beside the purple sea. The day was one of shadow and sunshine mingled, and from time to time, through passages of grey that lowered the glory of Estelle's sea garden, a sunburst came to set all glittering once more, to flash upon the river, lighten the masses of distant elm, and throw up the red roofs and grey church tower of Bridetown and her encircling hills.

"What a jolly place it is," he said taking out his cigar case.

Then they sat in the shadow of a fishing boat, drawn up here, and Raymond lamented the unlovely end of the river.

While he did so, the girl regarded him with affection and a secret interest and entertainment. For it amused her often to hear him echo thoughts that had come to her in the past. In a lesser degree her father did the like; but he belonged to a still older generation, and it was with Raymond that she found herself chiefly concerned, when he announced, as original, ideas and discoveries that reflected her own dreams in the past. Sometimes she thought he was catching up; sometimes, again, she distanced him and felt herself grown up and Raymond still a boy. Then, sometimes, he would flush a covey of ideas outside her reflections, and so remind her of the things that interested men, in which, as yet, women took no interest. When he spoke of such things, she strove to learn all that he could teach concerning them. But soon she found that was not much. He did not think deeply and she quickly caught him up, if she desired to do so.

Now he uttered just the same, trivial lament that she had uttered when she was a child. She was pleased, for she rather loved to feel herself older in mind than Raymond. It added a lustre to friendship and made her happy— why, she knew not.

"What a wretched end—to be choked up in the shingle like that," he said, "instead of dashing out gloriously and losing yourself in the sea!"

She smiled gently to herself.

"I thought that once, then I was ever so sorry for poor little Bride."

"A bride without a wedding," he said.

"No. She steals to him; she wins his salt kisses and finds them sweet enough. They mate down deep out of sight of all eyes. So you needn't be sorry for her really."

"It's like watching people try ever so hard to do something and never bring it off."

"Yes—even more like than you think, Ray; because we feel sad at such apparent failures, and yet what we are looking at may be a victory really, only our dull eyes miss it."

"I daresay many people are succeeding who don't appear to be," he admitted.

"Goodness can't be wasted. It may be poured into the sand all unseen and unsung; but it conquers somehow and does something worth doing, even though no eye can see what. Plenty of good things happen in the world—good and helpful things—that are never recorded, or even recognised."

"Like a stonewaller in a cricket match. The people cuss him, but he may determine who is going to win."

She laughed at the simile.

They went homeward presently, Estelle quietly content to have shown Raymond the flower-sprinkled strand, and he well pleased to have pleasured her.

CHAPTER III

A TWIST FRAME

Raymond Ironsyde grumbled sometimes at the Factory Act and protested against grandmotherly legislation. Yet in some directions he anticipated it. He went, for example, beyond the Flax Mill Ventilation Regulations. He loved fresh air himself, and took vast pains to make his works sweet and wholesome for those who breathed therein. Even Levi Baggs could not grumble, for the exhaust draught in his hackling shop was stronger than the law demanded, and the new cyclone separators in the main buildings served to keep the air far purer than of old.

Ironsyde had established also the Kestner System of atomising water, to regulate temperature and counteract the electrical effects of east wind, or frost, on the light slivers. He was always on the lookout for new automatic means to regulate the drags on the bobbins. He had installed an automatic doffing apparatus, and made a departure from the usual dry spinning in a demi-sec, or half-dry, spinning frame, which was new at that time, and had offered excellent results and spun a beautifully smooth yarn.

These things all served to assist and relieve the workers in varying degree, but, as Raymond often pointed out, they were taken for granted and, sometimes, in his gloomier moments, he accused his people of lacking gratitude. They, for their part, were being gradually caught up in the growing movements of labour. The unintelligent forgot to credit the master with his consideration; while those who could think, were often soured by suspicion. These ignorant spirits doubted not that he was seeking to win their friendship against the rainy days in store for capital.

Ironsyde came to the works one morning to watch a new Twist Frame and a new operator. The single strand yarn for material from the spinners was coming to the Twist Frame to be turned into twines and fishing lines. Four full bobbins from the spinning machine went to each spindle of the Twist Frame, and from it emerged a strong 'four-ply.' It was a machine more complicated than the spinner; and, as only a good billiard player can appreciate the cleverness of a great player, so only a spinner might have admired the rare technical skill of the woman who controlled the Twist Frame.

The soul of the works persisted, though the people and the machines were changed. The old photographs and old verses had gone, but new pictures and poems took their places in the workers' corners; and new fashion-plates hung where the old ones used to hang. The drawers, and the rovers, the spreaders and the spinners still, like bower-birds, adorned the scenes of their toil. A valentine or two and the portrait of a gamekeeper and his dog hung beside the carding machine; for Sally Groves had retired and a younger woman was in her place. She, too, fed the Card by hand, but not so perfectly as Sally was wont to do.

Estelle had come to see the Twist Frame. She cared much for the Mill women and spent a good portion of her hours with them. A very genuine friendship, little tainted with time-serving, or self-interest, obtained for her in the works. On her side, she valued the goodwill of the workers as her best possession, and found among them a field for study in human nature and, in their work, matter for poetry and art. For were not all three Fates to be seen at their eternal business here? Clotho attended the Spread Board; the can-minders coiling away the sliver, stood for Lachesis; while in the spinners, who cut the thread when the bobbin was full, Estelle found Atropos, the goddess of the shears.

Mr. Best, grown grizzled, but active still and with no immediate thoughts of retirement, observed the operations of the new spinner at the Twist Frame. She was a woman from Bridport, lured to Bridetown by increase of wages.

John, who was a man of enthusiasms, turned to Estelle.

"The best spinner that ever came to Bridetown," he whispered.

"Better than Sabina Dinnett?" she asked; and Best declared that she was. So passage of time soon deadens the outline of all achievement, and living events that happen under our eyes, offer a statement of the quick and real with which beautiful dead things, embalmed in the amber of memory, cannot cope.

"Sabina, at her best, never touched her, Miss Waldron."

"Sabina braids still in her spare time. Nobody makes better nets."

"This is a cousin of Sarah Roberts," explained the foreman. "Spinning runs in the Northover family, and though Sarah is a spreader and never will be anything else, there have been wondrous good spinners in the clan. This girl is called Milly Morton, and her mother and grandmother spun before her. Her father was Jack Morton, one of the last of the old hand spinners. To see him walking backwards from his wheel, and paying out fibre from his waist with one hand and holding up the yarn with the other, was a very good sight. He'd spin very nearly a hundred pounds of hemp in a ten hours' day, and turn out seven or eight miles of yarn, and walk every yard of it, of course. The rope makers swore by him."

"I'm sure spinning runs in the blood!" agreed Estelle. "Both Sarah's little girls are longing for the time when they can come into the Mill and mind cans; and, of course, the boy wants to do his father's work and be a lathe hand."

Best nodded.

"You've hit it," he declared. "It runs in the blood in a very strange fashion. Take Sabina's child. By all accounts, his old grandmother did everything in her power to poison his mind against the Mill as well as the master. She was a lot bitterer than Sabina herself, as the years went on; and if you could look back and uncover the past, you'd find it was her secret work to make that child what he is. But the Mill draws him like cheese draws a mouse. I'll find him here a dozen times in a month—just popping in when my back's turned. Why he comes I couldn't say; but I think it is because his mother was a spinner and the feeling for the craft is in him."

"His father is a spinner, too, for that matter," suggested Estelle.

"In the larger sense of ownership, yes; but it isn't that that draws him. His father's got no great part in him by all accounts. It's the mother in him that brings him here. Not that she knows he comes so often, and I dare say she'd be a good deal put about if she did."

"Why shouldn't he come, John?"

He shrugged his shoulders.

"I see no reason against. One gets so used to the situation that its strangeness passes off, but it's very awkward, so to say, that nothing can be done for Abel by his father. Sabina's wrong to hold out there, and so I've told her."

"She doesn't influence Abel one way or the other. The child seems to hate Mister Ironsyde."

"Well, he loves the Mill, though you'd think he might hate that for his father's sake."

"He's hard for a little creature of ten years old," said Estelle. "He won't make friends with me, but holds off and regards me—just as rabbits and things regard one, before they finally run away. I pretend I don't notice it. He'll listen and even talk if I meet him with his mother; but if I meet him alone, he flies. He generally bolts through a hole in the hedge, or somewhere."

"He links you up with Mister Raymond," explained Mr. Best. "He knows you live at North Hill House, and so he's suspicious. You can disarm him, however, for he's got reasoning parts quite up to the average if not above.

He's the sort of boy that if you don't want him to steal your apples, you've only got to give him a few now and then; and then he rises to the situation and feels in honour bound to be straight, because you've lifted him to be your equal."

"I call that a very good character."

"It might be a lot worse, no doubt."

"I wanted him to come to our outing, but he won't do that, though his mother asked him to go."

The outing, an annual whole holiday, was won for the Mill by Estelle, and for the past four years she had taken all who cared to come for a long day by the sea. They always went to Weymouth, where amusement offered to suit every taste.

"More than ever are coming this year," John told her. "In fact, I believe pretty well everybody's going but Levi Baggs."

"I'm glad. We'll have the two wagonettes from 'The Seven Stars' as usual. If you are going into Bridport you might tell Missis Legg."

"The two big ones we shall want, and they must be here sharp at six o'clock," declared Mr. Best. "There's nothing like getting off early. I'll speak to Job Legg about it and tell him to start 'em off earlier. You can trust it to Job as to the wagonettes being opened or covered. He's a very weather-wise person and always smells rain twelve hours in advance."

CHAPTER IV

THE RED HAND

The Mill had a fascination for all Bridetown children and they would trespass boldly and brave all perils to get a glimpse of the machinery. The thunder of the engines drew them, and there were all manner of interesting fragments to be picked up round and about. That they were not permitted within the radius of the works was also a sound reason for being there, and many boys could tell of great adventures and hairbreadth escapes from Mr. Best, Mr. Benny Cogle and, above all, Mr. Baggs. For Mr. Baggs, to the mind of youth, exhibited ogre-like qualities. They knew him as a deadly enemy, for which reason there was no part of the works that possessed a greater or more horrid fascination than the hackling shop. To have entered the den of Mr. Baggs marked a Bridetown lad as worthy of highest respect in his circle. But proofs were always demanded of such a high achievement. When Levi caught the adventurer, as sometimes happened, proofs were invariably apparent and a posterior evidence never lacked of a reverse for the offensive; but youth will be served, even though age sometimes serves it rather harshly, and the boys were untiring. Unless Levi locked the shop, when he went home at noon to dinner, there was always the chance of a raid with a strick or two possibly missing as proof of success.

Sabina had told Abel that he must keep away from the works, but he ignored her direction and often revolved about them at moments of liberty. He was a past master in the art of scouting and evading danger, yet loved danger, and the Mill offered him daily possibilities of both courting and escaping peril. Together with other little boys nourished on a penny journal, Abel had joined the 'Band of the Red Hand.' They did no harm, but hoped some day, when they grew older, to make a more' painful impression on Bridetown. At present their modest ambition was to leave the mark of their secret society in every unexpected spot possible. On private walls, in church and chapel, or the house-places of the farms, it was their joy to write with chalk, 'The Red Hand has been here.' Then followed a circle and a cross— the dark symbol of the brotherhood. Once a former chief of the gang had left his mark in the hackling shop and more than one member had similarly adorned the interior of the Mill; but the old chief had gone to sea at the age of thirteen, and, though younger than some of the present members, Abel was now appointed leader and always felt the demand to attempt things that should be worthy of so high a state.

They were not the everyday boys who thus combined, but a sort of child less common, yet not uncommon. Such lads scent one another out by parity of taste and care less for gregarious games than isolated or lonely adventures. They would rather go trespassing than play cricket; they would organise a secret raid before a public pastime. Intuitively they desire romance, and feeling that law and order is opposed to romance, find the need to flout law and order in measure of their strength, and, of course, applaud the successful companion who does so with most complete results.

Now 'the old Adam'—a comprehensive term for independence of view and unpreparedness to accept the tried values of pastors and masters—was strong in Abel Dinnett. He loved life, but hated discipline, and for him the Mill possessed far more significance than it could offer to any lesser member of the band, since his father owned it. For that much Abel apprehended, though the meaning of paternity was as yet hidden from him.

That Raymond Ironsyde was his father he understood, and that he must hate him heartily he also understood: his dead grandmother had poured this precept into his young mind at its most receptive period. For the present he was still too youthful to rise beyond this general principle, and he was far too busy with his own adventures to find leisure to hate any one more than fitfully. He told the Red Handers that some day he designed a terrific attack on Raymond Ironsyde; and they promised to assist and support him; but they all recognised their greater manifestations must be left until they attained more weight in the cosmic and social schemes, and, for the moment, their endeavour rose little higher than to set their fatal sign where least it might be expected.

To this end came dark-eyed Abel to the Mill at an hour when he should have been at his dinner. Ere long his activities might be curtailed, for he was threatened with a preparatory school in the autumn; but before that happened, the Red Hand must be set in certain high places, and the hackling shop of Levi Baggs was first among them.

Abel wore knickerbockers and his feet and legs were bare, for he had just waded across the river beyond the Mill, and meant to retreat by the same road. He had hidden in a may bush till the people were all gone to their meal, and then crossed the stream into the works. That the door of the hackler's would be open he did not expect, for Levi locked it when he went home; but there was a little window, and Abel, who had a theory that where his head could go, his body could follow, believed that by the window it would be possible to make his entrance. The contrary of what he expected happened, however, for the window was shut and the door on the latch. Fate willed that on the very day of Abel's attack, Mr. Baggs should be spending the dinner-hour in his shop. His sister, who looked after him, was from home until the evening, and Levi had brought his dinner to the works. He was eating it when the boy very cautiously opened the door, and since Mr. Baggs sat exactly behind the door, this action served to conceal him. The intruder therefore thought the place empty, and proceeded with his operations while Levi made no sound, but watched him.

Taking a piece of chalk from his pocket Abel wrote the words of terror, 'The Red Hand has been here,' and set down the circle and cross. Then he picked up one of the bright stricks, that lay beside the hackling board, and was just about to depart in triumph, when Mr. Baggs banged the door and revealed himself.

Thus discomfited, Abel grew pale and then flushed. Mr. Baggs was a very big and strong man and the culprit knew that he must now prepare for the pangs that attended failure. But he bore pain well. He had been operated upon for faulty tendons when he was five and proved a Spartan patient. He stood now waiting for Mr. Baggs. Other victims had reported that it was Levi's custom to use a strap from his own waist when he beat a boy, and Abel, even at this tense moment, wondered whether he would now do so.

"It's you, is it?" said Mr. Baggs. "And the Red Hand has been here, has it? And perhaps the red something else will go away from here. You're a darned young thief—that's what you are."

"I ain't yet," argued Abel. His voice fluttered, for his heart was beating very fast.

"You're as good, however, for you was going to take my strick. The will was there, though I prevented the deed."

"I had to show the Band as I'd been here."

"Why did you come? What sense is there to it?"

Abel regarded Mr. Baggs doubtfully and did not reply.

"Just to show you're a bit out of the common, perhaps?"

Abel clutched at the suggestion. His eyes looked sideways slyly at Mr. Baggs. The ogre seemed inclined to talk, and through speech might come salvation, for he had acted rather than talked on previous occasions.

"We want to be different from common boys," said the marauder.

"Well, you are, for one, and there's no need to trouble in your case. You was born different, and different you've got to be. I suppose you've been told often enough who your father is?"

"Yes, I have."

"Small wonder then that you've got your knife into the world at large, I reckon. What thinking man, or boy, has not for that matter? So you're up against the laws and out for the liberties? Well, I don't quarrel with that. Only you're too young yet to understand what a lot you've got to grumble at. Some day you will."

Abel said nothing. He hardly listened, and thought far less of what Mr. Baggs was saying than of what he himself would say to his companions after this great adventure. To make friends with the ogre was no mean feat, even for a member of the Red Hand.

What motiveless malignity actuated Levi Baggs meanwhile, who can say? He was now a man in sight of seventy, yet his crabbed soul would exude gall under pressure as of yore. None was ever cheered or heartened by anything he might say; but to cast a neighbour down, or make a confident and contented man doubtful and discontented, affected Mr. Baggs favourably and rendered him as cheerful as his chronic pessimism ever permitted him to be.

He bade the child sit and gave him his portion of currant dumpling.

"Put that down your neck," he said, "and don't you think so bad of me in future. I treat other people same as they treat me, and that's a rule that works out pretty fair in practice, if you've got the power to follow it. But some folks are too weak to treat other people as they are treated—you, for example. You're one of the unlucky ones, you are, Abel Dinnett."

Abel enjoyed the pudding; and still his mind dwelt more on future narration of this great incident than on the incident itself. With unconscious art, he felt that the moment when this tale was told, would be far greater for him than the moment when it happened.

"I ain't unlucky, Mister Baggs. I would have been unlucky if you'd beat me; but you've give me your pudding, and I'm on your side till death now."

"Well, that's something. I ain't got many my side, I believe. The fearless thinker never has. You can come and see me when you mind to, because I'm sorry for you, owing to your bad fortune. You've been handicapped out of winning the race, Abel. You know what a handicap is in a race? Well, you won't have no chance of winning now, because your father won't own you."

"I won't own him," said the boy. "Granny always told me he was my bitterest enemy, and she knew, and I won't trust him—never."

"I should think not—nor any other wise chap wouldn't trust him. He's a bad lot. He only believes in machines, not humans."

The boy began to be receptive.

"He wants to be friends, but I won't be his friend, because I hate him. Only I don't tell mother, because she don't hate him so much as me."

"More fool her, then. She ought to hate him. She's got first cause. Do you know who ought to own these works when your father dies?"

"No, Mister Baggs."

"You. Yes, they did ought to belong to you in justice, because you are his eldest son. Everything ought to be yours, if the world were run by right and fairness and honour. But it's all took from you and you can't lift a finger to better yourself, because you're only his natural son, and Nature may go to hell every time for all the Law and the Church care. Church and Law both hate Nature. So that's why I say you're an unlucky boy; and that's why I say that, despite your father's money and fame and being popular and well thought on and all that, he's a cruel rogue."

Abel was puzzled but interested.

"If I'm his boy, why ain't my mother his wife, like all the other chaps' fathers have got wives?"

"Why ain't your mother his wife? Yes, why? After ten years he'll find that question as hard to answer as it was before you were born, I reckon. And the answer to the question is the same as the answer to many questions about Raymond Ironsyde. And that is, that he is a crooked man who pretends to be a straight one; in a word, a hypocrite. And you'll grow up to understand these things and see what should be yours taken from you and given to other people."

"When I grow up, I'll have it out with him," said Abel.

"No, you won't. Because he's strong and you're weak. You're weak and poor and nobody, with no father to fight for you and give you a show in the world. And you'll always be the same, so you'll never stand any chance against him."

The boy flushed and showed anger.

"I won't be weak and poor always."

"Against him you will. Suppose you went so far as to let him befriend you, could he ever make up for not marrying your mother? Can he ever make you anything but a bastard and an outcast? No, he can't; and he only wants to educate you and give you a bit of money and decent clothes for the sake of his own conscience. He'll come to you hat in hand some day—not because he cares a damn for you, but that he may stand well in the eyes of the world."

Abel now panted with anger, and Mr. Baggs was mildly amused to see how easily the child could be played upon.

"I'll grow up and then—"

"Don't you worry. You must take life as you find it, and as you haven't found it a very kind thing, you must put up with it. Most people draw blanks, and that's why it's better to stop out of the world than in it. And if we could see into the bottom of every heart, we should very likely find that all draw blanks, and even what looks like prizes are not."

Levi laughed after this sweeping announcement. It appeared to put him in a good temper. He even relaxed in the gravity of his prophecies.

"However, life is on the side of youth," he said, "and you may come to the front some day, if you've got enough brains. Brains is the only thing that'll save you. Your mother's clever and your father's crafty, so perhaps you'll go one better than either. Perhaps, some day, if you wait long enough, you'll get back on your father, after all."

"I will wait long enough," declared Abel. "I don't care how long I wait, but I'll best him, Mister Baggs."

"You keep in that righteous spirit and you'll breed a bit of trouble for him some day, I daresay. And now be off, and if you want to come and see me at work and learn about hackling and the business that ought to be yours but won't be, then you can drop in again when you mind to."

"Thank you, sir," said Abel. "I will come, and if I say you let me, nobody can stop me."

"That's right. I like brave boys that ain't frightened of their betters—so called."

Then Abel went off, crossed Bride among the sedges and put on his shoes and stockings again. He had a great deal to think about, and this brief conversation played its part in his growing brain to alter old opinions and waken new ideas. That he had successfully stormed the hackling shop and found the ogre friendly was, of course, good; but already, and long before he could retail the incident, it began to lose its rare savour. He perceived this himself dimly, and it made him uncomfortable and troubled. Something had happened to him; he knew not what, but it dwarfed the operations of the Red Hand, and it even made his personal triumph look smaller than it appeared a little while before.

Abel stared at the Mill while he pulled on his stockings and listened to the bell calling the people back to work.

By right, then, all these wonders should be his some day; but his father would never give them to him now. He vaguely remembered that his grandmother had said something like this; but it remained for Mr. Baggs to rekindle the impression until Abel became oppressed with its greatness.

He considered the problem gloomily for a long time and decided to talk to his mother about it. But he did not. It was characteristic of him that he seldom went to Sabina for any light on his difficulties. Indeed he attached more importance to Mr. Churchouse's opinions than his mother's. He determined to see Levi Baggs again and, meantime, he let a sense of wrong sink into him. Here the Band of the Red Hand offered comfort. It seemed proper to his dawning intelligence that one who had been so badly treated as he, should become the head of the Red Hand. Yet, as the possible development of the movement occurred to Abel, the child began to share the uneasiness of all conspiracy and feel a weakness inherent in the Band. Seen from that modest standard of evil-doing which belonged to Tommy and Billy Keep, Amos Whittle and Jacky Gale, the Red Handers appeared a futile organisation even in Abel's eyes. He felt, as greater than he have felt, that an ideal society should embrace one member only: himself. There were far too many brothers of the Red Hand, and before he reached home he even contemplated resignation. He liked better the thought of playing his own hand, and keeping both its colour and its purpose secret from everybody else in the world. His head was, for the moment, full of unsocial thoughts; but whether the impressions created by Mr. Baggs were likely to persist in a mind so young, looked doubtful.

He told his mother nothing, as usual. Indeed, had she guessed half that went on in Abel's brains, she might have sooner undertaken what presently was indicated, and removed herself and her son to a district far beyond their native village.

But the necessity did not exist in her thoughts, and when she recognised it, since the inspiration came from without, she was moved to resent rather than accept it.

CHAPTER V

AN ACCIDENT

There was a cricket luncheon at 'The Tiger' when Bridport played its last match for the season against Axminster. The western township had won the first encounter, and Bridport much desired to cry quits over the second.

Raymond played on this occasion, and though he failed, the credit of Bridetown was worthily upheld by Nicholas Roberts, the lathe-worker. He did not bowl as fast as of yore, but he bowled better, and since Axminster was out for one hundred and thirty in their first innings, while Bridport had made seventy for two wickets before luncheon, the issue promised well.

Job Legg still helped Richard Gurd at great moments as he was wont to do, for prosperity had not modified Job's activity, or diminished his native goodwill. Gurd carved, while Job looked after the bottles. Arthur Waldron, who umpired for Bridport, sat beside Raymond at lunch and condoled with him, because the younger, who had gone in second wicket down, had played himself in very carefully before the interval.

"Now you'll have to begin all over again," said Waldron. "I always say luncheon may be worth anything to the bowlers. It rests them, but it puts the batsman's eye out."

"Seeing how short of practice you are this year, you were jolly steady, Ray," declared Neddy Motyer, who sat on the other side of Ironsyde. "You stopped some very hot ones."

Neddy preserved his old interest in sport, but was now a responsible member of society. He had married and joined his father, a harness-maker, in a prosperous business.

"I can't time 'em, like I could. That fast chap will get me, I expect."

And Raymond proved a true prophet. Indeed far worse happened than he anticipated.

Estelle came to watch the cricket after luncheon. She had driven into Bridport with her father and Raymond in the morning and gone on to Jenny Ironsyde for the midday meal. Now she arrived in time to witness a catastrophe. A very fast bowler went on immediately after lunch. He was a tall and powerful youth with a sinister reputation for bowling at the man rather than the wicket. At any rate he pitched them short and with his lofty delivery bumped them very steeply on a lively pitch. Now, in his second over, he sent down a short one at tremendous speed, and the batsman, failing to get out of the way, was hit on the point of the jaw. He fell as though shot and proved to be quite unconscious when picked up.

They carried him to the pavilion, and it was not until twenty minutes had passed that Raymond came round and the game went on. But Ironsyde could take no further part. There was concussion of doubtful severity and he found himself half blind and suffering great pain in the neck and head.

Estelle came to him and advised that he should go to his aunt's house, which was close at hand. He could not speak, but signified agreement, and they took him there in an ambulance, while the girl ran on to advise his aunt of the accident.

A doctor came with him and helped to get him to bed. His mind seemed affected and he wandered in his speech. But he recognised Estelle and begged her not to leave him. She sat near him, therefore, in a darkened room and Miss Ironsyde also came.

Waldron dropped in before dusk with the news that Bridport had won, by a smaller margin than promised, on the first innings. But he found Raymond sleeping and did not waken him. Estelle believed the injured man would want her when he woke again. The doctor could say nothing till some hours had passed, so she went home, but returned a few hours later to stop the night and help, if need be, to nurse the patient. A professional nurse shared the vigil; but their duties amounted to nothing, for Raymond slept through the greater part of the night and declared himself better in the morning.

He had to stop with his aunt, however, for two or three days, and while Estelle, her ministration ended, was going away after the doctor pronounced Raymond on the road to recovery, the patient begged her to remain. He appeared in a sentimental vein, and the experience of being nursed was so novel that Ironsyde endured it without a murmur. To Estelle, who did not guess he was rather enjoying it, the spectacle of his patience under pain awoke admiration. Indeed, she thought him most heroic and he made no effort to undeceive her.

Incidentally, during his brief convalescence the man saw more of his aunt than he had seen for many days. She also must needs nurse him and exhaust her ingenuity to pass the time. The room was kept dark for eight-and-forty hours, so her method of entertaining her nephew consisted chiefly in conversation.

Of late years Raymond seldom let a week elapse without seeing Miss Ironsyde if only for half an hour. Her waning health occupied him on these occasions and, at his suggestion, she had gone to Bath to fight the arthritis that slowly gained upon her. But during his present sojourn at Bridport as her guest, Raymond let her lead their talk as she would, indeed, he himself sometimes led it into channels of the past, where she would not have ventured to go.

Life had made an immense difference to the man and he was old for his age now, even as until his brother's death he had been young for his age. She could not fail to note the steadfastness of his mind, despite its limitations. As Estelle had often done, she perceived how he set his faith on material things—the steel and steam—to bring about a new order and advance the happiness of mankind; but he was interested in social questions far more than of old time, and she felt no little surprise to hear him talk about the future.

"The air is full of change," she said, on one occasion.

"It always is," he answered. "There is always movement, although the breath of advance and progress seems to sink to nothing, sometimes. Now it's blowing a stiff breeze and may rise to a hurricane in a few years."

"It is for the stable, solid backbone of the nation—we of the middle-class—to withstand such storms," she declared, and he agreed.

"If you've got a stake in the world, you must certainly see its foundations are driven deep and look to the stake itself, that it's not rotting. Some stakes are certainly not made of stuff stout enough to stand against the storms ahead. Education is the great, vital thing. I often feel mad to think how I wasted my own time at school, and came to man's work a raw, ignorant fool. We talk of the education of the masses and what I see is this: they will soon be better educated than we ourselves; for we bring any amount of sense and modern ideas to work on their teaching, while our own prehistorical methods are left severely alone. I believe the boys who come to working age now are better taught than I was at my grammar school. I wish I knew more."

"Yet we see education may run us into great dangers," said Jenny Ironsyde. "It can be pushed to a perilous point. One even hears a murmur against the Bible in the schools. It makes my blood run cold. And we need not look farther than dear Estelle to see the peril."

"What do you think of Estelle?" he asked. "I almost welcome this stupid collapse, nuisance though it is, because it's made a sort of resting-place and brought me nearer to you and Estelle. You've both been so kind. A man such as I am, is so busy and absorbed that he forgets all about women; then suddenly lying on his back—done for and useless—he finds they don't forget all about him."

"You ask what I think about Estelle?" she said. "I never think about Estelle—no more than I do about the sunshine, or my comfortable bed, or my tea. She's just one of the precious things I take for granted. I love her. She is a great deal to me, and the hours she spends with a rather old-fashioned and cross-grained woman are the happiest hours I know."

"I'm like her father," he said. "I give Estelle best. Nothing can spoil her, because she's so utterly uninterested in herself. Another thing: she's so fair—almost morbidly fair. The only thing that makes her savage is injustice. If she sees an injustice, she won't leave it alone if it's in her power to alter it. That's her father in her. What he calls 'sporting,' she calls 'justice.' And, of course, the essence of sport is justice, if you think it out."

"I don't know anything about sport, but I suppose I have to thank cricket for your company at present. As for Estelle. I think she has a great idea of your judgment and opinion."

He laughed.

"If she does, it's probably because I generally agree with her. Besides—"

He broke off and lighted a cigarette.

"'Besides' what?" asked the lady.

"Well—oh I hardly know. I'm tremendously fond of her. Perhaps I've taken her too much as you say we take the sun and our meat and drink—as a matter of course. Yes, like the sun, and as unapproachable."

Miss Ironsyde considered.

"I suppose you're right. I can well imagine that to the average man a 'Una,' such as Estelle, may seem rather unapproachable."

"We're very good friends, though how good I never quite guessed till this catastrophe. She seemed to come and help look after me as a matter of course. Didn't think it a bit strange."

"She's simple, but in a very noble way. I've only one quarrel with her—the faith of her fathers—"

"Leave it. You'll only put your foot into it, Aunt Jenny."

"Never," she said. "I shall never put my foot into it where right and wrong are concerned—with Estelle or you, or anybody else. I'm nearly seventy, remember, Raymond, and one knows what is imperishable and to be trusted at that age."

Thus she negatived Mr. Churchouse's dictum—that mere age demanded no particular reverence, since many years are as liable to error as few.

Her nephew was doubtful.

"Right and wrong are a never-ending puzzle," he said. "They vary so from the point of view. And if you once grant there are more view points than one, where are you?"

"Right and wrong are not doubtful," she assured him, "and all the science in the world can't turn one into the other—any more than light can turn into darkness."

"Light can turn into darkness easily enough. I've learned that during the last three days," he answered. "If you fill this room with light, I can't see. If you keep it dark, I can."

Estelle came to tea and read some notes that Mr. Best had prepared for Raymond. They satisfied him, and the meal was merry, for he found himself free of pain and in the best spirits. Estelle, too, had some gossip that amused him. Her father was already practising at clay pigeons to get his eye in for the first of September; and he wished to inform Raymond that he was shooting well and hoped for a better season than the last. He had also seen a vixen and three cubs on North Hill at five o'clock in the morning of the preceding day.

"In fact, it's the best of all possible worlds so far as father is concerned," said Estelle, "and now he hears you're coming home early next week, he will go to church on Sunday with a thankful heart. He said yesterday that Raymond's accident had a bright side. D'you know what it is? Ray meant to give up cricket altogether after this year; but father points out that he cannot do so now. Because it is morally impossible for Ray to stop playing until he stands up again to that bowler who hurt him so badly. 'Morally impossible,' is what father said."

"He's quite right too," declared the patient. "Till I've knocked that beggar out of his own ground for six, I certainly shan't chuck cricket. We must meet again next season, if we're both alive. Everybody can see that."

CHAPTER VI

THE GATHERING PROBLEM

Sabina Dinnett found that her mind was not so indifferent to her fortunes as she supposed. Upon examining it, with respect to the problem of leaving Bridetown for Abel's sake, which Ernest had now raised, she discovered a very keen disinclination to depart. Here was the only home that she, or her child, had ever known, and though that mattered nothing, she shrank from beginning a new life away from 'The Magnolias' under the increased responsibility of sole control where Abel was concerned. Moreover, Mr. Churchouse had more power with Abel than anybody. The boy liked him and must surely win sense and knowledge from him, as Sabina herself had won them in the past. She knew that these considerations were superficial and the vital point in reason was to separate the son from the father; so that Abel's existing animus might perish. Both Estelle and Ernest Churchouse had impressed the view upon her; but here crept in the personal factor, and Sabina found that she had no real desire to mend the relationship. Considerations of her child's future pointed to more self-denial, but only that Abel might in time come to be reconciled to Raymond and accept good at his hands. And when Sabina thought upon this, she soon saw that her own indifference, where Ironsyde was concerned, did not extend to the future of the boy. She could still feel, and still suffer, and still resent certain possibilities. She trusted that in time to come, when Mr. Churchouse and Miss Ironsyde were gone, the measure of her son's welfare would be hers. She was content to see herself depending upon him; but not if his own prosperity came from his father. She preferred to picture Abel as making his way without obligations to that source. She might have married and made her own home, but that alternative never tempted her, since it would have thrust her off the pedestal which she occupied, as one faithful to the faithless, one bitterly wronged, a reproach to the good name—perhaps, even a threat to the sustained prosperity of Raymond Ironsyde. She could feel all this at some moments.

She determined now to let the matter rest, and when Ernest Churchouse ventured to remind her of the subject and to repeat the opinion that it might be wise for Sabina to take the boy away from Bridetown, she postponed decision.

"I've thought upon it," she said, "and I feel it can very well be left to the spring, if you see nothing against. I've promised to do some braiding in my spare time this winter for a firm at Bridport that wants netting in large quantities. They are giving it out to those who can do it; and as for Abel, he'll go to his day-school through the winter. And it means a great deal to me, Mister Churchouse, that you are as good and helpful to him as you were to me when I was young. I don't want to lose that."

"I wish I'd been more helpful, my dear."

"You taught me a great many things valuable to know. I should have been in my grave years ago, but for you, I reckon. And the child's only a child still. If you work upon him, you'll make him meek and mild in time."

"He'll never be meek and mild, Sabina—any more than you were. He has plenty of character; he's good material—excellent stuff to be moulded into a fine pattern, I hope. But a little leaven leavens the whole lump of a child, and what I can do is not enough to outweigh other influences."

"I don't fear for him. He's got to face facts, and as he grows he must use his own wits and get his own living."

"The fear is that he may be spoiled and come to settled, rooted prejudices, too hard to break down afterwards. He is a very interesting boy, just as you were a very interesting girl, Sabina. He often reminds me of you. There are the possibilities of beauty in his character. He is sentimental about some things and strangely indifferent about others. He is a mixture of exaggerated kindness in some directions and utter callousness in others. Sentimental people often are. He will pick a caterpillar out of the road to save it from death, and he will stone a dog if he has a grudge against it. His attitude to Peter Grim is one of devotion. He actually told me that it was very sad that Peter had now grown too old to catch mice. Again, he always brings me the first primrose and spares no pains to find it. Such little acts argue a kindly nature. But against them, you have to set his unreasoning dislike of human beings and a certain—shall I say buccaneering spirit."

"He feels, and so he'll suffer—as I did. The more you feel, the more you suffer."

"And it is therefore our duty to prevent him from feeling mistakenly and wanting to make others suffer. He may sometimes catch allusions in his quick ears that cause him doubt and even pain. And it is certain that the sight of his father does wake wrong thoughts. Removed from here, the best part of him would develop, and when the larger questions of his future begin to be considered in a few years time, he might then approach them with an open mind."

"There can be no harm in leaving it till the spring. He'd hate going away from here."

"I don't think so. The young welcome a change of environment. There is nothing more healthy for their minds as a rule than to travel about. However, we will get him used to the idea of going and think about it again in the spring."

So the subject was left, and when the suggestion of departing from Bridetown came to Abel, he belied the prophecy of Mr. Churchouse and declared a strong objection to the thought of going. His mother influenced him in this.

During the autumn he had a misfortune, for, with two other members of the 'Red Hand,' he was caught stealing apples at the time of cider-making. Three strokes of a birch rod fell on each revolutionary, and not Ernest Churchouse nor his mother could console Abel for this reverse. He gleaned his sole comfort at a dangerous source, and while the kindly ignored the event and the unkindly dwelt upon it, only Levi Baggs applauded Abel and preached privi-conspiracy and rebellion. Raymond Ironsyde was much perturbed at the adventure, but his friend Waldron held the event desirable. As a Justice of the Peace, it was Arthur who prescribed the punishment and trusted in it.

Thus he, too, incurred Abel's enmity. The company of the 'Red Hand' was disbanded to meet no more, and if his fellow sufferers gained by their chastisement, it was certain that Sabina's son did not. Insensate law fits the punishment to the crime rather than to the criminal, as though a doctor should only treat disease, without thought of the patient enduring it.

Neither did Abel's mother take the reverse with philosophy. She resented it as cruel cowardice; but it reminded her of the advantages to be gained by leaving her old home.

Then fell an unexpected disaster and Mr. Churchouse was called to suffer a dangerous attack of bronchitis.

The illness seemed to banish all other considerations from Sabina's mind and, while the issue remained in doubt, she planned various courses of action. Incidentally, she saw more of Estelle and Miss Ironsyde than of late, for Mr. Churchouse, whose first pleasure on earth was now Estelle, craved her presence during convalescence, as Raymond in like case had done; and Miss Ironsyde also drove to see him on several occasions. The event filled all with concern, for Ernest had a trick to make friends and, what is more rare, an art to keep them. Many beyond his own circle were relieved and thankful when he weathered danger and began to build up again with the lengthening days of the new year.

Abel had been very solicitous on his behalf, and he praised the child to Jenny and Estelle, when they came to drink tea with him on a day in early spring.

"I believe there are great possibilities in him and, when I am stronger, I shall resume my attack on Sabina to go away," he said. "The boy's mind is being poisoned and we might prevent it."

"It's a most unfortunate state of affairs," declared Miss Ironsyde. "Yet it was bound to happen in a little place like this. Raymond is not sensitive, or he would feel it far more than he does."

"He can't do more and he does feel it a great deal," declared Estelle. "I think Sabina sees it clearly enough, but it's very hard on her too, to have to go from Mister Churchouse and her home."

"Nothing is more mysterious than the sowing and germination of spiritual seed," said the old man. "The enemy sowed tares by night, and what can be more devilish than sowing the tares of evil on virgin soil? It was done long ago. One hesitates to censure the dead, though I daresay, if we could hear them talking in another world, we should find they didn't feel nearly so nice about us and speak their minds quite plainly. We know plenty of people who must be criticising. But truth will out, and the truth is that Mary Dinnett planted evil thoughts and prejudices in Abel. He was not too young, unfortunately, to give them room. A very curious woman— obstinate and almost malignant if vexed and quite incapable of keeping silence even when it was most demanded. If you are going to give people confidences, you must have a good memory. Mary would confide all sorts of secrets to me and then, perhaps six months afterwards, be quite furious to find I knew them! She came to me for advice on one occasion and I reminded her of certain circumstances she had confided to me in the past, and she lost her temper entirely. Yet a woman of most excellent qualities and most charitable in other people's affairs."

"The question is Abel, and I have told Sabina she must decide about him," said Jenny. "We are all of one mind, and Raymond himself thinks it would be most desirable. As soon as you are well again, Sabina must go."

"I shall miss her very much. To find anybody who will fall into my ways may be difficult. When I was younger, I used to like training a domestic. I found it was better to rule by love than fear. You may lose here and there, but you gain more than you lose. Human character is really not so profoundly difficult, if you resolutely try to see life from the other person's standpoint. That done, you can help them—and yourself through them."

"People who show you their edges, instead of their rounds, are not at all agreeable," said Miss Ironsyde. "To conquer the salients of character is often a very formidable task."

"It is," he admitted, "yet I have found the comfortable, convex and concave characters often really more difficult in the long run. You must have some hard and durable rock on which to found understanding and security. The soft, crumbling people may be lovable; but they are useless as sand at a crisis. They are always slipping away and threatening to smother their best friends with the debris."

He chattered on until a fit of coughing stopped him.

"You mustn't talk so much," warned Estelle. "It's lovely to hear you talking again; but it isn't good for you, yet."

Then she turned to Miss Ironsyde.

"The first time I came in and found him reading a book catalogue, I knew he was going to be all right."

"By the same token another gift has reached me," he answered; "a book on the bells of Devon, which I have long wanted to possess."

"I'm sure it is not such a perfect book as yours."

"Indeed it is—very excellently done. The bell mottoes in Devonshire are worthy of all admiration. But a great many of the bells in ancient bell-chambers are crazed—a grave number. People don't think as much of a ring of bells in a parish as they used to do."

Miss Ironsyde brought the conversation back to Abel; but Ernest was tired of this. He viewed Sabina's departure with great personal regret.

"Things will be as they will, my dears," he told them, "and I have such respect for Sabina's good sense that I shall be quite content to leave decision with her. It would not become me to dictate or command in such a delicate matter. To return to the bells, I have received a rather encouraging statement from the publishers. Four copies of my book have been sold during the last six months."

CHAPTER VII

THE WALK HOME

Upon a Bank Holiday Sabina took Abel to West Haven for a long day on the beach and pier. He enjoyed himself very thoroughly, ate, drank and played to his heart's content. But his amusements brought more pleasure to the child than his mother, for he found the wonderful old stores and discovered therein far more entertaining occupation than either sea or shore could offer.

The place was deserted to-day, and while Sabina sat outside in a corner of the courtyard and occupied herself with the future, Abel explored the mysteries of the ancient building and found all manner of strange nooks and mysterious passages. He wove dreams and magnified the least incident into an adventure. He inhabited the dark corners and sombre, subterranean places with enemies that wanted to catch him; he most potently believed that hidden treasures awaited him under the hollow-echoing floors. Once he had a rare fright, for a bat hanging asleep in its folded wings, was wakened by him and suddenly flew into his face. He climbed and crawled and crept about, stole a lump of putty and rejoiced at the discovery of some paint pots and a brush. The 'Red Hand' no longer existed; but the opportunity once more to set up its sinister symbol was too good to resist. He painted it on the walls in several places and then called his mother to look at the achievement.

She climbed up a long flight of stone steps that led to the lofts, and suffered a strange experience presently, for the child was playing in the chamber sacred to her surrender. She stood where twelve years before she had come with Raymond Ironsyde after their day at Golden Cap.

Light fell through a window let into the roof. It was broken and fringed with cobwebs. The pile of fishermen's nets had vanished and a carpenter's bench had taken its place. On the walls and timbers were scrawled names and initials of holiday folk, who had explored the old stores through many years.

Sabina, perceiving where she stood, closed her eyes and took an involuntary step backward. Abel called attention to his sign upon the walls.

"The carpenter will shiver when he sees that," he said.

Then he rambled off, whistling, and she sat down and stared round her. She told herself that deep thoughts must surely wake under this sudden experience and the fountains of long sealed emotion bubble upwards, to drown her before them. Instead she merely found herself incapable of thinking. A dull, stale, almost stagnant mood crept over her. Her mind could neither walk nor fly. After the first thrill of recognition, the light went out and she found herself absolutely indifferent. Not anger touched her, nor pain. That the child of that perished passion should play here, and laugh and be merry was poignant, but it did not move her and she felt a sort of surprise that it should not. There was a time when such an experience must have shaken her to the depths, plunged her into some deep pang of soul and left indelible wounds; now, no such thing happened.

She gazed mildly about her and almost smiled. Then she rose from her seat on the carpenter's bench, went out and descended the staircase again.

When she called him to a promised tea at an inn, Abel came at once. He was weary and well content.

"I shall often come here," he said. "It's the best place I know—better than the old kiln on North Hill. I could hide there and nobody find me, and you could bring me food at night."

"What do you want to hide for, pretty?" she asked.

"I might," he answered and looked at her cautiously For a moment he seemed inclined to say more, but did not.

After tea they set out for home, and the fate, which, through the incident of the old store, had subtly prepared and paved a way to something of greater import, sent Raymond Ironsyde. They had passed the point at which the road from West Haven converges into that from Bridport, and a man on horseback overtook them. They were all going in the same direction and Abel, as soon as he saw who approached, left his mother, went over a convenient gate upon their right and hastened up a hedge. Thus he always avoided his father, and when blamed for so doing, would silently endure the blame without explanation or any offer of excuse. Raymond had seen him thus escape on more than one occasion, and the incident, clashing at this moment upon his own thoughts, prompted him to a definite and unusual thing. The opportunity was good; Sabina walked alone, and if she rebuffed him, he could endure the rebuff.

He determined to speak to her and break a silence of many years. The result he could not guess, but since he was actuated by friendly motives alone, he hoped the sudden inspiration might prove fertile of good. At worse she could only decline his advance and refuse to speak with him.

Their thoughts that day, unknown to each, had been upon the other and there was some emotion in the man's voice when he spoke, though none in hers when she answered. For to him that chance meeting came as a surprise and prompted him to a sudden approach he might not have ventured on maturer consideration; to her it seemed to carry on the experience of the day and, unguessed by Raymond, brought less amazement than he imagined. She was a fatalist—perhaps, had always been so, as her mother before her; yet she knew it not. They had passed and repassed many times during the vanished years; but since the moment that she had dismissed him with scorn and hoped her child would live to insult his grave, they had never spoken.

He inquired now if he might address her.

"May I say a few words to you?" he asked.

Not knowing what was in her mind, he felt surprised at her conventional reply.

"I suppose so, if you wish to do so."

Her voice seemed to roll back time. Yet he guessed her to be less indifferent than her words implied.

He dismounted and walked beside her.

"I dare say you can understand a little what I feel, when I see that child run away whenever he sets eyes on me," he began; but she did not help him. His voice to her ear was changed. It had grown deeper and hardened. It was more monotonous and did not rise and fall as swiftly as of old.

"I don't know at all what you feel about him. I didn't know that you felt anything about him."

This was a false note and he felt pained.

"Indeed, Sabina, you know very well I want his friendship—I need it even. Before anything I wish to befriend him."

"You can't help him. He's a very affectionate child and loves me dearly. You wouldn't understand him. He's all heart."

He marked now the great change in Sabina. Her voice was cold and indifferent. But a cynic fate willed this mood. Had she not spent the day at West Haven and stood in the old store, it is possible she might have listened to him in another spirit.

"I know he's a clever boy, with plenty of charm about him. And I do think, whatever you may feel, Sabina, it is doubtfully wise of you to stand between him and me."

"If you fancy that, it is a good thing you spoke," she answered. "Because nothing further from the truth could be. I don't stand between him and you. I've never influenced him against you. He's heard nothing but the fact that you're his father from me. I've been careful to leave it at that, and I've never answered more than the truth to his many questions."

"It is a very great sorrow to me, and it will largely ruin my life if I cannot win his friendship and plan his future."

"A child's friendship is easily won. If he denies it, you may be sure it is for a natural instinct."

"Such an instinct is most unnatural. He has had nothing but friendly words and friendly challenges from me."

She felt herself growing impatient. It was clear that he had spoken out of interest for the child alone, and any shadowy suspicion that he designed to declare interest in herself departed from Sabina's mind.

"Well, what's that to me? I can't alter him. I can't make him regard you as a hero and a father to be proud of. He's not hard-hearted or anything of that. He's pretty much like other boys of his age—more sensitive, that's all. He can suffer very sharply and bitterly and he did when that cruel, blundering fool at North Hill House had him whipped. He gets the cursed power to suffer from his mother. And, such is his position in the world, that his power to suffer no doubt will be proved to the utmost."

"I don't want him to suffer. At least it is in my reach to save him a great deal of needless suffering."

"That's just what it isn't—not with his nature. He'd rather suffer than be beholden to you for anything. Young as he is, he's told me so in so many words. He knows he's different from other boys—already he knows it—and that breeds bitterness. He's like a dog that's been ill-treated and finds it hard to trust anybody in consequence. Unfortunately for you, he's got brains enough to judge; and the older he grows, the harder he'll judge."

"That's what I want to break down, Sabina. It's awfully sad to feel, that for a prejudice against things that can't be altered, he should stand in his own light and be a needless martyr and make me a greater villain than I am."

"Are you a villain? If you are, it isn't my child that made you one—nor me, either. No doubt it's awkward to see him running about and breathing the same air with you."

He felt an impulse of anger, but easily checked it.

"You're rather hard on me, I think. It's a great deal more than awkward to have my child take this line. It's desperately sad. And you must know—

thinking purely and only of him—that nothing can be gained and much lost by it. You say he'll hate me more as he grows older. But isn't that a thing to avoid? What good comes into the world with hate? Can't you see that it's your place, Sabina, to use your influence on my side?"

"My God!" she said, "was there ever such a selfish man as you! Out of your own mouth you condemn yourself, for it's your inconvenience and discomfort that's troubling you—not his fate. He's a living witness against you—a running sore in your side—and that's why you want his friendship, to ease yourself and heal your conscience. Anybody could see that."

He did not answer; but this indictment astonished him. Could she still be so stern after the years that had swept over their quarrel?

"You wrong me there, Sabina. Indeed, it's not for my own comfort only, but much more largely for his that I am so much concerned. Surely we can meet on the common ground of his welfare and leave the rest?"

"What common ground is there? Why must I think your friendship and your money are the best possible things for him? Why should I advise him to take what I refused for myself twelve years and more ago? You offered me your friendship and your money—as a substitute for being your wife. You were so stark ignorant of the girl you'd promised to marry, that you offered her cash and the privilege of your company after your child was born. And now you offer your child cash and the privilege of your company—that's all. You deny him your name, as you denied his mother your name; and why should he pick up the crumbs from your table that his mother would have starved rather than eaten? I've never spoken against you to him and never shall, but I'm not a fool now—whatever I was—and I'm not going to urge my son to seek you and put his little heart into your keeping; because well I know what you do with hearts. I'm outside your life and so is he; and if he likes to come into your life, I shan't prevent it. I couldn't prevent it. He'll do about it as he chooses, when he's old enough to measure it up. But I'm not for you, or against you. I'm only the suffering sort, not the fighting sort. You know whether you deserve the love and worship of that little, nameless boy."

He was struck into silence, not at her bitter words, but at his own thoughts. For he had often speculated on future speech with her and wondered when it would happen and what it would concern. He had hoped that she would let the past go and be his friend again on another plane. He had pictured some sort of amity based on the old romance. He had desired nothing so much in life as a friendly understanding and the permission to contribute to the ease and comfort of Sabina and the prosperity of his son. He hoped that in course of time and faced with the rights of the child, she would come round. He had pictured her coming round. But now it seemed that he was not to plan their future on his own terms. What he offered had not grown sweeter to her senses. No gifts that he could devise would be anything but poor in the light of the unkind past. And that light burned steadfastly still. She was not changed. As he listened to her, it seemed that she was merely picking up the threads where they were dropped. He feared that if he stopped much longer beside her, she would come back to the old anger and wake into the old wrath.

"I'd dearly hoped that you didn't feel like that, any more. You've got right on your side up to a point, though human differences are so involved that it very seldom happens you can get a clean cut between right and wrong. However, the time is past for arguing about that, Sabina. Granted you are right in your personal attitude, don't carry it on into the next generation and assume I cannot even yet, after all these years, be trusted to befriend my own child."

"He's only your child in nature. He's only your child because your blood's in his veins. He's my child, not yours."

"But if I want to make him mine? If I want to lift him up and assure his future? If I want to assume paternity—claim it, adopt him as my son—to succeed me some day?"

"He must decide for himself whether that's the high-water mark for his future life—to be your adopted son. We can't have it all our own way in this world—not even you, I suppose. A child has to have a mother as well as a father, and a mother's got her rights in her child. Even the law allows that."

"Who'd deny them, Sabina? You're possessed, as you always were, with the significance of legal marriage. You don't know that marriage is merely a human contrivance and, nine times out of ten, an infernally clumsy makeshift and a long-drawn pretence. Like every other human shift, it is a thing that gets out-grown by the advance of humanity towards higher ideals and cleaner liberties. We are approaching a time when the edifice will be shaken to its mouldering foundations, and presently, while the Church and the State are wrangling and quibbling, as they soon must be, over the loathsome divorce laws, these mandarins will wake up to find the marriage laws themselves are being threatened by a new generation sick of the archaic tomfoolery that controls them. If you could only take a larger view and not let yourself be bound down by your own experience—"

"You'd better go," she said. "If you'd spoken, so twelve years ago on Golden Cap, and not hid your heart and lied to me and promised what you never meant to perform, I'd not be walking the world a lonely, despised woman to-day. And law, or no law, the law of the natural child is the law of the land—cruel and vile though it may be."

"I'll go, Sabina; but I must say what I want to say, first. I must stand up for Abel—even against you. Childish impressions and dislikes can be rooted out if taken in time; if left to grow, they get beyond reach. So I ask you to think of him. And don't pretend to yourself that my friendship is dangerous, or can do him anything but good. I'm very different from what I was. Life hasn't gone over me for nothing. I know what's right well enough, and I know what I owe your son and my son, and I want to make up to him and more than make up to him for his disadvantages. Don't prevent me from doing that. Give me a chance, Sabina. Give me a chance to be a good father to him. Your word is law with him, and if you left Bridetown and took him away from all the rumours and unkind things he may hear here, it would let his mind grow empty of me for a few years; and then, when he's older and more sensible, I think I could win him."

"You want us away from this place."

"I do. I never should have spoken to you until I knew you wished it, but for this complication; but since the boy is growing up prejudiced against me, I do feel that some strong effort should be taken to nip his young hatred in the bud—for his sake, Sabina."

"Are you sure it's all for his sake? Because I'm not. They say you think of nothing on God's earth but machinery nowadays, and look to machines to do the work of hands, and speak of 'hands' when you ought to speak of 'souls.' They say if you could, you'd turn out all the people and let everything be done by steam and steel. There's not much humanity in you, I reckon. And why should you care for one little, unwanted boy? Perhaps, if you looked deeper into yourself, you'd find it was your own peace, rather than his, that's making you wish us away from Bridetown. At any rate, that's how one or two have seen and said it, when they heard how everybody was at me to go. I've had to live down the past for long, slow, heart-breaking years and seen the fingers pointed at me; and now, with the child growing up, it's your turn I daresay, and you—so strong and masterful—have had enough of pointing fingers and mean to pack us out of our home—for your comfort."

He stared at her in the gathering dusk and stood and uttered a great sigh from deep in his lungs.

"I'm sorry for you, Sabina—sorrier than I am for myself. This is cruel. I didn't know, or dream, that time had stood still for you like this."

"Time ended for me—then."

"For me it had to go on. I must think about this. I didn't guess it was like this with you. Don't think I want you away; don't think you're the only thorn in my pillow and that I'm not used to pain and anxiety, or impatient of all the implicit meaning of your lonely life. Stop, if you want to stop. I'll see you again, Sabina, please. Now I'll be gone."

When he had mounted his horse and ridden away without more words from her, Abel, who had been lurking along on the other side of the hedge, crept through it and rejoined his mother.

They walked on in silence for some time. Then the child spoke.

"Fancy your talking to Mister Ironsyde, mother!"

"He talked to me."

"I lay you dressed him down then?"

"I told him the truth, Abel. He wants everything for nothing, Mister Ironsyde does. He wants you—for nothing."

"He's a beast, and I hate him, and he'll know I hate him some day."

"Don't hate him. He's not worth hating."

"I will hate him, I tell you. But for him I'd be the great man in Bridetown when he dies. Mister Baggs told me that."

"You mustn't give heed to what people say. You've got mother to look after you."

The boy was tired and spoke no more. He padded silently along beside her and presently she heard him laugh to himself. His thoughts had wandered back to the joy of the old store.

And she was thinking of what had happened. She, too, even as Raymond, had imagined what speech would fall out between them after the long years and wondered concerning the form it would take. She had imagined no such conversation as this. Half of her regretted it; but the other half was glad. He had gone on, but it was well that he should know she had stood still. Could there be any more terrible news for him than to hear that she had stood still—to feel that he had turned a living woman into a pillar of stone?

CHAPTER VIII

EPITAPH

It cannot be determined by what train of reasoning Abel proceeded from one unfortunate experience to create another, or why the grief incidental on a loss should now have nerved him to an evil project long hidden in his thoughts. But so it was; he suffered a sorrow and, under the influence of it, found himself strong enough to attempt a crime.

There was no sort of connection between the two, for nothing could bear less upon his evil project than the death of Mr. Churchouse's old cat; yet thus it fell out and the spirit of Abel reacted to his own tears.

He came home one day from school to learn how the sick cat prospered and was told to go into the study. His mother knew the child to be much wrapped up in Peter Grim, and dreading to break the news, begged Mr. Churchouse to do so.

"Your old playfellow has left us, daddy," said Ernest. "I am glad to say he died peacefully while you were at school. I think he only had a very little bit of his ninth and last life left, for he was fifteen years old and had suffered some harsh shocks."

"Dead?" asked Abel with a quivering mouth.

"And I think that we ought to give him a nice grave and put up a little stone to his memory."

Thus he tried to distract the boy from his loss.

"We will go at once," he said, "and choose a beautiful spot in the garden for his grave. You can take one of those pears and eat it while we search."

But Abel shook his head.

"Couldn't eat and him lying dead," he answered. He was crying.

They went through the French window from the study.

"Do you know any particular place that he liked?"

Slowly the child's sorrow lessened in the passing interest of finding the grave.

"You must dig it, please, when you come back from afternoon school."

Abel suggested spots not practical in the other's opinion.

"A more secluded site would be better," he declared. "He was very fond of shade. In fact, rather a shady customer himself in his young days. But not a word against the dead. His old age was dignified and blameless. You don't remember the time when he used to steal chickens, do you?"

"He never did anything wrong that I know of," said Abel. "And he always came and padded on my bed of a morning, like as if he was riding a bicycle—and—and—"

He wept again.

"If I thought anybody had poisoned him, I'd poison them," he said.

"Think no such thing. He simply died because he couldn't go on living. You shall have another cat, and it shall be your own."

"I don't want another cat. I hate all other cats but him."

They found a spot in a side walk, where lily of the valley grew, and later in the day Abel dug a grave.

Estelle happened to visit Mr. Churchouse and he explained the tragedy.

"If you attend the funeral, the boy might tolerate you," he said. "Once break down his suspicion and get to his wayward heart, good would come of it He is feeling this very much and in a melting mood."

"I'll stop, if he won't be vexed."

Mr. Churchouse went into the garden and praised Abel's energies.

"A beautiful grave; and it is right and proper that Peter Grim should lie here, because he often hunted here."

"He caught the mice that live in holes at the bottom of the wall," said Abel.

"If you are ready, we will now bury him. Mother must come to the funeral, and Estelle must come, because she was very, very fond of poor Peter and she would think it most unkind of us if we buried him while she was not there. She will bring some flowers for the grave, and you must get some flowers, too, Abel. We must, in fact, each put a flower on him."

The boy frowned at mention of Estelle, but forgot her in considering the further problem.

"He liked the mint bed. I'll put mint on him," he said.

"An excellent thought. And I shall pluck one of the big magnolias myself."

Returning, Ernest informed Estelle that she must be at the funeral and she went home for a bunch of blossoms to grace the tomb. She picked hot-house flowers, hoping to propitiate Abel. There woke a great hope in her to win him. But she failed.

He glowered at her when she appeared walking beside his mother, while before them marched Mr. Churchouse carrying the departed. When the funeral was ended and Abel left alone, he sat down by the grave, cried, worked himself into a very mournful mood and finally exhibited anger. Why he was angry he did not know, or against whom his temper grew; but his great loss woke resentment. When he felt miserable, somebody was always blamed by him for making him feel so. No immediate cause for quarrel with anything smaller than fate challenged his unsettled mind; then his eyes fixed upon Estelle's flowers, and since Estelle was always linked in his thoughts with his father, and his father represented an enemy, he began to hate the flowers and wish them away. He heard his mother calling him, but hid from her and when she was silent, came back to the grave again.

Meantime Estelle and Ernest drank tea and spoke of Abel.

"When grief has relaxed the emotions, we may often get in a kindly word and give an enemy something to think about afterwards," he said. "But the boy was obdurate. He is the victim of confused thinking—precocious to a degree in some directions, but very childish in others. At times he alarms me. Poor boy. You must try again to win him. The general sentiment is that the young should be patient with the old; but for my part I think it is quite as difficult sometimes for the old to be patient with the young."

He turned to his desk.

"When I found my dear cat was not, I composed an epitaph for him, Estelle. I design to have it scratched on a stone and set above his sleeping place."

"Do let me hear it," she said, and Ernest, fired with the joy of composition, read his memorial verse.

"Criticise freely," he said. "I value your criticism and you understand poetry. Not that this is a poem—merely an epitaph; but it may easily be improved, I doubt not."

He put on his glasses and read:

"'Ended his mingled joy and strife,
  Here lies the dust of Peter Grim.
  Though life was very kind to him,
  He proved not very kind to life.'"

Estelle applauded.

"Perfect," she said. "You must have it carved on his tombstone."

"I think it meets the case. I may have been prejudiced in my affection for him, owing to his affection for me. He came to me at the age of five weeks, and his attitude to me from the first was devoted."

"Cats have such cajoling ways."

"He was not himself honest, yet, I think, saw the value of honesty in others. Plain dealers are a temptation to rogues and none, as a rule, is a better judge of an honest man than a dishonest cat."

"He wasn't quite a rogue, was he?"

"He knew that I am respected, and he traded on my reputation. His life has been spared on more than one occasion for my sake."

"On the whole he was not a very model cat, I'm afraid," said Estelle.

"Yes, that is just what he was: a model—cat."

They went out to look at the grave again, and something hurried away through the bushes as they did so.

"Friends, or possibly enemies," suggested Mr. Churchouse, but Estelle, sharper-eyed, saw Abel disappear. She also noted that her bouquet of flowers had gone from Peter's mound.

"Oh dear, he's taken away my offering," she said.

"What a hard-hearted boy! Are there no means of winning him?"

They spoke of Abel and his mother.

"We all regretted her decision to stop. It would have been better if she had gone away."

"Raymond saw her some time ago."

"So she told me; and so did he. Misfortune seems to dog the situation, for I believe Sabina was half in a mind to take our advice until that meeting. Then she changed. Apparently she misunderstood him."

"Ray was very troubled. Somehow he made Sabina angry—the last thing he meant to do. He's sorry now that he spoke. She thought he was considering himself, and he really was thinking for Abel."

"We must go on being patient. Next year I shall urge her to let Abel be sent to a boarding-school. That will be a great advantage every way."

So they talked and meantime Abel's sorrow ran into the channels of evil. It may be that the presence of Estelle had determined this misfortune; but he was ripe for it and his feeling prompted him to let his misery run over, that others might drink of the cup. He had long contemplated a definite deed and planned a stroke against Raymond Ironsyde; but he had postponed the act, partly from fear, partly because the thought of it was a pleasure. Inverted instincts and a mind fouled by promptings from without, led him to understand that Ironsyde was his mother's enemy and therefore his own. Baggs had told him so in a malignant moment and Abel believed it. To injure his enemy was to honour his mother. And the time had come to do so. He was ripe for it to-night. He told himself that Peter Grim would have approved the blow, and with his mind a chaos of mistaken opinions, at once ludicrous and mournful, he set himself to his task. He ate his supper as usual and went to bed; but when the house was silent in sleep, he rose, put on his clothes and hastened out of doors. He departed by a window on the ground floor and slipped into a night of light and shade, for the moon was full and rode through flying clouds.

The boy felt a youthful malefactor's desire to get his task done as swiftly as possible. He was impatient to feel the deed behind him. He ran through the deserted village, crossed a little bridge over the river, and then approached the Mill by a meadow below them. Thus he always came to see Mr. Baggs, or anybody who was friendly.

The roof of the works shone in answer to fitful moonlight, and they presented to his imagination a strange and unfamiliar appearance. Under the sleight of the hour they were changed and towered majestically above him. The Mill slept and in the creepy stillness, the river's voice, which he had hardly heard till now, was magnified to a considerable murmur. From far away down the valley came the song of the sea, where a brisk, westerly wind threw the waves on the shingle.

A feeling of awe numbed him, but it was not powerful enough to arrest his purpose. His plans had been matured for many days.

He meant to burn down the Mill.

Nothing was easier and a match in the inflammable material, of which the hackler's shop was usually full, must quickly involve the mass of the buildings.

It was fitting that where he had been impregnated by Mr. Baggs with much lawless opinion, Abel should give expression to his evil purpose. From the tar-pitched work-room of the hackler, fire would very quickly leap to the main building against which it stood, and might, indeed, under the strong wind, involve the stores also and John Best's dwelling between them. But it was fated otherwise. A very small incident served to prevent a considerable catastrophe, and when Abel broke the window of the hackling room, turned the hasp, raised it, and got in, a man lay awake in pain not thirty yards distant. The lad lighted a candle, which he had brought with him, and it was then, while he collected a heap of long hemp and prepared to set it on fire, that John Best, in torture from toothache, went downstairs for a mouthful of brandy.

Upon the staircase he passed a window and, glancing through it, he saw a light in the hackling shop. It was not the moon and meant a presence there that needed instant explanation. Mr. Best forgot his toothache, called his sailor son, who happened to be holiday-making at home, and hastened as swiftly and silently as possible over the bridge to the Mill. John Best the younger, an agile man of thirty, may be said to have saved the situation, for he was far quicker than his father could be and managed to anticipate the disaster by moments. Half a minute more might have made all the difference, for the heap of loose hemp and stricks once ignited, no power on earth could have saved a considerable conflagration; but the culprit had his back turned to the window and was still busily piling the tow when Best and his son looked in upon him, and the sailor was already half through the window before Abel perceived him. The youngster dashed for his candle, but he was too late, a pair of strong hands gripped his neck roughly enough, and he fainted from the shock.

They took him out as he had gone in, for the door was locked and Levi Baggs had the key. Then the sailor went back to his home, dressed himself and started for a policeman, while Mr. Best kept guard over Abel.

When he came to his senses, the boy found himself in the moonlight with a dozen turns of stout fisherman's twine round his hands and ankles The foreman stood over him, and now that the house was roused, his wife had brought John a pair of trousers and a great coat, for he was in his night shirt.

"You'll catch your death," she said.

"It's only by God's mercy we didn't all catch our death," he answered. "Here's Sabina Dinnett's boy plotted to destroy the works, and we've yet to find whether he's the tool of others, or has done the deed on his own."

"On my own I did it," declared Abel; "and I'll do it yet."

"You shut your mouth, you imp of Satan!" cried the exasperated man. "Not a word, you scamp. You've done for yourself now, and everybody knew you'd come to it, sooner or later."

In half an hour Abel was locked up, and when Mr. Baggs heard next morning concerning the events of the night, he expressed the utmost surprise and indignation.

"Young dog! And after the friend I've been to him. Blood will tell. That's his lawless father coming out in the wretch," he said.

CHAPTER IX

THE FUTURE OF ABEL

Issues beyond human sight or calculation lay involved in the thing that Abel Dinnett had done. He had cast down a challenge to society, and everything depended on how society answered that challenge. Not only did the child's own future turn on what must follow, but vital matters for those who were called to act hung on their line of action. That, however, they could not know. The tremendous significance of the sinner's future training and the result of what must now happen to him lay far beyond their prescience.

It became an immediate question whether Abel might, or might not, be saved from the punishment he had deserved. Beyond that rose another problem, not less important, and his father doubted whether, for the child's own sake, it would be well to intervene. Waldron strongly agreed with him; but Estelle did not, and she used her great influence on the side of intervention. Miss Ironsyde and Ernest Churchouse were also of her opinion. Indeed, all concerned, save his mother and Arthur Waldron, begged Raymond to interfere, if possible.

He did not decide immediately.

"The boy will be sent to a reformatory for five years if I do nothing," he told Estelle, "and that's probably the very best thing on earth that can happen to him. It will put the fear of God into him and possibly obliterate his hate of me. He's bad all through, I'm afraid."

"No he isn't—far from it. That's the point," she argued. "These things are a legacy—a hateful legacy from his grandmother. Mister Churchouse knows him far better than anybody else, and he says there is great sensibility and power of feeling in him. He's tender to animals."

"That's not much good if he's going to be tough to me. Tell me why his mother doesn't come to me about him."

"Mister Churchouse says she's in a strange state and doesn't seem to care. She told him the sins of the fathers were being visited on the children."

"The sins of the fathers are being visited on the fathers, I should think."

"That's fair at any rate," she said. "I know just how you must feel. You've been so patient, Ray, and taken such a lot of trouble. But I believe it's all part of the fate that links you to the child. His future is made your business now, whether you will or no. It is thrust upon you. Nobody but you would be listened to by the law; but you can give an undertaking and do something to save him from the horror of a reformatory."

Estelle and Raymond were having tea together at 'The Seven Stars' during this conversation. Her father was returning home to Bridport by an evening train and she had driven to meet him. Nelly Legg waited upon them, and knowing the matter occupied many tongues, Raymond spoke to her.

"You can guess this is a puzzler, Nelly," he said. "What would you do? Miss Waldron says it's up to me to try and get the boy off; but the question is shall I be serving him best that way?"

"My husband and me have gone over it," she confessed; "of course, everybody has done so. You can't pretend the people aren't interested, and if one has asked Job his opinion, a hundred have. People bring him their puzzles and troubles as a sort of habit. From a finger ache to the loss of a fortune they pour their difficulties into his wise head, and for patience he's a very good second to the first of the name. And I may tell you a curious thing, Mister Raymond, for I've seen it happen. As the folks talk and talk to Legg, they get more and more cheerful and he gets more and more depressed. Then, after they've let off all their woes on the man, sometimes they'll have the grace to apologise and say it's too bad to give him such a dose. And they always wind up by assuring him he's done them a world of good; but they never stop to think what they have done to him."

"Vampires of sympathy—blood-suckers," declared Raymond. "Such kindly men as your husband must pay for their virtues, Nelly."

"Sympathetic people have to work hard," added Estelle.

"Not that he wants the lesser people's gratitude, so long as he has my admiration," explained Mrs. Legg. "And that he always will have, for he's more than human in some particulars. And only I know the full extent of his wonders. A master of stratagems too—the iron hand in the velvet glove—though if you was to tell half the people in Bridport he's got an iron hand, they never would believe it. And as to this sad affair, he's given his opinion and won't change it. You may think him right or wrong, but so it is."

"And what does he say, Nelly?"

"He says the child may be saved as a brand from the burning if the law takes its course. He thinks that if you, or anybody, was to go bail for the child and save him from the consequences of his wicked deed, that a great mistake would be made. In justice to you I should say that they don't all agree. Some hope you'll interfere—mostly women."

"What do you think?" asked Raymond.

"As Missis Legg, I think the same as him; and I'll tell you another thing you may not know. The young boy's mother is by no means sure if she don't feel the same. My married niece is her friend, and last time she saw her, Sabina spoke about it. From what Sarah says I think she feels it might be better for the boy to put him away. I can't say as to her motives. Naturally she's only concerned as to the welfare of the child and knows he'll never be trained to any good where he is."

That Sabina had expressed so strong an opinion interested Raymond. But Estelle refused to believe it.

"I'm sure Sarah misunderstood," she said. "Sabina couldn't mean that."

They went to the station presently, met Arthur Waldron and drove him home. Estelle urged Raymond to see Sabina before he decided what to do; and since little time was left before he must act, he went to 'The Magnolias' that evening and begged for an interview.

Sabina had a small sitting-room of her own in which evidence of Abel did not lack. Drawings that he had made at school were hung on the walls, and a steam-engine—a present from Mr. Churchouse on his twelfth birthday—stood upon the mantel-shelf.

"It's just this, Sabina," he said; "I won't keep you; but I feel the future of the boy is in the balance and I can't do anything without hearing your opinion. And first I want you to understand I have quite forgiven him. He's not all to blame. Certain fixed, false ideas he has got. They were driven into him at his most impressionable age; and until his reason asserts itself no doubt he'll go on hating me. But that'll all come right. I don't blame you for it."

"You should blame me all the same," she said. "It's as much me in his blood as his grandmother at his ear, that turned him to hate you. I don't hate you now—or anybody, or anything. I've not got strength and fight in me now to hate, or love either. But I did hate you and I was full of hate before he was born, and the milk was curdled with hate that fed him. Now I don't care what happens. I can't prevent the future of my child from shaping itself. The time for preventing things and doing things and fixing character and getting self-respect is over and past. What he's done is the natural result of what was done to him. And who'll blame him? Who'll blame me for being bad and indifferent—wicked if you like? Life's made me so—hard—cold to others. But I should have been different if I'd had love and common justice. So would he. It's natural in him to hate you; and now the poor little wretch will get what he deserves—same as his mother did before him, and so all's said. What we deserved, that's all."

"I don't think so. I'm very willing to fight for him if I can do him good by fighting. The situation is unusual. You probably do not realise what this means to me. Is there to be no finality in your resentment? Honestly I get rather tired of it."

"I got rather tired of it twelve years ago."

"You're not prepared to help me, then, or make any suggestion—for the child's sake?"

"I'll not help, or hinder. I've been looking on so long now that I'm only fit to look on. My child has everything against him, and he knows it; and you can't save him from his fate any more than I can. So what's the good of wasting time talking as though you could? Fate's fate—beyond us."

"We make our own fate. I may tell you that I should have been largely influenced by you, Sabina. The question admits of different answers and I recognise my responsibility. Some say that I must intervene now and some say that I should not."

"And the only one not asked to give an opinion is Abel himself. A child is never asked about his own hopes and fears."

"We know what his hopes were—to burn down the Mill. So we may take it for the present he's not the best judge of what's good for him."

"I've done my duty to him," she said, "and that's all I could do. I'm very sorry for him, and what love I've got for him is the sort that's akin to pity. It's contrary to reason that I should take any deep joy in him, or worship the ground he walks on, like other mothers do towards their children. For he stands there before me for ever as the sign and mark of my own failure in life. But I don't think any less of him for trying to destroy the works. I'd decided about him long ago."

Raymond found nothing to the purpose in this illusive talk. It argued curious impassivity in Sabina he thought, and he felt jarred to find the conventional attitude of mother to son was not acknowledged by her. Estelle had showed far more feeling, had taken a much more active part in the troubles of Abel. Estelle had spared no pains in arguing for the child and imploring Ironsyde to exhaust his credit on Abel's behalf.

He told Sabina this and she explained it.

"I dare say she has. A woman can see why, though doubtless you cannot. It isn't because he's himself that she's active for him; and it isn't because he's my child, either. It's because he's your child. Your blood's sacred in her eyes you may be sure. She was a child herself when you ruined me; she forgets all that. Why? Because ever since she's grown to womanhood and intelligence to note what happens, you have been a saint of virtue and the friend of the weak and the champion of the poor. So, of course, she feels that such a great and good man's son only wants his father's care to make him great and good too."

"To think you can talk so after all these years, Sabina," he said.

"How should I talk? What are the years to me? You never knew, or understood, or respected the stuff I was made of; and you'll never understand your child, either, or the stuff he's made of; and you can tell the young woman that loves you so much, that she's wrong—as wrong as can be. Nothing's gained by your having any hand in Abel's future. You won't win him with sugarplums now, any more than you will with money later on. He's made of different stuff from you—and better stuff and rarer stuff. There's very little of you in him and very little of me, either. He's himself, and the fineness that might have made him a useful man under fair conditions, is turned to foulness now. Your child was ruined in the making—not by me, but by you yourself. And such is his mind that he knows it already. So be warned and let him alone."

"If anything could make me agree with Miss Waldron, Sabina, it would be what you tell me," he answered. "And if I can live to show you that you are terribly wrong I shall be glad."

"That you never will."

"At least you'll do nothing to come between us?"

"I never have. I was very careful not to do that. If he can look at you as a friend presently, I shan't prevent it. I shan't warn him against you—though I've warned you against him. The weak use poisonous weapons, because they haven't got the strength to use weapons of might. That's why he tried to burn down the Mill. He'll be stronger some day."

"He's clever, I'm told, and if we can only interest him in some intelligent business and find what his bent is, we may fill his mind to good purpose. At any rate, I thank you for leaving me free to act. Now I can decide what course to take. It was impossible until I heard what you felt."

She said no more and he left her to make up his mind. Doubt persisted there, for he still suspected, that five years in a reformatory might be better for Abel than anything else. Such an experience he felt would develop his character, crush his malignant instincts and leave him only too ready to accept his father as his friend; but against such a fate for Abel, was his own relationship to the culprit, and the question whether Raymond would not suffer very far-reaching censure if he made no effort to come to the boy's rescue. Truest wisdom might hold a severe course of correction very desirable; but sentiment and public opinion would be likely to condemn him if he did nothing. People would say that he had taken a harsh revenge on his own, erring child.

He fumed at a situation intolerable and was finally moved to accept Estelle's advice. From no considerations for Bridport, or Bridetown, did she urge his active intervention. For Abel's sake she begged it and was more insistent than before, when she heard of Sabina's indifference.

"He's yours," she said. "You've been so splendidly patient. So do go on being patient, and the result will be a fine character and a reward for you. It isn't what people would say; but if he goes to a reformatory, far from wanting you and your help when he comes out again, he'll know in the future that you might have saved him from it and given him a first-rate education among good, upright boys. But if he went to a reformatory, he must meet all sorts of difficult boys, like himself, and they wouldn't help him, and he'd come out harder than he went in."

His heart yielded to her at last, even though his head still doubted, for Raymond's attitude to Estelle had begun insensibly to change since his accident in the cricket field. From that time he won a glimpse of things that apparently others already knew. Sabina, in their recorded conversation, had bluntly told him that Estelle loved him; and while the man dismissed the idea as an absurdity, it was certain that from this period he began to grow somewhat more sentimentally interested in her. The interest developed very slowly, but this business of Abel brought them closer together, for she haunted him during the days before the child came to his trial, and when, perhaps for her sake as much as any other reason, Raymond decided to undertake his son's defence, her gratitude was great.

He made it clear to her that she was responsible for his determination.

"I've let you over-rule me, Estelle," he told her. "Don't forget it, Chicky. And now that the boy will, I hope, be in my hands, you must strengthen my hands all you can and help me to make him my friend."

She promised thankfully.

"Be sure I shall never, never forget," she said, "and I shall never be happy till he knows what you really are, and what you wish him. You must win him now. It's surely contrary to all natural instinct if you can't. The mere fact that you can forgive him for what he tried to do, ought to soften his heart."

"I trust more to you than myself," he answered.

CHAPTER X

THE ADVERTISEMENT

Raymond Ironsyde had his way, and local justices, familiar with the situation, were content not to commit Abel, but leave the boy in his father's hands. He took all responsibility and, when the time came, sent his son to a good boarding-school at Yeovil. Sabina so far met him that the operation was conducted in her name, and since the case of Abel had been kept out of local papers, his fellow scholars knew nothing of his errors. But his difficulties of character were explained to those now set over him, and they were warned that his moral education, while attempted, had not so far been successful.

Perhaps only one of those concerned much sympathised with Ironsyde in his painful ordeal. Those who did not openly assert that he was reaping what he had sown, were indifferent. Some, like Mr. Motyer, held the incident a joke; one only possessed imagination sufficient to guess what these public events must mean to the father of Abel. Indeed, Estelle certainly suffered more for Raymond than he suffered for himself. She pictured poignantly his secret thoughts and sorrows at this challenge, and she could guess what it must be to have a child who hated you. In her maiden mind, however, the man's emotions were exaggerated, and she made the mistake of supposing that this grievous thing must be dominating Raymond's existence, instead of merely vexing it. In truth he suffered, but he was juster than Estelle, and, looking back, measured his liabilities pretty accurately. He had none but himself to thank for these inconveniences, and when he weighed them against the alternative of marriage with Sabina, he counted them as bearable. Abel tried him sorely, but he did not try him as permanent union with Abel's mother must have tried him. Since he had renewed speech with her, his conviction was increased that supreme disaster must have followed marriage. Moreover, there began to rise a first glimmer of the new situation already indicated. It had grown gradually and developed more intensely during his days of enforced idleness in his aunt's house. From that time, at any rate, he marked the change and saw his old regard and respect for Estelle wakening into something greater. Her sympathy quickened the new sentiments. He thought she was saner over Abel than anybody, for she never became sentimental, or pretended that nothing had happened which might not have been predicted. Her support was both human and practical. It satisfied him and showed him her good sense.

Miss Ironsyde had often reminded her nephew that he was the last of his line, and urged him to take a wife and found a family. That Raymond should marry seemed desirable to her; but she had not considered Estelle as a wife for him. Had she done so, Jenny must have feared the girl too young and too doubtful in opinions to promise complete success and safety for the master of the Mill. He would marry a mature woman and a steadfast Christian—so hoped Miss Ironsyde then.

There came a day when Raymond called on Mr. Churchouse. Business brought him and first he discussed the matter of an advertisement.

"In these days," he said, "the competition grows keener than ever. And I rather revel in it—as I do in the east wind. It's not pleasant at the time, but, if you're healthy, it's a tonic."

"And if you're not, it finds the weak places," added Mr. Churchouse. "No man over sixty has much good to say of the east wind."

"Well, the works are healthy enough and competition is merely a tonic to us. We hold our own from year to year, and I've reached a conviction that my policy of ruthlessly scrapping machinery the moment it's even on the down grade, is the only sound principle and pays in the long run. And now I want something new in the advertisement line—something not mechanical at all, but human and interesting—calculated to attract, not middlemen and retailers, but the person who buys our string and rope to use it. In fact I want a little book about the romance of spinning, so that people may look at a ball of string, or shoe-thread, or fishing-line, intelligently, and realise about one hundredth part of all that goes to its creation. Now you could do a thing like that to perfection, Uncle Ernest, because you know the business inside out."

Mr. Churchouse was much pleased.

"An excellent idea—a brilliant idea, Raymond! We must insist on the romance of spinning—the poetry."

"I don't want it to be too flowery, but just interesting and direct. A glimpse of the raw material growing, then the history of its manufacture."

Ernest's eyes sparkled.

"From the beginning—from the very beginning," he said. "Pliny tells us how the Romans used hemp for their sails at the end of the first century. Is not the English word 'canvas' only 'cannabis' over again? Herodotus speaks of the hempen robes of the Thracians as equal to linen in fineness. And as for cordage, the ships of Syracuse in 200 B.C.—"

He was interrupted.

"That's all right, but what I rather fancy is the development of the modern industry—here in Dorset."

"Good—that would follow with all manner of modern instances."

Mr. Churchouse drew a book from one of his shelves.

"In Tudor times it was ordered by Act of Parliament that ropes should be twisted and made nowhere else than here. Leland, that industrious chronicler, came to grief in this matter, for he calls Bridport 'a fair, large town,' where 'be made good daggers.' He shows the danger of taking words too literally, since a 'Bridport dagger' is only another name for the hangman's rope."

"That's the sort of thing," said Raymond. "An article we can illustrate, showing the hemp and flax growing in Russia and Italy, then all the business of pulling, steeping and retting, drying and scutching. That would be one chapter."

"It shall be done. I see it—I see the whole thing—an elegant brochure and well within my power. I am fired with the thought. There is only one objection, however."

"None in the world. I see you know just what I'm after—a little pamphlet well illustrated."

"The objection is that Estelle Waldron would do it a thousand times better than I can. She has a more modern outlook and a more modern touch. I feel confident that with me to supply the matter, she would produce a much more attractive and readable work."

Raymond considered.

"I suppose she would. I hadn't thought of her."

"Believe me, she would succeed to admiration. For your sake as well as mine, she would produce a little masterpiece."

"She'd do anything to please you, we all know; but I've no right to bother her with details of business. Of course, if you do it, it is a commission and you would name your honorarium, Uncle Ernest."

The old man laughed.

"We'll see—we'll see. Perhaps I should ask too high a price. But Estelle will not be so grasping. And as to your right to bother her with the details of business, anything she can do for you is a very great privilege to her."

"I believe I owe her more than a man can ever pay a woman, already."

"Most men are insolvent to the other sex. Woman's noble tradition is to give more than she gets, and let us off the reckoning, quite well knowing it beyond our feeble powers to cry quits with her."

Raymond was moved at this challenge, for in the light that Estelle threw upon them, women interested him more to-day than they had for ten years.

"One takes old Arthur's daughter for granted rather too much," he said; "we always take good women for granted too much, I suppose. It's the other sort who look out we shan't take them for granted, but at their own valuation. Estelle—she's so many-sided—difficult, too, in some things."

"She is," admitted Ernest. "And just for this reason. She always argues on her own basis of perfect ingenuous honesty. She assumes certain rational foundations for all human relations; and if such bases really existed, then it would be the best possible world, no doubt, and we should all do to our neighbour as we would have him do to us. But the Golden Rule doesn't actuate the bulk of mankind, unfortunately. Men and women are not as good as Estelle thinks them."

Raymond agreed eagerly.

"You've hit it," he said. "It is just that. She's right in theory every time; and if people were all as straight and altruistic and high-principled as she is, there'd really be no more bother about morals in the world. Native good sense would decide. Even as it is, the native good sense of mankind is deciding certain questions and will presently push the lawyers into codifying their mouldy laws, and then give reason a chance to cleanse the whole archaic lump of them; but as it is, Estelle—Take Marriage, for example. I agree with her all the way—in theory. But when you come to view the situation in practice—you're up against things as they are, and you never want people you love to be martyrs, however noble the cause. Estelle says the law of sex relationships is barbaric, and that marriage is being submitted to increasing rational criticism, which the law and the Church both conspire to ignore. She thinks that these barriers to progress ought to be swept away, because they have a vicious effect on the institution and degrade men and women. She's always got her eye on the future, and the result is sometimes that she doesn't focus the present too exactly. It's noble, but not practical."

"The institution of marriage will last Estelle's time, I think," declared Mr. Churchouse.

"One hopes so heartily—for her own sake. One knows very well it's an obsolescent sort of state, and can't bear the light of reason, and must be reformed, so that intelligent people can enter it in a self-respecting spirit; but if there is one institution that defies the pioneers, it is marriage. The law's far too strong for us there. And I don't want to see her misunderstood."

They parted soon after this speech, and the older man, who had long suspected the fact, now perceived that Raymond was beginning to think of Estelle in new terms and elevating her to another place in his thoughts.

It was the personal standpoint that challenged Ironsyde's mind. His old sentiments and opinions respecting the marriage bond took a very different colour before the vision of an Estelle united to himself. Thus circumstances alter opinions, and the theories he had preached to Sabina went down the wind when he thought of Estelle. The touchstone of love vitiates as well as purifies thinking.

CHAPTER XI

THE HEMP BREAKER

Ironsyde attached increasing importance to the fullest possible treatment of the raw material before actual spinning, and was not only always on the lookout for the best hemps and flaxes grown, but spared no pains to bring them to the Card and Spread Board as perfect as possible.

To this end he established a Hemp Break, a Hemp Breaker and a Hemp Softener. The first was a wooden press used to crush the stalks of retted hemp straw, so that the harl came away and left the fibre clean. The second shortened long hemp, that it might be more conveniently hackled and drawn. The third served greatly to improve the spinning quality of soft hemps by passing them through a system of callender rollers. There were no hands available for the breakers and softeners, so Raymond increased his staff. He also took over ten acres of the North Hill House estate, ploughed up permanent grass, cleaned the ground with a root crop, and then started to renew the vanishing industry of flax growing. He visited Belgium for the purpose of mastering the modern methods, found the soil of North Hill well suited to the crop, and was soon deeply interested in the enterprise. He first hoped to ret his flax in the Bride river, as he had seen it retted on the Lys, but was dissuaded from making this trial and, instead, built a hot water rettery. His experiments did not go unchallenged, and while the women always applauded any change that took strain off their muscles and improved the possibility of rest, the men were indifferent to this advantage. Mr. Baggs even condemned it.

He came to see the working of the Hemp Breaker, and perceived without difficulty that its operations must directly tend to diminish his own labour.

"You'll pull tons less of solid weight in a day, Levi," said Best, "when this gets going."

"And why should I be asked to pull tons less of solid weight? What's the matter with this?"

He thrust out his right arm with hypertrophied muscles hard as steel.

"It seems to me that a time's coming when the people won't want muscles any more," he said. "Steam has lowered our strength standards as it is, and presently labour will be called to do no more than press buttons in the midst of a roaring hell of machines. The people won't want no more strength than a daddy-long-legs; they that do the work will shrink away till they're gristle and bones, like grasshoppers. And the next thing will be that they'll not be wanted either, but all will be done by just a handful of skilled creatures, that can work the machines from their desks, as easy as the organist plays the organ in church. God help the human frame then!"

"We shall never arrive at that, be sure," answered Best; "for that's to exalt the dumb material above the worker, and if things were reduced to such a pitch of perfection all round, there would be no need of large populations. But we're told to increase and multiply at the command of God, so you needn't fear machines will ever lower our power to do so. If that happened, it would be as much as to say God allowed us to produce something to our own undoing."

"He allows us to produce a fat lot of things to our own undoing," answered the hackler. "Ain't Nature under God's direction?"

"Without doubt, Levi."

"And don't Nature tickle us to our own undoing morning, noon, and night? Ain't she always at it—always tempting us to go too far along the road of our particular weakness? And ain't laziness the particular weakness of all women and most men? 'Tis pandering to laziness, these machines, and for my part I wish Ironsyde would get a machine to hackle once and for all. Then I'd leave him and go where they still put muscles above machinery."

"Funny you should say that," answered the foreman. "He's had the thought of your retirement in his mind for a good bit now. Only consideration for your feelings has prevented him dropping a hint. He always likes it to come from us, rather than him, when anybody falls out."

Mr. Baggs took this with tolerable calm.

"I'll think of it next year," he said. "If I could get at him by a side wind as to the size of the pension—"

"That's hid with him. He'll follow his father's rule, you may be sure, and reward you according to your deserts."

"I don't expect that," said Mr. Baggs. "He don't know my deserts."

"Well, I shouldn't be in any great hurry for your own sake," advised Best. "You're well and hard, and can do your work as it should be done; but you must remember you've got no resources outside your hackling shop. Take you away from it and you're a blank. You never read a book, or go out for a walk, or even till your allotment ground. All you do is to sit at home and criticise other people. In fact, you're a very ignorant old man, Baggs, and if you retired, you'd find life hang that heavy on your hands you'd hardly know how to kill time between meals. Then you'd get fat and eat too much and shorten your days. I've known it to happen, where a man who uses his muscles gives up work before his flesh fails him."

Raymond Ironsyde joined them at this juncture and presently, when Levi went back to his shop and the Hemp Breaker had been duly applauded, the master took John Best aside and discussed a private matter.

"The boy has come back for his holidays," he said; and Best, who knew that when Raymond spoke of 'the boy' he meant Sabina's son, nodded.

"I hope all goes well with him and that you hear good accounts," he answered.

"The reports are all much the same, term after term. He's said to have plenty of ability, but no perseverance."

"Think nothing of that," advised the foreman. "Schoolmasters expect boys to persevere all round, which is more than you can ask of human nature. The thing is to find out what gets hold of a boy and what he does persevere at—then a sensible schoolmaster wouldn't make him waste half his working hours at other things, for which the boy's mind has got no place. Mechanics will be that boy's strong point, if I know anything about boys. And I believe all the fearful wickedness that prompted him to burn the place down is pretty well gone out of him by now."

"I've left him severely alone," said Raymond. "I've said to myself that not for three whole years will I approach him again. Meantime I don't feel any too satisfied with the school. I fancy they are a bit soft there. Private schools are like that. They daren't be too strict for fear the children will complain and be taken away. But there are others. I can move him if need be. And I'll ask you, Best, to keep your eye on him these holidays, as far as you reasonably can, when he comes here. It is understood he may. Try and get him to talk and see if he's got any ideas."

"He puts me a good bit in mind of what poor Mister Daniel was at that age. He's keen about spinning, and if I was to let him mind a can now and again he'd be very proud of himself."

"Rum that he should like the works and hate me. Yes, he hates me all right still, for Mister Churchouse has sounded him and finds that it is so. It's in the young beggar's blood and there seems to be no operation that will get it out."

Best considered.

"He'll come round. No doubt his schooling is making his mind larger, and, presently, he'll feel the force of Christianity also; and that should conquer the old Adam in him. By the same token the less he sees of Levi, the better.

Baggs is no teacher for youth, but puts his own wrong and rebellious ideas into their heads, and they think it's fine to be up against law and order. I'll always say 'twas half the fault of Baggs the boy thought to burn us down; yet, of course, nobody was more shocked and scandalised than Levi when he heard about it. And until the boy's come over to your side, he'll do well not to listen to the seditious old dog."

"Keep him out of the hackling shop, then. Tell him he's not to go there."

Best shook his head.

"The very thing to send him. He's like that. He'd smell a rat very quick if he was ordered not to see Baggs. And then he'd haunt Baggs. I shan't trust the boy a yard, you understand. You mustn't ask me to do that after the past. But I'm hopeful that his feeling for the craft will lift him up and make him straight. To a craftsman, his work is often more powerful for salvation than his faith. In fact, his work is his faith; and from the way things run in the blood, I reckon that Sabina's son might rise into a spinner."

"I don't want anything of that sort to happen, and I'm sure she doesn't."

"There's a hang-dog look in his eyes I'd like to see away," confessed John. "He's been mismanaged, I reckon, and hasn't any sense of righteousness yet. All for justice he is, so I hear he tells Mister Churchouse. Many are who don't know the meaning of the word. I'll do what I can when he comes here."

"He's old for his age in some ways and young in others," explained Raymond. "I feel nothing much can be done till he gets friendly with me."

"You're doing all any man could do."

"At some cost too, John. You, at any rate, can understand what a ghastly situation this is. There seems no end to it."

"Consequences often bulk much bigger than causes," said Best. "In fact, to our eyes, consequences do generally look a most unfair result of causes; as a very small seed will often grow up into a very big tree. You'll never find any man, or woman, satisfied with the price they're called to pay for the privilege of being alive. And in this lad's case, him being built contrary and not turned true—warped no doubt by the accident of his career—you've got to pay a far heavier price than you would have been called to pay if you'd been his lawful begetter. But seeing the difficulty lies in the boy's nature alone, we'll hope that time will cure it, when he's old enough to look ahead and see which side his bread's buttered, if for no higher reason."

Ironsyde left the Mill depressed; indeed, Abel's recurring holidays always did depress him. As yet no hoped-for sign of reconciliation could be chronicled.

To-day, however, a gleam appeared to dawn, for on calling at 'The Magnolias' to see Ernest Churchouse, Raymond was cheered by a promised event which might contain possibilities. Estelle had scored a point and got Abel to promise to come for a picnic.

"He made a hard bargain though," she said. "He's to light a fire and boil the kettle. And we are to stop at the old store in West Haven for one good hour on the road home. I've agreed to the terms and shall give him the happiest time I know how."

"Is his mother going?"

"Yes—he insists on that. And Sabina will come."

"But don't hope too much of it," said Ernest. "I regard this as the thin end of the wedge—no more than that. If Estelle can win his confidence, then she may do great things; but she won't win it at one picnic. I know him too well. He's a mass of contradictions. Some days most communicative, other days not a syllable. Some days he seems to trust you with his secrets, other days he is suspicious if you ask him the simplest question. He's still a wild animal, who occasionally, for his own convenience, pretends to be tame."

"I shan't try to tame him," said Estelle. "I respect wild things a great deal too much to show them the charms of being tame. But it's something that he's coming, and if once he will let me be his chum in holidays, I might bring him round to Ray."

She planned the details of the picnic and invited Raymond to imagine himself a boy again. This he did and suggested various additions to the entertainment.

"Did Sabina agree easily?" he asked, still returning to the event as something very great and gratifying.

"Not willingly, but gradually and cautiously."

"She's softer and gentler than she was, however. I can assure you of that," said Mr. Churchouse.

"She thought it might be a trap at first," confessed Estelle.

"A trap, Chicky! You to set a trap?"

"No, you, Ray. She fancied you might mean to surprise the boy and bully him."

"How could she think so?"

"I assured her that you'd never dream of any such thing. Of course I promised, as she wished me to do so, that you wouldn't turn up at the picnic. I reminded her how very particular you were, and how entirely you leave it to Abel to come round and take the first step."

"Be jolly careful what you say to him. He's a mass of prejudice, where I'm concerned, and doesn't even know I'm educating him."

"I'll keep off you," she promised. "In fact, I only intend to give him as good a day as I can. I'm not going to bother about you, Ray; I'm going to think of myself and do everything I can to get his friendship on my own account. If I can do that for a start, I shall be satisfied."

"And so shall I," declared Ernest. "Because it wouldn't stop at that. If you succeed, then much may come of it. In my case, I can't lift his guarded friendship for me into enthusiasm. He associates me with learning to read and other painful preliminaries to life. Moreover, I have tried to awaken his moral qualities and am regarded with the gravest suspicion in consequence. But you come to him freshly and won't try to teach him anything. Join him in his pleasure and add to it all you can. There is nothing that wins young creatures quicker than sharing their pleasures, if you can do so reasonably and are not removed so far from them by age that any attempt would be ridiculous. Fifteen and twenty-seven may quite well have a good deal in common still, if twenty-seven is not too proud to confess it."

CHAPTER XII

THE PICNIC

For a long day Estelle devoted herself whole-heartedly to winning the friendship of Abel Dinnett. Her chances of success were increased by an accident, though it appeared at first that the misadventure would ruin all. For when Estelle arrived at 'The Magnolias' in her pony carriage, Sabina proved to be sick and quite unequal to the proposed day in the air.

Abel declined to go without his mother, but, after considerable persuasion, allowed the prospect of pleasure to outweigh his distrust.

Estelle promised to let him drive, and that privilege in itself proved a temptation too great to resist. His mother's word finally convinced him, and he drove an elderly pony so considerately that his hostess praised him.

"I see you are kind to dumb things," she said. "I am glad of that, for they are very understanding and soon know who are their friends and who are not."

"If beasts treat me well," he answered, "then I treat them well. And if they treated me badly, then I'd treat them badly."

She did not argue about this; indeed, all that day her care was to amuse him and hear his opinions without boring him if she could avoid doing so.

He remained shy at first and quiet. From time to time she was in a fair way to break down his reserve; but he seemed to catch himself becoming more friendly and, once or twice, after laughing at something, he relapsed into long silence and looked at her from under his eyelids suspiciously when he thought she was not looking at him. Thus she won, only to lose what she had won, and when they reached the breezy cliffs of Eype, Estelle reckoned that she stood towards him pretty much as she stood at starting. But slowly, surely, inevitably, before such good temper and tact he thawed a little. They tethered the pony, gave it a nosebag and then spread their meal. Abel was quick and neat. She noticed that his hands were like his mother's—finely tapered, suggestive of art. But on that subject he seemed to have no ideas, and she found, after trying various themes, that he cared not in the least for music, or pictures, but certainly shared his father's interest in mechanics.

Abel talked of the Mill—self-consciously at first; yet when he found that Estelle ignored the past, and understood spinning, he forgot himself entirely for a time under the spell of the subject.

They compared notes, and she saw he was more familiar than she with detail. Then, while still forgetting his listener, Abel remembered himself and his talk of the Mill turned into a personal channel. There is no more confidential thing, by fits and starts, than a shy child; and just as Estelle felt the boy would never come any closer, or give her a chance to help him, suddenly he startled her with the most unexpected utterance.

"You mightn't know it," he said, "but by justice and right I should have the whole works for my very own when Mister Ironsyde died. Because he's my father, though I daresay he pretends to everybody he isn't."

"I'm very sure Mister Ironsyde doesn't feel anything but jolly kind and friendly to you, Abel. He doesn't pretend he isn't your father. Why should he? You know he's often offered to be friends, and he even forgave you for trying to burn down the Mill. Surely that was a pretty good sign he means to be friendly?"

"I don't want his friendship, because he's not good to mother. He served her very badly. I understand things a lot better than you might think."

"Well, don't spoil your lunch," she said. "We'll talk afterwards. Are you ready for another bottle of gingerbeer? I don't like this gingerbeer out of glass bottles. I like it out of stone bottles."

"So do I," he answered, instantly dropping his own wrongs. "But the glass bottles have glass marbles in them, which you can use; and so it's better to have them, because it doesn't matter so much about the taste after it's drunk."

She asked him concerning his work and he told her that he best liked history. She asked why, and he gave a curious reason.

"Because it tells you the truth, and you don't find good men always scoring and bad men always coming to grief. In history, good men come to grief sometimes and bad men score."

"But you can't always be sure what is good and what is bad," she argued.

"The people who write the histories don't worry you about that," he answered, "but just tell you what happened. And sometimes you are jolly glad when a beast gets murdered, or his throne is taken away from him; and sometimes you are sorry when a brave chap comes to grief, even though he may be bad."

"Some historians are not fair, though," she said. "Some happen to feel like you. They hate some people and some ideas, and always show them in an unfriendly light. If you write history, you must be tremendously fair and keep your own little whims out of it."

After their meal Estelle smoked a cigarette, much to Abel's interest.

"I never knew a girl could smoke," he said.

"Why not? Would you like one? I don't suppose a cigarette once in a way can hurt you."

"I've smoked thousands," he told her. "And a pipe, too, for that matter. I smoked a cigar once. I found it and smoked it right through."

"Didn't it make you ill?"

"Yes—fearfully; but I hid till I was all right again."

He smoked a cigarette, and Estelle told him that his father was a great smoker and very fond of a pipe.

"But he wouldn't let you smoke, except now and again in holiday times—not yet. Nobody ought to smoke till he's done growing."

"What about you, then?" asked Abel.

"I've done growing ages ago. I'm nearly twenty-eight."

He looked at her and his eyes clouded. He entered a phase of reserve. Then she, guessing how to enchant him, suggested the next step.

"If you help me pack up now, we'll harness the pony and go down to West Haven for a bit. I want to see the old stores I've heard such a lot about. You must show them to me."

"Yes—part. I know every inch of them, but I can't show you my own secret den, though."

"Do. I should love to see it."

He shook his head.

"No good asking," he said. "That's my greatest secret. You can't expect me to tell you. Even mother doesn't know."

"I won't ask, then. I've got a den, too, for that matter—in fact, two. One on North Hill and one in our garden."

"D'you know the lime-kiln on North Hill?"

"Rather. The bee orchis grows thereabout."

He thought for a moment. "If I showed you my den in the store, would you swear to God never to tell?"

"Yes, I'd swear faithfully not to."

"Perhaps I will, then."

But when presently they reached his haunt, he had changed his mood. She did not remind him, left him to his devices and sat patiently outside while he was hidden within. Occasionally his head popped out of unexpected places aloft, then disappeared again. Once she heard a great noise, followed by silence. She called to him and, after a pause, he shouted down that he was all right.

When an hour had passed she called out again to tell him to come back to her.

"We're going to Bridport to tea," she said.

He came immediately and revealed a badly torn trouser leg.

"I fell," he explained. "I fell through a rotten ceiling, and I've cut my leg. When I was young the sight of blood made me go fainty, but I laugh at it now."

He pulled up his trousers and showed a badly barked shin.

"We'll go to a chemist and get him to wash it, and I'll get a needle and thread and sew it up," said Estelle.

She condoled with him as they drove to Bridport, but he was impatient of sympathy.

"I don't mind pain," he said. "I've tried the Red Indian tests on myself before to-day. Once I had to see a doctor after; but I didn't flinch when I was doing it."

A chemist dressed the wounded leg and presently they arrived at 'The Seven Stars,' where the pony was stabled and tea taken in the garden. Mrs. Legg provided a needle and thread and produced a very excellent tea.

Abel enjoyed the swing for some time, but would not let Estelle help him.

"I can swing myself," he said, "but I'll swing you afterwards."

He did so until they were tired. Then he walked round the flower borders and presently picked Estelle a rose.

She thanked him very heartily and told him the names of the blossoms which he did not know.

Job came and talked to them for a time, and Estelle praised the garden, while Abel listened. Then Mr. Legg turned to the boy.

"Holidays round again, young man? I dare say we shall see you sometimes, and, if you like flowers, you can always come in and have a look."

"I don't like flowers," said the boy. "I like fruit."

He went back to the swing and Job asked after Mr. Waldron.

Estelle reminded him that he had promised to come and see her garden some day.

"Be sure I shall, miss," he answered, "but, for the minute, work fastens on me from my rising up to my going down."

"However do you get through it all?"

"Thanks to method. It's summed up in that. Without method, I should be a lost man."

"You ought to slack off," she said. "I'm sure that Nelly doesn't like to see you work so hard."

"She'd work hard too, but Nature and not her will shortens her great powers. She grows into a mountain of flesh and her substance prevents activity; but the mind is there unclouded. In my case the flesh doesn't gain on me and work agrees with my system."

"You're a very wonderful man," declared Estelle; "but no doubt plenty of people tell you that."

"Only by comparison," he explained. "The wonder is all summed up in the one word 'method,' coupled with a good digestion and no strong drink. I'd like to talk more on the subject, but I must be going."

"And tell them to put in the pony. We must be going, too."

On the way home Estelle tried to interest Abel in sport. She had been very careful all day to keep Raymond off her lips, but now intentionally she spoke of him. It was done with care and she only named him casually in the course of general remarks. Thus she hoped that, in time, he would allow her to mention his father without opposition.

"I think you ought to play some games with your old friends at Bridetown these holidays," she said.

"I haven't any old friends there. I don't want friends. I never made that fire you promised."

"You shall make it next time we come out; and everybody wants friends. You can't get on without friends. And the good of games is that you make friends. I'm very keen on golf now, though I never thought I should like sport. Did you play any cricket at school?"

"Yes, but I don't care about it."

"How did you play? You ought to be rather a dab at it."

"I played very well and was in the second eleven. But I don't care about it. It's all right at school, but there are better things to do in the holidays."

"If you're a good cricketer, you might get some matches. Your father is a very good cricketer, and would have played for the county if he'd been able to practise enough. And Mister Roberts at the mill is a splendid player."

His nervous face twitched and his instant passion ran into his whip hand. He gave the astonished pony a lash and made it start across the road, so that Estelle was nearly thrown from her seat.

"Don't! Don't!" she said. "What's the matter?"

But she knew.

He showed his teeth.

"I won't hear his name—I won't hear it. I hate him, I hate him. Take the reins—I'll walk. You've spoilt everything now. I always wish he was dead when I hear his name, and I wish he was dead this minute."

"My dear Abel, I'm sorry. I didn't think you felt so bad as that about him. He doesn't feel at all like that about you."

"I hate him, I tell you, and I'm not the only one that hates him. And I don't care what he feels about me. He's my greatest enemy on earth, and people who understand have told me so, and I won't be beholden to him for anything—and—and you can stick up for him till you're black in the face for all I care. I know he's bad and I'll be his enemy always."

"You're a little fool," she said calmly. "Let me drive and you can listen to me now. If you listen to stupid, wicked people talking of your father, then listen to me for a change. You don't know anything whatever about him, because you won't give him a chance to talk to you himself. If you once let him, you'd very soon stop all this nonsense."

"You're bluffing," he said. "You think you'll get round me like that, but you won't. You're only a girl. You don't know anything. It's men tell me about my father. You think he's good, because you love him; but he's bad, really—as bad as hell—as bad as hell."

"What's he done then? I'm not bluffing, Abel. There's nothing to bluff about. What's your father done to you? You must have some reason for hating him?"

"Yes, I have."

"What is it, then?"

"It's because the Mill ought to be mine when he dies—there!"

She did not answer immediately. She had often thought the same thing. Instinct told her that frankness must be the only course. Through frankness he might still be won.

He did not speak again after his last assertion, and presently she answered in a manner to surprise him. Directness was natural to Estelle and both her father and her friend, Mr. Churchouse, had fostered it. People either deprecated or admired this quality of her talk, for directness of speech is so rare that it never fails to appear surprising.

"I think you're right there, Abel. Perhaps the Mill ought to be yours some day. Perhaps it will be. The things that ought to happen really do sometimes."

Then he surprised her in his turn.

"I wouldn't take the Mill—not now. I'll never take anything from him. It's too late now."

She realised the futility of argument.

"You're tired," she said, "and so am I. We'll talk about important things again some day. Only don't—don't imagine people aren't your friends. If you'd only think, you'd see how jolly kind people have been to you over and over again. Didn't you ever wonder how you got off so well after trying to burn down the works? You must have. Anyway, it showed you'd got plenty of good friends, surely?"

"It didn't matter to me. I'd have gone to prison. I don't care what they do to me. They can't make me feel different."

"Well, leave it. We've had a good day and you needn't quarrel with me, at any rate."

"I don't know that. You're his friend."

"You surely don't want to quarrel with all his friends as well as him? We are going to be friends, anyway, and have some more good times together. I like you."

"I thought I liked you," he said, "but you called me a little fool."

"That's nothing. You were a little fool just now. We're all fools sometimes. I've been a fool to-day, myself. You're a little fool to hate anybody. What good does it do you to hate?"

"It does do me good; and if I didn't hate him, I should hate myself," the boy declared.

"Well, it's better to hate yourself than somebody else. It's a good sign I should think if we hate ourselves. We ought to hate ourselves more than we do, because we know better than anybody else how hateful we can be. Instead of that, we waste tons of energy hating other people, and think there's nobody so fine and nice and interesting as we are ourselves."

"Mister Churchouse says the less we think about ourselves the better. But you've got to if you've been ill-used."

In the dusk twinkled out a glow-worm beside the hedge, and they stopped while Abel picked it up. Gradually he grew calmer, and when they parted he thanked her for her goodness to him.

"It's been a proper day, all but the end," he said, "and I will like you and be your friend. But I won't like my father and be his friend, because he's bad and served mother and me badly. You may think I don't understand such things, but I do. And I never will be beholden to him as long as I live— never."

He left her at the outer gate of his home and she drove on and considered him rather hopelessly. He had some feeling for beauty on which she had trusted to work, but it was slight. He was vain, very sensitive, and disposed to be malignant. As yet reason had not come to his rescue and his emotions, ill-directed, ran awry. He was evidently unaware that his father had so far saved the situation for him. What would he do when he knew it?

Estelle felt the picnic not altogether a failure, yet saw little signs of a situation more hopeful at present.

"I can win him," she decided; "but it looks as though his father never would."

CHAPTER XIII

THE RUNAWAY

Estelle was as good as her word and devoted not a few of his holidays to the pleasure of Sabina's son. Unconsciously she hastened the progress of other matters, for her resolute attempt to win Abel, at any cost of patience and trouble, brought her still deeper into the hidden life and ambitions of the boy's father.

She was frank with Raymond, and when Abel had gone back to school and made no sign, Estelle related her experiences.

"He's sworn eternal friendship with me," she said, "but it's not a friendship that extends to you, or anybody else. He's very narrow. He concentrates in a terrifying way and wants everything. He told me that he hated me to have any other friends but him. It took him a long time to decide about me; but now he has decided. He extracts terrific oaths of secrecy and then imparts his secrets. Before giving the oaths, I always tell him I shan't keep them if he's going to confide anything wicked; but his secrets are harmless enough. The last was a wonderful hiding-place. He spends many hours in it. I nearly broke my neck getting there. That's how far we've reached these holidays; and after next term I shall try again."

"He's got a heart, if one could only reach it, I suppose."

"A very hot heart. I shall try to extend his sympathies when he comes back."

Her intention added further fuel to the fire burning in Raymond's own thoughts. He saw both danger and hope in the situation, as it might develop from this point. The time was drawing nearer when he meant to ask Estelle to marry him, and since he looked now at life and all its relations from this standpoint, he began to consider his son therefrom.

On the whole he was cheered by Estelle's achievements and argued well of them. The danger he set aside, and chose rather to reflect on the hope. With Abel back at school again and his mother in a more placid temper, there came a moment of peace. Ironsyde was able to forget them and did so thankfully, while he concentrated on the task before him. He felt very doubtful, both of Estelle's response and her father's view. The girl herself, however, was all that mattered, for Waldron would most surely approve her choice whatever it might be. Arthur had of late, however, been giving it as his opinion that his daughter would not marry. He had decided that she was not the marrying sort, and told Raymond as much.

"The married state's too limited for her: her energies are too tremendous to leave any time for being a wife. To bottle Estelle down to a husband and children is impossible. They wouldn't be enough for her intellect."

This had been said some time before, when unconscious of Ironsyde's growing emotions; but of late he had suspected them and was, therefore, more guarded in his prophecies.

Then came a shock, which delayed progress, for Abel thrust himself to the front of his mind again. Estelle corresponded with her new friend, and the boy had heard from her that in future he must thank his father for his education. She felt that it was time he knew this, and hoped that he would now be sane enough to let the fact influence him. It did, but not as she had expected. Instead there came the news that Abel had been expelled. He deliberately refused to proceed with his work, and, when challenged, explained that he would learn no more at his father's expense.

Nothing moved him, and Estelle's well-meant but ill-judged action merely served to terminate Abel's education for good and all.

The boy was rapidly becoming a curse to his father. Puritans, who knew the story, welcomed its development and greeted each phase with religious enthusiasm; but others felt the situation to be growing absurd. Raymond himself so regarded it, and when Abel returned home again he insisted on seeing him.

"You can be present if you wish to be," he told Sabina, but she expressed no such desire. Her attitude was modified of late, and, largely under the influence of Estelle, she began to see the futility of this life-enmity declared against Raymond by her son. Of old she had thought it natural, and while not supporting it had made no effort to crush it out of him. Now she perceived that it could come to nothing and only breed bitterness. She had, therefore, begun to tone her indifference and withhold the little bitter speeches that only fortified Abel's hate. She had even argued with him— lamely enough—and advised him not to persist in a dislike of his father that could not serve him in after life.

But he had continued to rejoice in his hatred. While Estelle hoped with Sabina to break down his obstinacy, he actually looked forward to the time when Estelle would hate his enemy also. He had been sorry to see his mother weakening and even blaming him for his opinions.

But now he was faced with his father under conditions from which there was no escape. The meeting took place in Mr. Churchouse's study and Abel was called to listen, whether he would or no. Raymond knew that the child understood the situation and he did not mince words. He kept his temper and exhausted his arguments.

"Abel," he said, "you've got to heed me now, and whatever you may feel, you must use your self-control and your brains. I'm speaking entirely for your sake and I'm only concerned for your future. If you would use your reason, it would show you that the things you have done and are doing can't hurt me; they can only hurt yourself; and what is the good of hurting yourself, because you don't like me? If you had burned down the works, the insurance offices would have paid me back all the money they were worth, and the only people to suffer would have been the men and women you threw out of work. So, when you tried to hurt me, you were only hurting other people and yourself. Boys who do that sort of thing are called embryo criminals, and that's what they are. But for me and the great kindness and humanity of other men—my friends on the magistrates' bench—you would have been sent to a reformatory after that affair; but your fellow creatures forgave you and were very good to me also, and let you go free on consideration that I would be responsible for you. Then I sent you to a good school, where nothing was known against you. Now you have been expelled from that school, because you won't work, or go on with your education. And your reason is that I am paying for your education and you won't accept anything at my hands.

"But think what precisely this means. It doesn't hurt me in the least. As far as I am concerned, it makes not a shadow of difference. I have no secrets about things. Everybody knows the situation, and everybody knows I recognise my obligations where you are concerned and wish to be a good father to you. Therefore, if you refuse to let me be, nobody is hurt but yourself, because none can take my place. You don't injure my credit; you only lose your own. The past was past, and people had begun to forget what you did two years ago. Now you've reminded them by this folly, and I tell you that you are too old to be so foolish. There is no reason why you should not lead a dignified, honourable and useful life. You have far better opportunities than thousands and thousands of boys, and far better and more powerful friends than ninety-nine boys out of a hundred.

"Then why fling away your chances and be impossible and useless and an enemy to society, when society only wants to be your friend? What is the good? What do you gain? And what do I lose? You're not hurting me; but you're hurting and distressing your mother. You're old enough to understand all this, and if your mother can feel as I know she feels and ask you to consider your own future and look forward in a sensible spirit, instead of looking back in a senseless one, then surely, for her sake alone, you ought to be prepared to meet me and turn over a new leaf.

"For you won't tire out my patience, or break my heart. I never know when I'm beat, and since my wish is only your good, neither you, nor anybody, will choke me off it. I ask you now to promise that, if I send you to another school, you'll work hard and complete your education and qualify yourself for a useful place in the world afterwards. That's what you've got to do, and I hope you see it. Then your future will be my affair, for, as my son, I shall be glad and willing to help you on in whatever course of life you may choose.

"So that's the position. You see I've given you the credit of being a sane and reasonable being, and I want you to decide as a sane and reasonable being. You can go on hating me as much as you please; but don't go on queering your own pitch and distressing your mother and making your future dark and difficult, when it should be bright and easy. Promise me that you'll go back to a new school and work your hardest to atone for this nonsense and I'll take your word for it. And I don't ask for my own sake—always remember that. I ask you for your own sake and your mother's."

With bent head the boy scowled up under his eyebrows during this harangue. He answered immediately Raymond had finished and revealed passion.

"And what, if I say 'no'?"

"I hope you won't be so foolish."

"I do say 'no' then—a thousand times I say it. Because if you bring me up, you get all the credit. You shan't get credit from me. And I'll bring myself up without any help from you. I know I'm different from other boys, because you didn't marry my mother. And that's a fearful wrong to her, and you're not going to get out of that by anything I can do. You're wicked and cowardly to my mother, and she's Mister Churchouse's servant, instead of being your wife and having servants of her own, and I'm a poor woman's son instead of being a rich man's son, as I ought to be. All that's been told me by them who know it. And you're a bad man, and I hate you, and I shall always hate you as long as you live. And I'll never be beholden to you for anything, because my life is no good now, and my mother's life is no good neither. And if I thought she was taking a penny of your money, I'd—"

His temper upset him and he burst into tears. The emotion only served to increase his anger.

"I'm crying for hate," he said. "Hate, hate, hate!"

Raymond looked at the boy curiously.

"Poor little chap, I wish to God I could make you see sense. You've got the substance and are shouting for the shadow, which you can never have. You talk like a man, so I'll answer you like a man and advise you not to listen to the evil tongue of those who bear no kindly thought to me, or you either. What is the sense of all this hate? Granted wrong things happened, how are you helping to right the wrong? Where is the sense of this blind enmity against me? I can't call back the past, any more than you can call back the tears you have just shed. Then why waste nervous energy and strength on all this silly hate?"

"Because it makes me better and stronger to hate you. It makes me a man quicker to hate you. You say I talk like a man—that's because I hate like a man."

"You talk like a very silly man, and if you grow up into a man hating me, you'll grow up a bitter, twisted sort of man—no good to anybody. A man with a grievance is only a nuisance to his neighbours; and seeing what your grievance is, and that I am ready and willing to do everything in a father's power to lessen that grievance and retrieve the mistakes of the past—remembering, too, that everybody knows my good intentions—you'll really get none to care for your troubles. Instead, all sensible people will tell you that they are largely of your own making."

"The more you talk, the more I hate you," said the boy. "If I never heard your voice again and never saw your face again, still I'd always hate you. I don't hate anything else in the world but you. I wouldn't spare a bit of hate for anything but you. I won't be your son now—never."

"Well, run away then. You'll live to be sorry for feeling and speaking so, Abel. I won't trouble you again. Next time we meet, I hope you will come to me."

The boy departed and the man considered. It seemed that harm irreparable was wrought, and a reconciliation, that might have been easy in Abel's childhood, when he was too young to appreciate their connection, had now become impossible, since he had grown old enough to understand it. He would not be Raymond's son. He declined the filial relationship—doubtless prompted thereto from his earliest days, first on one admonition, then at another. The leaven had been mixed with his blood by his mother, in his infant mind by his grandmother, in his soul by fellow men as he grew towards adolescence.

Yet from Sabina herself the poison had almost passed away. In the light of these new difficulties she grew anxious, and began to realise how fatally Abel's possession was standing in his own light. She loved him, but not passionately. He would soon be sixteen and her point of view changed. She had listened long to Estelle and began to understand that, whatever dark memories and errors belonged to Raymond Ironsyde's past, he designed nothing but generous goodness for their son in the future.

After the meeting with Abel, Raymond saw Sabina and described what had occurred; but she could only express her regrets. She declared herself more hopeful than he and promised to reason with the boy to the best of her power.

"I've never stood against you with him, and I've never stood for you with him. I've kept out of it and not influenced for or against," she said. "But now I'll do more than that; I'll try and influence him for you."

Raymond was obliged.

"I shall be very grateful to you if you can. If there's any human being who carries weight with him, you do. Such blistering frankness—such crooked, lightning looks of hate—fairly frighten me. I had no idea any young creature could feel so much."

"He's going through what I went through, I suppose," she said. "I don't want to hurt you, or vex you any more. I'm changed now and tired of quarrelling with things that can't be altered. When we find the world's sympathy for us is dead, then it's wiser to accept the situation and cease to run about trying to wake it up again. So I'll try to show him what the world will be for the likes of him if he hasn't got you behind him."

"Do—and don't do it bitterly. You can't talk for two minutes about the past without getting bitter—unconsciously, quite unconsciously, Sabina. And your unconscious bitterness hurts me far more than it hurts you. But don't be bitter with him, or show there's another side of your feelings about it. Keep that for me, if you must. My shoulders are broad enough to bear it. He is brimming with acid as it is. Sweeten his mind if it is in your power. That's the only way of salvation, and the only chance of bringing him and me together."

She promised to attempt it.

"And if I'm bitter still," she said, "it is largely unconscious, as you say. You can't get the taste of trouble out of your mouth very easily after you've been deluged with it and nigh drowned in it, as I have. It's only an echo and won't reach his ear, though it may reach yours."

"Thank you, Sabina. Do what you can," he said, and left her, glad to get away from the subject and back to his own greater interests.

He heard nothing more for a few days, then came the news that Abel had disappeared. By night he had vanished and search failed to find him.

Sabina could only state what had gone before his departure. She had spoken with him on Raymond's behalf and urged him to reconsider his attitude and behave sensibly and worthily. And he, answering nothing, had gone to bed as usual; but when she called him next morning, no reply came and she found that he had ridden away on his bicycle in the night. The country was hunted, but without result, and not for three days did his mother learn what had become of Abel. Then, in reply to police notices of his disappearance, there came a letter from a Devonshire dairy farm, twenty miles to the west of Bridport. The boy had appeared there early in the morning and begged for some breakfast. Then he asked for something to do. He was now working on trial for a week, but whether giving satisfaction or no they did not learn.

His mother went to see him and found him well pleased with himself and proud of what he had accomplished. He explained to her that he had now taken his life into his own hands and was not going to look to anybody in future but himself.

The farmer reported him civil spoken, willing to learn, and quick to please. Indeed, Abel had never before won such a good character.

She left him there happy and content, and took no immediate steps to bring the boy home.

It was decided that a conference should presently be held of those interested in Abel.

"Since he is safe and cheerful and doing honest work, you need not be in distress about him at present, Sabina," said Ernest Churchouse; "but Raymond Ironsyde has no intention that the boy should miss an adequate education, and wishes him to be at school for a couple of years yet, if possible. It is decided that we knock our heads together on the subject presently. We'll meet and try to hit upon a sensible course. Meantime this glimpse of reality and hard work at Knapp Farm will do him good. He may show talent in an agricultural direction. In any case, you can feel sure that whatever tastes he develops, short of buccaneering, or highway robbery, will be gratified."

CHAPTER XIV

THE MOTOR CAR

Raymond Ironsyde felt somewhat impatient of the conference to consider the situation of his son. But since he had no authority and Sabina was anxious to do something, he agreed to consult Mr. Churchouse.

They met at 'The Magnolias,' where Miss Ironsyde joined them; but her old energy and forcible opinions had faded. She did little more than listen.

Ironsyde came first and spoke to Ernest in a mood somewhat despondent. They were alone at the time, for Sabina did not join them until Estelle came.

"Is there nothing in paternity?" asked Raymond. "Isn't nature all powerful and blood thicker than water? What is it that over-rides the natural relationship and poisons him against me? Isn't a good father a good father?"

"So much is implied in this case," answered the elder. "He's old enough now to understand what it means to be a natural child. Doubtless the disabilities they labour under have been explained to him. That fact is what poisons his mind, as you say, and makes him hate the blood in his veins. We've got to get over that and find antidotes for the poison, if we can."

"I'm beginning to doubt if we ever shall, Uncle Ernest."

Sabina and Estelle entered at this moment and heard Mr. Churchouse make answer.

"Be sure it can be done. Every year makes it more certain, because with increase of reasoning power he'll see the absurdity of this attitude. It is no good to him to continue your enemy."

"Increase of reason cuts both ways. It shows him his grievances, as well as what will pay him best in the future. He's faced with a clash of reason."

"Reason I grant springs from different inspirations," admitted Ernest. "There's the reason of the heart and the reason of the head—yes, the heart has its reasons, too. And though the head may not appreciate them, they exercise their weight and often conquer."

Soon there came a carriage from Bridport and Miss Ironsyde joined them.

"Oh! I'm glad to see a fire," she said, and sat close beside it in an easy chair.

Then Raymond spoke.

"It is good of you all to come and lend a hand over this difficult matter. I appreciate it, and specially I thank Sabina for letting us consider her son's welfare. She knows that we all want to befriend him and that we all are his friends. It's rather difficult for me to say much; but if you can show me how to do anything practical and establish Abel's position and win his goodwill, at any cost to myself, I shall thank you. I've done what I could, but I confess this finds me beaten for the moment. You'd better say what you all think, and see if you agree."

The talk that followed was inconsequent and rambling. For a considerable time it led nowhere. Miss Ironsyde was taciturn. It occupied all her energies to conceal the fact that she was suffering a good deal of physical pain. She made no original suggestions. Churchouse, according to his wont, generalised; but it was through a generalisation that they approached something definite.

"He has yet to learn that we cannot live to ourselves, or design life's pattern single-handed," declared Ernest. "Life, in fact, is rather like a blind man weaving a basket: we never see our work, and we have to trust others for the material. And if we better realised how blind we were, we should welcome and invite criticism more freely than we do."

"No man makes his own life—I've come to see that," admitted Raymond. "The design seems to depend much on your fellow creatures; your triumph or failure is largely the work of others. But it depends on your own judgment to the extent that you can choose what fellow creatures shall help you."

Estelle approved this.

"And if we could only show Abel that, and make him feel this determination to be independent of everybody is a mistake. But he told me once, most reasonably, that he didn't mind depending on those who were good to him. He said he would trust them."

"Trust's everything. It centres on that. Can I get his trust, or can't I?"

"Not for the present, Ray. I expect his mind is in a turmoil over this running away. It's all my fault and I take the blame. Until he can think calmly you'll never get any power over him. The thing is to fill his mind full with something else."

"Find out if you can what's in his thoughts," advised Sabina. "We say this and that and the other, and plan what must be done, but I judge the first person to ask for an opinion is Abel himself. When people are talking about the young, the last thought in their minds is what the young are thinking themselves. They never get asked what's in their minds, yet, if we knew, it might make all the difference."

"Very sound, Sabina," admitted Mr. Churchouse; "and you should know what's in his mind if anybody does."

"I should no doubt, but I don't. I've never been in the boy's secrets, or I might have been more to him. But that's not to say nobody could win them. Any clever boy getting on for sixteen years should have plenty of ideas, and if you could find them, it might save a lot of trouble."

She turned to Estelle as she spoke.

"He's often told me things," said Estelle, "and he's often been going to tell me others and stopped—not because he thought I'd laugh at him; but because he was doubtful of me. But he knows I can keep secrets now."

"He must be treated as an adult," decided Ernest. "Sabina is perfectly right. We must give him credit for more sense than he has yet discovered, and appeal directly to his pride. I think there are great possibilities about him if he can only be brought to face them. His ruling passion must be discovered. One has marked a love of mystery in him and a wonderful power of make-believe. These are precious promises, rightly guided. They point to imagination and originality. He may have the makings of an artist. Without exaggeration, I should say he had an artist's temperament without being an artist; but art is an elastic term. It must mean creative instinct, however, and he has shown that. It has so far taken the shape of a will to create disaster; but why should we not lead his will into another channel and help it to create something worthy?"

"He's fond of machinery," said Sabina, "and very clever with his hands."

"Could your child be anything but clever with his hands, Sabina?" said Estelle.

"Or mine be anything but fond of machinery?" asked Raymond.

He meant no harm, but this blunt and rather brutal claim to fatherhood made Sabina flinch. It was natural that she never could school herself to accept the situation in open conversation without reserve, and all but Ironsyde himself appreciated the silence which fell upon her. His speech, indeed, showed lack of sensibility, yet it could hardly be blamed, since only through acceptation of realities might any hopeful action be taken. But the harm was done and the delicate poise of the situation between Abel's parents upset. Sabina said no more, and in the momentary silence that followed she rose and left them.

"What clumsy fools even nice men can be," sighed Miss Ironsyde, and Churchouse spoke.

"Leave Sabina to me," he said. "I'll comfort her when you've gone. There is a certain ingrained stupidity from which no man escapes in the presence of women. They may, or may not, conceal their feelings; but we all unconsciously bruise and wound them. Sabina did not conceal hers. She is quick in mind as well as body. What matters is that she knows exceedingly well we are all on her side and all valuable friends for the lad. Now let us return to the point. I think with Estelle that Abel may have something of the artist in him. He drew exceedingly well as a child. You can see his pictures in Sabina's room. Such a gift if developed might waken a sense of power."

"If he knew great things were within his reach, he would not disdain the means to reach them," said Miss Ironsyde. "I do think if the boy felt his own possibilities more—if we could waken ambition—he would grow larger-minded. Hate always runs counter to our interests in the long run, because it wastes our energy and, if people only knew it, revenge is really not sweet, but exceedingly bitter."

"I suggest this," said Ironsyde: "that Uncle Ernest and Estelle visit the boy—not in any spirit of weakness, or with any concessions, or attempts to change his mind; but simply to learn his mind. Sabina was right there. We'll approach him as we should any other intelligent being, and invite his opinion, and see if it be reasonable, or unreasonable. And if it is reasonable, then I ought to be able to serve him, if he'll let me do so."

"I shall certainly do what you wish," agreed Ernest. "Estelle and I will form a deputation to this difficult customer and endeavour to find out what his lordship really proposes and desires. Then, if we can prove to him that he must look to his fellow creatures to advance his welfare; if we can succeed in showing him that not even the youngest of us can stand alone, perhaps we shall achieve something."

"And if he won't let me help, perhaps he'll let you, or Estelle, or Aunt Jenny. Agree if he makes any possible stipulation. It doesn't matter a button where he supposes help is coming from: the thing is that he should not know it is really coming from me."

"I hope we may succeed without craft of that sort, Raymond," declared Mr. Churchouse; "but I shall not hesitate to employ the wisdom of the serpent—if the olive branch of the dove fails to meet the situation. I trust, however, more to Estelle than myself. She is nearer Abel in point of time, and it is very difficult to bridge a great gulf of years. We old men talk in another language than the young use, and the scenery that fills their eyes—

why, it has already vanished beneath our horizons. Narrowing vision too often begets narrowing sympathies and we depress youth as much as youth puzzles us."

"True, Ernest," said Miss Ironsyde. "Have you noticed how a natural instinct makes the young long to escape from the presence of age? The young breathe more freely out of sight of grey heads."

"And the grey heads survive their absence without difficulty," confessed Mr. Churchouse. "But we are a tonic to each other. They help us to see, Jenny, and we must help them to feel."

"Abel shall help us to see his point of view, and we'll help him to feel who his best friends are," promised Estelle.

Raymond had astonished Bridport and staggered Bridetown with a wondrous invention. The automobile was born, and since it appealed very directly to him, he had acquired one of the first of the new vehicles at some cost, and not only did he engage a skilled mechanic to drive it, but himself devoted time and pains to mastering the machine. He believed in it very stoutly, and held that in time to come it must bulk as a most important industrial factor. Already he predicted motor traction on a large scale, while yet the invention was little more than a new toy for the wealthy.

And now this car served a useful purpose and Mr. Churchouse, in some fear and trembling, ventured a first ride. Estelle accompanied him and together they drove through the pleasant lands where Dorset meets Devon, to Knapp Farm under Knapp Copse, midway between Colyton and Ottery St. Mary, on a streamlet tributary of the Sid.

Mr. Churchouse was amazed and bewildered at this new experience; Estelle, who had already enjoyed some long rides, supported him, lulled his anxieties and saw that he kept warm.

Soon they sighted the ridge which gave Knapp its name, and presently met Abel, who knew that they were coming. He stood on the tumuli at the top of the knoll and awaited them with interest. His master, from first enthusiasms, now spoke indifferently of him, declared him an average boy, and cared not whether they took him, or left him. As for Abel himself, he slighted both Estelle and Mr. Churchouse at first, and appeared for a time quite oblivious to their approaches. He was only interested in the car, which stood drawn up in an open shed at the side of the farmyard. He concentrated here, desired the company of the driver alone, and could with difficulty be drawn away to listen to the travellers and declare his own ambitions.

He was, however, not sorry to see Estelle, and when, presently, they lured him away from the motor, he talked to them. He bragged about his achievement in running away and finding work; but he was not satisfied with the work itself.

"It was only to see if I could live in the world on my own," he said, "and now I know I can. Nobody's got any hold on me now, because if you can earn your food and clothes, you're free of everybody. I don't tell them here, but I could work twice as hard and do twice as much if it was worth while; only it isn't."

"If you get wages, you ought to earn them," said Estelle.

"I do," he explained. "I get a shilling a day and my grub, and I earn all that. But, of course, I'm not going to be a farmer. I'm just learning about the land—then I'm going. Nobody's clever here. But I like taking it easy and being my own master."

"You oughtn't to take it easy at your time of life, Abel," declared Estelle. "You oughtn't to leave school yet, and I very much hope you'll go back."

"Never," he said. "I couldn't stop there after I knew he was paying for it. Or anywhere else. I'm not going to thank him for anything."

"But you stand in the light of your own usefulness," she explained. "The thing is for a boy to do all in his power to make himself a useful man, and by coming here and doing ploughboy's work, when you might be learning and increasing your own value in the world, you are being an idiot, Abel. If you let your father educate you, then, in the future, you can pay him back splendidly and with interest for all he has done for you. There's no obligation then—simply a fair bargain."

His face hardened and he frowned.

"I may pay him for all he's done for me, whether or no," he answered. "Anyway, I don't want any more book learning. I'm a man very nearly, and a lot cleverer, as it is, than the other men here. I shall stop here for a bit. I want to be let alone and I will be let alone."

"Not at all," declared Mr. Churchouse. "You're going back on yourself, Abel, and if you stop here, hoeing turnips and what not, you'll soon find a great disaster happening to you. You will indeed—just the very thing you don't want to happen. You pride yourself on being clever. Well, cleverness can't stand still, you know. You go back, or forward. Here, you'll go back and get as slow-witted as other ploughboys. You think you won't, but you will. The mud on your boots will work up into your mind, and instead of being full of great ideas for the future, you'll gradually forget all about them. And that would be a disgrace to you."

Abel showed himself rather impressed with this peril.

"I shall read books," he said.

"Where will you get them?" asked Estelle. "Besides, after long days working out of doors, you'll be much too tired to read books, or go on with your studies. I know, because I've tried it."

"Quies was the god of rest in ancient Rome," proceeded Mr. Churchouse, "but he was no god for youth. The elderly turned their weary bodies to his shrine and decorated his altars—not the young. But for you, Abel, there are radiant goddesses, and their names are Stimula and Strenua. To them you must pay suit and service, and your motto should be 'Able and Willing.'"

"Of course," cried Estelle; "but instead of that, you ask to be let alone, to turn slowly and surely into a ploughboy! Why, the harm is already beginning! And you may be quite sure that nobody who cares for you is going to see you turn into a ploughboy."

They produced some lunch presently and Abel enjoyed the good fare. For a time they pressed him no more, but when the meal was taken, let him show them places of interest. While Estelle visited the farm with him and heard all about his work, Mr. Churchouse discussed the boy with his master. Nothing could then be settled, and it was understood that Abel should stop at Knapp until the farmer heard more concerning him.

Estelle advanced the good cause very substantially, however, and felt sanguine of the future; for alone with her, Abel confessed that farming gave him no pleasure and that his ambition was set on higher things.

"I shall be an engineer some day," he said. "Presently I shall go where there is machinery, and begin at the bottom and work up to the top. I know a lot more about it than you might think, as it is."

"I know you do," she said. "And there's nothing your mother would like better than engineering for you. Besides, a boy begins that when he's young, and I believe you ought to be in the shops soon."

"I shall be soon. Very likely the next thing you hear about me will be that I have disappeared again. Then I shall turn up in a works somewhere. Because you needn't think I'm going to be a ploughboy. I shouldn't get level with my father by being a ploughboy."

"Your father would be delighted for you to get level with him and know as much as he does," she answered, pretending to mistake his meaning. "If you said you wanted to know as much about machinery and machines in general as he does, then he would very soon set to work to help you on."

Abel considered.

"I won't take any help from him; but I'll do this—to suit myself, not him. I'd do it so as I could be near mother and could look after her. Because, when Mister Churchouse dies, I'll have to look after her."

"You needn't be anxious about your mother, Abel. She's got plenty of friends."

"Her friends don't count if they're his friends, because you can't be my mother's friend and his friend, too. But I'll go into the spinning Mill, and be like anybody else, and work for wages—just the same wages as any other boy going in. That won't be thanking him for anything."

Estelle could hardly hide her satisfaction at this unexpected concession. She dared not show her pleasure for fear that Abel would see it and draw back.

"Then you could live with mother and Mister Churchouse," she said. "It would be tremendously interesting for you. I wonder if you would begin with Roberts at the lathes, or Cogle at the engines?"

"I don't know. Before I ran away, Nicholas Roberts wanted somebody to help him turning. I've turned sometimes. I'd begin like that and rise to better things."

She was careful not to mention his father again.

"I believe Mister Roberts would like to have you in his shop very much. Sarah, his wife, hopes that her son will be a lathe-worker some day, but he's too young to go yet."

"He'll never be any good at machinery," declared Abel. "I know him. He's all for the sea."

They took their leave presently, after Ernest had heard the boy's offer. He, too, was careful, but applauded the suggestion and assured Abel he would be very welcome at his old home.

"I like you, you know; in fact, as a rule, we have got on very well together. I believe you'll make an engineer some day if you remember the Roman goddesses. To be ambitious is the most hopeful thing we can wish for youth. Always be ambitious—that's the first essential for success."

But the old man surprised Estelle by failing to share her delight at Abel's decision. She for her part felt that the grand difficulty was passed, and that once in his father's Mill, the boy must sooner or later come to reason, if only by the round of self-interest; but Mr. Churchouse reminded her that another had to be reckoned with.

"A most delicate situation would be created in that case," he said. "Of course I can't pretend to say how Raymond will regard it. He may see it with your eyes. He sees so many things with your eyes—more and more, in fact—that I hope he will; but you mustn't be very disappointed if he does not. This cannot look to him as it does to you, or even to me. His point of view may reject Abel's suggestion altogether for various reasons; and Sabina, too, will very likely feel it couldn't happen without awakening a great many painful memories."

"She advised us to consult Abel and hear what he thought."

"We have. We return with the great man's ultimatum. But I'm afraid it doesn't follow that his ultimatum will be accepted. Even if Sabina felt she could endure such an arrangement, it is doubtful in the extreme whether Raymond will. Indeed I'll go so far as to prophesy that he won't."

Estelle saw that she had been over-sanguine.

"There's one bright side, however," he continued. "We have got something definite out of the boy and should now be able to help him largely in spite of himself. Every day he lives, he'll become more impressed with the necessity for knowledge, and if, for the moment, he declines any alternative, he'll soon come round to one. He knows already that he can't stop at Knapp, so this great and perilous adventure of the automobile has been successful—though how successful we cannot tell yet."

He knew, however, before the day was done, for Sabina felt very definitely on the subject. Yet her attitude was curious: she held it not necessary to express an opinion.

Mr. Churchouse came home very cold, and while she attended to his needs, brought him hot drink and lighted a fire, Sabina listened.

"The boy is exceedingly well," he said. "I never saw his eye so bright, or his skin so clear and brown. But a farmer he won't be for anybody. Of course, one never thought he would."

When she had heard Abel's idea, she answered without delay.

"It's a thousand pities he's set his heart on that, because it won't happen. What I think doesn't matter, of course, but for once you'll find his father is of a mind with me. He'll not suffer such an arrangement for a moment. It's bringing the trouble too near. He doesn't want his skeleton walking out of the cupboard into the Mill, and whatever happens, that won't."

She was right enough, for when Raymond heard all that Estelle could tell him, he decided instantly against any such arrangement.

"Impossible," he said. "One needn't trouble even to argue about it. But that he would like to be an engineer is quite healthy. He shall be; and he shall begin at the beginning and have every advantage possible—not his way, but mine. I argue ultimate success from this. It eases my mind."

"All the same, if you don't do anything, he'll only run away again," said Estelle, who was disappointed.

"He won't run far. Let him stop where he is for a few months, till he's heartily sick of it and ready to listen to sense. Then perhaps I'll go over and see him myself. You've done great things, Estelle. I feel more sanguine than I have ever felt about him. I wish I could do what he wants; but that's impossible his way. However, I'll do it in my own. Sense is beginning in him, and that is the great and hopeful discovery you've made."

"I'm ever so glad you're pleased about it," she said. "He loved the motor car much better than the sight of us. Yet he was glad to see us too. He's really a very human boy, you know, Ray."

CHAPTER XV

CRITICISM

Upon a Sunday afternoon, Sarah Roberts and her husband were drinking tea at 'The Seven Stars.' They sat in Nelly Legg's private room, and by some accident all took rather a gloomy view of life.

As for Nelly, she had been recently weighed, and despite drastic new treatment, was found to have put on two pounds in a month.

"Lord knows where it'll end," she said. "You can't go on getting heavier and heavier for ever more. Even a vegetable marrow, and such like things, reach their limit; and if they can it's hard that a creature with an immortal soul have got to go growing larger and larger, to her own misery and her husband's grief. To be smothered with your own fat is a proper cruel end I call it; and I haven't deserved it; and it shakes my faith in an all-wise God, to feel myself turning into a useless mountain of flesh. Worse than useless in fact, because them that can't work themselves are certain sure to make work for others. Which I do."

"I never knew anything so aggravating, I'm sure," assented Nicholas; "but so far as I can see, if life don't fret you from within, it frets you from without. It can't leave you alone to go on your way in a dignified manner. It's always intruding, so to speak. In fact, life comes between us and our living, if you understand me, and sometimes for my part I can look on to the end of it with a lot of resignation."

Sentiments so unusual from her husband startled Mrs. Roberts as well as her aunt.

"Lor, Nicholas! What's the matter with you?" asked Sarah.

"It ain't often I grumble," he answered, "and if anybody's better at taking the rough with the smooth than me, I'd like to see him; but there are times when nature craves for a bit of pudding, and gets sick to death of its daily meal of bread and cheese. I speak in a parable, however, because I don't mean the body but the mind. Your body bothers you, Missis Legg, as well it may; but your mind, thanks to your husband, is pretty peaceful year in year out. In my case, my body calls for no attention. Thin as a rake I am and so shall continue. But the tissue is good, and no man is made of better quality stuff. It's my mind that turns in upon itself and gives me a pang now and again. And the higher the nature of the mind, the worse its troubles. In fact the more you can feel, the more you are made to feel; and what the mind is built to endure, that, seemingly, it will be called to endure."

But Nelly had no patience with the philosophy of Mr. Roberts.

"You're so windy when you've got anything on your chest," she said. "You keep talking and don't get any forwarder. What's the fuss about now?"

"You've been listening to Baggs, I expect," suggested the wife of Nicholas. "Baggs has got the boot at last and leaves at Christmas, and his pension don't please him, so he's fairly bubbling over with verjuice. I should hope you'd got too much sense to listen to him, Nick."

"So should I. He's no more than the winter wind in a hedge at any time," answered Mr. Roberts. "Baggs gets attended to same as a wasp gets attended to—because of his sting. All bad-tempered people win a lot more attention and have their way far quicker than us easy and amiable ones. Why, we know, of course. Human nature's awful cowardly at bottom and will always choose the easiest way to escape the threatened wrath of a bad temper. In fact, fear makes the world go round, not love, as silly people pretend. In my case I feel much like Sabina Dinnett, who was talking about life not a week ago in the triangle under the sycamore tree. And she said, 'Those who do understand don't care, and those who don't understand, don't matter'—so there you are—one's left all alone."

"I'm sure you ain't—more's Sabina. She's got lots of friends, and you've got your dear wife and children," said Nelly.

"I have; but the mind sometimes takes a flight above one's family. It's summed up in a word: there's nothing so damned unpleasant as being took for granted, and that's what's the matter with me."

"Not in your home, you ain't," declared Sarah. "No good, sensible wife takes her husband for granted. He's always made a bit of a fuss over under his own roof."

"That's true; but in my business I am. To see people—I'll name no names—to see other people purred over, and then to find your own craft treated as just a commonplace of Nature, no more wonderful than the leaves on a bush—beastly, I call it."

Mr. Legg had joined them and he admitted the force of the argument.

"We're very inclined to put our own job higher in the order of the universe than will other people," he said; "and better men than you have hungered for a bit of notice and a pat on the back and never won it. But time covers that trouble. I grant, all the same, that it's a bit galling when we find the world turns a cold shoulder to our best."

"It's a human weakness, Nicholas, to want to be patted," said Nelly, and her husband agreed.

"It is. We share it with dogs," he declared. "But the world in general is too busy to pat us. I remember in my green youth being very proud of myself once and pointing to a lot of pewter in a tub, that I'd worked up till it looked like silver; and I took some credit, and an old man in the bar said that scouring pots was nothing more than scouring pots, and that any other honest fool could have done them just as well as me."

"That's all right and I don't pretend my work on the lathe is a national asset, and I don't pretend I ought to have a statue for doing it," answered Nicholas; "but what I do say is that I am greater than my lathe and ought to get more attention according. I am a man and not a cog-wheel, and when Ironsyde puts cog-wheels above men and gives a dumb machine greater praise than the mechanic who works it—then it's wrong and I don't like it."

"He can't make any such mistake as that," argued Job. "It's rumoured he's going to stand for Parliament at the next General Election, so his business is with men, not machines, and he'll very soon find all about the human side of politics."

"He'll be human enough till he gets in. They always are. They'll stoop to anything till they're elected," said Mrs. Legg, "but once there, the case is often altered with 'em."

"I want to be recognised as a man," continued Roberts, "and Ironsyde don't do it. He isn't the only human being with a soul and a future. And now, if he's for Parliament, I dare say he'll become more indifferent than ever. He may be a machine himself, with no feelings beyond work; but other people are built different."

"A man like him ought to try and do the things himself," suggested Sarah. "If employers had to put in a day laying the stricks on the spreadboard, or turning the rollers on the lathe, or hackling, or spinning, they'd very soon get a respect for what the workers do. In fact, if labour had its way, it ought to make capital taste what labour means, and get out of bed when labour gets out, and do what labour does, and eat what labour eats. Then capital would begin to know it's born."

"It never will happen," persisted Nicholas. "Nothing opens the eyes of the blind, or makes the man who can buy oysters, eat winkles. The gulf is fixed between us and it won't be crossed. If he goes into Parliament, or stops out, he'll be himself still, and look on us doubtfully and wish in his soul that we were made of copper and filled with steam."

"A master must follow his people out of the works into their homes if he's worth a rap," declared Job. "Your aunt always did so with her maidens, and I do so with the men. And it's our place to remember that men and women are far different from metal and steam. You can't turn the power off the workers and think they're going to be all right till you turn it on again. They go on all the time—same as the masters and mistresses do. They sleep and eat and rest; they want their bit of human interest, and bit of fun, and pinch of hope to salt the working day. And as for Raymond Ironsyde, I've seen his career unfolding since he was a boy and marked him in bad moments and seen his weakness; which secrets were safe enough with me, for I'd always a great feeling for the young. And I say that he's good as gold at heart and his faults only come from a lack of power to put himself in another man's place. He could never look very much farther than his own place in the world and the road that led to it. He did wrong, like all of us, and his faults found him out; which they don't always do. But he's the sort that takes years and years to ripen. He's not yet at his best you'll find; but he's a learner, and he may learn a great many useful things if he goes into Parliament—if it's only what to avoid."

"There's one thing that will do him a darned sight more good than going into Parliament, and that's getting married," said Sarah. "In fact, a few of us, that can see further through a milestone than some people, believe it's in sight."

"Miss Waldron, of course?" asked Nelly.

"Yes—her. And when that happens, she'll make of Mister Ironsyde a much more understanding man than going into Parliament will. He's fair and just—not one of us, bar Levi Baggs, ever said he wasn't that—but she's more—she's just our lady, and our good is her good, and what she's done for us would fill a book; and if she could work on him to look at us through her eyes, then none of us, that deserved it, as we all do, would lose our good word."

"What do you say to that, Job?" asked Mrs. Legg.

"I say nothing better could happen," he answered. "But don't feel too hopeful. The things that promise best to the human eye ain't the things that Providence very often performs. To speak in a religious spirit and without feeling, there's no doubt that Providence does take a delight in turning down the obvious things and bringing us up against the doubtful and difficult and unexpected ones. That's why there's such a gulf between story books and real life. The story books that I used to read in my youth, always turned out just as a man of good will and good heart and kindly spirit would wish them to do; but you'd be straining civility to Providence and telling a lie if you pretended real life does. Therefore I say, hope it may happen; but don't bet on it."

Job finished his tea and bustled away.

"The wisdom of the man!" said Nicholas. "He's the most comforting person I know, because he don't pretend. There's some think that everything that happens to us is our own fault, and they drive you silly with their bleating. Job knows it ain't so."

"A far-seeing man," admitted Nelly, "and a great reader of the signs of the times. People used to think he was a simple sort—God forgive me, I did myself; but I know better now. All through that business with poor Richard Gurd, Job understood our characters and bided his time and knew that the crash must come between us. He's told me since that he never really feared Gurd, because he looked ahead and felt that two such natures as mine and Richard's were never meant to join in matrimony. Looking back, I see Job's every move and the brain behind it. Talk about Parliament! If Bridport was to send Legg there, they'd be sending one that's ten times wiser than Raymond Ironsyde—and ten times deeper. In fact, the nation's very ill served by most that go there. They are the showy, rich, noisy sort, who want to bulk in the public eye without working for it—ciphers who do what they're told, and don't understand the inner nature of what they're doing more than a hoss in a plough. But men like Job, though not so noisy, would get to the root, and use their own judgment, and rise superior to party politics and the pitiful need to shout with your side, right or wrong."

"Miss Waldron is very wishful for him to get in, and she says he's got good ideas," replied Nicholas.

"If so, he has to thank her for them," added Sarah.

"And I hope," continued Nicholas, "that if he does get in, he'll be suffered to make a speech, and his words will fall stone dead on the ears of the members, and his schemes will fail. Then he'll know what it is to be flouted and to see his best feats win not a friendly sign."

"Electors are a lot too easy going in my opinion," said Nelly. "I'm old enough to have seen their foolish ways in my time, and find, over and over again, that they are mostly gulls to be took with words. They never ask what a man's record is and turn over the pages of his past. They never trouble about what he's done, or how he's made his money, or where he stands in public report. It isn't what he has done, but what he's going to do. Yet you can better judge of a man from his past than his promises, and measure, in the light of his record, whether he's going to the House of Commons for patriotic, decent reasons, or for mean ones. And never you vote for a lawyer, Nicholas Roberts. 'Tis a golden rule with Job that never, under any manner of circumstances, will he help to get a lawyer into Parliament. They stand in the way of all progress but their own; they suck our blood in every affair of life; they baffle all honest thinking with their cunning, and look at right and wrong only from the point of expediency. Job says there ought to be a law against lawyers going in at all. But catch them making it! In fact, we're in their clutches more than the fly in the web, because they make the laws; and they'll never make any laws to limit their own powers over us, though always quick enough to increase them. Job says that the only bright side to a revolution would be that the law and the lawyers would be swept into the street orderly bin together. Then we'd start clean and free, and try to keep clean and free."

Upon this subject Mrs. Legg always found plenty to say. Indeed she continued to open her mind till they grew weary.

"We must be moving if we're going to church," said Sarah. "I think we'd better go and pick up a bit of charity to our neighbour—Sunday and all."

CHAPTER XVI

THE OFFER OF MARRIAGE

Raymond met Estelle on his way from the works and together they walked home. Here and there in the cottage doorways sat women braiding. Among them was Sally Groves—now grown too old and slow to tend the 'Card'— and accident willed that she should make an opening for thoughts that now filled Ironsyde's mind. They stopped, for Sally was an old acquaintance of both, and Estelle valued the big woman for her resolute character and shrewd sense. Now Sally, on strength of long-standing friendship, grew personal. It was an ancient joke to chaff Miss Groves about marriage, but to-day, when Raymond asked if the net she made was to catch a husband, Sally retorted with spirit.

"All very fine for you two to be poking fun at me," she said. "But what about you? It's time you made up your minds I'm sure, for everybody knows you're in love with each other—though you don't yourselves seemingly."

"Give us a lead, Sally," suggested Raymond; but she shook her head.

"You're old enough to know your own business," she answered; "but don't you go lecturing other people about matrimony while you're a bachelor yourself—else you'll get the worst of it—as you have now."

They left her and laughed together.

"Yet I've heard you say she was the most sensible woman that ever worked in the mills," argued Raymond.

Estelle made no direct reply, but spoke of Sally in the past at one of her parties, when the staff took holiday and spent a day at Weymouth.

Their conversation faded before they reached North Hill House, and then, as they entered the drive, Raymond reminded Estelle of a time long vanished and an expedition taken when she was a child.

"Talking of good things, d'you remember our walk to Chilcombe in the year one? Or, to be more exact, when you were in short frocks."

"I remember well enough. How my chatter must have bored you."

"You never bored me in your life, Chicky. In fact, you always seem to have been a part of my life since I began to live. That event happened soon after our walk, if I remember rightly. You really seem as much a part of my life as my right hand, Estelle."

"Well, your right hand can't bore you, certainly."

"Some of the things that it has done have bored me. But let's go to Chilcombe again—not in the car—but just tramp it as we did before. How often have you been there since we went?"

She considered.

"Twice, I think. My friends there left ten years ago and my girl friend died. I haven't been there since I grew up."

"Well, come this afternoon."

"It's going to rain, Ray."

"Since when did rain frighten you?"

"I'd love to come."

"A walk will do me good," he said. "I'm getting jolly lazy."

"So father thinks. He hates motors—says they are going to make the next generation flabby and good-for-nothing."

They started presently under low grey clouds, but the sky was not grey for them and the weather of their minds made them forget the poor light and sad south-west wind laden with rain. It held off until they had reached Chilcombe chapel, entered the little place of prayer and stood together before the ancient reredos. The golden-brown wood made a patch of brightness in the little building. They were looking at it and recalling Estelle's description of it in the past, when the storm broke and the rain beat on the white glass in the windows above them.

"How tiny it's all grown," said Estelle. "Surely everything has shrunk?"

They had the chapel to themselves and, sitting beside her in a pew, Raymond asked her to marry him. Thunder had wakened in the sky, and the glare of lightning touched their faces now and then. But they only remembered that afterwards.

"Sally Groves was no more than half right," he said, "so her fame for wisdom is shaken. She told us we didn't know we loved one another, Estelle. But I know I love you well enough, and I've been shaking in my shoes to tell you so for months and months. I knew I was getting too old every minute and yet couldn't say the word. But I must say it now at any cost. Chicky, I love you—dearly, dearly I love you—because I'm calm and steady, that doesn't mean I'm not in a blaze inside. I never thought of it even while you were growing up. But a time came when I did begin to think of it like the deuce; and when once I did, the thought towered up like the effreet let out of the bottle—that story you loved when you were small. But my only fear and dread is that you've always been accustomed to think of me as so much older than you are. If you once get an idea into your head about a person's age, you can't get it out again. At least, I can't; so I'm afraid you'll regard me as quite out of the question for a husband. If that's so, I'll begin over again."

Her eyes were round and her mouth a little open. She did not blink when the lightning flashed.

"But—but—" she said.

"If I'm not too old, there are no 'buts' left," he declared firmly. "Ten years is no great matter after all, and from the point of view of brains, I'm an infant beside you. Then say 'yes,' my darling—say 'yes' to me."

"I wonder—I wonder, Ray?"

"Haven't you ever guessed what I felt?"

"Yes, in a vague way. At least I knew there was something growing up between us."

"It was love, my beautiful dear."

She smiled at him doubtfully. The colour had come back to her face, but she did not respond when he lifted his arms to her.

"Are you sure—can you be sure, Ray? It's so different,—so shattering. It seems to smash up all the past into little bits and begin the world all over again—for you and me. It's such a near thing. I've seen the married people and wondered about it. You might get so weary of always having me so close."

"I want you close—closer and closer. I want you as the best part of myself—to make me happier first and, because happier, more useful in the world. I want you at the helm of my life—to steer me, Chicky. What couldn't we do together! It's selfish—? it's one-sided, I know that. I get everything—you only get me. But I'll try and rise to the occasion. I worship you, and no woman ever had a more devout worshipper. I feel that your father wouldn't be very mad with me. But it's for you to decide, nothing else matters either way."

"I love to think you care for me so much," she said. "And I care for you, Ray, and have cared for you—more than either of us know. Yes, I have. Sally Groves knew somehow. I should like to say 'yes' this moment; but I can't. I know I shall say it presently; but I'm not going to say it till I've thought a great many thoughts and looked into the future and considered all this means—for you as well as for me. It's life or death really, for both of us, and the more certain sure we are before, the happier we should be afterwards, I expect."

"I'm sure enough, Estelle. I've been sure enough for many a long day. I know the very hour I began to be sure."

"I think I am too; but I can't say 'yes' and mean 'yes' for the present. I've got to thresh out a lot of things. I dare say they'd be absurd to you; but they're not to me."

"Can I help you?"

"I don't know. You can, I expect. I shall come to you again to throw light on the difficult points."

"How long are you going to take?"

"How can I tell? But I *can* all the same, I'm not going to take long."

"Say you love me—do say that."

"I should have told you if I didn't."

"That's all right, but not so blessed as hearing you say with your own lips you do. Say it—say it, Chicky. I won't take advantage of it. I only want to hear it. Then I'll leave you in peace to think your thoughts."

"I do love you," she said gently and steadily. "It can be nothing smaller than that. You are a very great part of my life—the greatest. I know that, because when you go away life is at evening, and when you come back again life is at morning. Let me have a little time, Ray—only a very little. Then I'll decide."

"I hope your wisdom will let you follow your will, then, and not forbid the banns."

"You mustn't think it cold and horrid of me."

"You couldn't be cold and horrid, my sweet Estelle. We're neither of us capable of being cold, or horrid. We are not babies. I don't blame you a bit for wanting to think about it. I only blame myself. If I was all I might have been, you wouldn't want to think about it."

This challenge shook her, but did not change her.

"Nobody's all they might be, Ray; but many people are a great deal more than they might be. That's what makes you love people best, I think—to see how brave and patient and splendid men and women can be. Life's so difficult even for the luckiest of us; but it isn't the luckiest who are the pluckiest generally—is it? I've had such a lot more than my share of luck already. So have you—at least people think so. But nobody knows one's luck really except oneself."

"It's the things that are going to happen will make our good luck," he said. "You'll find men are seldom satisfied with the past, whatever women may be. God knows I'm not."

"You were always one of my two heroes when I was a child; and father was the other. He is still my hero—and so are you, Ray."

"A pretty poor hero. I wouldn't pretend that to my dog. I only claim to have something worth while in me that you might bring out—raw material for you to turn into the finished article."

She laughed to hear this.

"Come—come—you're not as modest as all that. You're much too clever even to pretend any such thing. Women don't turn strong men into finished articles. At best, perhaps, they can only decorate a little of the outside."

"You laugh," he answered, "but you know better. If you love me, be ambitious for me. That's the most helpful love a woman can give a man— to see his capabilities better than he can, and fire him on the best and biggest he can do, and help him to grasp his opportunities."

"So it is."

"You've got to decide whether it's worth while marrying me, Chicky. You do love me, as I love you—because you can't help it. But you can help marrying me. You've got to think of your own show as well as mine. I quite understand that. You must be yourself and make your own mark, and take advantage of all the big new chances offered to the rising generation of women. I love you a great deal too much to want to lessen you, or drift you into a back-water. It's just a question whether my work, and the Mill, and so on, give you the chance you want—if, working together, we can each help on the other. You could certainly help me hugely and you know it; but whether I could help you—that's what you've got to think about I suppose."

"Yes, I suppose it is, Ray."

"Your eyes say 'yes' already, and they're terrible true eyes."

But she only lowered them and neither spoke any more for a little while. The worst of the storm had passed, and its riot and splash gave place to a fine drizzle as the night began to close in.

They started for home and, both content to think their own thoughts, trudged side by side. For Raymond's part, he knew the woman too well to suffer any doubt of the issue and he was happy. For he felt that she was quietly happy too, and if instincts had brought grave doubts, or prompted her to deny him, she would not have been happy.

Estelle did not miss the romance from his offer of marriage. She had dreamed of man's love in her poetry-reading days, but under the new phase and the practical bent, developed by a general enthusiasm for her kind, personal emotions were not paramount. There could be but little sex in her affection for Raymond: she had lived too near him for that. Indeed, she had grown up beside him, and the days before he came to dwell at North Hill seemed vague and misty. Thus his challenge came as an experience both less and greater than love. It was less, in that no such challenge can be so urgent and so mighty as the call of hungry hearts to each other; it was greater, because the interests involved were built on abiding principles. They arrested her intellectual ambitions and pointed to a sphere of usefulness beyond her unaided power. What must have made his prosaic offer flat in the ear of an amorous woman, edged it for her. He had dwelt on the aspect of their union that was likely most to attract her.

There was a pure personal side where love came in and made her heart beat warmly enough; but, higher than that, she saw herself of living value to Raymond and helping him just where he stood most in need of help. She believed that they might well prove the complement of each other in those duties, disciplines, and obligations to which life had called them.

That night she went closely, searchingly over old ground again from the new point of vision. What had always been interesting to her, became now vital, since these characteristics belonged to the man who wanted to wed her. She tried to be remorseless and cruel that she might be kind. But the palette of thought was only set with pleasant colours. She had been intellectually in love with him for a long time, and he had offered problems which made her love him for the immense interest they gave her. Now came additional stimulus in the knowledge that he loved her well enough to share his life, his hopes, and his ambitions with her.

She believed they might be wedded in very earnest. He was masterful and possessed self-assurance; but what man can lead and control without these qualities? His self-assurance was less than his self-control, and his instinct for self-assertion had nearly always been counted by a kind heart. It seemed to her that she had never known a man who balanced reason and feeling more judicially, or better preserved a mean between them.

She had found that men could differentiate in a way beyond woman's power and be unsociable if their duty demanded it. But to be unsociable is not to be unsocial. Raymond took long views, and if his old, genial and jolly attitude to life was a thing of the past, there had been substituted for it a wiser understanding and saner recognition of the useful and useless. Men did take longer views than women—so Estelle decided: and there Raymond would help her; but the all-important matter that night was to satisfy herself how much she could help him. In this reverie she found such warmth and light as set her glowing before dawn, for she built up the spiritual picture of Raymond, came very close to its ultimate realities, quickened by the new inspiration, and found that it should be well within her power to serve him generously. She took no credit to herself, but recognized a happy accident of character.

There were weak spots in all masculine armour, that only a woman could make strong, and by a good chance she felt that her particular womanhood might serve this essential turn for Raymond's manhood. To strengthen her own man's weak spots—surely that was the crown and completion of any wedded life for a woman. To check, to supplement, to enrich: that he would surely do for her; and she hoped to deal as faithfully with him.

She was not clear-sighted here, for love, if it be love at all, must bring the rosy veil with it and dim the seeing of the brightest eyes. While the fact that she had grown up with Raymond made her view clear enough in some directions, in others it served, of course, to dim judgment. She credited him with greater intellect than he possessed, and dreamed that higher achievements were in his power than was the truth. But there existed a mean, below her dream yet above his present ambition, that it was certainly possible with her incentive he might attain. She might make him more sympathetic and so more synthetic also, and show him how his own industry embraced industrial problems at large—how it could not be taken by itself, but must hold its place only by favour of its progress, and command respect only as it represented the worthiest relation between capital and labour. Thus, from the personal interest of his work, she would lift him to measure the world-wide needs of all workers. And then, in time to come, he would forget the personal before the more splendid demands of the universal. The trend of machinery was towards tyranny; he must never lose sight of that, or let the material threaten the spiritual. Private life, as well as public life, was open to the tyranny of the machine; and there, too, it would be her joyful privilege to fight beside him for added beauty, added liberty, not only in their own home, but all homes wherein they had power to increase comfort and therefore happiness. The sensitiveness of women should be linked to the driving force of men, as the safety valve to the engine. Thus, in a simile surely destined to delight him, she summed her intentions and desires.

She had often wondered what must be essential to the fullest employment of her energies and the best and purest use of her thinking; and now she saw that marriage answered the question—not marriage in the abstract, but just marriage with this man. He, of all she had known, was the one with whom she felt best endowed to mingle and merge, so that their united forces should be poured to help the world and water with increase the modest territory through which they must flow.

She turned to go to sleep at last, yet dearly longed to tell Raymond and amaze her father with the great tidings.

An impulse prompted her to leave her lover not a moment more in doubt. She rose, therefore, and descended to his room, which opened beside his private study on the ground floor. The hour was nearly four on an autumn morning. She listened, heard him move restlessly and knew that he did not sleep. He struck a match and lighted a cigarette, for he often smoked at night.

Then she knocked at the door.

"Who the devil's that?" he shouted.

"I," she said, opening the door an inch and talking softly. "Stop where you are and stop worrying and go to sleep. I'm going to marry you, Ray, and I'm happier than ever I was before in all my life."

Then she shut the door and fled away.

CHAPTER XVII

SABINA AND ABEL

Now was Raymond Ironsyde too busy to think any thought but one, and though distractions crowded down on the hour, he set them aside so far as it was possible. His betrothal very completely dominated his life and the new relation banished the old attitude between him and Estelle. The commonplace existence, as of sister and brother, seemed to perish suddenly, and in its place, as a butterfly from a chrysalis, there reigned the emotional days of prelude to marriage. The mere force of the situation inspired them and they grew as loverly as any boy and girl. It was no make-believe that led them to follow the immemorial way and glory only in the companionship of each other; they felt the desire, and love that had awakened so tardily and moved in a manner so desultory, seemed concerned to make up for lost time.

Arthur Waldron was not so greatly astonished as they expected, and whatever may have been his private hopes and desires for his daughter, he never uttered them, but seeing her happiness, echoed it.

"No better thing could have happened from my point of view," he declared, "for if she'd married anybody else in the world, I should have been called to say 'good-bye' to her. Since she's chosen you, there's no necessity for me to do so. I hope you're going on living at North Hill, and I trust you're going to let me do the same. Of course, it would be an impossible arrangement if you were dealing with anybody but me; but since we are what we are in spirit and temper and understanding, I claim that I may stop. The only difference I can see is this: that whereas at present, when we dine, you sit between Estelle and me, in future I shall sit between Estelle and you."

"Not even that," vowed the lover. "Why shouldn't I go on sitting between you?"

"No—you'll be the head of the house in future."

"The charm of this house is that there's no head to it," said Estelle, "and Raymond isn't going to usurp any such position just because he means to marry me."

But distractions broke in upon their happiness. Ernest Churchouse fell grievously ill and lacked strength to fight disease; while there came news from Knapp that the farmer was tired of Abel and wished him away.

For their old friend none could prolong his life; in the case of the boy, Raymond decided that Sabina had better see him and go primed with a definite offer. Abel's father did not anticipate much more trouble in that quarter. He guessed that the lad, now in his seventeenth year, was sufficiently weary of the land and would be glad to take up engineering. He felt confident that Sabina must find him changed for the better, prepared for his career and willing to enter upon it without greater waste of time. He invited the boy's mother to learn if he felt more friendly to him, and hoped that Abel had now revealed a frame of mind and a power of reasoning, that would serve to solve the problem of his career, and finally abolish his animosity to his father.

Sabina went to see her son and heard the farmer first. He was not unfriendly, but declared Abel a responsibility he no longer desired to incur.

"He's just at a tricky age—and he's shifty and secret—unlike other lads. You never know what's going on in his mind, and he never laughs, or takes pleasure in things. He's too difficult for me, and my wife says she's frightened of him. As to work, he does it, but you always feel he's got no love for it. And I know he means to bolt any day. I've marked signs; so it will be better for you people to take the first step."

The farmer's wife spoke to similar purpose and added information that made Sabina more than uneasy.

"It's about this friend of his, Miss Waldron, that came to see him backalong," she explained. "He'd talk pretty free about her sometimes and was very proud of it when he got a letter now and again. But since she's wrote and told him she's going to be married, he's turned a gloomier character than ever. He don't like the thought of it and it makes him dark. 'Tis almost as if he'd been in love with the lady. You do hear of young boys falling in love before their time like that."

Sabina was on the point of explaining, but did not do so. Her first care was to see Abel and learn the truth of this report. Perhaps she felt not wholly sorry that he resented this conclusion. Not a few had spoken of Ironsyde's marriage before her: it was the gossip of Bridetown; but none appeared to consider how it must affect her, or sympathise with her emotions on the subject. What these emotions were, or whither they tended, she hardly knew herself. Unowned even to her innermost heart, a sort of dim hope had not quite died, that he might, after all, come back to her. She blushed at the absurdity of the idea now, but it had struck in her subconsciously and never wholly vanished. Before the engagement was announced she had altered her attitude to Raymond and used him civilly and shared his desire that Abel should be won over by his father. The old hatred at receiving anything from Ironsyde's hands no longer existed. She felt indifferent and, before her own approaching problems, was not prepared to decline the offers of help that she knew would quickly come when Ernest Churchouse died.

She intended to preach patience and reason in the ears of Abel, and she hoped he would not make her task difficult; but now it was clear that Estelle's betrothal had troubled the boy.

She saw him and they spoke together for a long time; but already his force of character began to increase beyond his mother's. Despite her purpose and sense of the gravity of the situation, he had more effect upon her than she had upon him. Yet her arguments were rational and his were not. But the old, fatal, personal element of temper crept in and, during her speech with him, Sabina found fires that she believed long quenched, were still smouldering in the depths of memory. The boy could not indeed fan them to flame again; but the result of his attitude served to weaken hers. She did not argue with conviction after finding his temper. By some evil chance, that seemed more like art than accident, he struck old wounds, and she was interested and agitated to find that now he knew all there was to be known of the past and its exact significance. The dream hidden so closely in her heart: that there might yet be a reconciliation—the dream finally killed when she perceived that Ironsyde had fallen in love with Estelle Waldron— was no dream in her son's mind. What she knew was impossible, till now represented no impossibility to him. He actually declared it as a thing which, in his moral outlook, ought to be. Only so could the past be retrieved, or the future made endurable. But to that matter they did not immediately come. She dined at the farmer's table with Abel and three men. Then he was told that he might make holiday and spend the afternoon with his mother where he pleased. He took her therefore to the old barrows nigh Knapp, and there on a stone they sat, watched the sun sink over distant woodlands and talked together till the dusk was down.

"I ought never to have trusted her," he said. "But I did. And, if I'd thought she would ever have married him, I wouldn't have trusted her. I thought she was the right sort; but if she was, she would never have married a man who had sworn to marry you."

"Good gracious, Abel! Whatever are you talking about?" she asked, concerned to find the matter in his mind.

"I'm talking about things that happened," he answered. "I'm not a child now. I'm nearly seventeen and older than that, for I overheard two of the men say so. You needn't tell me these things; I found them out for myself, and I hated Raymond Ironsyde from the time I could hate anybody, because the honest feeling to hate him was in me. And nobody has the right to marry him but you, and he's got no right to marry anybody but you. But he doesn't know the meaning of justice, and she is not fine, or brave, or clever, or any of the things I thought she was, because she wants to marry him."

His mother considered this speech.

"It's no good vexing yourself about the past," she said. "You and me have got to look to the future, Abel, and not to dwell on all that don't make the future any easier. It's difficult enough, but, for us, the luxury of pride and hate isn't possible. I know very well what you feel. It all went through me like fire before you were born—and after; but we've got to go on living, and things are going to change, and we must cut our coats according to our cloth—you and me."

"What does that mean?" he asked.

"It means we're not independent. There's not enough for your education and my keep. So it's got to be him, or one other, and the other is an old woman—his aunt. But it's all the same really, and he'll see that it comes out of his pocket in the end. He's all powerful and we must do according. Christianity's a very convenient thing for the likes of us. It teaches that the meek are blessed and the weak the worthy ones. You must look to your father if you want to succeed in the world."

"Never," he said. "He's got everything else in the world, but he shan't have me. I don't care much about being alive at best, seeing I must be different from other people all my life; but I'd rather die twenty times than owe anything to him. He knew before I was born that he was going to wreck my life, and he did it, and he wrecked yours, and his marriage with any other woman but you is a lie and a sham, and Estelle knows it very well. Now I hate her as much as him, and I hate those who let her marry him, and I hate the clergyman that will do it; and if I could ruin them by killing myself on their doorstep, I would. But he wouldn't care for that. If I was to do that, it would just suit the devil, because he'd know I'd gone and could never rise up against him any more."

She made a half-hearted attempt to distract his thoughts. She began to argue and, as usual, ended in bitterness.

"You mustn't talk nonsense, like that. He means well by you, and you mustn't cut off your nose to spite your face. You'll find plenty of people to take his side and you mustn't only listen to his enemies. There's always wise people to stand up for young men and excuse them, though not many to stand up for young women."

"Let them stand up for me and excuse me, then," he answered. "Let them explain me and tell me why I should think different, and why I should take his filthy money just to set his mind at rest. What has he done for me that I should ease him and do as he pleases? Is it out of any care for me he'd lift me up? Not likely. It's all to deceive the people and make them say he's a good man. And until he puts you right, he's not a good man, and soon or late I'll have it out with him. God blast me if I don't. But I'll revenge myself clean on him. He shan't make out to the world that he's done what a father should do for a son. He's my natural father and no more, and he never wanted or meant to be more. And no right will take away that wrong. And I'll treat him as other natural creatures treat their fathers."

"You can't do that," she said. "You're a human, and you've got a conscience and must answer to it."

"I will—some day. I know what my conscience says to me. My conscience tells me the truth, not a lot of lies like yours tells you. I know what's right and I know what's justice. I gave the man one chance. I offered to go in his works—my works that ought to be some day. But that didn't suit him. I must always knuckle under and bend to his will. But never—never. I'd starve first, or throw myself into the sea. He don't want me near him for people to point to, so I must be drove out of Bridetown to the ends of the earth if he chooses. And if the damned world was straight and honest and looked after the women and innocent children, 'tis him, not me, would have been drove out of Bridetown."

He spoke with amazing bitterness for youth, and echoed much that he had heard, as well as what he had thought. His mother felt some astonishment to find how his mind had enlarged, and some fear, also, to see the hopelessness of the position.

Already she considered in secret what craft might be necessary to bring him to a more reasonable mind.

"You'll have to think of me as well as yourself," she said. "Life's hard enough without you making it so much harder. Two things will happen in a few weeks from now and nothing can stop them. First you've got to leave here, because farmer don't want you any more, and then poor Mister Churchouse is going to pass away. He's just fading out like a night-light—flickering up and down and bound to be called. And the best man and the truest friend to sorrow that ever trod the earth."

"I was going from here," he answered. "And you can look to me for making a pound a week, and you can have it all if you'll take nothing from any of my enemies. If you take money from my enemies, then I won't help you."

"You're a man in your opinions seemingly, though I wish to God you hadn't grown out of childhood so quick, if you were going to grow to this. It'll drive you mad if you're not careful. Then where shall I be?"

"I'll drive other people mad—not you. I'll come back home, and then I'll find work at Bridport."

"Where's home going to be—that's the question?" Sabina answered. "There's only one choice for you—between letting him finish your education and going out to work."

"We'll live in Bridport, then," he told her, "and I'll go into something with machinery. I'll soon rise, and I might rise high enough to ruin him yet, some day. And never you forget he had my offer and turned it down. He didn't know what he was doing when he did that."

"He couldn't trust you. How was he to know you wouldn't try to burn the works again—and succeed next time?"

Abel laughed.

"That was a fool's trick. If they'd gone, he'd only have built 'em again, better. But there are some things he can't insure."

"I know a good few spinners at Bridport. Shall I have a look round for you?" she asked, as they rose to return.

He considered and agreed.

"Yes, if it's only through you. I trust you not to go to him about it. If you did and I found you had—"

"No, no. I'll not go to him."

He came and looked again at the motor car that had brought her. It interested him as keenly as before.

"That's for him to go about the country in, because he's standing for Parliament," explained Sabina.

But his anger was spent. He heeded her no more, and even the fact that his father owned the car did not modify his deep interest.

He rode a mile or two with her when she started to return and remained silent and rapt for the few minutes of the experience.

His mother tried to use the incident.

"If you was to be good and patient and let the right thing be done, I daresay in a few years you'd rise to having a motor of your own," she said, when they stopped and he started to trudge back.

"If ever I do, I'll get it for myself," he answered. "And when you're old, I'll drive you about, very likely."

He left her placidly, and it was understood that in a month he would return to her as soon as she had determined on their immediate future.

For herself she knew that it would be necessary to deceive him, yet feared to attempt it after the recent conversation. She felt uneasily proud of him.

CHAPTER XVIII

SWAN SONG

The doctor said Mr. Churchouse was dying because he didn't wish to go on living, and when Estelle taxed the old man with his indifference, he would not deny it.

"I have lived long enough," he said. "The machine is worn out. My thinking is become a painful effort. I forget the simplest matters, and before you are a nuisance to yourself, you may feel very certain you have long been a nuisance to other people."

He had for some months grown physically weaker, and both Raymond and others had noticed an inconsequence of utterance and an inability to concentrate the mind. He liked friends to come and see him and would listen with obvious effort to follow any argument, or grasp any fresh item of news. But he spoke less and less. Nor could Sabina tempt him to eat adequate food. He ignored the doctor's drugs and seemed to shrink physically as well as mentally.

"I'm turning into my chrysalis," he said once to Estelle. "One has to go through that phase before one can be a butterfly. Remember, my pretty girl, you are only burying an empty chrysalis when this broken thing is put into the ground."

"You're very unkind to talk so," she declared. "You might go on living if you liked, and you ought to try—for the sake of those who love you."

But he shook his head.

"One doesn't control these things. You know I've always told you that the length of the thread is no part of our business, but only the spinning. I should have liked to see you married; yet, after all, why not? I may be there. I shall hope to beg a holiday on that occasion and be in church."

He always spoke thus quite seriously. Death he regarded as no discontinuity, or destruction, of life, but merely an alteration of environment.

At some personal cost Miss Ironsyde came to take leave of him, when it seemed that his end was near. He kept his bed now, and by conserving his strength gained a little activity of mind.

He was troubled for Jenny's physical sufferings; while she, for her part, endeavoured to discuss Sabina's problems, but she could not interest the old man in them.

"Abel is safe with his father," said Mr. Churchouse. "As for Sabina, I have left her a competency, and so have you. One has been very heartily sorry for her. She will have no anxiety when my will is read. I am leaving you three books, Jenny. I will leave you more if you like. My library as a whole is bequeathed to Estelle Waldron, since I know nobody who values and respects books so well."

"But Abel," she said.

"I have tried to establish his character and we may find, after all, I did more than we think. Providence is ever ready to water and tend the good seed that we sow. But he must be made to abandon this fatal attitude to his father. It is uncomfortable and inconvenient and helps nobody. I shall talk to him, I hope, before I die. He is coming home in a day or two."

But Abel delayed a week, at his master's request, that he might help pull a field of mangels, and Mr. Churchouse never saw him again.

During his last days Estelle spent much time with him. He seldom mentioned any other person but himself. He wandered in a disjointed fashion over the past and mixed his recollections with his dreams. He remembered jests and sometimes uttered them, then laughed; but often he laughed to himself without giving any reason for his amusement.

He was thoughtful and apologetic. Indeed, when he looked up into any face, he always said, "I mourn to give you so much trouble." Latterly he confused his visitors, but kept Estelle and Sabina clear in his mind. He fancied that they had quarrelled and was always seeking to reconcile them. Every morning he appeared anxious and distressed until they stood by him together and declared that they were the best of friends. Then he became tranquil.

"That being so," he said, "I shall depart in peace."

Estelle relieved the professional nurse and would read, talk, or listen, as he wished. He spoke disjointedly one day and wove reality and imagination together.

"Much good marble is wasted on graves," he declared. "But it doesn't bring the dead to life. Do you believe in the resurrection of the body, Estelle? I hope you find it easy. That is one of the things I never was honestly able to say I had grasped. Reason will fight against the nobler tyranny of faith. The old soul in a glorified body—yet the same body, you understand. We shan't all be in one pattern in heaven. We shall preserve our individuality; and yet I deprecate passing eternity in this tabernacle. Improvements may be counted upon, I think. The art of the Divine Potter can doubtless make beautiful the humblest and the most homely vessel."

"Nobody who loves you would have you changed," she assured him.

Then his mind wandered away and he smiled.

"I listened to a street preacher once—long, long ago when I was young—and he said that the road to everlasting destruction was lined with women and gin shops. Upon which a sailor-man, who listened to him, shouted out, 'Oh death, where is thy sting?' The meeting dissolved in a very tornado of laughter. Sailors have a great sense of humour. It can take the place of a fire on a cold day. One touch of humour makes the whole world kin. If you have a baby, teach it to laugh as well as to walk. But I think your baby will do that readily enough."

On another occasion he laughed suddenly to himself and explained his amusement to Sabina, who sat by him.

"Eunominus, the heretic, boasted that he knew the nature of God; whereupon St. Basil instantly puzzled him with twenty-one questions about the body of the ant!"

Estelle also tried to make Mr. Churchouse discuss Abel Dinnett. She told him of an interesting fact.

"I have got Ray to promise a big thing," she said. "He hesitated, but he loved me too well to deny me. Besides, feeling as I do, I couldn't take any denial. You see Nature is so much greater than all else to me, and contrasted with her, our little man-made laws, often so mean and hateful in their cowardly caution and cruel injustice, look pitiful and beneath contempt. And I don't want to come between Raymond and his eldest son. I won't—I won't do it. Abel is his first-born, and it may be cold-blooded of me—Ray said it was at first—but I insist on that. I've made him see, and I've made father see. I feel so much about it, that I wouldn't marry him if he didn't recognize Abel first and treat him as the first-born ought to be treated."

"Abel—Abel Dinnett," said the other, who had not followed her speech. "A good-looking boy, but lawless. He wants the world to bend to him; and yet, if you'll believe me, there is a vein of fine sentiment in his nature. With tears in his eyes he once told me that he had seen a fellow pupil at school cruelly killing insects with a burning glass; and he had beaten the cruel lad and broken his glass. That is all to the good. The difficulty for him is that he was born out of wedlock. This great disability could have been surmounted in America, Scotland, Ireland, Germany, or, in fact, anywhere but in England. The law of the natural child in this country would bring a blush to the cheek of a gorilla. But neither Church nor State will lift a finger to right the infamy."

"We are always wanting to pluck the mote out of our neighbour's eyes, and never see the beam in our own," she answered. "Women will alter that some day—and the disgusting divorce laws, too. Perhaps these are the first things they will alter, when they have the power."

"Who is going into Parliament?" he asked. "Somebody told me, but I forget. He was a friend of mine. I remember that much."

"Ray hopes to get in. I am going to help him, if I can."

"It is a great responsibility. Tell him, if he is elected, to fight for the natural child. It would well become him to do so. Let him rise to it. Our Saviour said, 'Suffer the little children to come unto Me.' The State, on the contrary, says, 'Suffer the little children to be done to death and put out of the way.'"

"Yes," she answered, "suffer fifty thousand little children to be lost every year, because it is kinder to let them perish, than help them to live under the wicked laws we have planned to govern them."

But his mind collapsed and when she strove to bring it back again, she could not.

Two days before he died, Estelle found him in deep distress. He begged to see her alone, and explained that he had to confess a great sin.

"I ought to tell a priest," he said, "but I dare think that you will do as well. If you absolve me, I shall know I may hope to be forgiven. I have lived a double life, Estelle. I have pretended what was not true—not merely once or twice, but systematically, deliberately, callously."

"I don't believe it, dear Mister Churchouse. You couldn't."

"I should never have believed it myself. But even the old can surprise themselves, painfully sometimes. I have lived with this perfidy for many years; but I can't die with it. There's always an inclination to confess our sins to a fellow creature. To confess them to our Maker is quite needless, because He knows them; but it's a quality of human nature to feel better after imparting its errors to another ear."

He broke off.

"What was I saying? I forget."

"That you'd done something ever so wicked and nobody knew it."

"Yes, yes. The books—the books I used to receive from unknown admirers by post. My child, there were no unknown admirers! Nobody ever admired me, either secretly or openly. Why should they? I used to send the books to myself—God forgive me."

"If I'd only known, I'd have sent you hundreds of books," she said. "I did send you one or two."

"I know it—they are my most precious possessions. They served in some mysterious way to soothe my bad conscience. It would be interesting to examine and find out how they did. But my brain can't look into anything subtle now. I knew you sent the books. My good angel has recorded my thanks. You always increased my vitality, Estelle. You are keeping me alive at present. You have risen in the autumn of my life as a gracious dawn; you have been the sun of my Indian summer. You will be a good wife to Raymond. It seems only yesterday that he was a little thing in short frocks, and Henry so proud of him. Now Henry is dead, and Raymond wife-old and in Parliament. A sound Liberal, like his father before him."

"The election isn't till next year. But I hope he'll get in. They say at Bridport he has a very good chance."

The day before he died, Mr. Churchouse seemed better and talked to Estelle of another visit from her father.

"I always esteem his great good humour and fine British instinct to live and let live. That is where our secret lies. We ride Empire with such a loose rein, Estelle—the only way. You cannot dare to put a curb on proud people. A paradox that—that those who fast bind don't fast find. The instinct of England's greatness is in your father; he is an epitome of our virtues. He has no imagination, however. Nor has England. If she had, doubtless she would not do the great deeds that beggar imagination. That reminds me. There is one little gift that you must have from my own hand. A work of imagination—a work of art. Nobody in the world would care about it but you. A poem, in fact. I have written one or two others, but I tore them up. I sent them to newspapers, hoping to astonish you with them; but when they were rejected I destroyed them. This poem I did not send. Nobody has seen it but myself. Now I give it to you, and I want you to read it aloud to me, that I may hear how it sounds."

"How clever of you! There's nothing you can't do. I know I shall love it."

He pointed to a sheaf of papers on a table.

"The top one. It is a mournful subject, yet I hope treated cheerfully. I wrote it before death was in sight; but I feel no more alarmed or concerned about death now than I did then. You may think it is too simple. But simplicity, though boring to the complex mind, is really quite worth while. The childlike spirit—there is much to be said for it. No doubt I have missed a great deal by limiting my interests; but I have gained too—in directness."

"There is a greatness about simplicity," she said.

"To be simple in my life and subtle in my thought was my ambition at one time; but I never could rise to subtlety. The native bent was against it. The poem—I do not err in calling it a poem—is called 'Afterwards'—unless you can think of a better title. If any obvious and glaring faults strike you, tell me. No doubt there are many."

She read the two pages written in his little, careful and almost feminine hand.

"When I am dead, the storm and stress
Of many-coloured consciousness
Like blossom petals fall away
And drops the calyx back to clay;
A man, not woman, makes the bed
When our night comes and we are dead.

"When I am dead, the ebb and flow
Of folk where I was wont to go,
Will never stay a moment's pace,
Or miss along the street my face.
Yet thoughts may wake and things be said
By one or two when I am dead.

"When I am dead, the sunset light
Will fill the gap upon the height
In summer time, but on the plain
Sink down as winter comes again
And none who sees the evening red
Will know I loved it, who am dead.

"When I am dead, upon my mound
Exotic flow'rs may first be found,
And not until they've blown away
Will other blossoms come to stay.
A daisy growing overhead
Brings gentle pleasure to the dead.

"When I am dead, I'd love to see
An amber thrush hop over me
And bend his ear, as he would know
What I am whispering down below.

May many a song-bird find his bread
Upon my grave when I am dead.

"When I am dead, and years shall pass,
The scythe will cut the darnel grass
Now and again for decency,
Where we forgotten people lie.
O'er ancient graves the living tread
With great impertinence on the dead.

"When I am dead, all I have done
Must vanish, like the evening sun.
My book about the bells may stay
Behind me for a fleeting day;
But will not very oft be read
By anybody when I'm dead."

She stopped and smiled with her eyes full of tears.

"I had meant to write another verse," he explained, "but I put it off and it's too late now. Such as it is, it is yours. Does it seem to you to be interesting?"

"It's very interesting indeed, and very beautiful. I shall always value it as my greatest treasure."

"Read it to your children," he said, "and if the opportunity occurs, take them sometimes to see my grave. The spot is long chosen. Let there be no gardening upon it out of good heart but bad taste. I should wish it left largely to Nature. There will be daisies for your babies to pick. I forget the text I selected. It's in my will."

He bade her good-bye more tenderly than usual, as though he knew that he would never see her again, and the next morning Bridetown heard that the old man had died in his sleep. The people felt sorry, for he left no enemies, and his many kindly thoughts and deeds were remembered for a little while.

CHAPTER XIX

NEW WORK FOR ABEL

With a swift weaver's knot John Best mended the flying yarn. Then he turned from a novice at the Gill Spinner and listened, not very patiently, to one who interrupted his lesson.

"It's rather a doubtful thing that you should always be about the place now you've left it, Levi," he said to Mr. Baggs. "It would be better judgment and more decent on your part if you kept away."

"You may think so," answered the hackler, "but I do not. And until the figure of my pension is settled, I shall come and go and take no denial."

"It is settled. He don't change. He's said you shall have ten shillings a week and no more, so that it will be."

"And what if I decline to take ten shillings a week, after fifty years of work in his beastly Mill?"

"Then you can do the other thing and go without. You want it both ways, you do."

"I want justice—no more. Common justice, I suppose, can be got in Dorset as elsewhere. I ought to have had a high testimonial when I left this blasted place—a proper presentation for all to see, and a public feed and a purse of sovereigns at the least."

"That's what I mean when I say you can't have it both ways," answered Mr. Best. "To be nice and pick words and consider your feelings is waste of time, so I tell you that you can't grizzle and grumble and find fault with everything and everybody for fifty years, and then expect people to bow down and worship you and collect a purse of gold when you retire. If we flew any flags about you, it would be because we'd got rid of you. Mister Ironsyde don't like you, and why should he? You've always been up against the employer and you've never lost a chance to poison the minds of the employed. There's no good will in you and never was, and where you could hang us up in the Mill and make difficulties without getting yourself into trouble, you've always took great pleasure in so doing. Did you ever pull with me, or anybody, if you could help it? Never. You pulled against. You'd often have liked to treat us like the hemp and tear us to pieces on your rougher's hackle. And how does such a man expect anybody to care about him? There was no reason why you should have had a pension at all, in my opinion. You've been blessed with good health and no family, and you've never spent a shilling on another fellow creature in your life. Therefore, it's more than justice that you get ten shillings, and not less as you seem to think."

Mr. Baggs glowered at John during this harangue. His was the steadfast attitude of the egoist, who sees all life in terms of his own interest alone.

"We've got to fight for ourselves in this world since there's none other to fight for us," he said, "and, of course, you take his side. You've licked Ironsyde boots all your life, and nothing an Ironsyde can do is wrong. But I might have known the man that's done the wickedness he's done, and deserts his child and let his only son work on the land, wouldn't meet me fair. There's no honour or honesty in the creature, but if he thinks I'm going to take this slight without lifting my voice against it, he's wrong. To leave the works and sneak out of 'em unmourned and without a bit of talk and a testimonial was shameful enough; but ten shilling a week—no! The country shall ring about that and he'll find his credit shaken. 'Tis enough to lose him his election to Parliament, and I hope it will do so."

Best stared.

"You're a cracked old fool, and not a spark of proper pride or gratitude in you. Feeling like that, I wonder you dare touch his money; but you're the sort who would take gifts with one hand and stab the giver with the other. I hope he'll change his mind yet and give you no pension at all."

Levi, rather impressed with this unusual display of feeling from the foreman, growled a little longer, then went his way; while in John there arose a determination to prevent Mr. Baggs from visiting the scene of his old activities. At present force of habit drew the old man to spend half his time here; and now, when Best had returned to the Gill Spinner, Levi prowled off to his old theatre of work, entered the hackling shop and criticised the new hackler. His successor was young and stood in awe of him at first; but awe was not a quality the veteran inspired for long. Already Joe Ash began to grow restive under Levi's criticisms, and dimly to feel that the old hackler was better away. To-day Mr. Baggs allowed the resentment awakened by Best's criticisms to take shape in offensive comments at the expense of his young successor. He was of that order of beings who, when kicked, rests not until he has kicked somebody again.

But to-day the evil star of Mr. Baggs was in ascendant, and when he told the youth that he wasted half his strength and had evidently been taught his business by a fool, Levi was called to suffer a spirited retort. Joe Ash came from the Midlands; his vocabulary was wider than that of Mr. Baggs, and he soon had the old man gasping. Finally he ordered him out of the shop, and told him that if he did not go he would be put out.

"Strength or no strength," he said, "I've got enough for you, so hop out of this and don't come back. If you're to be free of my shop, I leave; and that's all there is to it."

Mr. Baggs departed, having hoped that he might live to see the young man hung with his own long line. He then pursued his way by the river, labouring under acute emotions, and half a mile down stream met a lad engaged in angling.

Abel Dinnett had returned home and was making holiday until his mother should discover work for him, or he himself be able to get occupation.

For the moment Sabina found herself sufficiently busy packing up her possessions and preparing for the forthcoming sale at 'The Magnolias.'

She was waiting to find a new home until Abel's future labour appeared; but, in secret, Raymond Ironsyde had undertaken to obtain it, and she knew that henceforth she would live at Bridport.

Mr. Baggs poured out his wrongs, but he did not begin immediately. Failing adult ears, Abel's served him, and he proceeded to declare that the new hackler was a worthless rogue, who did not know his business and would never earn his money.

Abel, however, had reached a standard of intelligence that no longer respected Mr. Baggs.

"I don't go to the works now," he said, "and never shall again. I don't care nothing about them. My mother and me are going to leave Bridetown when I get a job."

"No doubt—no doubt. Though I dare say your talk is sour grapes—seeing as you'll never come by your rights."

Abel lifted his eyes to the iron-roofed buildings up the valley.

"Oh yes, I could," he said. "That man wants to win me now. He's going to be married, and she—her he's going to marry—told my mother that he's wishful for me to be his proper son and be treated according. But I won't have his damned friendship now. It's too late now. You can't drive hate out of a man with gifts."

"They ain't gifts—they're your right and due. 'Tis done to save his face before the people, so they'll forgive his past and help send him into Parliament. Look at me—fifty years of service and ten shillings a week pension! It shall be known and 'twill lose him countless votes, please God.

A dog like that in Parliament! 'Twould be a disgrace to the nation. And you go on hating him if you're a brave boy. Every honest man hates him, same as I do. Twenty shillings I ought to have had, if a penny."

"Fling his money back in his face," said Abel. "Nobody did ought to touch his money, or work for it. And if every man and woman refused to go in his works, then he'd be ruined."

"The wicked flourish like the green bay tree in this country, because there's such a cruel lot of 'em, and they back each other up against the righteous," declared Levi. "But a time's coming, and you'll live to see it, when the world will rise against their iniquity."

"Don't take his money, then."

"It ain't his money. It's my money. He's keeping back my money. When that John Best drops out, as he ought to do, for he's long past his work, will he get ten shillings a week? Two pound, more like; and all because he cringes and lies and lets the powers of darkness trample on him! And may the money turn to poison in his mouth when he does get it."

"Everything about Ironsyde is poison," added Abel. "And that girl that was a friend to me—he's poisoned her now, and I won't know her no more. I won't neighbour with anybody that has a good word for him, and I won't breathe the same air with him much longer; and I told my mother if she took a penny from him, I'd throw her over, too."

"Quite right. I wish you was strong enough to punish him; but if you was, he'd come whining to you and pray you not to. Men like him only make war on women and the weak."

Abel listened.

"I'll punish him if he lives long enough," he said. "That's what I'm after. I'll bide my time."

"And for him to dare to get up and ask the people to send him to Parliament. But they won't. He's too well known in these parts for that. Who's he that he should be lifted up to represent honest, God-fearing men?"

"If there was anything to stop him getting in, I'd do it," declared Abel.

"'Tis for us, with weight of years and experience, to keep him out. All sensible people will vote against him, and the more that know the truth of him the fewer will support him. And Republican though I am, I'd rather vote for the Tory than him. And as for you, if you stood up at his meetings when the time comes, while they were all cheering the wretch, and cried out that you was his son—that would be sure to lose him a good few God-fearing votes. You think of it; you might hinder him and even work him a mint of harm that way."

The old man left Abel to consider his advice and the angler sat watching his float for another hour. But his thoughts were on what he had heard; and he felt no more interest in his sport.

Presently he wound up his line and went home. He was attracted by Levi's suggestion and guessed that he might create great feeling against his father in that way. Himself, he did not shrink from the ordeal in imagination; indeed his inherent vanity rather courted it. But when he told his mother what he might do, she urged him to attempt no such thing. Indeed she criticised him sharply for such a foolish thought.

"You'll lose all sympathy from the people," she said, "and be flung out; and none will care twopence for you. When you tried to burn the place down and he forgave you, that made a feeling for him, and since then 'tis well known by those that matter, that he's done all he could for you under the circumstances."

"That's what he hasn't."

"That's what he would if you'd let him. So it's silly to think you've got any more grievances, and if you get up and make a row at one of his meetings, you'll only be chucked into the street. You're nobody now, through your own fault, and you've made people sorry for your father instead of sorry for you, because you're such a pig-headed fool about him and won't see sense."

The boy flushed and glared at his mother, who seldom spoke in this vein.

"If you wasn't my mother, I'd hit you down for that," he said, clenching his fists. "What do you know about things to talk to me like that? Who are you to take his side and cringe to him? If you can't judge him, there's plenty that can, and it's you who are pig-headed, not me, because you don't see I'm fighting your battle for you. It may seem too late to fight for you; but it's never too late to hate a wicked beast, and if I can help to keep him from getting what he wants I will, and I don't care how I do it, either."

She looked at him with little love in her eyes.

"You're only being a scourge to me—not to him," she answered. "You can't hurt him, however much you want to, and you can't hurt his name or reputation, because time heals all and he's done much to others that will make them forget what he did to me. I forget myself sometimes, so 'tis certain enough the people do. And if I can, surely to God you can, if only for my sake. You're punishing me for being your mother, not him for being your father—just contrary to what you want."

"That's all I get, then, for standing up for you against him, and keeping it before him and the people what he's done against you. Didn't you tell me years and years ago I'd fight your battles some day? And now, when I'm got clever enough to set about it, you curse me."

"I don't curse you, Abel. But time is past for fighting battles. There's nothing to fight about now."

"We're punishing him cruel by not taking his money; but there's more to do yet," he said. "And I'll do it if I can. And you mind that I'm fighting against him for your sake, and if you're grown too old and too tired to hate the man any more, I haven't. I can hate him for you as well as myself."

"And the hate comes back on you," she said. "It's long past the time for all that. You've got plenty of brains and you know that this passion against him is only harming yourself. For God's sake drop it. You say you're a man now. Then be a man and take man's views and look on ahead and think of your future life. Far from helping me, you're only hindering me. We've come to a time when life's altered and the old life here is done. We're going to begin life together—you and me—and you're going to make our fortunes; but it's a mad lookout if you mean to put all your strength into hating them that have no hate for you. It will make you bitter and useless, and you'll grow up a sour, friendless creature, like Levi Baggs. What's he got out of all his hate and unkindness to the world?"

Abel considered.

"He hates everybody," he said. "It's no use to hate everybody, because then everybody will hate you. I don't hate everybody. I only hate him."

She argued, but knew that she had not changed her son. And then, when he was gone again, fearing that he might do what he threatened, she went to see Estelle Waldron.

They met on the way to see each other, for Estelle had heard from Raymond that work was found for Abel and, as next step in the plot, it was necessary for Sabina to go to a small spinning mill in Bridport herself. Ironsyde's name was not to transpire.

Gladly enough the mother undertook her task.

"He's out of hand," she said, "and away from home half his time. He roams about and listens to bad counsellors. He's worse than ever since he's idle. He's got another evil thought now, for his thoughts foul his reason, as well I know thoughts can."

She told Estelle what Abel had declared he would do.

"You'd best let Mister Ironsyde know," she said, "and he'll take steps according. If the boy can be kept out from any meeting it would be wisest. But I'm powerless. I've wearied my tongue begging and blaming and praying to him to use his sense; but it's beyond my power to make him understand. There's a devil in him and nobody can cast it out."

"He won't speak to me now. Poor Abel—yes, it's something like a devil. I'll tell his father. We were very hopeful about the future until—But if he gets to work, it may sweeten him. He'll have good wages and meet nice people."

"I wish it had been farther off."

"So did I," answered Estelle; "but his father wants him under his own eye and will put him into something better the moment he can. You won't mention this to Abel, and he won't hear it there, because the workers don't know it; but Raymond has a large interest in the Mill really."

"I'll not mention it. I'll go to-morrow, and the boy will know nothing save that I've got him a good job."

"He can begin next month; and that will help him every way, I hope."

So things fell out, and within a month Abel was at work. He believed his mother solely responsible for this occupation. She had yet to find a home at Bridport, so he came and went from Bridetown.

He was soon deeply interested and only talked about his labours with a steam engine. Of his troubles he ceased to speak, and for many days never mentioned his father's name.

CHAPTER XX

IDEALS

An event which seemed more or less remote, came suddenly to the forefront of Raymond Ironsyde's life, for ill-health hastened the retirement of the sitting member and a parliamentary bye-election was called for.

Having undertaken the constituency he could not turn back, though the sudden demand had not been expected. But he found plenty of enthusiastic helpers and his own personality had made him many friends.

It was indeed upon the significance of personality that much turned, and incidentally the experiences into which he now entered served to show him all that personality may mean. Estelle rejoiced that he should now so swiftly learn what had so long been apparent to her. She always declared an enthusiasm for personality; to her it seemed the force behind everything and the mainspring of all movement. Lack of personality meant stagnation; but granted personality, then advance was possible—almost inevitable.

He caught her meaning and appreciated what followed from it. But he saw that personality demands freedom before its fullest expression and highest altitude are attainable. That altitude had never been reached as yet even by the most liberty-loving people.

"There's no record in all the world of what man might do under conditions of real liberty," said Estelle. "It has never been possible so far; but I do believe history shows that the nearer we approach to it, the more beautiful life becomes for everybody."

Raymond admitted so much and agreed that the world had yet to learn what it might achieve under a nobler dispensation of freedom.

"Think of the art, the thought, the leisure for good things, if the ceaseless fight against bad things were only ended; think of the inspirations that personality will be free to express some day," she said.

But he shattered her dreams sometimes. She would never suffer him to declare any advance impossible; yet she had to listen, when he explained that countless things she cried for were impracticable under existing circumstances.

"You want to get to the goal without running the race, sweetheart," he told her once. "Before this and this can possibly happen, that and that must happen. House-building begins at the cellars, not the roof."

She wrestled with political economy and its bearings on all that was meant by democracy. She was patient and strove to master detail and keep within the domain of reality. But, after all, she taught him more than he could teach her; because her thoughts sprung from an imagination touched with genius, while he was contented to take things as he found them and distrust emotion and intuition.

She exploded ideas in the ordered chambers of his mind. The proposition that labour was not a commodity quite took him off his balance. Yet he proved too logical to deny it when Estelle convinced his reason.

"That fact belongs to the root of all the future, I believe," she said. "From it all the flowers and seed we hope for ought to come, and the interpretation of everything vital. Labour and the labourer aren't two different things; they're one and the same thing. His labour is part of every man, and it can no more be measured and calculated away from him than his body and soul can. But it is the body and soul that must regulate labour, not labour the body and soul. So you've got to regard labour and the rights of labour as part of the rights of man, and not a thing to be bought and sold like a pound of tea. You see that? Labour, in fact, is as sacred as humanity and its rights are sacred too."

"So are the rights of property," he answered, but doubtfully, for he knew at heart that the one proposition did not by any means embrace the other. Indeed Estelle contradicted him very forcibly.

"Not the least bit in the world," she declared. "They are as far apart as the poles. There's nothing the least sacred about property. The rights of property are casual. They generally depend on all sorts of things that don't matter. They happen through the changes and chances of life, and human whims and fads and the pure accident of heredity and descent. They are all on a lower level; they are all suspect, whereas the rights of labour are a part of humanity."

But he followed her parry with a sharp *riposte*.

"Remember what happened when somebody promised to marry me," he said. "Remember that, as a principle of rectitude, I have recognised my son and accepted your very 'accident of descent' as chief reason for according him all a first-born's rights. That was your instinct towards right—his rights of property."

"It was righteousness, not rights of property that made you decide," she assured him. "Abel has no rights of property. The law ignores his rights to be alive at all, I believe. The law calls him 'the son of none,' and if you have no parents, you can't really exist. But the rights of labour are above human law and founded in humanity. They are Abel's, yours, everybody's. The man who works, by that fact commands the rights of labour. Besides, circumstances alter cases."

"Yes, and may again," he replied. "We can't deny the difficulties in this personal experience of mine. But I'm beginning to think the boy's not normal. I very much fear there's a screw loose."

"Don't think that. He's a very clever boy."

"And yet Sabina tells me frankly that his bitterness against me keeps pace with his growing intelligence. Instead of his wits defeating his bad temper, as they do sooner or later with most sane people, the older he gets, the more his dislike increases and the less trouble he takes to control it."

"If that were so, of course circumstances might alter the case again," she admitted. "But I don't believe there's a weak spot like that. There's something retarded—some confusion of thought, some kind of knot in his mind that isn't smoothed out yet. You've been infinitely patient and we'll go on being infinitely patient—together."

This difficult matter she dropped for the present; but finding him some days later in a recipient mood, followed up her cherished argument, that labour must be counted a commodity no more.

"Listen to me, Ray," she said. "Very soon you'll be too busy to listen to me at all—these are the last chances for me before your meetings begin. But really what I'm saying will be splendidly useful in speeches."

"All very well if getting in was all that mattered," he told her. "I can't echo all your ideas, Chicky, and speeches have a way of rising up against one at awkward moments afterwards."

"At any rate, you grant the main point," she said, "and so you must grant what follows from it; and if you grant that, and put it in your manifesto, you'll lose a few votes, but you'll gain hundreds. If labour's not a commodity, but to be regulated by body and soul, then wages must be regulated by body and soul too. Or, if you want to put it in a way for a crowd to understand, you can say that we give even a steam-engine the oil it must have before it begins to work, so how can we deny a man the oil he wants before he begins to work?"

"That means a minimum of wages."

"Yes, a minimum consistent with human needs, below which wages cannot and must not fail. That minimum should be just as much taken for granted as the air a man breathes, or the water he drinks, or the free education he gets as a boy. It isn't wages really; it's recognition of a man's right to live and share the privileges of life, and be self-respecting, just because he is a man. Everybody who is born, Ray, ought to have the unquestioned right to live, and the amplest opportunity to become a good and useful citizen. After that is granted, then wages should begin, and each man, or woman, should have full freedom and opportunity to earn what he, or she, was worth. That does away with the absurd idea of equality, which can only be created artificially and would breed disaster if we did create it."

"There's no such thing as equality in human nature, any more than in any other nature, Estelle. Seeds from the same pod are different—some weak, some strong. But I grant the main petition. The idea's first rate—a firm basis of right to reasonable life, and security for every human being as our low-water mark; while, on that foundation, each may lift an edifice according to their power. So that none who has the power to rise above the minimum would be prevented from doing so, and no Trades Union tyranny should interfere to prevent the strong man working eight hours a day if he desires to do so, because the weaker one can only work seven."

"I think the Trades Unions only want to prevent men being handicapped out of the race at the start," she answered. "They know as well as we do, that men are not born equal in mind or body; but rightly and reasonably, they want them all to start equal as far as conditions go. The race is to the strong and the prize is to the strong; but all, at least, should have power to train for the race and start with equal opportunities to win. There's such a lot to be done."

"There is," he admitted. "The handicap you talk of is created for thousands and thousands before they are born at all."

"Think of being handicapped out of the race before you are born!" she cried. "What could be more unjust and cruel and wicked than that?"

"Very few will put the unborn before the living, or think of a potential child rather than the desires of the parents—selfish though they may be. It's a free country, and we don't know enough to start stopping people from having a hand in the next generation if they decide to do so."

But her enthusiasm was not quenched by difficulties.

"We want science and politics and good will to work together," she said.

He returned to the smaller argument.

"It's a far cry to what you want, yet I for one don't shrink from it. The better a man is, the larger share he should have of the profits of any enterprise he helps to advance. Then wages would take the shape of his share in the profits, and you might easily find a head workman of genius drawing more out of a business than—say, a junior partner, who is a fool and not nearly so vital to the enterprise as he. But, you see, if we say that, we argue in a circle, for the junior partner, ass though he is, represents oil and fuel, which are just as important as the clever workman's brains—in fact, his brains can't work without them. Capital and labour are two halves of a whole and depend upon each other, as much as men depend on women and women on men. Capital does a great deal more than pay labour wages, remember. It educates his children, builds his houses and doctors his ailments. Soon—so they tell me—capital will be appropriated to look after labour's old age also, and cheer his manhood with the knowledge that his age is safe."

"You don't grudge any of these things, Ray?"

"Not one. Every man should have security. But, after all, capital cannot be denied its rights. It has got rights of some sort, surely? Socialists would kill the goose that lays the golden eggs; but though they lack power yet to kill the goose, they possess plenty of power to frighten it away to foreign shores, where it can build its nest a bit more hopefully than here. Many, who scent repudiation and appropriation, are flying already. Capital is diminishing, and there seems a fair chance of labour being over-coddled, at the expense of capital, when the Liberals come in again. If that happens, labour is weakened as well as capital. But both are essential to the power and well-being of the State. If we ever had another war, which God forbid, labour and capital would have to sink all differences and go to battle together unless we meant to be defeated. Both are vital to our salvation."

"Then give labour an interest in the blessing of capital," she said. "Open labour's eyes to the vital values of capital—its strength as well as weakness. Let the units of labour share the interests of their employers and each become a capitalist in their own right. What does it matter where the capital is as long as the nation has got it safe? You might make England a thousand times richer if all those in the country, who want to save money, had the power to save."

"How can we? There's not enough to go round," he told her. But she declared that no argument.

"Then create conditions under which there might be much more. Let the workers be owners, too. If the owners only took their ownership in a different spirit and felt no man is more than a trustee for all—if they were like you, Ray, who are a worker and an owner both, what great things might happen! Make all industry co-operation, in reality as well as theory, and a real democracy must come out of it. It's bound to come."

"Well, I suppose nothing can help it coming. We are great on free institutions in this country and they get freer every year."

So they argued, much at one in heart, and an impartial listener had felt that it was within the power of the woman's intelligence and the man's energy and common sense, to help the world as far as individuals can, did chance and the outcome of their union afford them opportunity.

But Estelle knew that good ideas were of little value in themselves. Seed is of no account if the earth on which it falls be poisoned, and a good idea above all, needs good will to welcome it. Good will to the inspirations of man is as sunshine, rain, sweet soil to the seed; without good will all thinking must perish, or at best lie dormant. She wondered how much of good seed had perished under the bad weather of human weakness, prejudice and jealousy. But she was young, and hope her rightful heritage. The blessed word 'reconstruction' seemed to her as musical as a ring of bells.

"There are some things you never will be able to express in political terms, and life is one of them," Ernest Churchouse had assured her; but she was not convinced of it. She still reverenced politics and looked to it to play husbandman, triumph over party and presently shine out, like a universal sun, whose sole warmth was good will to man.

And as she felt personally to Raymond's work, so did she want the world of women to feel to all men's work. She would not have them claim their rights in the argument of parity of intellect, for that she felt to be vain. It was by the virtue of disparity that their equality should appear. Their virtue and essential aid depended on the difference. The world wanted women, not to do what men had done, but to bring to the task the special qualities and distinctive genius of womanhood to complement and crown the labour of manhood. The mighty structure was growing; but it would never be finished without the saving grace of woman's thought and the touch of woman's hand. The world's work needed them—not for the qualities they shared with men, but for the qualities men lacked and they possessed. If Raymond represented the masculine worker, she hoped that she might presently stand in the ranks of the women, and doubted not that great women would arise to lead her.

She remembered that the Roman element of humanity was described as representing the male spirit, while the Greek stood for the female; and she could easily dream a blend of the two destined to produce a spirit greater than either. Love quickened her visions and added the glow of life to her hopes.

So together she and her future husband prepared for their wedded days, and if ever a man and woman faced the future with steadfast determination to do justly and serve their kind with the best of their united powers, this man and woman did.

They were to be married after the election, and that would take place early in the coming year.

CHAPTER XXI

ATROPOS

Ironsyde for once found himself part of a machine, and by no means the most important part. He fought the election resolutely and spared no energy. The attraction of the contest grew upon him, and since he contended against a personal acquaintance, one who rated sportsmanship as highly as Arthur Waldron himself, the encounter proceeded on rational lines. It became exceedingly strenuous in the later stages and Raymond's agent, from an attitude of certainty, grew more doubtful. But the personal factor told for the Liberal. He was popular in the constituency and Waldron, himself a strong Conservative, whose vote must necessarily be cast against his future son-in-law, preached the moral.

"If you beat us, Ray, it will be entirely owing to the fact that you played cricket and football in the public eye for twenty years," he asserted and believed.

The Liberal Committee room was at 'The Seven Stars,' for Mr. Legg supported the cause of democracy and pinned his highest hopes thereto. He worked hard for Ironsyde and, on the sole occasion when painful incidents threatened to spoil a public meeting, Job exercised tact and saved the situation.

At one of the last of his gatherings, in the great, new public room of 'The Seven Stars,' Ironsyde had been suddenly confronted with his son. Abel attended this meeting of his father's supporters and attempted to interrupt it. He had arrived primed with words and meant to declare himself before the people; but when the time came, he was nervous and lost his head. Sitting and listening grew to an agony. He could not wait till question time and felt a force within him crying to him, to get upon his feet and finish the thing he had planned to do. But Job, who was among the stewards, kept watchful eyes upon the benches, and Abel had hardly stood up, when he recognised him. Before the boy had shouted half a dozen incoherent words, Mr. Legg and a policeman were at his side.

He sat far down the hall and the little disturbance he had been able to create was hardly appreciated. For Raymond now neared the end of his speech and it had contained matter which aroused attention from all who listened to it, awakened disquiet in some, but enthusiasm among the greater number. He was telling of such hopes and desires as he and Estelle shared, and though an indifferent speaker, the purity of his ambitions and their far-reaching significance challenged intelligent listeners.

In less than half a minute Abel was removed. He did not struggle, but his first instinct was great relief to be outside. Not until later did his reverse breed wrath. His father had not seen him and when Ironsyde inquired afterwards, what the trouble was, Mr. Legg evaded the facts. But he looked to it that Abel should be powerless to renew disturbances. He warned those who controlled the remaining meetings not to admit him, and henceforth kept at the doors a man who knew Abel. Mr. Legg also saw Sabina, who was now much in Bridport concerned with a little house that she had taken, and the boy's mother implored him to do no more evil. To her surprise he admitted that he had been wrong. But he was dark and stormy. She saw but little of him and did not know how he occupied his leisure, or spent his wages.

There is no doubt that, at this time, Abel sank out of mind with those most interested in him. Estelle was entirely preoccupied with the election, and when once the lad's new work had been determined and he went to do it, Raymond dismissed him for the present from his thoughts. He felt grateful to Sabina for falling in with his wishes and hoped that, since she was now definitely on his side, a time might soon come when she would be able to influence her son. Indeed Sabina herself was more hopeful, and when Estelle came to see her in Bridport, declared that Abel kept regular hours and appeared to be interested in his work.

Neither she nor anybody belonging to him heard of the boy's escapade at the meeting, for upon that subject Job Legg felt it wisest to be silent. And when the penultimate meeting passed, the spirit of it was such that those best able to judge again felt very sanguine for Ironsyde. He had created a good impression and won a wide measure of support. He had worked hard, traversed all the ground and left the people under no shadow of doubt as to his opinions. Bridetown was for him; West Haven and Bridport were said to be largely in his favour, but the outlying agricultural district inclined towards his rival. Raymond had, however, been at great pains to win the suffrage of the farmers, and his last meeting was on their account.

Before him now lay the promise of two days' rest, and he accepted them very thankfully, for he began to grow weary in mind and body. He had poured his vitality into the struggle which, started more or less as a sporting event, gradually waxed into a serious and all-important matter. And as his knowledge increased and his physical energy waned, a cloud dulled his enthusiasm at times and more than once he asked himself if it was all worth while—if this infinite trouble and high tension were expended to the wisest purpose on these ambitions. He had heard things from politicians, who came to speak for him, that discouraged him. He had found that single-mindedness was not the dominant quality of those who followed politics as a profession. The loaves and fishes bulked largely in their calculations, and he heard a distinguished man say things at one of his meetings which Raymond knew that it was impossible he could believe. For example, it was clearly a popular catchword that party politics had become archaic, and that a time was near when party would be forgotten in a larger and nobler spirit. Speakers openly declared that great changes were in sight, and the constitution must be modified; but, privately, they professed no such opinions. All looked to their party and their party alone for personal advance. It seemed to Ironsyde that their spirits were mean spirits; that they concealed behind their profession a practice of shrewd calculation and a policy of cynical self-advance. The talk behind the scenes was not of national welfare, but individual success, or failure. The men who talked the loudest on the platform of altruism and the greatest good to the greatest number, were most alive in private conversation to the wire-pulling and intrigue which proceeded unseen; and it was in the machinery they found their prime interest and excitement, rather than in the great operations the machine was ostensibly created to achieve. The whole business on their lips in private appeared to have no more real significance than a county cricket match, or any other game.

Thanks largely to the woman he was to wed, Ironsyde took now a statesman-like rather than a political view as far as his inexperience could do so. He had no axe to grind, and from the standpoint of his ignorance, progress looked easy and demanded no more than that good will of which Estelle so often spoke. But in practice he began to perceive the gulf between ideal legislation and practical politics and, in moments of physical depression, as the election approached, his heart failed him. He grew despondent at night. Then, after refreshing sleep, the spirit of hope reawakened. He felt very certain now that he was going to get in; and still with morning light he hailed the victory; while, after a heavy day, he doubted of its fruits and mistrusted himself. His powers seemed puny contrasted with the gigantic difficulties that the machine set up between a private member and any effective or independent activity in the House.

He was cast down as he rode home after his last meeting but one, and his reflections were again most deeply tinged with doubt as to the value of these heroic exertions. Looked at here, in winter moonlight under a sky of stars, this fevered strife seemed vain, and the particular ambition to which he had devoted such tremendous application appeared thin and doubtful—almost unworthy. He traversed the enterprise, dwelt on outstanding features of it and comforted himself, as often he had done of late, by reflecting that Estelle would be at his right hand. If, after practical experience and fair trial, he found himself powerless to serve their common interests, or advance their ideals, then he could leave the field of Parliament and seek elsewhere for a hearing. His ingenuous hope was to interest his leaders; for he believed that many who possessed power, thought and felt as he did.

He had grown placid by the time he left South Street and turned into the road for home. The night was keen and frosty. It braced him and he began to feel cheerful and hungry for the supper that waited him at North Hill.

Then, where the road forked from Bridetown and an arm left it for West Haven, at a point two hundred yards from outlying farm-houses, a young, slight figure leapt from the hedge, stood firmly in the road and stopped Raymond's horse. The moonlight was clear and showed Ironsyde his son. Abel leapt at the bridle rein, and when the rider bade him loose it, he lifted a revolver and fired twice pointblank.

Ten minutes later, on their way back from the meeting and full of politics, there drove that way John Best, Nicholas Roberts and a Bridetown farmer. They found a man on his back in the middle of the road and a horse standing quietly beside him. None doubted but that Raymond Ironsyde was dead, yet it was not possible for them to be sure. They lifted him into the farmer's cart therefore, and while Best and Roberts returned with him to Bridport Hospital, the farmer mounted Ironsyde's horse and galloped to North Hill with his news. Arthur Waldron was from home, but Estelle left the house as quickly as a motor car could be made ready, and in a quarter of an hour stood at Raymond's side.

He was dead and had, indeed, died instantly when fired upon. He had been shot through the lung and heart, and must have perished before he fell from his horse to the ground.

They knew Estelle at the hospital and left her with Raymond for a little while. He looked ten years younger than when she had seen him last. All care was gone and an expression of content rested upon his beautiful face.

The doctor feared to leave her, judging of the shock; but when he returned she was calm and controlled. She sat by the dead man and held his hand.

"A little longer," she said, and he went out again.

CHAPTER XXII

THE HIDING-PLACE

No doubt existed as to the murderer of Raymond Ironsyde, for on the night of his death, Abel Dinnett did not return home. He had left work at the usual time, but had not taken his bicycle; and from that day he was seen no more.

It appeared impossible that he could evade the hue and cry, but twenty-four hours passed and there came no report of his capture. Little mystery marked the matter, save that of Abel's disappearance. His animosity towards his father was known and it had culminated thus. None imagined that capture would be long delayed; but forty-eight hours passed and still there came no news of him.

Estelle Waldron fled from all thought of him at first; then she reflected upon him—driven to do so by a conviction concerning him that commanded action from her.

On the day after the coroner's inquest, for the first time she sought Sabina. The meeting was of an affecting character, for each very fully realised the situation from the standpoint of the other. Sabina was the more distressed, yet she entertained definite convictions and declared herself positive concerning certain facts. Estelle questioned her conclusions and, indeed, refused to believe them.

"I hope you'll understand my coming, Sabina," she said.

She was clad, as usual, in a grey Harris tweed, and the elder wondered why she did not wear black. Estelle's face was haggard and worn, with much suffering. But it seemed that the last dregs of her own cup were not yet drunk, for an excruciating problem faced her. There was none to help her solve it, yet she took it to Sabina.

"I thought you'd come, sooner or later. This is a thing beyond any human power to make better. God knows I mourn for you far more than I mourn for myself. I don't mourn for myself. Long ago I saw that the living can't be happy, though the dead may be. The dead may be—we'll hope it for them."

"It's death to me as well as to him," said Estelle simply. "As far as I'm concerned, I feel that I'm dead from now and shall live on as somebody different—somebody I don't know yet. All that we were and had and hoped—everything is gone with him. The future was to be spent in trying to do good things. We shared the same ideas about it. But that's all over. I'm left—single-handed, Sabina."

"Yes, I know how you feel."

"I can't bear to think of it yet. I didn't come to talk about him, or myself. I came to talk about Abel."

"I can't tell you anything about him."

"I know you know nothing. I think I know more than you do."

"Know more of him than I do?" asked the mother. There was almost a flash of jealousy in her voice. But it faded and she sighed.

"No, no. You needn't fret for him. They may find him, or they may not; but they'll not find him alive."

Estelle started. She believed most steadfastly that Abel was alive, and felt very certain that she knew his hiding-place.

"Why do you think that?" she asked. "You might hope it; but why do you think it? Have you any good reason for thinking it?"

"There are some things you know," answered the mother. "You know them without being told and without any reason. You neither hope nor fear— you know. I might ask you how you know where he is. But I don't want to ask you. I've taken my good-bye of him, poor, wasted life. How had God got the heart to let him live for this? People will say it was fitting, and happened by the plan of his Maker. No man's child—not even God's. It's all hidden, all dark to me. It's worked itself out to the bitter end. Men would have been too kind to work it out like this. Only God could. I can't say much to you. I'm very sorry for you. You were caught up into the thing and didn't know, or guess, what you were thrusting yourself into. But now it's your turn, and you'll have to wait long years, as I did, before you can look at life again without passion or sorrow."

"It doesn't matter about me. But, if you feel Abel is dead, I feel just as strongly that he is alive, and that this isn't the end of him."

Sabina considered.

"I know him better than you, and I know Providence better than you do," she answered. "It's like the wonder you are—to think on him without hate. But you're wasting your time and showing pity for nothing. He's beyond pity. Why, I don't pity him—his mother."

"I'm only doing what Raymond tried to do so often and failed—what he would have me do now if he'd lived. And if I know something that nobody else does, I must use that knowledge. I'm sorry I do know, Sabina, but I do."

"You waste your time, I expect. If the hunt that's going on doesn't find him, how shall you do it? He's at the bottom of the sea, I hope."

They parted and the same night Estelle set out to satisfy her will. She told nobody of her purpose, for she knew that her father would not have allowed her to pursue it. Waldron was utterly crushed by the death of his friend and could not as yet realise the loss.

Nor did Estelle realise it, save in fitful and fleeting agonies. As yet the full significance of the event was by no means weighed by her. It meant far more than she could measure and receive and accept in so brief a space of time. Seen from the standpoint of this death, every plan of her life, every undertaking for the future, was dislocated. She left that complete ruin for the present. There was no hurry to restore, or set about rebuilding the fabric of her future. She would have all her life to do it in.

The thought of Abel came as a demand to her justice. Her knowledge, amounting to a conviction, required action. The nature of the action she did not know, but something urged her to reach him if she could. For she believed him mad. Great torture of spirit had overtaken her under her loss; but upon this extreme grief, ugly and incessant, obtruded the thought of Abel, the secret of his present refuge and the impulse to approach him. Her personal suffering established rather than shook her own high standards. She had promised the boy never to tell anybody of the haunt he had shown her under the roof in the old store at West Haven; and if most women might now have forgotten such a promise, Estelle did not. But she very strenuously argued against the spiritual impulse to seek him, for every physical instinct rose against doing so. To do this was surely not required of her, for whereunto would it lead? What must be the result of any such meeting? It might be dreadful; it could not fail to be futile. Yet all mental effort to escape the task proved vain. Her very grief edged her old, austere, chivalrous acceptance of duty. She felt that justice called her to this ordeal, and she went—with no fixed purpose save to see him and urge him to surrender himself for his own peace if he could understand. No personal fear touched her reflections. She might have welcomed fear in these unspeakable moments of her life, for she was little enamoured of living after Raymond Ironsyde died. The thought of death for herself had not been distasteful at that time.

She went fearlessly, when all slept and her going and coming would not be observed. She left her home at a moonless midnight, took candle and matches, dressed in her stoutest clothes and walked over North Hill towards Bridport. But at the eastern shoulder of the downs she descended through a field and struck the road again just at the fork where Raymond had perished.

Then she struck into the West Haven way and soon slipped under the black mass of the old store. The night was cloudy and still. No wind blew and the sigh of the sea beneath the shelving beaches close at hand, had sunk to a murmur. West Haven lay lost in darkness. The old store had been searched, as many other empty buildings, for the fugitive; but he was not specially associated with this place, save in the mind of Estelle. The police had hunted it carefully, no more, and she guessed that his eerie under the roof, only reached by a somewhat perilous climb through a broken window, would not be discovered.

She remembered also that there were some students of Raymond's murder who did not associate Abel with it. Such held that only accident and coincidence had made him run away on the night of Ironsyde's end. They argued that in these cases the obvious always proved erroneous, and the theory most transparently rational seldom led the way to the truth.

But she had never doubted about that. It seemed already a commonplace of knowledge, a lifetime old, that Abel had destroyed his father, and that he must be insane to have ruined his own life in this manner.

She ascended cautiously through the darkness, reached a gap—once a window—from which her ascent must be made, and listened for a few moments to hear if anything stirred above her.

It seemed as though the old store was full of noises, for the fingers of decay never cease from picking and, in the silence of night, one can best hear their stealthy activities. Little falls of fragments sounded loudly, even echoed, in this great silence. There was almost a perpetual rustle and whisper; and once a thud and skurry, when a rat displaced a piece of mortar which fell from the rotting plaster. Dark though the heaven was and black the outer night, it had the quality that air never loses and she saw the sky as possessed of illumination in contrast with its setting of the broken window. Within all was blankly black; from above there came no sound.

She climbed to the window ledge, felt for the nails that Abel had hammered in to hold his feet and soon ascended through a large gap under the eaves of the store. Some shock had thrown out a piece of brickwork here. Seen from the ground the aperture looked trifling and had indeed challenged no attention; but it was large enough to admit a man.

For a moment Estelle stood in this aperture before entering the den within. She raised her voice, which fluttered after her climb, and called to him.

"Abel! Abel! It's Estelle."

There came the thought, even as she spoke, that he might answer with a bullet; but he answered not at all. She felt thankful for the silence and hoped that he might have deserted his retreat. Perhaps, indeed, he had never come to it; and yet it seemed impossible that he had for two days escaped capture unless here concealed. It occurred to her that he might wander out by night and return before day. He might even now be behind her, to intercept her return. Still no shadow of fear shook her mind or body. She felt not a tremor. All that concerned her conscience was now completed and she hoped that it would be possible to dismiss from her thoughts the fellow creature who had destroyed her joy of life and worked evil so far reaching. She could leave him now to his destiny and feel under no compulsion to relate the incidents of her nocturnal search. Had he been there, she would have risked the meeting, urged him to surrender and then left him if he allowed her to do so. She would never have given him up, or broken her promise to keep his secret.

But the chamber under the roof was large and she did not leave it without making sure that he was neither hiding nor sleeping within it. She entered, lighted her candle and examined a triangular recess formed by the converging beams of the roof above her and the joists under her feet.

The boy had been busy here. There were evidences of him—evidences of a child rather than a man. Boyish forethought stared her in the face and staggered her by its ghastly incongruities with the things this premeditating youth had done. Here were provisions, not such as a man would have selected to stand a siege, but the taste of a schoolboy. She looked at the supplies spread here—tins of preserved food, packets of chocolate, bottles of ginger beer, bananas, biscuits. But it seemed that the hoard had not been touched. One tin of potted salmon had been opened, but no part of the contents was consumed. Either accident had changed his purpose and frightened him elsewhere at the last moment, or the energies and activities that had gone to pile this accumulation were all spent in the process and now he did not need them.

Then she looked further, to the extremity of the den he had made, and there, lying comfortably on a pile of shavings, Estelle found him.

She guessed that the storm and stress of his crime had exhausted him and thrown him into heaviest possible physical slumber after great mental tribulation. She shuddered as she looked down on him and a revulsion, a loathing tempted her to creep away again before he awakened. She did not think of him as a patricide, nor did her own loss entirely inspire the emotion; she never associated him with that, but kept him outside it, as she would have kept some insensible or inanimate object had such been responsible for Ironsyde's end. It was the sudden thought of all Raymond's death might mean—not to her but the world—that turned her heart to stone for a fearful second as she looked down upon the unconscious figure. Her own sorrow was sealed at its fountains for the time. But her sorrow for the world could not be sealed. And then came the thought that the insensible boy at her feet, escaping for a little while through sleep's primeval sanctity, was part of the robbed world also. Who had lost more than he by his unreason? If her heart did not melt then, it grew softer.

But there was more to learn before she left him and the truth can be recorded.

Abel had killed his father and hastened to his lair exultant. He had provided for what should follow and vaguely hoped that presently, before his stores were spent, the way would be clearer for escape. He assured himself safe from discovery and guessed that when a fortnight was passed, he might safely creep out, reach a port, find work in a ship and turn his back upon England for ever.

That was his general plan before the deed. Afterwards all changed for him. He then found himself a being racked and over-mastered by new sensations. The desirable thing that he had done changed its features, even as death changes the features of life; the ideal, so noble and seemly before, when attained assumed such a shape as, in one of Abel's heredity, it was bound to assume. Not at once did the change appear, but as a cloud no bigger than a man's hand in the clear, triumphant sky of his achievement. Even so an apple, that once he had stolen and hidden, was bruised unknown to him and thus contained the seed of death, that made it rot before it was ripe. The decay spread and the fruit turned to filth before he could win any enjoyment from it.

He shook off the beginnings of doubt impatiently. He retraced his grievances and dwelt on the glory of his revenge as he reached his secret place after the crime. But the stain darkened in the heart of his mind; and before dawn crept through cracks in the roof above his lair, dissolution had begun.

Through the hours of that first day he lay there with his thoughts for company and a process, deepening, as dusk deepened, into remorse began to horrify him. He fought with all his might against it. He resented it with indignation. His gorge rose against it; he would have strangled it, had it been a ponderable thing within his power to destroy; but as time passed he began to know it was stronger than he. It gripped his spirit with unconquerable fingers and slowly stifled him. Time crept on interminable. When the second night came, he was faint and turned to his food. He struggled with himself and opened a tin of salmon. But he could not eat. He believed that he would never eat again. He slept for an hour, then woke from terrifying dreams. His mind wandered and he longed to be gone and tear off his clothes and dip into the sea.

At dawn of the second day men were hunting the old stores, from its cellars to the attics below him. He heard them speaking under his feet and listened to two men who cursed him. They speculated whether he was too young to hang and hoped he might not be. Yet he could take pride in their failure to find him. There was, as he remembered, only one person in the world who knew of his eerie; but terror did not accompany this recollection. His exultation at the defeat of the searchers soon vanished, and he found himself indifferent to the thought that Estelle might remember.

He knew that his plans could not be fulfilled now: it was impossible for him to live a fortnight here. And then he began stealthily, fearfully, to doubt of life itself. It had changed in its aspect and invitation. Its promises were dead. It could hold nothing for him as he had been told by Levi Baggs. The emotions now threatening his mind were such that he believed no length of days would ever dim them; from what he suffered now, it seemed that time's self could promise no escape. Life would be hell and not worth living. At this point in his struggles his mind failed him and became disordered. It worked fitfully, and its processes were broken with blanks and breaks. Chaos marked his mental steps from this point; his feet were caught and he fell down and down, yet tried hard for a while to stay his fall. His consciousness began to decide, while his natural instincts struggled against the decision. Not one, but rival spirits tore him. Reason formed no part in the encounter; no arbiter arose between the conflicting forces, between a gathering will to die and escape further torment, and the brute will to live, that must belong to every young creature, happy or wretched.

The trial was long drawn out; but it had ended some hours before Estelle stood beside him.

She considered whether she should waken Abel and determined that she must do so, since to speak with him, if possible, she held her duty now. He was safe if he wished to be, for she would never tell his secret. So she bent down with her light—to find him dead. He had shot himself through the right temple after sunset time of the second day.

Estelle stood and looked at him for a little while, then climbed back to earth and went away through the darkness to tell his mother that she was right.

THE END